PRINCE OF SUMBA

Husband to Many Wives

An End Times Novel by

Pastor Don Milton

Born Again Publishing, Inc.

To My Wife, Laura: May Our Lives Ever Be
An Epic Adventure With God At The Center.

And

In Loving Memory of My Parents
Who Have Gone To Be With the Lord
Their Love for God's Word Was a Great Gift

Trust in the LORD with all thine heart;
and *lean not unto thine own understanding*.
In all thy ways *acknowledge Him, and He shall direct thy paths.*
Proverbs 3:5-6

About the Author

It's impossible to tell you about Don Milton without discussing the Philippines. On his first visit there, long before the Internet, he was kidnapped by his penpal. On his second visit, he came face to face with a wild eyed cannibal. His travels have taken him from the Islamic City of Marawi to mountain top villages where corn fields thrive on spring water.

Don learned Tagalog, the Philippine National Language, at the University of Washington where he received his Bachelor of Arts in Linguistics. He's been a taxi driver, an insurance agent, a minister of the gospel, and always a story teller.

For the last ten years Don has pastored ChristianMarriage.com, an online ministry dedicated to providing theological answers to questions about marriage. Pastor Don has published numerous books dealing with the topics of Courtship and Christian Marriage as well as Law & Justice. Don is currently working on a historical novel.

Don has a wonderful wife and three children. He would like to have more.

Author - Pastor Don Milton

Contents

In order to assure accuracy,
this novel contains 385 footnotes.

Many readers have told me that reading the footnotes
along with the story increases the impact of its message.

If you find any inaccuracies please let me know.
Your questions and comments are appreciated.

Pastor Don Milton
WWW.DonMilton.Com

PRINCE OF SUMBA
HUSBAND TO MANY WIVES

An Introductory Message From Pastor Ishmael David

This story is about a simple mission trip that turned into a great awakening as God poured out His Spirit on millions of Christians.[1] He also poured out His Spirit on millions of new believers who follow Him today with an honest and good heart. Having heard the word, they keep it, and tell others about God's love.[2]

There were some however, who called themselves brothers, yet like Jonah were *angry with us enough to die* and would have preferred to continue wasting water on a *withering vine*.[3]

But it came to pass that when the Lord's Spirit was poured out on us, He softened our hearts so that we might *take away the reproach* of our women[4] and *prepare the way of the Lord*.[5]

All of us who were there, wish to express our gratitude that we weren't alone on our mission but that some of you prayed for us as the miraculous events I'm about to describe unfolded.

To those of you who've thwarted us in this work of the Lord, the prophet says, *come out of her*[6] for if you don't know that *it's not the Lord's will that anyone should perish, but everyone come to repentance* then you've lost sight of the Lord's love and of His patience.[7]

Let's give thanks and praise to the Lord whose Spirit moved upon us so that those who'd sought in vain to find a righteous witness were finally presented with His pure gospel, untainted by cultural bigotry.[8]

Let's be thankful and in awe of God's great mercy in that He has been patient with our stubbornness so that we've lived to see the day that *the Branch of the Lord* would be restored.[9]

Let's be thankful that after many years of hardened hearts the Lord has seen fit to open us to His will so that His Spirit could be poured out on our new brothers and sisters in the Lord as was His plan from the beginning.[10]

Finally, I praise God that He has seen fit to let me be part of that great moving of His Spirit. Singing praises to His Name in the presence of millions of newborn believers has left me with a most indescribable joy!

If you still have not *come out of her*, that great apostate church, that *great whore of Babylon*,[11] which includes those who protest[12] yet revel in her abominations, listen to the words of the prophet:

And I heard another voice from heaven, saying, Come out of her, my people, that ye be not partakers of her sins, and that ye receive not of her plagues.[13]

Let the Lord judge your heart and find it true for He has said, *If you are not with Me you are against Me.*[14] Our prayers and the prayers of our new found brothers and sisters in the Lord, and there are millions, are with you who read these pages. May you be with the Lord as His plan continues to unfold, always guided by His holy Word for *He will lift you up.*[15]

Footnotes

1. Joel 2:28 And it shall come to pass afterward, [that] I will pour out my spirit upon all flesh; and your sons and your daughters shall prophesy, your old men shall dream dreams, your young men shall see visions.

2. Luke 8:15 But that on the good ground are they, which in an honest and good heart, having heard the word, keep [it], and bring forth fruit with patience.

3. Jonah 3:10-Jonah 4:1 And God saw their works, that they turned from their evil way; and God repented of the evil, that he had said that he would do unto them; and he did [it] not. But it displeased Jonah exceedingly, and he was very angry.

Jonah 4:5-7 So Jonah went out of the city, and sat on the east side of the city, and there made him a booth, and sat under it in the shadow, till he might see what would become of the city. And the LORD God prepared a gourd, and made [it] to come up over Jonah, that it might be a shadow over his head, to deliver him from his grief. So Jonah was exceeding glad of the gourd. But God prepared a worm when the morning rose the next day, and it smote the gourd that it withered.

Psalm 37:2 For they shall soon be cut down like the grass, and wither as the green herb.

4. Isaiah 4:1 And in that day seven women shall take hold of one man, saying, We will eat our own bread, and wear our own apparel: only let us be called by thy name, to take away our reproach.

Note: Mass conversions of women to Christianity began in the 20th century. By the arrival of the 21st century there were more than double the number of Born-Again Christian women in the Philippines than Born-Again Christian men.

5. Isaiah 40:3 The voice of him that crieth in the wilderness, Prepare ye the way of the LORD, make straight in the desert a highway for our God.

6. Revelation18:4 And I heard another voice from heaven, saying, Come out of her, my people, that ye be not partakers of her sins, and that ye receive not of her plagues.

7. 2 Peter 3:9 The Lord is not slack concerning his promise, as some men count slackness; but is longsuffering to us-ward, not willing that any should perish, but that all should come to repentance.

8. Hebrews 11:4 *By faith* Abel offered unto God a more excellent sacrifice than Cain, by which he obtained *witness that he was righteous*, God testifying of his gifts: and by it he being dead yet speaketh.

Jam 3:17 But the *wisdom that is from above is first pure*, then peaceable, gentle, [and] easy to be intreated, full of mercy and good fruits, *without partiality, and without hypocrisy.*

9. Isaiah 4:2-6 In that day shall the branch of the LORD be beautiful and glorious, and the fruit of the earth [shall be] excellent and comely for them that are escaped of Israel. And it shall come to pass, [that he that is] left in Zion, and [he that] remaineth in Jerusalem, shall be called holy, [even] every one that is written among the living in Jerusalem: When the Lord shall have washed away the filth of the daughters of Zion, and shall have purged the blood of Jerusalem from the midst thereof by the spirit of judgment, and by the spirit of burning. And the LORD will create upon every dwelling place of mount Zion, and upon her assemblies, a cloud and smoke by day, and the shining of a flaming fire by night: for upon all the glory [shall be] a defence.

And there shall be a tabernacle for a shadow in the daytime from the heat, and for a place of refuge, and for a covert from storm and from rain.

10. Joel 2:28-29 And it shall come to pass afterward, that I will pour out my spirit upon all flesh; and your sons and your daughters shall prophesy, your old men shall dream dreams, your young men shall see visions: And also upon the servants and upon the handmaids in those days will I pour out my spirit.

Isaiah 44:3-8 For I will pour water upon him that is thirsty, and floods upon the dry ground: I will pour my spirit upon thy seed, and my blessing upon thine offspring: And they shall spring up as among the grass, as willows by the water courses. One shall say, I am the LORD'S; and another shall call himself by the name of Jacob; and another shall subscribe with his hand unto the LORD, and surname himself by the name of Israel. Thus saith the LORD the King of Israel, and his redeemer the LORD of hosts; I am the first, and I am the last; and beside me there is no God. And who, as I, shall call, and shall declare it, and set it in order for me, since I appointed the ancient people? and the things that are coming, and shall come, let them show unto them. Fear ye not, neither be afraid: have not I told thee from that time, and have declared it? ye are even my witnesses. Is there a God beside me? yea, there is no God; I know not any.

11. Revelation 17:5 And upon her forehead [was] a name written, MYSTERY, BABYLON THE GREAT, THE MOTHER OF HARLOTS AND ABOMINATIONS OF THE EARTH.

12. *Those who protest yet revel in her abominations* -

This includes any group claiming to have broken from the false traditions of man but that has taken up those false traditions once again. Some of the false, even blasphemous, traditions include the placement of graven images outside or inside the church and the use of Sunday school books that include such images or that even teach children to create graven images. Such things are found in nearly every Christian church. Other abominations include the rejection of God's moral laws concerning chastity to replace them with government laws that permit every sin that the Bible forbids and that forbid many things that the Bible commands. Such groups revel in tolerance, that is, they revel in these abominations.

13. Revelation 18:4 And I heard another voice from heaven,

saying, Come out of her, my people, that ye be not partakers of her sins, and that ye receive not of her plagues.

14. Matthew 12:30 He that is not with me is against me; and he that gathereth not with me scattereth abroad.

15. James 4:10 Humble yourselves in the sight of the Lord, and he shall lift you up.

The narrative you are about to read has been written as if the Great Awakening has not yet taken place. You will be presented with facts and figures as well as descriptions of places that may no longer be the same. It has been many years since I first set foot on Mindanao but we shall begin there. May you be blessed.

MISSION MINDANAO

As our plane circled to touch down, I felt inadequately prepared for my mission. Mindanao was a huge island, larger than many countries. Its population was in the tens of millions and still there were vast areas of uninhabited jungle. Well over half its population were Roman Catholic, about an eighth were Muslim, and another eighth were born-again Christians. The remaining fraction was made up of a scattering of *other Christian* as well as clearly non-Christian religions. If there were a place on earth where the pure gospel of our Lord and Savior could cause an instant reaction it was here. I was anxious to see the results. Just then I remembered my grandfather's prophecy, that I would become a missionary to the Asiatic peoples. My mind and heart collided in the realization that this prophecy was about to be fulfilled.

"Praise God!" I was thinking half out loud.

My wife, Mary, read my lips. "Amen!" She concurred.

Our plane eased across the runway at Cagayan de Oro Airport just as the midday equatorial sun took its place above us. When the crew opened the door of the plane we were greeted by a burst of heat and humidity. By the time we descended the stairs and walked across the airport runway to the lobby I was sweating profusely.

I took out my handkerchief and wiped my forehead. Well, we were here, Mindanao. I looked across the landing strip and saw nothing familiar except for a few tufts of grass stubbornly poking their way through the cracks in the runway. A water buffalo was yanking them out as he grazed. The field beyond the airport apparently didn't supply a choice enough variety for his tastes. Well, I guess for water buffalo as well as cattle, the grass is always greener; something the Christian world had ignored in recent years when it came to evangelizing distant lands.

At the airport dozens of drivers of various sorts and sizes of taxis were arguing over fares. By the looks of some of the vehicles, they'd have to pay me to get in. I was glad that we were expected and that our ride would be along soon, but before we had a chance to take a seat in the waiting area, a man approached us.

"May I be so rude as to bother you?" He asked. That was a curious way of putting it and how could I say no. He continued,

"Are you Mr. David?"

"That's right, and you?"

"I'm Tony. Pastor sent me. He knew there wouldn't be enough room for us all to fit into my vehicle so pastor and his family are waiting for you back at his house."

I looked at what Tony had referred to as his vehicle. It was a tricycle. *Yes, I said tricycle.* His tricycle was a four wheeled contraption with a motorcycle welded into the center. If you can imagine a Chinese rickshaw with four wheels and a motorcycle pulling it instead of a man then you not only have a wild imagination but you're close to visualizing what these actually looked like.

"Will it be all right with you if we go now?" Tony asked.

I was trying to figure out a polite way to get out of riding with Tony and to find some safer way to get to Pastor Sam's house when Mary spoke.

"Sure Tony, We'd love to. Is this your tricycle?"

"Yes, my brother-in-law in the States bought it for me!" Tony beamed with pride.

After loading up our luggage we got into Tony's tricycle for the five mile ride to the pastor's house. Tony had to shout to be heard over the din of his motorcycle. He would halt mid-sentence as his engine revved then as it glided into the next gear he would begin speaking again.

"We only have two brown outs per day now. That's what we call our scheduled power outages. We have only enough power to supply *most* of our needs so we have brownouts."

Tony then related a story of one missionary who checked into a local hotel during a brownout. Having assumed that the power could be out for hours, the missionary climbed the ten flights of stairs to his room. The bell hop came out of the elevator with his baggage just as he arrived. Upon realizing that he'd been allowed to climb the stairs, even though the bellhop knew the power was about to return, he lost his temper in such a fit that the church he'd been sent to wouldn't accept him. The bell hop was simply being polite, *according to local etiquette*. The missionary had told him to bring his baggage up after the power returned and that's exactly what he'd done. He didn't want to insult the intelligence of the missionary by telling him what anyone on Mindanao should have known. *Brownouts were part of the landscape*. They came and went as consistently as the sun rose and set. The bell hop simply figured the missionary was like other Americans; taking the stairs to keep fit. Some of the things the missionary said to the hotel staff were so personal as to be seen not just as anger but as bigotry so he was called back to the States despite his protestations.[1]

I was familiar with this missionary. He'd come from the old school that said regardless of the message it was the messenger that counted and if you were a Doctor of Divinity then you must be a messenger of truth. All that mattered was that you had credentials. What you preached was incidental. Our mission board had taken very seriously the trouble this man had brought upon his denomination and wasn't about to let it happen to ours. Because of this, they leaned heavily on multilingual missionaries such as myself. We were generally more interested in the people we met than our highly educated but language illiterate counterparts. Can you imagine how Americans would receive a foreign missionary who refused to speak English? Yet to this day, *most American missionaries who go abroad cannot speak the language of the people to whom they're sent*. Instead of spending their time studying the local language, many missionaries spend their free time playing racket ball with their rich English speaking buddies. The people they're sent to evangelize get little more than a Sunday sermon delivered in English. It's the local pastor who ends up delivering the sermon and counseling those who don't speak English.

I was beginning to enjoy our ride to the pastor's house along that bumpy little highway. We drove through little barangays (communities) that ended just minutes after they'd begun. Each barangay had its own mix of stores. Each store had a sign or banner that told its specialty. One such sign read:

"We make authentic brand name jeans, you pick the label."

Apparently trademark laws weren't enforced here.

About now I was beginning to feel guilty for having wanted to find another mode of transportation. This certainly wasn't going to be the most dangerous ride I'd ever taken and Tony had been so kind as to pick us up. Besides, being a missionary to remote places was going to entail more dangers than a tricycle ride.

I never liked holding things in, so I said, "Tony, I wanted to let you know how much we appreciate your having come out to the airport to pick us up."

But before Tony had a chance to respond, an explosion went off behind us. Judging from the way the tricycle careened to the side, we'd been hit. Mary held even more tightly to my now sticky arm. I wasn't sweating as profusely as before but that was because what I'd already sweated just remained on my skin. The humidity was so high that it couldn't evaporate. Luckily the *explosion* was only a flat tire.

Tony now responded to my thanks, "I'm glad to know I can be of service to the Lord's work. I'll just change the tire."

I noticed that the tire Tony was swapping for the flat was no less bald than the one that had just blown. Well, as the locals were fond of saying, *bahala na*, translated, *in God's hands* or *come what may*. I knew the wisdom of this saying for things can go at such a slow pace at the equator that an impatient attitude is a sign of either low intelligence or extreme rudeness.[2]

There was a little sari-sari store at the side of the road where we got the flat and while Tony was changing it we had a soda and snacks. A sari-sari store is a little shack that sells candy, snacks, and drinks. They also sell little packets of soap, shampoo, and other sundries. I always liked these little places where you could get a snack and a drink. They were a great place to hang out and get the local tsismis (gossip). The cost of our soda and pastries was only fifteen pesos (thirty cents) and Suni, the girl behind the counter, appeared determined to get her wages in conversation. It wasn't every day that an American and his wife stopped by to have a snack. For that matter, it was unlikely that it had ever happened.

Suni, in sharp contrast to the dilapidated little sari-sari store, looked more like a fashion model than a poor roadside vendor. Her lips were glossed and her fingernails glistened in the sun. When she walked, her toes would peek out from her long skirt, revealing their stylish pedicure, then hide themselves again. Her hips swayed each time she came around the corner to put another snack in front of us. I know; such things are to be far from a missionary's mind, but that was why I was so blessed to have Mary, my wife. It seems my youthful drive had never left me. I knew that I must be a married man or face the possibility of fornication and disgrace each time a beauty such as Suni sauntered by.[3]

Suni's feminine charms were nearly matched by her skills as an interrogator. She wanted to know our whole life story; how long we'd been married, how we'd met each other, whether it was love at first sight and whether we'd been married before. Had Tony not finished changing the tire, the conversation would have continued for hours, if you could call it a conversation. Suni was asking all the questions. In America we tend to think that questions such as these are rude or nosey. *In the Philippines they are indications that someone is simply curious about you and no harm is intended.* They certainly won't forget any of the things you've told them as so many of us who converse more superficially do.

Suni was looking at some of the pictures Mary had brought of our family when Mary showed her one of our wedding pictures.

"Oh, you got him!" Suni exclaimed, then apologized, "*Sorry hah*, it's just the dream of every single girl to get their man. You're so blessed!"

Mary wasn't used to being told that she was blessed to get me. In the States it's the man who's told he's lucky to have gotten his bride.

Not wanting Mary to feel slighted, I responded quickly. "And I was so blessed to get her! And now I must take her again."

I took Mary's arm and helped her back into the tricycle since Tony had finished fixing the flat.

"It must be wonderful to have such a strong husband." Suni

shouted as we drove away.

Wonderful indeed! I thought to myself as I basked in the praise of Suni's comments.

Mary, having gotten over the unintended insult of being told that she was lucky to have me, shouted to me above the motor of the tricycle, "Wouldn't it be nice just to have Tony drive us all over the city getting flats and chatting with people at sari-sari stores?"

It was as if she'd read my mind. It would be great fun meeting all those people one by one, but next time I wanted to be the interrogator. Suni's longing to have a husband had triggered my curiosity. Wouldn't someone with her beauty and personality have lots of suitors? Maybe she did, but since we hadn't asked, she hadn't told us. I regretted that our conversation had been so lopsided. It seemed a shame that we were the adventurers but had learned so little from our first encounter with one of the locals. I promised myself that next time, such an opportunity wouldn't be wasted.

Chapter 1 Footnotes

1. Proverbs 19:19 A man of great wrath shall suffer punishment: for if thou deliver him, yet thou must do it again.

2. Proverbs 14:29 He that is slow to wrath is of great understanding: but he that is hasty of spirit exalteth folly.

Proverbs 16:32 He that is slow to anger is better than the mighty; and he that ruleth his spirit than he that taketh a city.

Proverbs 15:18 A wrathful man stirreth up strife: but he that is slow to anger appeaseth strife.

3. 1 Corinthians 7:9 But if they cannot contain, let them marry: for it is better to marry than to burn.

Chapter 2

THE ARRIVAL

Tony suddenly pulled the tricycle to the side of the road and announced, "We're here!"

I surveyed the neighborhood, my eyes moist with tears. I was overwhelmed having finally arrived at my mission. My grandfather used to tell me that I had the eyes of an evangelist. He'd say, "Just shout the gospel news and they'll be pierced to the heart when they see the joy in your tears."[1]

I wondered now if he was simply humoring an over emotional boy. Well, I now had the chance to find out. Evangelism was my mission. Would the locals think I was an over emotional fanatic or would they indeed see the joy in my tears.

At that moment the truth for my being here hit me. I loved attention. I was selfish. Had the Lord used my desire for friends and attention to carry out His purpose? I felt ashamed but the Lord always knew my heart. He knew my heart and my reasons before I'd left on this mission. I often prayed that He would be gentle in chastening me for my selfishness but this time I wasn't so sure how gentle He would be. After all, the pastor's house was just a few hours drive from The Islamic City of Marawi. Could that city, made up of over ninety percent Muslims, be my end? I couldn't spend time worrying about it. The Lord was going to have His way and I simply had to follow Him. Yes, my selfishness had brought me here but it was no more than the vehicle that the Lord had used to start me out on this journey.

I remembered my professor's words, "Mindanao is one of the few places on earth where Christian and Muslim worlds intersect."

I pondered how its people would respond to the Lord's message of love and hope[2] and what part in delivering that message I would play. Would the local Born-Again Christians grasp the epic nature of the prophesies concerning Mindanao. Would they even take part in them or would the Lord raise up new converts to carry out that task; new wine into new bottles.[3] Could I love this people? Could they love each other?

From Pastor Sam's front yard I could see a mosque in the distance. It was imposing. Its gold dome was polished to a glass like finish. What would happen to the people who prayed there? Would they realize that they could not find salvation in their works?[4] Would they know the joy of salvation or would they go to their graves in a so-called Jihad? By what method would the Lord bring His way to be held in high esteem there?[5]

Now that Tony had turned off the engine of his tricycle I could hear other tricycles in the distance. The sounds of their engines would rise then fade like the ocean surf beating against the shores. Mary could never understand how I identified city sounds with nature. Well, to me, the cities were alive. These were the sounds of Cagayan de Oro; the tricycles, children laughing, a rooster crowing in the afternoon, I should say a *confused rooster crowing in the afternoon*, the clip clop of hooves as a farmer wearing a turban sat atop a wagon pulled by a huge water buffalo on his way to market.

"Hiya, hiya," he shouted.

I could hear the keys of an antique typewriter slapping paper from the window of a nearby school. I would remember these sounds.

Pastor Sam was outside waiting for us as we got down from the tricycle.

"*Pastor Ishmael David*, How was your ride? Not too many flats, I hope?"

"We really enjoyed the ride." I answered. "Actually, we enjoyed the flat. It gave us an opportunity to have a chat with Suni, a girl at the sari-sari store next to the market."

"Oh you met her? She's been looking forward to your coming. She's a member of our choir."

"That's odd, she didn't say a thing about it."

"Maybe she thought she'd like to meet the real Ishmael David, not the one who comes here as a missionary. Did she ask your occupation?"

"Mostly she just asked a lot of personal questions. No, she didn't ask my occupation."

"She must have enjoyed that. In fact, I'd bet that you're the first foreigners she's spoken to outside of the missionaries she's met here at church. All the other girls are going to be envious of her."

I was tired from the trip and didn't want to stand outside till dark so I asked, "Is your wife at home?"

"Yes, Sarisa is at home, and this is *your* wife, Mary?"

"Yes, I'm Mary." She answered for herself. "Nice to meet you, Pastor Sam. I hope you won't mind that I don't try to pronounce your last name."

"Oh, not in the least. Everyone here calls me Pastor Sam or just Pastor, and I'm the one who's been rude."

Pastor Sam motioned Tony to take our bags inside, then quipped, "Come in to my humble adobo er abode."[6]

I think I was the only one who got the joke. Adobo is a type of meat dish that is sautéed in red wine vinegar and soy sauce.

Chapter 2 Footnotes

1. Psalm 126:5-6 They that sow in tears shall reap in joy. He that goeth forth and weepeth, bearing precious seed, shall doubtless come again with rejoicing, bringing his sheaves [with him].
2. Romans 5:5 And hope maketh not ashamed; because the love of God is shed abroad in our hearts by the Holy Ghost which is given unto us.
3. Matthew 9:17 Neither do men put new wine into old bottles: else the bottles break, and the wine runneth out, and the bottles perish: but they put new wine into new bottles, and both are preserved.
4. Ephesians 2:8-9 For by grace are ye saved through faith; and that not of yourselves: [it is] the gift of God: Not of works, lest any man should boast.
5. Acts 18:25-28 This man was instructed in ***the way of the Lord***; and being fervent in the spirit, he spake and taught diligently the things of the Lord, knowing only the baptism of John. And he began to speak boldly in the synagogue: whom when Aquila and Priscilla had heard, they took him unto them, and expounded unto him the way of God more perfectly. And when he was disposed to pass into Achaia, the brethren wrote, exhorting the disciples to receive him: who, when he was come, helped them much which had believed through grace: For he mightily convinced the Jews, and that publicly, ***showing by the scriptures that Jesus was Christ***.

6. Among themselves pastors tend to be fond of joking and making puns. A pastor's congregation often takes him so seriously that it isn't kosher to kid and so he relishes getting visits from other pastors who can cut the mustard and in this way he avoids getting into a pickle with his flock.

Chapter 3

HUMBLE ABODE

Pastor Sam's house was built into the side of a hill. Its large foyer opened up to an expansive living room where four huge plate windows framed a postcard view of the harbor. The dining area was equally spacious and had both hillside and harbor views. The floors were made of oversized rectangular cuts of marble.

Upon entering, I could see the maids moving about the giant pantry on the other side of the kitchen. This was the first pastor I'd ever visited who had such accommodations, not to mention servants. He could see we were in awe of his home so he took us on a tour. There was a master suite, a sewing room, a den, several multi-purpose rooms, and twelve additional bedrooms. There were also a number of guestrooms that resembled the master suite. I noticed that every room had mahogany panels covering the walls and the only seams I could make out were at the corners where the panels joined.

Sam responded to my obvious curiosity.

"The man who owned this home before it was given to the church built it with the hope of having a large family. He and his wife had planned to have many sons, just like Jacob. Unfortunately, she was barren, and after a few years of living here they could no longer stand to be reminded of her barrenness by the empty rooms. Every one of those single cut panels of mahogany you've been admiring were put together with love. The entire home was a gift of love. It's such a shame that they were unable to fill it with the fruit of that love. As a matter of fact, I keep telling my wife, Sarisa, that she must bear me children again soon. This house was given to the church with the stipulation that they can't put a pastor out of it as long as his wife is pregnant, or before their youngest reaches his first birthday - Mortgage Protection." Sam smiled broadly.

"Now let me get this straight." I said. "You and Sarisa keep popping out kids and this house is yours, no matter what?

No monthly payments? No landlord? That's a good way to make sure all the rooms get filled. How many children do you have so far?"

"Only four," he said, "we have eight to go before the home is paid off."

"Paid off?" I asked.

"Yes, that's the last stipulation the owner made when he gave this house to the church. If the pastor who lives in it fills all twelve bedrooms with his own children then the house is his!"

"I would love to meet the man who gave this house to the church. He must have interesting thoughts. Who is he?" I asked.

"Nobody knows. It was given anonymously." Sam said. "Every rich barren couple in town is suspect."

"Wait a minute," Mary protested, "You just told us that the couple lived here for a while. How is it that none of the neighbors know who they are."

"Neighbors? Twenty years ago, when this home was built, there were no neighbors. All of the homes you see around here are built on land leased from the church. Mr. Tigas gave this home, along with the entire hillside, to the church before any other homes were built."

"But you just said it was Mr. Tigas," Mary protested.

"Well, we do know his name but there are hundreds of families by that name living in the area and every one of them lives up to their name."

"Lives up to their name?"

Mary was now beginning to suspect Pastor Sam was teasing her. Pastor Sam clarified, "The meaning of tigas is hard, some say hard, as in hard headed. Mary, I don't want you to think I'm kidding because I'm not. I know it sounds strange but surely there are donors in your country who wish to remain anonymous. What if one of their names was Smith or Jones? Would you have any idea who they were?"

"Well, you're right about that." Mary said. "It's just that Ish is such a kidder that I thought the two of you might have conspired to make up some unbelievable story so that you could have fun making me believe it."

"Mary," I said, "Tigas does mean hard, and it's not that uncommon of a surname. I'll get you my dictionary."

"No need to do that." Mary said. "I believe Sam. It's such a nice story to believe anyway. Well, not so nice for the couple that couldn't have kids, but it's nice the way it's turning out for you folks."

I hadn't conspired with Sam as Mary had suspected. I was as fascinated by Sam's story as she was. Such a story; Mr. Tigas had actually *wanted* a dozen children. A story like this would never be believed in the States. The government schools had so brain washed the kids into believing there were too many of them, that by the time they'd grown up they actually believed the country was overpopulated. The United States was a country with less than one hundred people per square mile[1] and yet its people believed three children was too many. Too many children, ha! The Bible says, *Happy is the man whose quiver is full of them.*[2] As for Mindanao, it was still a place where families were large and where many children were rightly considered a blessing. The story of Mr. and Mrs. Tigas was an especially fitting tale. I knew that if Sam were really kidding, he'd tell us at dinner. To think how many American couples would never get this house given the same situation. Could you even pay them to have more than a few kids? What a wretched people indeed would consider blessings a curse![3] I was glad this mission would give me time to reflect on the prospects of a mission to my own people, to the people of America. A people that had begun to see the government as the provider, instead of understanding how greatly the Lord provides for each one of us, for He created us.[4]

"To Sarisa and me," Sam said, "having lots of kids has always been a dream. Now with my position as pastor of Tigas View Bible Church, we'll be rewarded for living that dream."

Sam walked us back to the living room where Sarisa had laid out a tray of pastries and coffee.

"I hope you don't mind if I leave you for a while." Sam said. "I have some things to prepare for tonight's meeting. I'll see you in a bit."

Mary and I were left alone in this immaculately kept living room while the maids went about getting everything ready for our dinner with the church board.

Then I smelled it; a stench!

I whispered to Mary, "Do you smell that?"

She sniffed. "Eww, what is it!"

We both sniffed again to determine the origin of the smell, then Mary looked at me with one of those crooked little expressions she gets, and said. "It's you!"

She was right. It *was* me! My body had not yet accustomed itself to the tropical climate, not to mention the fact that I hadn't changed my clothes since we boarded our flight in the States. I guess you could say my clothes were beginning to ferment. Fortunately, Tony had left our bags sitting next to the door so I got out a change of clothes and hurried to one of their many bathrooms and showered. Just as I came out of the bathroom wearing my clean change of clothing, one of the maids walked by.

"Excuse me," I asked her, "could you please put my clothes in the laundry?"

She looked at my clothes which were lying on the bathroom floor, poked at them with the end of her broomstick, and said, "Eww!"

Apparently she'd overheard Mary and me when we'd first noticed the smell. The other maid brought a dustpan and squatted down to hold it while the first tried to push my clothes into it with her broomstick. When the clothes fell out of the dustpan and nearly touched them they squealed, "Eww!" then tumbled backwards onto the floor laughing.

I couldn't help but laugh with them.

"I'm Ish." I said, reaching down with both hands to help them to their feet.

"I'm Rosemary, and this is Analyn." The maid armed with the broomstick said.

Analyn matter-of-factly lifted up my elbow and sniffed my armpit.

"Ah, much better. Your wives will be very happy now. Ah, sorry sir, I meant your *wife* will be very happy."

Analyn's slip of the tongue made them giggle all the more.

"Please just call me Ish." I said.

I wasn't sure whether Analyn was kidding with the *wives* comment or if it really was a slip of the tongue.

I remembered the missionary who was sent home for insulting the hotel clerk. I said a silent prayer for him right then that he'd stop taking the little things in life too seriously and start enjoying life's blessings.[5] How wonderful it is when the help can make fun without fearing for their jobs; my request to put my clothes in the laundry had become an introduction to a pair of adorable young ladies.

The members of the church board and their wives arrived a bit late, *Philippine time* they called it. When our dinner finally began, Pastor Sam joked, "Beloved, be not ignorant of this one thing, that one day is with the Filipino as a thousand years, and a thousand years as one day."[6]

The meal was tasty but Mary and I were suffering a bit too much from jet lag to enjoy it. Tony took us to the apartment that had been arranged for us a little sooner than planned since we were starting to nod off during the meal. We hadn't meant to be rude to the members of the church board but thirty six hours without sleep is a bit much, *even if you are a missionary.*

When we arrived at the apartment that would be our home for the next few months, Tony put all of our stuff inside; four large boxes containing everything we felt necessary to start our new life. Mary had crammed everything she could into those boxes. She'd brought our best china and silverware, even bed sheets that she'd gotten on sale the day before we left. Only a Filipino or customs official knows how much can be packed into one of those balikbayan[7] boxes. That's what they call the huge boxes that nearly everyone going to the Philippines takes with them.

I thanked Tony for picking us up at the airport and helping us get our stuff into the apartment, then gave him some money,

"It's for your children's educational expenses." I said in his native tongue. "It's our custom."

Tony was so shocked that I was speaking his language that he forgot Philippine custom, that he must object, *at least once*. He simply said, "Thank you sir. Thank you."

It was the least we could do, considering he'd forfeited a day's wages to cater to our transportation needs. I knew that if I'd directly offered to pay him that he would have refused it.

Now Tony rattled off something so fast in his dialect that I understood just one part of it; *he'd be back Sunday morning to take us to church.*

Mary and I were both so excited to settle in that as soon as Tony left we started to sort through our stuff. Mary set out to prepare our bedroom and to tidy up the bathroom while I put the rest of our belongings in place. We had barely enough energy left after unpacking to brush our teeth.

Mary was out the moment she laid down. I lay there, awake and alone for the first time since we'd arrived. I pondered. My vision of Mindanao had been one of grass huts and coconut palms blowing in the wind. Cagayan de Oro was so different from my expectations. It was a huge city with an international harbor and Sam's church was financially independent. For what reason had the Lord brought me here? Had I closed my eyes to the obvious or was my lack of vision a work of the Lord? Was He closing my eyes to something that He would show me only when I was ready? I dozed off, unaware of how prophetic my thoughts would turn out to be.

Chapter 3 Footnotes

1. CIA Factbook - United States
2. Psalm 127:5 Happy [is] the man that hath his quiver full of them: they shall not be ashamed, but they shall speak with the enemies in the gate.
3. Revelation 3:17 Because thou sayest, I am rich, and increased with goods, and have need of nothing; and knowest not that thou art wretched, and miserable, and poor, and blind, and naked.
4. Genesis 1:27-28a So God created man in his [own] image, in the image of God created he him; male and female created he them and God blessed them.
5. James 5:16 Confess [your] faults one to another, and pray one for another, that ye may be healed. The effectual fervent prayer of a righteous man availeth much.
6. 2 Peter 3:8 But, beloved, be not ignorant of this one thing, that one day [is] with the Lord as a thousand years, and a thousand years as one day.
7. Balikbayan - *One who returns to their country*. A balikbayan box is a card board box that in inches measures 20 X 20 X 22 and is carried by nearly every Filipino who returns to the Philippines. A family of five is allowed to carry ten such boxes without an additional charge. Ten boxes can weigh a total of seven hundred pounds! It's not unusual to witness frantic Filipinos at the airport, moving items between boxes to bring each one under the seventy

pound limit. If you ever need to borrow boxing tape at the airport just find the nearest flight leaving for the Philippines.

Chapter 4

SISTERS IN NEED

Mary and I had spent the couple of days since our arrival busily sprucing up our apartment so Sunday came quickly. Tony drove up as scheduled and dropped us off in front of Sam's church.

Sam's church was referred to as a *startup* church. Some startup church. It had over a thousand members and an assistant pastor who had more degrees from Western seminaries than my entire mission board put together. It was our first experience with this language group so we were surprised when, in perfect English, pastor Sam delivered a fire and brimstone sermon.[1]

It happened to be mother's day so toward the end of the service there was a special time when the mothers in the church were honored. Each mother walked to the front to have a freshly picked orchid pinned on her by her husband. It was at this point that I noticed those left sitting. The back twenty pews were filled with women! I learned later that most of these women were NBSB, *No Boyfriend Since Birth*, their way of saying that they were single and pure, having never been alone with a man. Off to one side were a few straggly looking single men; recent converts one would hope from the looks of them. I found out later that *all the best men were taken*. So I'd been told, but I'd not realized the profoundness of that saying till now. I wondered; what would become of these single women? Would God provide new men converts?

Pastor Sam told me later that this was of great concern to him. The single ladies had a hunger for fellowship that neither their own families nor the families at the church were providing. Their own families were still locked in the clutches of the *Great Whore of Babylon* yet the families of these *Born-Again* churches shunned them. The married women of the church felt threatened by the presence of so many single ladies since there were no single Christian men available for them.[2] Some claimed the single ladies *had eyes* for their husbands.

The only fellowship with families that the single ladies were allowed was to attend the coffees after the service. The coffees allowed them to mix with the married members and their children. *You could see the covetousness in the eyes of the single women for the children of the women who already had husbands.*[3] A covetousness I didn't begrudge them. What healthy young woman wouldn't want to be mother to such delightful children. How many times had godly women of the Bible thanked the Lord that He had *taken away their reproach* by giving them a son?[4] Not only did these single ladies have no children, they had no husband nor hope to find one. Many had already been taught the false doctrine of *the gift of singleness* in order to stop them from wondering if the Lord had forgotten them. This only led them to feel guilty for their natural desires.

I don't know why they called the after service get-togethers; *coffees*. The members put more cream into those cups than coffee.

One of the young ladies joked with me, "Do you take coffee in your cream or do you drink it white?"

"Black," I said.

"Black cream?" She giggled. "Whoever heard of such a thing."

She grasped my hand as she poured the hot coffee into my cup, not wanting to scald me with it. You could tell how much this opportunity to mingle and kid around meant to her. Was she flirting with me or was it simply my fertile imagination that noticed a slight wink as she turned to serve the others?

Pastor Sam noticed my look of concern and took me aside.

"I'm at wits end trying to deal with what has become *the issue of the single women*." He said. "More than one of the single women has even proposed becoming a second wife to me."

Not surprisingly, I expressed shock.

"Tell me you're kidding."

"I'm not, Ish. In fact, my wife Sarisa was at my side when she brought it up."

As Mary approached, Sam changed the subject.

"So what are your and Ish's plans for Tigas View, Mary?"

"Ish and I hadn't expected to be greeted by such a huge church and we've been wondering whether this is really where the Lord wants us. You've obviously been very effective in your evangelism." Mary said.

"Now let's not have any of that kind of talk. I have just the job for Ish. I'll discuss it with him in my office after the coffee."

"That's great Sam!" Mary said with excitement. "Ish and I had begun to wonder what we could do here. Everything looks so successful. I'm reassured now that you've told us you have a special task for Ish."

"Yes, a special task. That's what it is."

Normally Mary and I were on the same wavelength but she made no comment whatsoever about the huge numbers of single women. How could she not notice that over two thirds of the membership of Sam's church were single women? Had she noticed but was shocked into silence? I was certain I'd find out later.

I was glad when I saw Suni approaching. I wanted to return her hospitality and maybe get to know something about her. All she'd done at her sari-sari store was ask about us. It was our turn to ask about her. When Mary noticed her, she bubbled.

"Suni! You've got to let us return your hospitality! Come over to our new apartment with a few of your friends after the service and we can all prepare dinner together."

Sam put his hand on my shoulder.

"Ish, why not have Mary go back to the apartment with Suni and some of her friends right now and you and I will have that chat we talked about."

Mary answered for me, "Great! Let's go Suni."

Sam and I went back to his office. We began our meeting with a prayer. Listening to Sam pray made me painfully aware how little I'd known love in my own life. My wife loved me with all her heart as did my family but how much had I loved. This precious man, after praying for my wife and me, prayed for dozens of the single ladies by name. He'd taken it upon himself to take headship for these women, not as their husband but as their pastor.[5] They knew he loved them even more than the wives of the married women reviled them.

I began weeping uncontrollably as did Pastor Sam. We prayed in the spirit for guidance and the Lord's will in dealing with what seemed like an insurmountable problem.[6] Then I felt the shame. The shame, for I knew my own church, back home, had women in it like these. They were told to wait upon the Lord and He would give them a husband and all the time no head, no shepherd, no man to pray with them and for them. The Lord is our shepherd we shall not want but what if the Lord's own messengers stand in the way of the Lord, what then?[7] Doesn't Paul say to avoid immorality every woman should have her own husband?[8] I realized now that I had not even spent sufficient time praying for my own wife let alone praying for the dear single ladies in my church back home. Pastor Sam had inspired me. I asked him to pray with me about this too and he did.

After Sam's prayer I remembered the *special task* he'd mentioned and asked him,

"What's your special task for me?"

He replied,

"I have just seven tasks for you."

I thought to myself, seven tasks! He told me he had *a* special task but Pastor Sam was serious and I'd never met such a kind and thoughtful pastor before. This was my mission so I accepted without knowing what he was going to assign.

"Sure, no problem." I said.

I know now that it was the moving of the Spirit that prompted my response. Sure, no problem. Seven tasks? Never in my inward looking life had I accepted a request like that, nor had I ever prayed for so many people in one sitting.

"So what are these seven tasks?" I asked.

Then Pastor Sam said, "I have seven bios here with information about seven of the single women in the church. Will you take headship over them until they find a husband? I ask that you do this in all humility and purity of thought.[9] Will you encourage them to flee fornication?[10] Will you pray for them? Will you love them? Will you ask the Lord what is His will for them?[11] When the Lord answers you, will you believe Him and will you guide these women in accordance with what the Lord has laid upon your heart? Will you guide them in their prayer life? Will you explain Scripture to them? Will you lay down your life for them if needs be as Christ gave His body for the church?[12] Will you do all this?"

All I said was, "I will."

I thought to myself, am I nuts? I just became everything a man can be to these women short of actually marrying them.

Barely had I finished answering when Pastor Sam took out

another list of seven women and asked me the same questions.

Again, I answered, "I will."

This, he repeated until he had asked me and I had responded seven times. Seven lists, each of seven women, over whom I would have all the responsibilities of a husband but at a distance.

Sam handed me the lists. There were no names, just a picture of the back of each woman's head and a nickname. TinkaTwist read one, another, SweetieWinky, and so forth. Then Sam explained to me.

"This was put upon my heart by the Lord that you should pray neither knowing the name nor the face of the woman you were praying for. You'll receive her requests, her thanksgivings, and you'll share her sorrows but you shall not meet any of them in person until the time that the Lord will reveal to you."[13]

This sounded kind of wild to me, being somewhat reserved, but I felt the moving of the Spirit and couldn't refuse. Sam logged me into the system that I would use to communicate with the women. It reminded me of ChristianMarriage.com, one of my favorite ministries.

I left our meeting not fully understanding what Pastor Sam meant by *headship* but he assured me that over time I would come to recognize my role in the lives of these single ladies. I knew that none of the things he had asked of me was sinful so why was I doubting? Was it a sin to pray for blessings upon single women? Had the Western Church so slanted my views on women that I couldn't allow myself to love them as sisters in the Lord for fear that I might go against taboos not found in the Holy Scriptures?[14] In fact, all of the things he'd asked of me had already been asked of me by Jesus when He said, "Feed My sheep."[15] Certainly I loved the Lord and I would feed His sheep. These ladies were His flock and they needed special prayer and special attention. As I thought on these things, peace came upon my spirit.[16]

When I arrived home, Mary was busy washing the vegetables that she and the girls had bought at the market. This was the perfect time for a power Bible study. Some people take power naps, I take power Bible studies. The fifteen or twenty minutes I spend in these fast paced studies leave me more rested and clear of mind than any nap could.

Chapter 4 Footnotes

1. Revelation 21:8 But the fearful, and unbelieving, and the abominable, and murderers, and whoremongers, and sorcerers, and idolaters, and all liars, shall have their part in the lake which burneth with fire and brimstone: which is the second death.
2. Mass conversions of women to Christianity began in the 20th century. By the beginning of the 21st century there were more than double the number of Born-Again Christian women in the Philippines than Born-Again Christian men.
3. Genesis 30:1 And when Rachel saw that she bare Jacob no children, Rachel envied her sister; and said unto Jacob, Give me children, or else I die.
4. Genesis 30:23 And she conceived, and bare a son; and said, God hath taken away my reproach.
5. 1 Corinthians 11:3 But I would have you know, that the head of every man is Christ; and the head of the woman [is] the man; and the head of Christ [is] God.
6. Romans 8:26 Likewise the Spirit also helpeth our infirmities: for we know not what we should pray for as we ought: but the Spirit itself maketh intercession for us with groanings which cannot be uttered.
7. Psalm 23:1 [[A Psalm of David.]] The LORD [is] my shepherd; I shall not want.

2 Chronicles 36:16 But they mocked the messengers of God, and despised his words, and misused his prophets, until the wrath of the LORD arose against his people, till [there was] no remedy.

8. 1Corinthians 7:2 Nevertheless, [to avoid] fornication, let every man have his own wife, and let every woman have her own husband.
9. Philemon 4:8 Finally, brethren, whatsoever things are true, whatsoever things [are] honest, whatsoever things [are] just, whatsoever things [are] pure, whatsoever things [are] lovely, whatsoever things [are] of good report; if [there be] any virtue, and if [there be] any praise, think on these things.
10. 1Corinthians 6:18 Flee fornication. Every sin that a man doeth is without the body; but he that committeth fornication sinneth against his own body.
11. Hebrews 13:21 Make you perfect in every good work to do his will, working in you that which is well pleasing in his sight,

through Jesus Christ; to whom [be] glory for ever and ever. Amen.
12. Ephesians 5:25 Husbands, love your wives, even as Christ also loved the church, and gave himself for it;
13. Matthew 25:44-46 Then shall they also answer him, saying, Lord, when did we see thee hungered, or athirst, or a stranger, or naked, or sick, or in prison, and did not minister unto thee? Then shall he answer them, saying, Verily I say unto you, Inasmuch as ye did [it] not to one of the least of these, ye did [it] not to me. And these shall go away into everlasting punishment: but the righteous into life eternal.
14. Isaiah 5:20 Woe unto them that call evil good, and good evil; that put darkness for light, and light for darkness; that put bitter for sweet, and sweet for bitter!
15. John 21:17 He saith unto him the third time, Simon, [son] of Jonas, lovest thou me? Peter was grieved because he said unto him the third time, Lovest thou me? And he said unto him, Lord, thou knowest all things; thou knowest that I love thee. Jesus saith unto him, Feed my sheep.
16. Galatians 5:22-23 But the fruit of the Spirit is love, joy, peace, longsuffering, gentleness, goodness, faith, meekness, temperance: against such there is no law.

Chapter 5

THE BARBECUE

Suni came in to tell us that dinner was ready. She entered through a door that was previously hidden behind a wall hanging.

"Wow, there's a door there?" I said.

"Sure," Suni answered. "All of the units have them."

"All of the units? I've got to see this."

I went out the door and stood on the balcony which stretched the length of a basketball court. Below us was indeed a court, a courtyard, that is, with trees and shrubs and lots of benches. Suni's friends waved to us from below.

"Can you smell the barbecue?" Suni asked.

I nodded. Hunger took over where curiosity had begun. I walked down the stairs, sniffing my way to the barbecue. From the courtyard I could see that my unit was actually above another. The lower one had windows that looked out onto the courtyard and a private patio graced with a beautiful little table. Two cute chairs adorned it like a pair of ear rings.

"Bet you didn't know I lived right under you." Suni said. She went into her unit and came out with such a high stack of paper plates that she had to keep them in place with her chin.

"Nothing like having friends for neighbors." I said. "Here, let me help you with that."

Suni dumped the stack into my arms and went back inside to get more. Now we both had plates up to our chins. Kicking the door shut with her foot, she started toward the grill.

"Follow me." She said.

We set the plates down where the food was being served and made small talk.

"I've never seen such beautiful designs on paper plates." I said.

"That's right, Ish. I bet you never guessed you'd be holding that many beautiful dishes in your arms today." Suni kidded. "Hope you don't mind if I call you Ish? I heard Mary calling you that."

"Not at all, Suni. I'd prefer you call me Ish. Is Suni *your* nickname, or your real name?"

"Suni's my real name, as in Sue Nee. My mother was half Chinese. Nee was her maiden name. My nickname is *Sexy*."

At that moment Mary walked by.

"Ah, I see Sexy has shown you her apartment. Bet you didn't know we'd have *Sista Sexy* living just below us."

Mary kept on walking. She was having too much fun mingling with her new friends to stop now.

"I'd been wondering how Mary might react if I called you by your nickname, now I know... *Sexy*."

"There you go again, Ish. First you're holding beautiful dishes in your arms and now you're calling me *Sexy*."

Suni's face lit up to match her smiling eyes as she teased. I'd heard Sexy used as a nickname before and knew it was nothing more than that, a nickname. Filipinas are quick to kid about love but slow to act on it. Sure, there are exceptions, as in all cultures, but in general, they value their chastity.

As we approached Suni's friends, they raised their voices in unison, "Uh!"

"They say I have a crush on you." Suni said, averting her eyes from mine.

"I'll take that as a compliment." I assured her.

"*As well you should*." She responded., no longer ashamed.

A loud voice bellowed from a tiny lady standing a few tables away.

"Aren't you going to introduce us to your crush, Suni?"

How many friends did Suni have, I wondered. It looked like every one of the single ladies in Sam's church were there.

Sam walked across the courtyard and stood next to the tiny lady with the loud voice.

"May I introduce Asina." He said. "Her folks nicknamed her Asina for her salty remarks."

I remembered my lessons. Asin was their word for salt.

"I speak with grace, seasoned with an ample dash of salt, that I may answer every man." She said.

Asina had paraphrased Colossians 4:6 to suit her unique personality.[1]

"And she does give every man an answer." Sam said. "You ought to have seen her take on the atheists in the debate club at law school. Yes, the perfect career match, and Asina informed me this morning that she just received her bar exam results in the mail. Let's all congratulate her; *Attorney Asina*!"

The girls' applause drowned out even the sounds of traffic from the nearby streets.

"And you do give every man an answer," Sam looked at tiny Asina with admiration, "just as the Bible says every Christian must do." Then Sam put his arm around her shoulder and kidded. "Of course in Asina's case, one might call it *talking back*."

Pastor Sam acknowledged her uniqueness as he gave her shoulder a squeeze. For the moment, Asina appeared satisfied with the amount of seasoning she'd added to the occasion.

Suni had gotten over her embarrassment that the girls had revealed her crush on me. She peeked up at me like a child waiting for a gift. If it pleased her to have a crush on me, I wasn't going to stop her. She handed me a plateful of barbecued beef.

"Thanks so much that you picked out the best barbecue for me." I said.

Suni, her bubbly self again, responded. "I'm so glad you like it."

Suni and I found a seat at one of the tables. I'd barely shoveled down enough bites to stop the growls in my stomach when I sensed that someone was peering over my shoulder. I turned around and saw that the ladies had formed a long line leading to my table, each of them was carrying a copy of my book. Our barbecue had become an autograph signing.

"Your book is so poetic." One said.

Another sighed,

"I couldn't stand it! I was so excited reading it that you made me late for school."

While yet another gushed,

"I could just die dreaming. It's so romantic!"

This was beyond my expectations. Frankly, I didn't have any expectations. It was a theology book! I couldn't understand how young single ladies could be so taken with a text book.

Suni came back with her food and sat down next to me.

"You're a star." She said.

"I'm not a star. This is..." I halted mid-sentence. I was about to say ridiculous but then I realized their sincerity. "Now what's the word I'm looking for? Humbling. That's it. I'm very much humbled that there are so many of you who've gotten something from my book. I'm kind of a book worm. I'm not used to so much..."

"Adoration?" One of the single ladies completed my sentence. She looked like one of the women in a liquor ad. Actually, she made them look homely by comparison.

"W..well, I wouldn't call it that." I stuttered.

"*I would*." This silencer of mankind replied. *I'd never seen anyone that beautiful up close*. I mean it. I couldn't hope to describe her here. For that matter, I didn't really see her. I experienced her presence. Like the finest chocolate cake, baked by a king's chef for his favorite son's birthday, she also had been carefully prepared, *but her maker was the King Himself, Jehovah*; and she was meant for some lucky idiot who couldn't possibly deserve her. *Oops*, did I covet her? Well, not in the technical sense since she didn't belong to another, but still, I longed to taste the frosting on that cake.

"Oh, don't let Modelisa scare you. She's tame."

Suni took her handkerchief and wiped the sweat from my forehead. The ladies roared with laughter. I hadn't realized it but they'd all been waiting for Modelisa to approach and Suni's wiping the sweat from my forehead was just part of the show. I was certain that Modelisa was a nickname but it fit, just like each piece of perfectly tailored clothing that she wore. The girls loved seeing the affect she had on men. She knew who she was and what she had. She could turn even the most confident man into a little puppy on a leash. She could and did, that is, until she was born again. But for special occasions, such as this, she would entertain her friends by helping some important visitor face his own mortality; and to show him that no matter who he was, that there are some things that even the wisest man, cannot comprehend or explain.[2] Such was Modelisa.

The laughter was contagious. I found myself nervously laughing as well, and I'm sure I was even redder in the face than Suni had been earlier when the girls had teased her. So this was what getting to know Suni and her friends meant. How could I ever forget it.

A few minutes more of signing autographs and a simply dressed young lady came up and sat next to Suni and me. She had a kind face, one that no stranger would fear. She was asking questions about my book and did so in the most thorough fashion. Each time she got an answer she would apply it to her witnessing manual.

"I'm putting together a witnessing manual that helps single Christian ladies reach other single ladies for Christ. I'm approaching it from the method of showing them what the Bible says about chastity and helping them to realize that they fall short of the glory of God and need Jesus.[3] It's a lot like what you've laid out in your book."

I was impressed; so easy to be with and chat with.

"I'm sorry, I've been rude. I'm Ish, and you're?"

"Hope. At least that's what my parents named me. My friends call me Modelisa."

I was about floored.

"You didn't mind my teasing you a few minutes ago?" She asked.

"Mind? It was a treat. You're very talented, but what I can't figure out is how you did it? How did you make yourself look so totally different?"

"To tell you the truth, Ish, it's not how I *did* it but how I'm doing this."

Hope took my hand and lifted it to her face pushing one of my fingers into her cheek, which I now realized was covered with some kind of stage putty.

"My father invented it. We used to live far from the city, and since the mountain chiefs wouldn't take no for an answer when they found a girl they wanted for a wife, he wanted to make sure I was ugly."

"Well, you don't look ugly now," I said, "except for the hole I poked in your cheek."

"Oh, this is just my plain Jane face." She said. "You should see me when I put on my ugly face."

"To tell you the truth, Modelisa, I'd rather not." I kidded. "But what about your real face and, well, everything else about you."

"Ish, my real face is hidden beneath this and it looks just the way you saw it earlier, and what you refer to as *everything else*, well, that's just good genes."

"I find it hard to believe that a pair of jeans could do all that." I couldn't resist the temptation to make such an obvious pun, even at the price of appearing a bit corny.

Modelisa smiled politely, "Well Ish, I hope you'll excuse me. This goo will ruin my complexion if I leave it on too long. I'll see you in a bit."

"Okay, see you later." I said.

Sam was sitting close by so I couldn't help commenting to him.

"Is Modelisa the greatest actress in the world, or what?! How will her future husband ever know when she's telling the truth or when she's acting? She's incredible."

"You will know them by their fruit,"[4] Sam answered. "Modelisa was used of God to bring at least half of the women you see here to a saving knowledge of the Lord."[5]

I looked out at all the single ladies. It looked like all of those from his church were there; over seven hundred. My throat tightened from emotion and I was barely able to speak.

"You're telling me that Modelisa has brought over three hundred women to Christ?"

"I'd put it at well over a thousand." Sam responded. "There are other churches in Cagayan de Oro besides Tigas View. All of the churches in our city have been blessed by the fruit of Modelisa's ministry."

Tears gushed from my eyes. I managed to get out the words,

"Excuse me."

Suni took me to her apartment where I sat down for a few minutes and wept privately. Mary walked in and said,

"What's the problem, Ish?"

I tried to tell her but the tears started gushing again. Sam was standing outside the door so Mary went out to ask him.

"It's about Hope; how she's brought hundreds to a saving knowledge of our Savior."

I could hear Mary whisper to Sam, "Oh, Ish is always crying about some spiritual revelation he's had. He'll get over it."

Mary didn't realize I could hear her. It cut me deep. Not because it was disrespectful to me but because of the way my wife had reacted to Hope; the greatest evangelist I'd ever met. I was humbled at how the Lord had used Hope for such a great purpose and was ashamed at my own shallowness. How could it be that Mary had no awe for the great power that God had given that woman?

Sam walked over, "Now that you've gotten to know the ladies, don't you think it's time for a Bible study? The girls have been waiting for this moment."

"Sure," I said, "But I'll need some water first."

Suni had already poured it.

"Here you go, Ish," Suni consoled me, "My father used to cry when he preached. He said it was because he knew that he wasn't worthy. But you know, Ish, it was that humility in him that convinced me all the more that he was a man of God. If we ever think that we're great or that we're the reason someone was saved, then whatever power the Lord has given us to reach people will disappear. We won't be worshipping God anymore. We'll be worshipping our own ministry. Modelisa knows that and she needs our prayers. Think how difficult it must be to remain humble if you're Modelisa? Not only is she extremely beautiful but she has a gift of reaching women for the Lord. There's hardly a day that goes by that someone has not come to the Lord through her personal ministry. Anyway, my dad would go through two liters of water in one sermon, that's how much he cried. Don't ever be ashamed of your tears. They're the mark of a contrite heart."[6]

Suni's caring words warmed me.

Chapter 5 Footnotes

1. Colossians 4:6 Let your speech [be] alway with grace, seasoned with salt, that ye may know how ye ought to answer every man.

2. Proverbs 30:18-19 There be three things which are too wonderful for me, yea, four which I know not: The way of an eagle in the air; the way of a serpent upon a rock; the way of a ship in the midst of the sea; and the way of a man with a maid. When Solomon sets up verses this way, it is the last item mentioned which is contrasted to the others as being even more astounding. The last phrase is better rendered in modern English as follows:

"A fourth, which I cannot comprehend; the way of a man with a young woman."

3. Romans 3:23 For all have sinned, and come short of the glory of God. It is a Christians duty to know what the Bible teaches concerning fornication. We know it's wrong, of course, but we're supposed to know where fornication is defined in the Bible. All

cultures are not the same and our culture's definition of fornication is not always the same as the Bible's definition of fornication. The definition of the different types of fornication as spelled out in the Bible is what we are to teach and accept. Not only are we are to use biblical definitions of fornication to call sinners attention to their own sins but the primary duty of a minister to those already saved is spelled out in the following verse:

Acts 15:20 But that we write unto them, that they abstain from pollutions of idols, and [from] fornication, and [from] things strangled, and [from] blood.

Remember that Jesus taught the Ten Commandments. The above verse is therefore emphasizing a particular area where Christians must be especially mindful since they are no longer overseen by a priest who gives daily sacrifices for them at the temple. This verse clarifies that even though they are not required to give those daily sacrifices that there are still certain holy rules of behavior that they must follow and that their behavior as well as their avoidance of certain things reflects their reverence for God. Tattoos are a modern day example of fornication against God.

Leviticus 19:28 Ye shall not make any cuttings in your flesh for the dead, nor print any marks upon you: I [am] the LORD.

4. Matthew 7:16-20 Ye shall know them by their fruits. Do men gather grapes of thorns, or figs of thistles? Even so every good tree bringeth forth good fruit; but a corrupt tree bringeth forth evil fruit. A good tree cannot bring forth evil fruit, neither [can] a corrupt tree bring forth good fruit. Every tree that bringeth not forth good fruit is hewn down, and cast into the fire. Wherefore by their fruits ye shall know them.

5. 1Timothy 2:4-6 Who will have all men to be saved, and to come unto the knowledge of the truth. For [there is] one God, and one mediator between God and men, the man Christ Jesus; Who gave himself a ransom for all, to be testified in due time.

6. Psalm 34:18 The LORD [is] nigh unto them that are of a broken heart; and saveth such as be of a contrite spirit.

Psalm 51:17 The sacrifices of God [are] a broken spirit: a broken and a contrite heart, O God, thou wilt not despise.

Isaiah 57:15 For thus saith the high and lofty One that inhabiteth eternity, whose Name [is] Holy; I dwell in the high and holy [place], with him also [that is] of a contrite and humble spirit, to

revive the spirit of the humble, and to revive the heart of the contrite ones.
Isaiah 66:2 For all those [things] hath mine hand made, and all those [things] have been, saith the LORD: but to this [man] will I look, [even] to [him that is] poor and of a contrite spirit, and trembleth at my word.

Chapter 6

CHERRY THE HARLOT

"C'mon Ish. The other girls are waiting." Suni said.

She took my hand and led me to the center of the courtyard where Pastor Sam was standing on a raised platform. He motioned me to join him.

"Bring Suni with you. I'm sure you'll need an assistant."

"Suni, would you like to be my assistant today?"

"Sure, Ish. If you want me."

"Of course I want you. C'mon"

I hadn't realized till we stepped onto the platform that it was slowly turning. Sam could see my surprise and explained it to me.

"Ish, the platform turns so that we'll be able to face all of the audience every fifteen minutes or so. Don't worry. It doesn't spin fast enough to make you dizzy. Here, you'll need this." Pastor Sam fastened a tiny microphone to my lapel.

"Nothing could make me any dizzier than looking out over these seven hundred women and having all of them look back at me." I said to Pastor Sam.

I hadn't realized the microphone was live. My comment was met with laughter and applause so I went with the flow.

"Now that you've gotten my attention, I mean, well, you know what I mean. Anyway, it's time to tell you that I'm in love."

"Uh!" Came the familiar chorus from the ladies.

"Yes! I'm in love!" I shouted "*And so are you*. We're in love with the Lord!"

They all stood clapping. The clapping became a rhythm which continued till I began to pray.

"Let's open with a prayer." I said.

"*Lord, help us so that we do not become a strange and degenerate vine unto You.*[1] *Help us so that we will not close our eyes to Your Light. Help us so that we will not backslide but that we may joyfully accept Your deliverance from the hand of our enemies. Help us to serve You without fear. Strengthen our faith.*

Amen."[2]

"*Amen*!" Came the shout from the ladies.

After I'd prayed, I began to teach.

"Now, let's open our Bibles to..." but before I could finish my sentence the ladies shouted as with one voice:

"*Matthew 5:27 and 28!*"[3]

"So you *have* read my books." I said. "Okay, since you've read my books, you all must know that I like to put together little plays to demonstrate the meaning of various Bible verses. Today we'll be studying the topic of marriage, fornication, and harlotry. Suni's already volunteered and in a few minutes I'll be asking for a couple more volunteers. Come over here *Sexy*."

I was certain that calling Suni by her nickname, *Sexy*, would keep the ladies' attention, and it did. The familiar *uh* was hummed by the audience like a chorus.

"You're going to be the single lady, Sexy. Stand over there." I pointed.

Sexy put on a pouting face.

"I wanted to be the married lady!" She stomped her feet like a spoiled toddler.

"Yes, let her be the married lady!" The girls shouted.

No more had I gotten out the words, "Okay, so you're the married lady," than Suni popped out with, "Who's my husband?"

Exasperated I replied, "You want a husband? Let's see. Who do you argue with most?"

"I'm arguing with you right now." She snapped.

Running short of patience I replied.

"Okay, so I'm your husband."

"Whatcha want for dinner honey?" Suni didn't miss a cue.

I turned to the side shaking my head. Sexy was a natural when it came to tickling the crowd. I could barely keep a straight face. Mary was watching from the front row and was having just as much fun watching Sexy pretend to be my wife as Sexy was having playing the part.

"All right. All right. Let's get on with this." I said.

"Well we better. We're married. If we don't get on with this you'll have me to deal with when we get home."

The ladies roared with laughter. Sexy and I couldn't have put on a better show had we planned it. Just then, I realized that Suni *had* planned it. She was using her comedic talent to warm up the crowd for me. I was glad. Maybe this would be the first Bible study I held where nobody fell asleep. Suni signaled me with a nod that she was through with her antics and that it was up to me to keep them awake from here on out so I announced.

"Now, I need two more volunteers; one to play the part of a virgin and the other to play the part of a prostitute."

Modelisa came up to the stage and brought with her a shy girl who barely looked sixteen.

"I'll let the two of you decide which will play the prostitute and which will play the virgin." I said.

Modelisa and the girl started arguing over who would play the prostitute. This was the first time I'd seen Modelisa in anything but perfect composure.

Modelisa complained,

"But she wants to play the prostitute!"

The girl looked so innocent that I couldn't imagine her playing the prostitute either.

"But maybe she can act the part." I offered.

Modelisa sighed, "Introduce yourself to Ish."

The young girl said, "I'm *Cherry the Harlot.*"

"You mean that's what you want your character to be called?" I asked her.

"No. I *am* a harlot. *Puta*. I'm a *whore.*"[4]

It really hurt me to hear her say that. I'd written a lot on the subject of chastity but I'd never personally dealt with someone who'd come out of harlotry. Despite the words that came out of her mouth, I couldn't imagine her being a whore.

"Maybe Modelisa is right." Cherry said. "I can't even remember what it was like being a whore."

"You're a new creature." Modelisa insisted. "Old things are passed away."[5]

Cherry, by now in tears, blubbered, "But that doesn't change what I am!"

The ladies in the audience could hear the entire discussion over the loud speakers and so they shouted,

"*Testimony! Testimony! Testimony!*"

Sam handed Cherry a microphone.

"There's nothing good about the fact that I used to be a whore.

Nothing! It didn't teach me anything. That was a lost and worthless part of my life. I'm so ashamed."[6]

One of the girls in the crowd shouted,

"But now you're clean, you're washed,[7] you're like your name, a cherry all over again."

"Yeah right," Cherry responded, "Cherry in the ass."

There was dead silence. The girls from Sam's church winced at Cherry's words. Only a handful of them had even been kissed. It was as if Cherry's words had pierced a veil of innocence that had covered their ears. Then there were cries from the audience. Modelisa had managed to convince about a dozen of the girls who worked in the local bars to attend the gathering. Some of them started sobbing and shouting. One of them screamed:

"I'm a whore, I'm worthless! Help me."

The other girls with her started screaming and crying as well,

"Nobody can help us. We're disgusting!"

"There is nothing we can do. You heard Cherry."

Cherry, now composed, took out her Bible.

"They're right! In First Corinthians 6:9 Paul wrote:

Don't you know that the unrighteous won't get the kingdom of God?"[7]

Cherry now moved to the edge of the stage where the whores had cried out and looked them directly in the eyes.

"Don't pretend, if you're a whore, you won't get the kingdom of God. And that's what you are, whores!" She paused, "But you know what Paul wrote in the very next verse to the whores of his day who had repented? Paul said,

but you are washed[7], you are sanctified, you are justified in the Name of the Lord Jesus, and by the Spirit of our God.

Do you want to be washed through the Name of Jesus?"

"Yes!" "Yes!" came their cries, now overcome by the Lord's Spirit moving among them.

"Praise God! And you will be!" Cherry assured them. Then Cherry turned her attention to another group.

"I know that some of you other ladies here, think you're better than these whores because you gave yourself for free to your boyfriends and didn't ask money. You even gave your boyfriends presents, kind of like equals you felt. Do you know what God says about you?"

The girls of Sam's church now listened attentively to Cherry's words. They knew, as Sam had told me, that there were a dozen or so tares among them; girls who despite being warned, refused to *kiss dating goodbye*.[8]

Cherry's voice now hammered into the crowd.

"God says in Ezekiel 16:34

And you are the opposite of the other whores because nobody follows you to find you but it is you who gives gifts to your lover while he gives you none!"[9]

Cherry's voice was now shaking and yet it grew stronger. As each word found its mark another repentant voice would cry from the crowd.

"Help me!"[10]

Cherry's spiritual assault was unrelenting.

"If these whores don't get the kingdom of heaven, and God says you're worse than them. What do you think you get? Some of you already think you're Christians and yet you behave as whores of the worst kind! I say repent! Come down here to the front right now."

Cherry pointed accusingly. She knew which girls were having sex with their so-called Christian boyfriends and she was making it crystal clear to them that they were every bit the whore that she'd been, and worse.

"Don't wait. God will not wait for you when He arrives on a day and at an hour you cannot know!"[11]

The sobs which had begun slowly now echoed off the buildings that surrounded the courtyard. A few dozen of the ladies Cherry had been pointing to came forward in addition to the whores that Modelisa had brought. Then I noticed an awesome sight. Someone was wandering in from the street.

"What will I do?" She whimpered.

She started shaking uncontrollably as her tears gushed. One of the ladies helped her to a seat in front of the platform where Cherry stood.

Others were coming from outside the courtyard as well. The microphone hadn't been turned up that loud but Cherry had been able to bellow out her condemnations of harlotry into the nearby streets. The bar girls had just begun arriving for work in the tourist district adjacent to the courtyard and they'd heard Cherry's pleas and denunciations. They now began to fill up the courtyard.

Cherry's cry now pierced the air like the sigh of an animal's last gasp for life before going down in the jaws of a predator.

"What shall you do?" She rasped.

The whores' eyes were fixed on Cherry as she spoke, their faces streaked with mascara from tears.

"I was a whore. I told myself it was an accident, that I hadn't planned it and so that made it all right but I knew different. All those things I did. That's not pretend. You're not pretend. Your broken life, that's not pretend. Your body, maybe it's destroyed. What diseases do you have? If you still have your health, what unseen diseases does your filthy soul have? Yes, filthy soul. DIRT!"[12]

The sobs increased and there was now a wailing like the wind in a storm moving from one end of the courtyard to the other. It seemed no one else could possibly squeeze into the courtyard but they did.

"Ah, I hear some of you saying. *But I was raped by my boss and then he forced me to become a whore*. He made you become a whore? Where are the chains around your wrists? Where are the shackles on your ankles. If you hated it so much then why did you remain a whore? Could it be for the simple reason that you *are* a whore? Tell me, does anyone mistake you for being anything but a whore?"[13]

Cherry's face reddened as she screeched like a mother whose child has pushed her over the brink.

"You bought those clothes! Don't you know that you chose to remain a whore? Wasn't it enough for you to hate the man who raped you? No, your hatred was nothing compared to your envy and you became like him!"[14] Cherry stomped on the stage. The sound system hummed with the reverberation.

Screams now filled the courtyard.

"Yes! You're right!"

"Yes! I did it!"

The walls of the apartment buildings that surrounded us echoed with howls of repentance. It sounded hellish but it was heavenly. Cherry's voice, now soothing, sang through the broken cries of hundreds of repentant sinners.

"Here is what I want you to do. I want each of you to come

down here. You're not going back to those bars. You belong to Jesus now. The worthless whore hunters that have found out you're absent from work today; they don't love you. They don't even love themselves or why would they believe they're only worthy of a whore? They're fools.[15] Over the next few hours I'll help you to understand the joy of salvation that I have. I'll help you to understand that Jesus loves you and gave Himself for you so that you might have life and have it abundantly.[16] If you plan to go back to the streets, leave now."

Nobody left. Still, Cherry didn't let up.

"Here is what you need to know."

She spoke forcefully but no longer shouted.

"Repent! Turn from your sins and turn to God. Be converted, that your sins may be blotted out, when the times of refreshing shall come from the presence of the Lord."[17]

Cherry handed the microphone to Pastor Sam.

Pastor Sam began,

"You've heard a very powerful message today. I've known Cherry since she became a Christian but this is the first time I've ever heard her speak publicly. She still hasn't given us her testimony but the Lord has used her to bring hundreds to Him in just a few minutes and I'm sure that this is a testimony that you will remember. I know they'd still like to hear your testimony. Cherry?"

Pastor Sam handed the microphone back to Cherry.

"My testimony isn't pretty like some of yours."

Cherry looked toward that part of the audience made up of second generation Born-Again Christians. Her eyes were cast down as if ashamed, then she raised them back up and looked straight at the crowd.

"But what God has raised up, shall I cast down? What God has done shall I now forget?"[18]

"No!" The crowd shouted, "Tell us!"

"I was with a customer. I'd just finished, well, think of the worst thing that whores do. That's what I had just finished. Some of you don't know what the worst thing is, but it's worse than you think. But I would do anything for money. Nothing bothered me. I'd never gotten sick. I was counting the money my customer had already given me and hoping he'd go to sleep. The next thing I knew, I was waking up in a hospital bed. The nurses saw that I was awake and got the doctor. I could tell from the way he was looking at me that he knew I was a whore. He told me that my bill had been paid and he didn't know who'd paid it but that I was lucky. He said that at first they'd thought I had hepatitis but since my condition responded to antibiotics it was simply some kind of an infection. I didn't think I was lucky. I was in a hospital and I felt like I hadn't eaten for weeks. I told them that I was hungry and their response was that I had to leave. I left the hospital and went back to the bar where I'd worked. There was a notice on the door that said it had been closed for allowing minors to work there. I wondered if I had anything to do with it. I was just thirteen."

Some of the ladies in the crowd gasped. There was a girl who'd come up to the edge of the platform who was listening intently. She looked thirteen herself. She was made up like a whore and had a long tank top that she wore for a dress. A single tear rolled down her cheek. It was followed by a flood. Sarisa hurried over and wrapped her in a blanket, holding her. They both stood there, the girl trembling in Sarisa's arms. Cherry continued her testimony.

"I knew what I was doing. I don't blame the bar owner." Cherry paused to regain her composure. "I'm sorry, I've never given my testimonial before. It's so dirty. So I was walking down the street of bars looking for another place to work when I heard a woman preaching, saying. 'There is only one thing that you must do.' Then she looked straight at me. I looked around to see if there was anyone else she could be looking at but there was no one. She continued to speak to me. 'Walk away from sin and walk to God. He will show you the steps you must take.' I looked at myself. I was wearing a top too short to cover my stomach and jeans that stretched skin tight. I asked the lady preacher.

'How can I walk away from sin. I don't even have any decent clothes.' Did that just come out of my mouth? I was amazed. I'd never thought there was anything wrong with my clothing. My cousins all wore the same revealing stuff and they weren't whores. But I saw myself as never before. I saw myself for the first time. I didn't know this self that I had been. What were these rags I was wearing?

'You've got to get me into some decent clothes!' I pleaded with the preacher. She had a small booth next to where she was preaching and let me sit down there. The street of bars had lots of clothing shops and she walked into one of them. She came out with a simple dress and some under things.

After I'd changed in her booth, she took my old clothes back to the shop where she'd gotten the new ones. I could see from the shop owner's smile that she was very happy with the trade. The preacher lady, Sarisa, Pastor Sam's wife, came back and folded up her booth. I helped her put it into the back of her pickup truck. Then she said,

'Come on. We have someplace to go.'

I got in with her and we drove to a field meeting that was just a few blocks away. There was a preacher baptizing there. I'd never seen that kind of a baptism. He was putting a girl all the way down under the water. She came out of the water shouting and crying,

'Alleluia, Praise God, Thank you Jesus!'

It really seemed weird to me. Sarisa introduced me to the preacher. It was her husband, Pastor Sam.

'This is Cherry, Sam. I know that she has just had a heavy burden lifted from her heart.'[19]

Pastor Sam took me by the arm and led me to the microphone. He asked me where I'd come from and what had just happened. I spoke into the microphone,

'I was listening to your wife preach, and the moment she said to turn from sin and turn toward the Lord Jesus, I felt like I wasn't who I'd been anymore. My clothing, my makeup, nothing felt like me. I felt...'

'New?' Pastor Sam asked.

'Yes, new.' I looked up at Pastor Sam. 'Like something new!'

Tears started to flow from my eyes. Pastor Sam took out his Bible and read 2 Corinthians 5:17.

'Therefore if anyone be in Christ, she is a new creature: old things are passed away; behold, all things are become new.'

I was baptized that day and I haven't turned back to sin. Not because I'm good but because God worked a miracle in me. He took over when I was weak. That's my story."[20]

You could still hear sobs from the crowd in the courtyard but the sobs had changed to sobs of joy. Sam took back the microphone from Cherry and addressed those who were yearning to be new creations in Christ.

"That day, Cherry met the Lord. She was baptized in that field and in that baptismal much like the one you see here. The Lord promises to you today just as he promised to Cherry on that day,

If anyone be in Christ, he or she is a new creature: old things are passed away; behold, all things are become new.

Now I would like those of you who have accepted Jesus in your hearts today to come to the stage in an orderly procession. I want each one of you to come here and state publicly that you have accepted Jesus as your Savior and then show us by being baptized that you're turning away from sin and turning to the Lord Jesus for He said,

If you are ashamed of me and of my words, then I will be ashamed of you."21

The musicians began playing hymns as Pastor Joe, Sam's assistant, took over. He stood next to the pool which was at the center of the courtyard and called those who were repentant to come near.

"*Prepare your hearts to approach the Lord and He will come near you. Cleanse yourselves now of the filthiness that has filled your lives you sinners and purify your hearts, you double minded.*"22

I didn't understand how Sam's church could put everything into place so quickly but they'd apparently been expecting a great outpouring of the Spirit and this surely was. The ladies from the church were going to their apartments and getting clothing. They'd formed a tent to the side of the pool that was being used for a baptismal. Each of the girls was brought to the tent after her baptism to clean up and put on new clothes. Some of the ladies had built a fire where they were burning the prostitutes' clothing. I could see Pastor Joe baptizing. Each time a whore approached him to be baptized he spoke the same words,

"*Take away the filthy garments from her.*"23 At this, the whore would enter a curtained area and come out wearing a baptismal gown. Then the pastor would say to her,

"*Behold, the Lord has caused thine iniquity to pass from thee, and He will clothe thee with a change of raiment.*23 *For today, you have received His robes of righteousness which all the angels now see.*24 *Enter now through the narrow gate.*"25 Then the pastor would dunk her.

"*I baptize you in the Name of the Father, and of the Son, and of the Holy Spirit, Amen.*"26

Each new convert nearly leapt out of the pool, praising God. Then Pastor Joe would greet these new creatures, these lost lambs who had been found,27 these beloved of the Lord with the same admonition,

"*Greatly rejoice in the LORD this day and let your soul be joyful in our God; for he hath clothed you with the garments of salvation, he hath covered you with the robe of righteousness, as a bride adorneth [herself] with her jewels.*"28

Pastor Sam walked over to me with Cherry. I was glad. I wanted to say something to her.

"Cherry, remember what Pastor Sam quoted?"

"Yes, Ish, I was thinking about that."

"How you're a new creature and that all things are become new?"

"Yes, Ish."

"You're not a whore, Cherry. Someone was a whore but that's not you. You belong to Jesus and everything that belongs to Him is precious and perfect."

"I know. I don't know why I carried that burden with me so long."

Now it was Pastor Sam's turn to choke up.

"I know why, Cherry." Sam forced back his tears. "Look at all of them. Maybe if you hadn't carried that burden with you till this day, these sinners wouldn't have believed your message."

"*Praise God!*" Cherry exclaimed.

"*Amen*!" Pastor Sam and I concurred.

Chapter 6 Footnotes

1. Jeremiah 2:21 Yet I had planted thee a noble vine, wholly a right seed: how then art thou turned into the degenerate plant of a strange vine unto me?
2. Joel 2:32 And it shall come to pass, [that] whosoever shall call on the Name of the LORD shall be delivered: for in mount Zion and in Jerusalem shall be deliverance, as the LORD hath said, and in the remnant whom the LORD shall call.
3. Matthew 5:27-28 Ye have heard that it was said by them of old

time, Thou shalt not commit adultery: But I say unto you, That whosoever looketh on a woman to lust after her hath committed adultery with her already in his heart. *"Looketh on a woman to lust" = "covet thy neighbour's ... wife" Romans 7:7 I had not known ***lust***, except the law had said, ***Thou shalt not covet***.

4. Puta - Cebuano for prostitute.

Harlot - a woman who has engaged in sexual relations without the benefit of marriage. Harlots are in bondage to sin, in bondage to the men they have relations with and draw men into bondage with them. The harlot takes the place of God as head of the man.

5. 2 Corinthians 5:17 Therefore if any man [be] in Christ, [he is] a new creature: old things are passed away; behold, all things are become new.

6. Romans 3:20 Therefore by the deeds of the law there shall no flesh be justified in his sight: **for by the law [is] the knowledge of sin**.

We must not let the world teach us falsely that by sinning we gain knowledge of sin! Sin does not reveal sin. The law reveals sin and the prophet Malachi speaks of our Lord when he says,

"The law of truth was in his mouth, and iniquity was not found in his lips: he walked with me in peace and equity, and did turn many away from iniquity." Malachi 2:6

Those who brag that they grew up on the streets as if that gives them some special wisdom concerning sin are liars but there are so many who are fooled into believing that kind of liar that I am burdened to repeat the words of Paul to the Romans again: **"for by the *law* [is] the knowledge of sin."** Cherry, the girl in this book, acknowledges this very fact when she says,

"There's nothing good about the fact that I used to be a whore. Nothing! It didn't teach me anything. That was a lost and worthless part of my life. I'm so ashamed."

We must never forget this and we must teach our children that they will gain nothing whatsoever by sinful experiences nor by associating with sinful people.

2 Corinthians 6:17 Wherefore come out from among them, and be ye separate, saith the Lord, and touch not the unclean [thing]; and I will receive you.

7. 1 Corinthians 6:9-11 Know ye not that the unrighteous shall not inherit the kingdom of God? Be not deceived: neither fornicators,

nor idolaters, nor adulterers, nor effeminate, nor abusers of themselves with mankind, nor thieves, nor covetous, nor drunkards, nor revilers, nor extortioners, shall inherit the kingdom of God. **And such were some of you: but ye are washed**, but ye are sanctified, but ye are justified in the Name of the Lord Jesus, and by the Spirit of our God. (sanctified - absolutely clean and presentable as an offering to God)

8. Matthew 13:38 The field is the world; the good seed are the children of the kingdom; but the tares are the children of the wicked [one]. [Definition: tares - weeds]

9. Ezekiel 16:34 And the contrary is in thee from [other] women in thy whoredoms, whereas none followeth thee to commit whoredoms: and in that thou givest a reward, and no reward is given unto thee, therefore thou art contrary.

10. 2 Chronicles 20:9 If, [when] evil cometh upon us, [as] the sword, judgment, or pestilence, or famine, we stand before this house, and in thy presence, (for thy Name [is] in this house,) and cry unto thee in our affliction, then thou wilt hear and help.

The Lord hears and helps us when we cry unto Him in our troubles! He even helps us when we have created those troubles by our own actions. Praise God! He is a God of love!

11. Matthew 25:13 Watch therefore, for ye know neither the day nor the hour wherein the Son of man cometh.

12. Psalm 53:3-4 Every one of them is gone back: they are altogether become filthy; [there is] none that doeth good, no, not one. Have the workers of iniquity no knowledge? who eat up my people [as] they eat bread: they have not called upon God.

Proverbs 6:26a For by means of a whorish woman [a man is brought] to a piece of bread.

13. Proverbs 23:27-28 For a whore [is] a deep ditch; and a strange woman [is] a narrow pit. She also lieth in wait as [for] a prey, and increaseth the transgressors among men.

14. Proverbs 3:31 Envy thou not the oppressor, and choose none of his ways.

It's common among those who have been oppressed to choose to become an oppressor as well, in order to have the wealth of the oppressor, which they envy. A whore is an oppressor in that she "lieth in wait as [for] prey, and increaseth the transgressors among men." [see above] Certainly her diseases shall not be only for herself but for all the men who lay with her "receiving in themselves that recompence of their error which was meet." Romans 1:27b

15. Proverbs 7:22 He goeth after her straightway, as an ox goeth to the slaughter, or as a fool to the correction of the stocks.

16. John 10:10 I am come that they might have life, and that they might have it more abundantly.

17. Acts 3:19 Repent ye therefore, and be converted, that your sins may be blotted out, when the times of refreshing shall come from the presence of the Lord.

18. Ephesians 2:6-9 And hath raised [us] up together, and made [us] sit together in heavenly [places] in Christ Jesus: That in the ages to come he might show the exceeding riches of his grace in [his] kindness toward us through Christ Jesus. For by grace are ye saved through faith; and that not of yourselves: [it is] the gift of God: Not of works, lest any man should boast.

19. Psalm 55:22 Cast thy burden upon the LORD, and he shall sustain thee: he shall never suffer the righteous to be moved.

20. 2Corinthians 12:10 Therefore I take pleasure in infirmities, in reproaches, in necessities, in persecutions, in distresses for Christ's sake: for when I am weak, then am I strong.

21. Mark 8:38 Whosoever therefore shall be ashamed of me and of my words in this adulterous and sinful generation; of him also shall the Son of man be ashamed, when he cometh in the glory of his Father with the holy angels.

Luke 9:26 For whosoever shall be ashamed of me and of my words, of him shall the Son of man be ashamed, when he shall come in his own glory, and [in his] Father's, and of the holy angels.

Romans 10:9-10 That if thou shalt confess with thy mouth the Lord Jesus, and shalt believe in thine heart that God hath raised him from the dead, thou shalt be saved. For with the heart man believeth unto righteousness; and with the mouth confession is made unto salvation.

22. James 4:8 Draw nigh to God, and he will draw nigh to you. Cleanse [your] hands, [ye] sinners; and purify [your] hearts, [ye] double minded.

23. Zechariah 3:4 And he answered and spake unto those that stood before him, saying, Take away the filthy garments from him.

And unto him he said, Behold, I have caused thine iniquity to pass from thee, and I will clothe thee with change of raiment.
24. Luke 15:10 Likewise, I say unto you, there is joy in the presence of the angels of God over one sinner that repenteth.
25.] Matthew 7:14 Because strait [is] the gate, and narrow [is] the way, which leadeth unto life, and few there be that find it.
26. Matthew 28:19 Go ye therefore, and teach all nations, baptizing them in the Name of the Father, and of the Son, and of the Holy Ghost.
27. Luke 15:4-7 What man of you, having an hundred sheep, if he lose one of them, doth not leave the ninety and nine in the wilderness, and go after that which is lost, until he find it? And when he hath found [it], he layeth [it] on his shoulders, rejoicing. And when he cometh home, he calleth together [his] friends and neighbours, saying unto them, Rejoice with me; for I have found my sheep which was lost. I say unto you, that likewise joy shall be in heaven over one sinner that repenteth, more than over ninety and nine just persons, which need no repentance.
28. Isaiah 61:10 Greatly rejoice in the LORD this day and let your soul be joyful in our God; for he hath clothed you with the garments of salvation, he hath covered you with the robe of righteousness, as a bridegroom decketh [himself] with ornaments, and as a bride adorneth [herself] with her jewels.

You have just read:

CHERRY THE HARLOT

Many readers are prompted to make changes in their lives as a result of this story. The following space is provided so that you might remind yourself of the things that came to your mind as you read Cherry's testimony.

~NOTES~

Chapter 7

LOAVES OF BREAD, FISH!

News of the conversion of prostitutes, whores, and even the local vendors who made their money off of the spending of thousands of profligate sons, had spread quickly throughout Cagayan de Oro. The local Christian radio stations had picked up on it as well and announced the good news to their listeners. They in turn passed the news on with the result that dozens of buses were kept busy shuttling in an endless procession of people anxious to find out what was happening. A nearby park was set up to accommodate all the people and loud speakers were wired so that they could know what was going on inside the courtyard. All the while, the baptisms continued.

We now had an audience of thousands of new believers and thousands more onlookers so Pastor Sam suggested I deliver a sermon instead of a Bible study.

"You've been anointed by the Lord, Ish.[1] I've never seen anything like this in all my years living here in Cagayan de Oro. There's an outpouring of God's Spirit in this place today. We're going to have to follow God's lead as well as the leader He's put in charge of this event. And that's you, Ish. Now get out there and say whatever He puts on your lips."[2]

"But, it was Cherry's testimony that began all of this." I protested.

"Ish, this isn't over, believe me. You can't see it but we do. The anointing is on you."

Sam's wife Sarisa nodded as he spoke.

"But I don't have any idea where to start." I objected.

Sam and Sarisa were just silent. They motioned me forward.

A calm took over my mind and body as I readied myself to speak. I stepped to the front of the stage and looked out at the thousands of people, aware that there were tens of thousands more at the park that lay beyond the walls of the apartment complex. Then, out of my mouth, came the words;

"Loaves of bread! Fish!"[3]

I stepped back from the microphone. I didn't know what I was talking about. I hadn't planned those words. They just spilled out of my mouth. The words were not mine! I didn't know what the Lord wanted me to say, but I stepped up to the microphone again. This time the words flew from my lips.

"Loaves of bread! Fish!"

I still couldn't understand why the Lord wanted me to shout those words. I looked at Sam, bewildered, he looked back at me and shrugged. Then suddenly, God's message burst into my mind. I was *speaking* to loaves of bread and fish! They *were*, or would shortly *be*, the loaves of bread and fish!

"Yes, I'm speaking to you. I'm speaking to you. You *are* loaves of bread and fish!"

The audience was murmuring because they didn't get what I was saying. How could they, the Lord had only now placed this message on my lips and only through His Spirit speaking to me had I known the meaning. I took out my bible and read.

"It is written in Matthew 14:20

And they did all eat, and were filled: and they took up of the fragments that remained; twelve baskets full.' And again it is written in Matthew 15:37 'And they did all eat, and were filled: and they took up of the broken meat that was left; seven baskets full."

I explained,

"Did the people use knives and forks to eat that bread? Were they eating that bread on table cloths of fine linen? No! They were eating it with their hands. Kamayan![with hands][4] What do you suppose the pieces they gathered looked like? Why weren't the disciples concerned about gathering that bread and fish up into baskets to be eaten later? It had been touched by so many unclean people. Can you imagine how filthy that bread and fish must have been after being handled by thousands in a grassy field? Notice how Matthew writes, *fragments that remained, broken meat.* I don't know about you but I wouldn't want to take a chance eating such food. I would be afraid that because it was handled by so many unclean people that it would also be unclean. So why did the disciples gather those filthy fragments and broken pieces?"

At that moment the shout of one of the whores being baptized prophetically interjected itself.

"I've been touched by Jesus," she cried, "by Jesus. Praise God, I am washed!"5

"Amen!" I shouted to the audience lifting my hand in the direction of the baptismal, "She said it! Who touched that bread and fish, who broke it, who blessed it? JESUS! Listen again to what Matthew wrote.

'*And He commanded the multitude to sit down on the grass, and took the five loaves, and the two fish, and looking up to heaven, He blessed, and broke the bread*, and who broke it? and He broke it; Jesus, *and gave the loaves to His disciples, and the disciples to the multitude.*'

Now to you, I say, you who have come to the Lord today, the Lord has blessed you in that He has broken your proud spirit and He has given you to us and to this crowd, and we shall gather you for the Lord just like the Lord's disciples gathered those filthy fragments of bread and fish for the Lord. The scraps they gathered were for food but you, you shall be for spiritual nourishment to those who will hear your testimony! Yes, today, all you who have turned from your sinful ways and to Jesus have been made clean by the Lord Jesus Himself. You were filthy but now the Lord has made you clean. You were dirty, so dirty, handled like old bread and broken pieces of fish, by many hands, but now you are clean, washed," I shouted, "by the Almighty Himself through the blood of Jesus.

Now to my fellow servants in Christ I say, go now and gather up the pieces of bread and fish. Bring them here so that they may be baptized, giving evidence through this, their first act of obedience, that they belong to the Lord."6

As the members of Sam's church and the volunteers from other churches went among the crowd, the newly saved were crying out with sobs of repentance and praises to Jesus for His Free Gift of Salvation. Every time one of them would rise out of the baptismal pool they would shout praises to the Lord, "Alleluia," "Thank you Jesus!" How wonderful to see the mouths of new converts overflow with praises to God.7

Those who had come simply to see what all the noise was about were each having their own face to face with God's Spirit as the Lord's Presence continued to move powerfully through the crowd.[8]

"Unclean, I'm unclean!" A nun screamed as she ran to the front of the stage.

"I'm full of pride! Help me. I hate Born-Agains! I'm in bondage to rules but have never known the Lord. Pray for me father."

I stepped down for a moment to speak with her, microphone attached.

"I'm not your father."

I put my hand on her shoulder and felt a jolt like electricity leave my fingertips. Her hard exterior seemed to melt. I thought for a moment she would faint. I grasped her arm to keep her from falling while I steadied myself with the other hand on the stage. I explained to her.

"Other than the man who caused your mother to conceive, you have just one Father and He is in heaven."

"Blasphemy! Blasphemy! I'm a blasphemer!" She shouted. "I have called the pope Holy Father." Now louder than before she shouted, "The pope is a blasphemer!"[9]

The crowd was so hushed that you could hear the wind rustling through the trees and the slight buzz of the amplification system.

A little girl's voice was easily heard:

"Pray for the pope. Pray that he might be saved!"

The nun squeezed my arm and whispered.

"May I pray for the pope?"

Dare I let a nun who'd just now realized her own sins speak officially before this crowd? She took me by the arm and asked for one of the prayer shawls that she saw sitting on a table to the side of the stage. I handed it to her. She removed her habit to reveal the blouse and blue jeans that she wore underneath it then covered her head with the prayer shawl and prayed.

"Lord, this is my first prayer directly to you. Just me to you. How lonely I've been. Can you forgive me? Thank you. Thank you Jesus that you love me so much that now you're speaking to my heart and for the first time my heart is not hard. I can feel your words."

For a moment she lost her balance as she seemed overcome with grief and joy all at the same time. She continued.

"The pope sins by letting the world call him Holy Father, yes, he blasphemes by letting others call him by Your Name. I pray that his heart would be softened and that he too could hear Your voice."

As she spoke these words, lightning struck one of the poles that held the loud speakers. A clap of thunder followed that left a humming in our ears. I was about to head for cover from the certain downpour but saw that the sky was clear. A young woman ran out of the crowd to the nun, shouting.

"You've spoken with God and God answered you! Teach me to speak to God."

"Yes, teach me to speak to God." Others in the crowd shouted.

"I'm not the one to talk to you concerning prayers or holy things." The nun scolded. "I've only just met the Lord. Speak with Cherry. She has God's anointing."

"Puta!"[10] A few who'd approached the nun shouted at Cherry and spat.

Another sneered, "This nun must have been sleeping with the pastor. I've heard about those Born-Agains."

"Born to hell, that's what they are!" Someone from the crowd shouted.

A few more voices could be heard repeating,

"Born to hell, that's what they are!"

I was surprised that after this brief disorder, only a few dozen left. The rest of the mostly Roman Catholic audience stood motionless, in awe of what had just happened and what was continuing to happen.

The prostitutes were emerging from the curtain behind the baptismal having changed into the modest clothing that the single ladies of the church had brought for them.

"I've been healed!" Shouted one.

"I'm clean!" Shouted another.

They no longer looked like prostitutes. This was not simply because of their change in clothing. Their faces looked rested. The haughtiness and *naughtiness*, for lack of a better word, was *gone*, vanished. They were indeed new creatures. I looked forward to seeing what great task God had set before them for *to whom much is forgiven, much is expected* and *she who is forgiven much will love much.*[11] They took their places in the choir and joined in with those who had already begun singing Redeeming Love.[12]

'Ye, alas! who long have been
Willing slaves to death and sin,
Now from bliss no longer rove,
Stop and taste redeeming love.'

Now that portion of the crowd that had been silent came forward. Thousands of them. They were crying. Not all converts shout. Some were whispering,

"Thank you Jesus."

Others seemed to try to speak but could only bring forth tears. Over the next few hours, every unbeliever, both in and outside the courtyard, that had heard the message came forward to confess Jesus as Lord and be baptized. They were walking away from the church whose highest official called himself by God's Own Name, Holy Father. They were walking away so that they could live by faith as revealed to them through God's Holy Word.[13] They knew there was no turning back. Cardinal 'what's his name' would not take lightly what had happened today.

I was now very sleepy. In fact, I could barely keep my eyes open. I invited Sam to the stage. He would be better able to lead these new converts in what had become an outpouring of praise through song. These blessed converts had escaped out of the clutches of the Great Whore of Babylon[14] and for the first time felt free from the burden of sin. I slipped away across the square to my apartment. I fell asleep with my clothes on but in the few seconds before losing consciousness, I remembered the words that had come from the Lord, *Loaves of bread, fish!* What were the Lord's plans for the tens of thousands of new believers he'd just laid at our doorstep? I hummed,

"Grace, grace, God's grace,
grace that will pardon and cleanse within;
grace, grace, God's grace,
grace that is greater than all our sin!"[15]

Falling back on my bed I pushed my shoes off my feet with my toes. Thud, I was out.

Chapter 7 Footnotes

1. Hebrews 1:9 Thou hast loved righteousness, and hated iniquity; therefore God, [even] thy God, hath anointed thee with the oil of gladness above thy fellows.
2. Psalm 40:9 I have preached righteousness in the great congregation: lo, I have not refrained my lips, O LORD, thou knowest.

Psalm 141:3 Set a watch, O LORD, before my mouth; keep the door of my lips.

3. Matthew 14:15-21 And when it was evening, his disciples came to him, saying, This is a desert place, and the time is now past; send the multitude away, that they may go into the villages, and buy themselves victuals. But Jesus said unto them, They need not depart; give ye them to eat. And they say unto him, We have here but five loaves, and two fishes. He said, Bring them hither to me. And he commanded the multitude to sit down on the grass, and took the five loaves, and the two fishes, and looking up to heaven, he blessed, and brake, and gave the loaves to [his] disciples, and the disciples to the multitude. And they did all eat, and were filled: and they took up of the fragments that remained twelve baskets full. And they that had eaten were about five thousand men, beside women and children.
4. Kamayan - The Cebuano word for eating food with your hands.
5. Mark 1:40-45 And there came a leper to him, beseeching him, and kneeling down to him, and saying unto him, If thou wilt, thou canst make me clean. **And Jesus, moved with compassion, put forth [his] hand, and touched him, and saith unto him, I will; be thou clean.** And as soon as he had spoken, immediately the leprosy departed from him, and he was cleansed. And he straitly charged him, and forthwith sent him away; And saith unto him, See thou say nothing to any man: but go thy way, show thyself to the priest, and offer for thy cleansing those things which Moses commanded, for a testimony unto them. **But he went out, and began to publish [it] much, and to blaze abroad the matter**, insomuch that Jesus could no more openly enter into the city, but was without in desert places: and they came to him from every quarter.

May we be as this leper in our gratefulness to Jesus for the gift of

salvation that he has given to us!
6. Mark 16:16 He that believeth and is baptized shall be saved; but he that believeth not shall be damned.
7. Psalm 107:31 Oh that [men] would praise the LORD [for] his goodness, and [for] his wonderful works to the children of men!
Isaiah 25:1 O LORD, thou [art] my God; I will exalt thee, I will praise thy Name; for thou hast done wonderful [things; thy] counsels of old [are] faithfulness [and] truth.
8. Judges 13:25 And the Spirit of the LORD began to move him at times in the camp of Dan between Zorah and Eshtaol.
9. John 17:11 And now I am no more in the world, but these are in the world, and I come to thee. Holy Father, keep through thine own Name those whom thou hast given me, that they may be one, as we [are].
Matthew 23:9 And call no [man] your father upon the earth: for one is your Father, which is in heaven.
10. Puta - Cebuano for prostitute.
11. Luke 7:47 Wherefore I say unto thee, Her sins, which are many, are forgiven; for she loved much: but to whom little is forgiven, [the same] loveth little.
12. Redeeming Love - Written by Martin Madan during his ministry at the London Lock Hospital; a hospital in London that cared for women who were suffering the effects of venereal disease. [See the picture on the next page.] It was Martin Madan's hymnal on which the later hymnals were based.
13. 2 Timothy 3:16 All scripture [is] given by inspiration of God, and [is] profitable for doctrine, for reproof, for correction, for instruction in righteousness.
14. Revelation 17:1-5 And there came one of the seven angels which had the seven vials, and talked with me, saying unto me, Come hither; I will show unto thee the judgment of the great whore that sitteth upon many waters: With whom the kings of the earth have committed fornication, and the inhabitants of the earth have been made drunk with the wine of her fornication. So he carried me away in the spirit into the wilderness: and I saw a woman sit upon a scarlet coloured beast, full of names of blasphemy, having seven heads and ten horns. And the woman was arrayed in purple and scarlet colour, and decked with gold and precious stones and pearls, having a golden cup in her hand

full of abominations and filthiness of her fornication: And upon her forehead [was] a name written, MYSTERY, BABYLON THE GREAT, THE MOTHER OF HARLOTS AND ABOMINATIONS OF THE EARTH.

Revelation18:2-4 And he cried mightily with a strong voice, saying, Babylon the great is fallen, is fallen, and is become the habitation of devils, and the hold of every foul spirit, and a cage of every unclean and hateful bird. For all nations have drunk of the wine of the wrath of her fornication, and the kings of the earth have committed fornication with her, and the merchants of the earth are waxed rich through the abundance of her delicacies. And I heard another voice from heaven, saying, Come out of her, my people, that ye be not partakers of her sins, and that ye receive not of her plagues.

15. "Grace Greater than Our Sin" Words by Julia Harriette Johnston. Music by Daniel B. Towner.

The Lock Hospital was the first hospital built exclusively for the care and treatment of women with venereal disease. Many were healed in both body and spirit.

Lock Hospital as it stood in Madan's day.

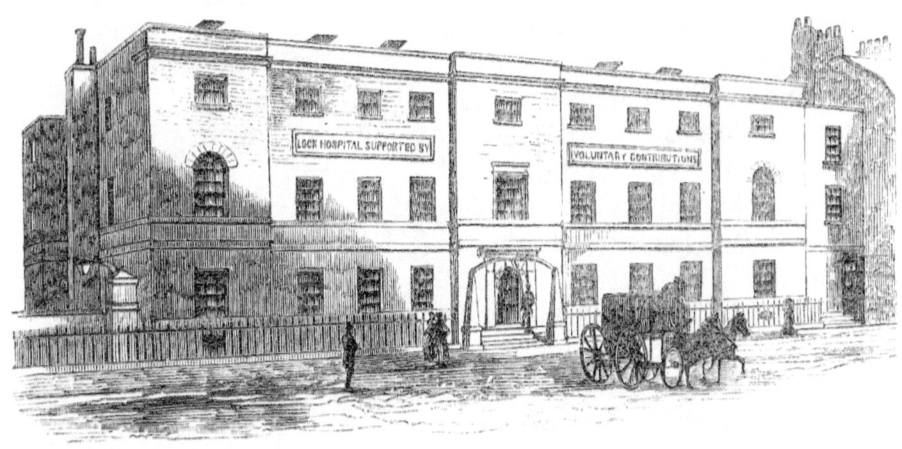

Chapter 8

THE MARKET

I woke up refreshed and ready for the new day. I felt every bit as cleansed as last night's converts must have felt, with two exceptions; my mouth tasted like garbage from going to sleep without brushing my teeth and my ankles itched from sleeping with my socks on.

Mary was already cooking breakfast when I heard a knock at the door. It was Sam and Sarisa. I hurried to the bathroom to clean myself up and a few minutes later came out.

Mary was following our family tradition of forcing food and beverage down our guests' throats, hungry or not. Mary's efforts were meeting little resistance since it was a Philippine tradition as well.

"Good morning, Sam, Sarisa." I nodded to Sarisa and reached out to shake Sam's hand.

"Good morning, Ish."

Sarisa replied for Sam whose mouth was stuffed with the missing brownie from the cookie tin at the center of the table. Washing down the brownie with a sip of coffee, Sam leaned back and stretched as if rising from a long nap.

"We need a change from the monotony of Cagayan de Oro." Sam yawned, "Wouldn't you agree?"

"Monotony? Are you kidding! If yesterday was monotonous, what kind of adventure do you have planned for today?"

"Just a little drive in the old Ford Fiera and there won't be a better time to leave than right now."

Mary couldn't contain her excitement.

"I've already packed our things, Ish. It might be a few days we'll be gone!"

Mary had packed more than a few days worth of belongings. Her telling me that it might be a few days was her way of shushing me about her excessive packing.

"Are you ready?" Mary asked.

"I haven't even had a chance to eat my breakfast and drink my morning coffee. Is this some kind of a conspiracy!" I repeated the words that a dear but overly dramatic pastor we knew had once shouted during a church board meeting.

"Well Ish, you might say it is." Suni nudged her way into the discussion. Suni, Asina and some of the other girls had been sitting uncharacteristically silent in the corner. "All of us decided to let you sleep late while we were preparing everything. You were so sleepy last night; we wanted you to have plenty of energy for today."

"Besides, we wanted to keep you humble." Asina quipped. "After the most fantastic revival that Cagayan de Oro has ever seen, we didn't want to give you time to bask in the accolades."

I remembered the song I'd hummed before falling to sleep, *Grace grace, God's grace*. It was then that I realized Asina was right, for as I hummed, I felt no small sense of pride in having been part of that revival.[1] I understood moreover, that Satan's plans for the destruction of a man's ministry go into high gear with the ministry's first great success. I prayed silently in my heart: '*Lord, keep my thoughts pure and toward you in all ways. Gently keep me humble and let me lean on You and Your word only. May I give You the glory and honor in all things.*'[2]

Grabbing my breakfast which had been waiting for me on a paper plate and a mug of freshly brewed coffee, I headed for the door.

"You couldn't be more right, Asina. We're outta here!"

Sam's vintage Ford Fiera was parked at the curb. It had benches in the truck bed that faced each other. I took my seat; Mary on one side of me and Suni on the other. Four of the girls from the church faced us, balancing out the load. There was Modelisa; resident actress, Cherry; the girl with the testimony about coming out of prostitution, Asina; her speech always with grace though seasoned with salt,[3] and Tisay; the young girl who'd just turned to the Lord after leaving a life of whoredom. I could barely recognize her. Wearing modest clothing and without makeup, she didn't look older than eleven. It was hard to acknowledge her without choking up, but I managed.

"Hi Tisay, it's nice to know that you'll be accompanying us." She smiled simply. I wondered what had happened to her folks.

"So where are we headed?" I asked Sam.

"We'll begin with the Marawi Brass Market. It's close to Lake Lanao." Then he added with a wink, "You would have been considered rude by local custom had you not accepted our invitation, so sit back and enjoy the ride. You really have no choice."

"Ha ha. You really have no choice!" Suni mimicked, sounding more like a parrot than a young lady.

We were all laughing now. Imagine me, laughing before I'd even finished my first cup of coffee. The excitement of going to the Islamic City of Marawi had obviously hastened the effect of the caffeine.

After Sam led us in prayer we were on our way.

Mary and the girls quickly went into their chatting mode. They were doing their best to hold a conversation but the rattling of the old Ford Fiera won out as we were all treated to a concerto in galvanized steel. I managed to move the food off of my plate and into my mouth without dropping so much as a crumb and guzzled down the last of my coffee. I smiled at Mary, assured of my neatness, but then that one last drop of coffee, with which I'd been having an ongoing battle over the years found its place on my shirt. Fortunately, I was wearing brown.

I'd heard about the brass market. It was a place where mountain men and lowlanders mixed in a clattering of brass from all over the island. Sam said we might inquire as to some remote places to go where the inhabitants weren't entirely hostile to *foreign missionaries*. Our purpose for coming here, after all, had been to go on a mission. What better way than to spontaneously set out in search of adventure.

As we got closer to the Marawi brass market the pot holes increased as well as the hammering from inside the market. I had a hard time telling between the clattering of Sam's truck and the chattering of my teeth. Had I really had that much dental work? Now I understood what Paul meant when he said in his letter to the Corinthians that practicing gifts without love is as sounding brass.[4] What a racket! Between the pounding in the brass market and Sam's Ford Fiera growing ever closer to its final bump, my aching ears were able to make out that one joyous sentence from Sam.

"There's a parking stall. Shall I pull in?"

"*PLEASE!*" We shouted in unison.

"Well it's good to hear that we're all of one voice!" Sam shouted back.

We beeped and edged our way past carts and vegetables laid out on woven mats to squeeze into what I was sure would be the final resting spot for Sam's truck. The sputtering sound when he turned off the key convinced me that we'd surely have to find another mode of transportation for our return home.

"I'll be back in a few minutes." Sam said.

He got out and walked up to an old man who was sitting behind the counter at one of the stalls. The man was wearing a kerchief wrapped around the upper part of his head like a turban. His teeth were like the rutted road we'd just come in on; clay colored and broken except for two; they were gold. They glistened as if signaling to each other. Beacons among hills of clay. He was selling bolos and butterfly knives. They glistened too.

There are stories of Moros attacking military compounds in the early 1900s armed only with such bolos.[5] They were usually able to hack up a dozen or more soldiers before falling dead from gunshot wounds. In order to give themselves that extra thirty seconds of life necessary to carry out their mission of death they would wrap their arms and even their chests with bands like tourniquets. The 1910 45 caliber pistol was designed specifically for defense against the Moros. After it was introduced on Mindanao, the attacks stopped.

My knowledge of these and other facts made me acutely aware of the divisions between Muslim and Christian. The Muslim's grandfathers had correctly told them that before the discovery of penicillin, Roman Catholic priests were seen unashamed in public with open syphilis sores on their faces, so until now, the Muslims had no reason to see any difference between Western decadence and Christianity. But these new Born-Again Christians weren't decadent and they were gaining more converts than the Muslims could breed. Truth told, it wasn't the decadence that the Muslims hated. They had decadence. They just kept it underground. It was the Christians they hated and they'd put them under ground too, if they had a chance.

Sam was still chatting with the blade vendor when I noticed *a tall mestiso*[6] *making his way through the aisle that divided the vendors' stalls*. He had a strong chin, a full head of hair and a Caucasian nose. I felt like I was viewing a scene in a movie. He looked like someone who could have starred in one of our American action films but there was something more about him than that. He had the air of royalty about him. All eyes were upon him as soon as walked into view. His steps were deliberate. His boots clopped on the wooden sidewalk which creaked under his weight. He was easily six foot and of no slight figure.

As he approached the place where Sam stood, the knife vendor greeted him,

"Mabuhay po, Datu!" (May you live long, Prince!)

To anyone else, mabuhay would simply have meant *welcome* but I was certain his greeting carried the more literal meaning. The vendor had some very large boxes waiting for this intriguing stranger. I wondered how many bolos and butterfly knives must be inside. The stranger now turned to Sam and shook his hand. They were conversing as if they'd known each other for years. Could this man have something to do with the adventure Sam had planned for us? I'd find out soon enough. He accompanied Sam as they walked over to us. Shaking my hand through the slats in the canopy of Sam's truck, he introduced himself.

"I'm John."

"Nice to meet you John. I'm Ishmael and this is my wife Mary and some of the girls from our church; Suni, Asina, Modelisa, Cherry, Tisay, and I'm sure you've already met Sarisa, Sam's wife?"

"Yes, nice to see you again Sarisa, and nice to meet you ladies too." John tipped his hat, then spoke to me again. "So you're an adventurer, are you?"

"Well, not unless you could call teaching Sunday school an adventure." I replied.

"Sunday school teacher or no, I have it on good word from a twelve foot tall angel that you have adventures in store for you that few men have even dreamed of. Isn't that right, Sam?"[7] John turned to Sam who'd taken his place again behind the wheel of his dilapidated Ford Fiera.

"One thing I can tell you for sure." Sam pronounced, "If John says he spoke with a twelve foot tall angel then he spoke with a twelve foot tall angel. And if that angel told him you'd have an adventure then we'll be praying you're ready for the ride."

I grabbed tightly to my seat cushion in comic fashion. The girls laughed at my comic relief but Sarisa cautioned,

"We're not kidding, Ish. John's had numerous visions concerning our ministry and all of them came true."

John motioned toward a nearby jeepney full of women and children.

"I only brought a few of my wives and children today. The rest are back at my place preparing lunch. Keep a distance Sam, I wouldn't want the dust to get you folks sick. We'll see you up at my place."

John patted me on the shoulder and walked over to his Jeepney. He backed it up to the vendor's stall till it bumped against one of the boxes where his sons had been keeping watch, then he got out and walked over to the old man. After a few minutes of animated discussion they opened each of the boxes. Pulling a machine gun out of the last box, the old man held it out and said, "NBSB," then winked. He was applying the Christian acronym for No Boyfriend Since Birth to the gun. I figured he must have meant that no cartridge had ever been chambered. John smiled, shook the old man's hand, then paid him. His sons loaded up the boxes and we were off to his place. I wasn't worried about the guns; John was a Christian and if anyone knew responsibility with weapons, a man with so many children would.

Sam started his truck then added, "It runs on gasoline and prayers, but mostly prayers."

Sam led us in prayer, then we were off to John's place, about thirty miles into the mountains. This may not seem like a long distance to Americans used to wide roads and freeways but the potholed pavement that began the journey soon became a dirt road. We arrived at John's place two flats and one radiator hose later, by the clock that's about three hours.

Sam pulled his truck to a stop inside the gates of John's property. This time the engine sputtered just once and was silent. Within moments the silence was replaced by the sounds of the jungle; birds chirping, parrots cawing, a monkey's angry call echoing across the canyon.

Chapter 8 Footnotes

1. Proverbs 11:2 When pride cometh, then cometh shame: but with the lowly is wisdom.

Proverbs 16:18 Pride goes before destruction, and a haughty spirit before a fall.

2. Proverbs 3:5-6 Trust in the LORD with all thine heart; and *lean not unto thine own understanding.* In all thy ways *acknowledge him, and he shall direct thy paths.*

3. Colossians 4:6 Let your speech be alway with grace, seasoned with salt, that ye may know how ye ought to answer every man.

4. 1 Corinthians 13:1 Though I speak with the tongues of men and of angels, and have not charity, I am become as sounding brass, or a tinkling cymbal.

5. Moro - Muslims in Mindanao were called Moros in the early 20th century.

Bolo - A small sword used by natives in the Philippines, mostly as a tool for clearing vegetation but also as a weapon.

6. Mestiso - A person of mixed Philippine and White ancestry.

7. Angels appeared to many of the apostles in the years after Jesus' resurrection and there is no reason to doubt that they're still appearing to various Christians around the world.

JOHN'S PLACE

John led us to a structure on the hillside of his estate that was overlooking the road we'd just come up. He'd converted the deck of an old ship into a gazebo of sorts, retaining the masts, wheel, and navigational instruments. John, his family, and the others sat down to take in the view while I took the helm. Turning the wheel this way and that, I wondered if this ship had been at sea or if it was just a novelty where a man could dream; to fly from one jungle mountain peak to another; suspended on the wings of his own imagination. When I stopped turning the wheel, Asina shouted.

"Don't stop, Ish, you've been fanning all of us with your day dreams. Dream on!"

Sam pointed to the fans above the seating.

"Don't be embarrassed, Ish. John had me fanning his whole family for half an hour before I realized the wheel was attached to these fans. I sailed this ship to that mountain and back before I woke from my daydream. How far did you get?"

Distracted from my daydream, I protested.

"Hey, no visitors allowed. You interrupted a perfectly good daydream."

"So what were you dreaming of?" Suni asked.

Asina couldn't resist.

"He was dreaming of you, Suni! Just don't forget you were only *pretending* to be his wife at the Bible study."

The other girls lifted their voices yet again. "Uh."

I wondered if Suni had noticed my leering as she sashayed about her Sari-Sari store on the day we arrived. If so, she certainly had reason to believe that the crush was mutual. It was surprising that such a feminine charmer had not been seriously courted. Then I remembered how few single Christian men there were in Sam's church. It was only yesterday that I'd attended my first after service coffee but now it seemed so distant. So much had happened in just one day. I prayed that Suni would soon find the right man. Why should she have to settle for less than she deserved.

Suni was silent in response to the teasing. She knew protesting would just encourage more of the same. Mary had told me that Suni's crush on me wasn't unusual, that she wouldn't be the last Christian girl on Mindanao to have eyes for me. Pastors were the ultimate catch. According to Mary, it was just one of the hazards of the job, but this was one hazard the mission board hadn't told me about.

John graciously interrupted the teasing.

"We'll be eating within a few minutes and I'd like to give you a chance to see more of our place before lunch."

He walked us up the steps to his palatial home and nodded in the direction of Lake Lanao.

"The city that you see in the distance is the Islamic City of Marawi, about ten miles as the crow flies. Those dots you see on the lake are fishing boats. We've got some binoculars around here somewhere and you can have a look after we eat. These trees growing on our mountain are redwoods. You know them as Philippine Mahogany. Probably not like the jungle you'd imagined, huh Ish?"

"I couldn't have imagined. It's beautiful. How high are we?"

"About four thousand feet. Even so, the storms don't touch us. They blow in from the other side of the mountain. We hope you folks will be able to stay for the night. It'll give you a chance to see our mountain sunset."

Sam answered for us, "Ish, Mary, this is the beginning of the adventure we promised. I hope you'll enjoy it."

Mary gushed in response to John's invitation, "It's wondrous. What a spectacular place you and your family have. Of course we'll stay."

One of John's wives now spoke, or was it one of his older daughters?

"Thank you Mary. Our home is your home. Please, ladies, come in."

The girls went inside while John escorted me and Sam to his armory. There was an impressive array of knives and guns. I'd seen some like them at gun shows; far beyond my price range.

Then he took us to a room at the center of the armory. I wondered if we'd find the contents of the boxes he'd brought from the market inside. Instead, the door opened to reveal a huge library. His collection included an enviable assortment of rare books. He had many of the major works of the 16th, 17th, and 18th centuries, written in German, Italian, English, and Latin.

"They were a gift to me." He said.

"Some gift! Do you mind?" I pointed to the books that were laid out on his table.

"Go right ahead."

I gently opened the cover of one of them.

"You've got Bernardino Ochino's *Seven Dialogs* with a 1539 print date?" I opened the cover of another book. "And John Milton's History of Britain, printed in 1670? These are incredible. What's this? Paradise Lost, printed in 1667? All of these look like first printings, printed during the lifetimes of their authors!"

"I did well then. Go ahead, page through them. They won't break."

While I was going through John's library, he and Sam were enjoying coffee and cookies and a leisurely conversation. I was too enlivened by my new discovery to take part. Just then I found something I could scarcely believe, another seven volumes of Paradise Lost with a 1667 print date, all in excellent condition.

"John!" I nearly shouted, "Do you realize that these eight books alone are worth well over a quarter of a million dollars?" I pointed to the eight identical issues of Paradise Lost.

"$327,672 the last time I priced them. You'll find they're in mint condition, printed by Simmons. My plan is to sell one every three years. I don't want to flood the market and deflate their value."

"Sorry John, I guess in my excitement, I forgot the obvious. What collector of rare books wouldn't know the value?"

"Don't feel bad, Ish. A jungle mountaintop isn't exactly the place you'd expect to find such a collection of rare books, but here they are. Haven't you noticed how dry the air is in my library?"

"The air does feel a bit dry."

"I have the humidity controlled. These books are nearly immortal."

"In more ways than one." I said.

The smell of ancient paper and ink filled my nostrils. It was as if the books' authors had invited me to sit with them for a while. I perused one of the books written by Bernardino Ochino[1], the great evangelist of the 16th century whose no less than three exiles set him on a path to preach in more places than any of his peers. Then I opened Paradise Lost, written by John Milton in the 17th century, this epic Christian poem is still unequalled in Christian history. Now I turned my mind toward music, picking up the first Evangelical Hymnal. Its dedication page read, "This collection of Hymn and Psalm Tunes is presented, as a Benefaction to the [Lock] Hospital, that the Profits arising from the Sale of it, may be applied for the Benefit of the Charity." Published in the Eighteenth Century by the founder of the Lock Hospital, the Reverend Martin Madan, (pronounced Madden) it contained nearly one hundred and forty hymns. Madan himself had composed nearly forty of them. With this work of love, he had indeed become the Father of the Evangelical Hymnal.[2] It was primarily the songs from his hymnal that enlivened the great revivals of the 18th and 19th century with songs of praise for the Lord. I was then struck with a great sadness. Why had 20th century America produced more vain tares (weeds among believers) than believers in God? How could America, the cradle of Evangelical thought, have become the cradle of depraved thought. How had so called Christian men become such idolaters that they would place those who play children's games on pedestals? How could so called Christian men revere those Cains of the modern world, those men who would risk their own lives and the lives of their brothers in the blood sport of NASCAR racing? How could the women of my own nation have become such harlots that over ninety percent of them had sex outside of marriage by the time they were thirty?[3] Oh, that this century could be different. Might that I could be blessed by the Lord to be his tool to open the path for a new awakening. There was my ego again, or was it the Lord's destiny calling me. I silently prayed that whatever my destiny was, I would trust in the LORD with all my heart; and lean not unto my own understanding.[4]

"I'm sure lunch is ready." John's words brought me back to the present. He motioned to the door.

As we stepped outside, the extraordinary aroma from the kitchen easily won out over the smell of old books, paper, and ink. My nostalgia was replaced by hunger. I could easily have found the food with my eyes shut.

John's dining hall was opulently furnished. The top of the banquet table was made of a single cut of mahogany and it had ornate carvings on its edges. It was inlaid with mother of pearl and had a glasslike finish. Never before had I beheld such a magnificent table.

John and his entire family were now seated around the table with me, Sam, Sarisa, Mary, and the girls. My appetite by this time had grown, and not just for food. I wanted to hear what must be an incredible tale of adventure and faith. Few men had John's riches, fewer still, a family such as his.

"Sam, will you lead us in prayer?" John asked.

"*Heavenly Father, I ask that You bless this food and this household. I ask that You bless Ish and Mary as well as the other guests. Guide our hearts as each new truth You reveal. I especially ask, Lord, that You will guide me and Ish and John as we are the heads of our wives. Guide our wives also as they submit to us in the Lord. In the precious Name of Our Lord and Savior Jesus, Who is Messiah, Amen.*"

"*Amen.*" We all agreed.

Nearly forty of us now sat around John's banquet table. His wives kept busy moving plates of food between us. Even a Hollywood set designer could not have produced a more inviting display. At one end of the table was a litson baka; that is to say, a small cow that has been roasted over coals till it's skin turns a caramel brown. There were at least two dozen native chickens; some basted with coconut milk and cloves, others with chopped tomato and onion sauce and of course all had just the right amount of garlic. There was Orange Chicken, Chinese style, and every type of vegetable dish you could imagine. The fruit was plentiful, much of which had names I couldn't pronounce.

"The way to a man's heart is through his stomach." Sam opened the conversation, "It looks like John's wives took that route. Wouldn't you agree, Ish?"

"A well worn path indeed!" I couldn't believe what I'd just said but everyone laughed, especially John.

Now that the ice was broken, the members of John's family went straight to making conversation with whoever sat nearest them.

They were wonderfully hospitable and the food was bountiful.

The beautiful young woman who'd earlier told us their home was our home came over to me.

"I'm sorry, Pastor Ish, I didn't introduce myself earlier. I'm Ruth, John's eldest daughter."

"Nice to meet you Ruth. Please, call me Ish. This is a wonderful lunch you all have prepared for us."

"Thank you, Ish. I brought a tray that has everything we've cooked so that you can decide what you like best."

"That was kind of you."

I thought she was simply going to put the tray on the table between me and Mary but instead she pulled up a chair, placing it between the two of us and sat down. Before I had a chance to consider what she was doing she lifted a piece of something to my mouth, feeding me.

"Snow peas and bamboo shoots in tamarind sauce. You like it?"

My mouth was full so I just nodded. It was tart and tangy without a hint of hot. The bamboo shoots and pea pods crunched lightly in the creamy sauce. Maybe if I'd had this as a boy I would have been able to finish my vegetables. As if reading my mind, Ruth said.

"The children love it. It's not too spicy."

She was about to stuff my mouth again so I covered it and asked, "So, how many children are there?" I let down my guard long enough for Ruth to scoop in another mouthful as she said,

"Stuffing made of ground beef, eggs, lemon, green peppers, crumbs from our native bread and a portion of love." I could taste the love.

"My father has twenty eight children." She said, "I'm the only daughter of marriageable age."

Suni, who'd been sitting on the other side of me, now picked up something from the platter and much less delicately than Ruth shoved a piece into my mouth.

"Our native fruit, langka, sweet to the taste and soft to the touch with a double portion of love." Suni recited this local proverb as if wanting to make sure I knew she could pamper me every bit as much as Ruth.

I placed my hand on Suni's to convey that I understood. It was enough. She went back to the conversation she'd been having with another of John's family as if Ruth and I didn't exist.

Mary was quietly shaking her head in disbelief over my encounter with Ruth, peering at me sideways. Then she smiled and nodded, as if to signal that she understood she dared not interfere with anything that might be local custom, and returned to her conversation with one of John's wives. Ah, local custom, sometimes a pain but today, a one of a kind experience! Well, not to leave Suni out; a two of a kind experience.

Ruth continued feeding me, telling me about each dish they'd prepared, and making sure that I knew which of them was her own contribution.

In the middle of the table was a huge kettle of kalabaw stew, Bisaya for water buffalo. I hadn't cared much for this when I'd tried it in the city but Ruth assured me that I'd like it.

"This one was made from a young and fat kalabaw, fed only on rice." She spoon fed me again.

"Mmm." I hummed.

I recognized only a few of the fruits that Ruth had adorning her platter. Some had simply been peeled. Others were in a sweet sauce that accentuated the taste.

"We call this the forbidden fruit." Ruth said. "You must not eat too much of it."

She held it to my lips first, teasing, then placed it in my mouth. It reminded me of the flavor of a candy I'd had as a child.

"So, why shouldn't I eat too much of it, Ruth?"

"A single lady with honor cannot discuss such things. Have Mary ask Sarisa about it later. I'm sure she knows."

I wondered what it could be, a love potion? And it was being fed to me by John's beautiful young, and, in her words, marriageable daughter? What could be next?

I could see now that Ruth was doing all she could to keep from laughing out loud.

"Silly," she said, "It's an apple."

She batted her eyes as if imitating Eve, then elbowed me.

"You're a character, Ish. I bet you weren't this easy to tease when you were a college boy."

She was right. In college I was an egotistical toad. Most college boys were. It didn't make any difference that I was a Christian. Any woman who sought my attention had to be flawless. A small defect could easily disqualify her; being too nice, being too mean, being too flirtatious, not being flirtatious enough. If I couldn't find an imperfection at first sight, I'd find one soon enough. That is, until I met Mary, who turned me from a toad into prince, at least in her eyes. I was thankful that this interchange with Ruth had reminded me of Mary, the great love of my life.

Ruth lifted the lid from a bowl to reveal a kind of oyster soup.

"Oysters in cashew sauce with ginger and diced lamb. This is our customary dish for a groom on his wedding night, and this time I'm not kidding, Ish."

As well I knew. All four ingredients were high in zinc. I remembered learning that the Israelite men had been so fertile because of their high intake of lamb. Why was Ruth feeding me as if it were my wedding night? Did she have plans for me, or did they simply have a custom to feed the guest of honor by the hand of their most beautiful maiden?

Ruth raised the spoon again to my lips. It was exquisite. I could taste each ingredient, yet they combined into something entirely different. I let her feed me till I'd finished all of it. She then put her delicate fingers into the sauce that remained at the bottom of the bowl to pull out a pearl. Wiping it with a cloth, she handed it to me.

"This is for you, to remember this day."

"Thank you Ruth, I will."

I wondered if there was some hidden meaning behind Ruth's gesture with the pearl. Nonetheless, I would remember this day. I couldn't help but think that John had given me the highest honor a guest could have; to be fed by the hand of his maiden daughter.

After Ruth had fed me a sample of everything on the platter, she asked.

"So which of these would you like me to bring you?"

"They all tasted fantastic Ruth, especially what you prepared, but I'm stuffed. You fed me so much. Thank you."

I bit my tongue to keep from saying anything more. I wanted to tell her that it had been one of the most sensual experiences I'd ever had. Just the same, I'm sure she saw it in my eyes.

"Thanks for letting me serve you, Ish."

Ruth left to clean up after the feast. My eyes followed her, feasting once again. Just before going through the kitchen doors she turned as if knowing our eyes would meet. They did. Her eyes were warm and full of love. I hadn't seen such eyes in many years. Did she know my hunger better than I? Was this simple desire the beginning of a series of steps that would lead to sin, or had I already sinned by desiring her?

I knew John would have been pleased to see me marry his daughter, and Suni was no longer hiding her own desire for me. I suddenly realized that I'd been studying how to witness to polygamouss peoples for so long that I was lost in confusion. I could no longer distinguish between the rules that applied to them and those that I must follow. I was even beginning to question how those two sets of rules could be different. I took a deep breath and let it out. Then I assured myself that once Mary and I were far from this place, my desire would be for her only. I remembered the verse that Mary so loved reading to me, Philippians 4:8:

"Whatsoever things are true, whatsoever things are honest, whatsoever things are just, whatsoever things are pure, whatsoever things are lovely, whatsoever things are of good report; if there be any virtue, and if there be any praise, think on these things."

My breathing grew shallow again as my chest tightened. Why did Mary's favorite verse have to come to mind right at this moment? Ruth fit the description in this verse precisely! Was the Lord speaking to me through Mary's favorite verse? Was I to think on Ruth or was I simply an over imaginative husband whose wife had forgotten the words my grandfather spoke at our wedding:

"The wife whose words no longer praise
A mistress fair, shall soon replace."

Chapter 9 Footnotes

1. Bernardino Ochino's Dialogi Sette is but one of his many writings for which he became famous.
2. Madan's Hymnal is regarded as the first Evangelical hymnbook. The Lock Hospital Chapel and its Music by Nicholas Temperley - Page 62
3. Trends in Premarital Sex in the United States, 1954--2003 Lawrence B. Finer, PhD
4. Proverbs 3:5 Trust in the LORD with all thine heart; and lean not unto thine own understanding.
5. Polygamous, polygamist, polygamy - the correct word for a marriage where one man has more than one wife is polygamy. Poly (many) gamy (marriages). Polygyny refers to a man who has many women whether they be his wives or not. Marriage is a man drawing a woman or more to him with the understanding that she may not leave without a Bill of Divorcement supplied by him. Harlotry is when a woman draws many men to her. Many of today's marriages resemble harlotry more than biblical marriage since the wives do not put themselves under the authority of their husbands.

Chapter 10

A HARD TEACHING

The main course had been removed from the table and it was time for dessert. This time John gave the blessing.

"Father in heaven, we thank You for this food, for this fellowship, and for Your love. In Jesus' Name, Amen."

John's simple blessing reminded me of Solomon's proverb. "In an abundance of words, sin is not lacking: but he who restrains his lips is wise."[1] I hoped to discover some of John's wisdom.

I thought I'd already had a taste of dessert but what lay before us now was something very different. Each dish was a design. It brought to mind the educational channel with chefs cooking up a storm. A cooking show for John's wives? Now that would be a first.

Ruth had kept my mouth so filled throughout the main course that I hadn't been able to hold a conversation with John, despite the fact that he sat only an arm's length away. I was determined not to let that happen again.

"Thanks." I said to Ruth who'd returned from the kitchen and was now pouring me a cup of freshly brewed coffee.

"Grown right here in these mountains." John said.

"Oh." I looked up at Ruth, "You grew up in these mountains?"

Ruth covered her mouth with her free hand, giggling.

John half whispered, "I meant the coffee, Ish, the coffee."

"Oh, of course John, *the coffee, the coffee.*"

I feigned seriousness as the girls watched in delight. John hadn't caught the fact that my mistake was premeditated.

"So, do you always tempt your guests with such dishes, John?"

Asina nearly choked on her juice. Suni kicked me under the table and I have to admit, I did steal her joke. The other girls were getting their own kick out of each of my pretended Freudian slips.

John was looking into his cup as if reading tea leaves, his serious demeanor a sharp contrast to mine.

"No, this is a special day."

"Really, what are we celebrating, John?"

"We're celebrating your arrival here, Ish. That is, you, Mary, and the girls. Up until now, Sam and Sarisa were the only Born-Again Christians who'd spent any time with us."

"Really, how long has it been since you came to know the Lord, John?" The girls now listened attentively.

"It's been nearly twenty five years." He said.

"And are you new to these parts?" I asked.

Sam answered for John;

"John and his family have been living on this mountain for the last twenty years. Born-Again Christians won't visit him because he has more than one wife. You aren't the first family that I've invited here. I didn't see the point in telling you folks ahead of time since you're expected to visit such families, after all, that's your mission, but local Christians won't have anything to do with John and his family."

At this, Mary spoke up, "That's horrible. Those Christians ought to be ashamed of themselves!"[2]

"Well, Mary, some were interested in fellowshipping with John and his family but when they found out he took additional wives *after* becoming a Christian, they wanted nothing to do with him."

Mary kept the cup of coffee she'd been sipping from up to her face, holding it with both hands as if to savor it. This way she was able to hide her shock that we weren't having lunch with polygamists who'd become Christians, as she had assumed. We were having lunch with Christians who, without reservation, practiced polygamy.

Sarisa then confessed, "I have to admit that at first, I wasn't any different than the Christians we'd invited here. I had a hard time understanding how John could have taken one wife after another when he was already a Christian but then I started to read. I even read your book Ish, *Adultery in the heart, it's not what you think*."

Mary laughed nervously, "Maybe I'd better start reading some of these books he's been writing."

This so animated Asina that she had to speak, "Oh Mary, you mean you haven't read Ish's books! I think every Christian girl on Mindanao has read them. Oh, you've got to read..." then she caught herself mid-sentence, realizing all eyes were on her. "I'm just going to say it, salty that I am, I still have to admit. Ish's books are brilliant. I just don't have anything to criticize about them, period!"

Whoa! What a compliment, considering it came from Asina.

"And I love his poetry." Suni chimed.

"Me too! Me too!" Cherry spouted.

"Ish, won't you read this please? It's my favorite." Modelisa handed me a well worn paperback I'd authored. *Love Poems and Other Lies*. She had opened it to *A Maiden's Footprints in the Sand*.

"Read it to us!" The girls pleaded.

"Well, if you insist." I said, pulling out my reading glasses.

"*A Maiden's Footprints in the Sand*

A poet's words though many
And his descriptions grand
Cannot contain the message
Of a maiden's footprints in the sand

His English that of kings
And his pen as many swords
Before a maiden's love
Seem faint, somehow untoward

And when at last in one attempt
To say what's in his heart
He gives a thrust with pen and soul
Yea, nearly comes apart

Now smitten sore and left undone
Knows he is just a man
Before the maiden's love
Before her footprints in the sand"

Everyone around the table was now clapping and cheering. "Bravo, bravo."

"I knew it would sound like that if you read it." Suni squealed. "I just love the way he read it, don't you, Modelisa."

"Wow! I did, I really did!" I wasn't sure if Modelisa was acting or what. She was such a mystery to me. I think she liked it that way, then I chided myself. Though she was a master of disguise, she wasn't plastic.

Mary wasn't going to let anything deter her from the subject at hand, even if it meant ignoring the girls overt advances toward me again.

"Back to your family, John. We want to make sure you know that even if we disagree with you concerning your marrying more than one wife," Mary paused and looked at me, as if seeking some signal that I agreed with her. I gave none. She finished her sentence, "We want to know *everything* about your family and couldn't imagine you having even *one wife less*."

The applause were now for Mary. Everyone stood and one of John's older sons shouted,

"A toast for Mary, *Favor is deceitful, and beauty is vain: but a woman that fears the LORD, she shall be praised*."[3]

"Here here," another son said, "*and give her of the fruit of her hands; and let her own works praise her in the gates*."[4]

Ruth completed the stream of thought by quoting one more verse from proverbs,

"*She opens her mouth with wisdom; and in her tongue is the law of kindness*."[5]

At that, a tear began to form in one of Mary's eyes. She wasn't used to such compliments and certainly was not used to being the center of attention. Asina now showed her softer side, using humor to get Mary out of the spotlight. She proudly quoted Proverbs again.

"*She lays her hands to the spindle, and with its rod she spins thread.*[6] Mary, you don't suppose you could help me sew this button back onto my blouse, could you?" Asina held up a button which she'd secretly removed just for effect.

Now Mary was laughing and so were the rest of us. I was impressed with Asina's character. In fact, I was impressed with the character of everyone I'd met since setting foot on Mindanao.

Mary had become more at ease now that the toast had broken the ice. She settled back into her chair and nibbled on a pastry.

"Tell the others about your first response to my having four wives, Sam."

"Well, I have to admit, when I met John I was shocked.

I'd heard of men with more than one wife converting, and of course keeping their wives, but I'd never heard of men who'd taken more wives after they'd converted. John wasn't pushy about what he believed and the fact that he showed such respect for each of his wives made me all the more curious. After he showed me his library and pointed out some of his books, I took it upon myself to study the topic further. It seems that the reformation didn't settle the issue of polygamy. Theologians simply stopped talking about it. Now I'm not sure everyone here has registered what I just said, so I'm going to repeat it. The Reformation did not settle the issue of polygamy. Theologians simply stopped talking about it, at least for a while, but every century the topic would come up again and it was always introduced by the most pious and famous Christians, famous during their lifetimes, that is; for as soon as a man would take the position that polygamy was lawful, the powers that be would make life very difficult for him. A little censorship here, a little exile there, a bit of slander to top it off and you can effectively silence about anyone. After the lives of the men who spoke in favor of polygamy were destroyed, the Chancellors of the seminaries set out to have them erased from their history books. Till this day, some of the most famous Christians in history are merely footnotes in the biographies of lesser men.[7]"

The girls were wide eyed and glued to every word that Sam uttered.

"I discovered that famous Christians such as Bernardino Ochino and John Milton, among others, had argued the case that nowhere in Scripture is a man condemned for having many wives. Now, wouldn't I be correct in saying that those two are among the most famous Christian writers?"

Asina answered, "There is no Christian writer more famous than John Milton! What Christian has never heard of Milton's Paradise Lost?"

"And what Christian theologian has never read Bernardino Ochino's Seven Dialogs?" Ruth added.

"Sam," Modelisa asked, "Did you say that many of the leaders of the Reformation saw nothing wrong with polygamy?"

"That's exactly what I said. Eight of the best known German reformers put their own signatures on a notarized letter to Philip

Hesse, a nobleman of their country, explaining in great detail how they approved of his polygamous marriage.[8] In fact, they attended his wedding. Who knows how many other famous Christians may have been outspoken in their zeal for polygamy but whose fame has been erased from the history books."

"But Sam," Mary objected, "I really don't care what any man says about polygamy. The Bible says, in 1 Timothy 3:2 'A bishop then must be blameless, the *husband of one wife*, vigilant, sober, of good behaviour, given to hospitality, apt to teach.'"[9]

I couldn't help it but I had to quote a funny poem I'd once heard.

"Bishop, man of one wife must be, cannot a layman have two or three?'"

Mary looked at me sourly. "Really Ish, must we be childish about this? The requirement for a Bishop shows the example of a godly marriage. All men should model their lives after that godly example."

"Mary," Sam countered, "your husband has done a tremendous amount of study on this subject for his book, 'Adultery in the Heart, It's not what you think.'" Sam pulled out my book. "Listen to what Ish has written here concerning the verse you quoted.

'Many lay people and homespun ministers have tried to say that 1 Timothy 3:2 and Titus 1:6 are written against polygamy. However, famous theologians throughout history have not claimed this. There are two major problems with considering 1 Timothy 3:2 and Titus 1:6 as injunctions against polygamy.

First, the question arises, why ban polygamy to become a Bishop, Elder, or Deacon but not to remain one. This question cannot be overlooked. There is nothing in the text that suggests that the man who becomes a Bishop, Elder, or Deacon may not, after having received this office, take more wives. In fact, there are no punishments outlined for anyone, whosoever, that takes more than one wife.

Second, if 1 Timothy 3:2 and Titus 1:6 are bans against polygamy, then what is 1 Timothy 5:9 for it says, *Let not a widow be taken into the number under threescore years old, having been the wife of one man*. This is why theologians throughout history have not considered 1 Timothy 3:2 or Titus 1:6 to have anything to do with polygamy. Paul wouldn't write something so silly; banning something that didn't exist in his time; a woman who claimed to be married to more than one husband at the same time? So what is the key to this verse? As always, it's found in the surrounding paragraphs. In 1 Timothy 5:3 Paul says regarding widows, "Honour widows that are widows indeed." What does Paul mean by widows indeed? What characteristics do most harlots and widows share?'"

Cherry spouted, "Children!"

"That's right, children."

Cherry's smile widened as she congratulated herself on the answer.

"You've apparently read Ish's book." Sam said.

"Well, yes, but it's true. Nearly all the girls at the bars where I used to work had children."

John and his family now looked with pity on Cherry.

"Oh, don't worry about me," Cherry said. "the Lord pulled me away from the path of sinners many years ago. I'm a new creation, washed by the blood of the Lamb."

The room erupted with alleluias and praises to God. John's wives started singing and their sons took up their instruments.

"There is pow'r, pow'r,
Wonder-working pow'r
In the blood of the Lamb;
There is pow'r, pow'r,
Wonder-working pow'r
In the precious blood of the Lamb"[10]

They continued singing until all the stanzas had been completed. There was obviously no separation between daily life and worship in John's household; no permission required to sing praises to the Lord. What a refreshing change from the compartmentalized living of Western Christianity where so few Christians could mix words of faith with their daily conversation.[11] How is it that they could claim a saving knowledge of our Savior and not feel naturally led to talk about Him. In fact, what kind of a question was the oft asked, *How can I witness in my daily life?* which begs the question, *How can a Christian NOT witness in their daily life?* This was a puzzle that baffled me still. Were there so many tares?[12]

Sam went back to reading my book aloud.

"'What Paul is saying here is NOT to treat a harlot the same as a widow just because she has children. Don't assume that she's a widow. Check things out. The woman is required to have been married to the father of her children and he must be deceased in order for her to be placed on the widow's list. She cannot be abandoned, a runaway bride, or a harlot.'"

Sam broke from the text for a moment to put in his two cents.

"In other words, she can't be a single mother as your countrymen so shamelessly call harlots."

He looked directly at Mary who couldn't resist taking up the challenge.

"I don't think all those single mothers take money for sex. In fact, I'll bet less than five percent of them do such things."

"Mary," Sam replied, "a harlot is someone who has sex without the benefit of marriage. Those who do it for free are even worse than prostitutes as Cherry so eloquently backed up with Scripture in her testimony yesterday."

Mary was at least now listening. This heartened me.

"I'll continue with what your husband wrote, Mary.

'The phrase in 1 Timothy 5:3 *Honour widows that are widows indeed* precedes and sets up the understanding for the phrase in 1 Timothy 5:9 *wife of one husband* making it clear that *wife of one husband* simply means that she has been married already; that she is a *widow indeed* and not a harlot or a runaway bride. You can't be a widow if you've never been married.

So 1 Timothy 5:3 & 5:9 clarify 1 Timothy 3:2 as well as Titus 1:6 since the phrases *wife of one husband* and *husband of one wife* are identical in form. What they clarify is that we are talking about someone who is married indeed, so pertaining to bishops, that we must only assign the position of bishop to men who are married indeed; that the man who becomes a bishop cannot be someone who is shacking up.'"

"Or celibate!" Modelisa spouted. "That means every elder or bishop has got to be married to *at least* one wife."

"Yes, *at least*!" Suni piped in delight.

Mary was leaning over the table, both hands holding up her forehead in disbelief. I could barely keep back my chuckles at the girls' enthusiasm.

Sam went back to reading my book aloud.

"'It's impossible for us to know how or why the expression *husband of one wife* or *wife of one husband* came to mean *married indeed* by the time Paul wrote it, but languages have subtleties that cannot be understood when separated by such great time periods, and we are around two thousand years from the time this was originally written. Now, if I say to you that you're *one sharp dude* it doesn't mean the number one, it means *a* and sharp doesn't mean sharp like a knife, it means *smart*, and dude doesn't mean a guy from the city. It just means a *guy*. Two thousand years from now you'd need a linguist by your side and many months studying comparative texts to find out the meanings of many simple phrases that we take for granted today, and many of them you could never figure out.'

Now that's how Ish explained it in his book, Mary, but I just want to clarify. Paul would not write that in order to be placed on the widow's list that a widow must have been the wife of one husband in the sense we understand that phrase. He says that young widows *should* remarry.[13] Why, then, would he penalize them if their second husband also dies? Why would he penalize them for losing two husbands? Why would he penalize them for doing exactly what he told them to do, to remarry? It's clear that when Paul uses the phrase wife of one husband that he's not limiting a woman to one husband at a time, that's already been forbidden and it's called adultery. Likewise, when Paul uses the phrase husband of one wife, he's not limiting a man to one wife at a time, there is no such limit found anywhere in Scripture. He's simply stating that any woman who is mother to his children must be married to him, *indeed.*"

Cherry raised her hand.

"Yes, Cherry?" Sam said.

"I don't get it. Why would anyone think it's a prohibition in the first place? Who'd want to be an Elder, Bishop or Deacon? Aren't those offices appointed because nobody wants them?"

"Yes, they're appointed, Cherry, but a lot of men seek those offices." Sam answered.

"But they weren't paid offices in Paul's day and the men in those offices were appointed and not necessarily called of God. Isn't that right?"

"Well yes, now that you mention it. They were appointed and even Paul was not paid for his services so certainly an Elder, Bishop, and Deacon would not have been paid. So you're right, Cherry."

"So, Ish, what exactly is an Elder, Bishop, and Deacon, and why would anyone want those offices?" Cherry asked.

"This *is* an interesting question that you've brought up." I said. "The churches have actually changed those offices from what they were when Paul wrote his words. An Elder is actually the equivalent of a District Attorney within the church and a Bishop is the equivalent of his deputy. A Deacon is simply an administrative assistant, a secretary. These positions involved a lot of work in Paul's day and were unpaid."

"Okay, so, am I stupid or something?" Cherry said. "Is there something that I'm not understanding? I can't imagine anyone wanting those church offices in the first place. They sound like *Chief Busybody*, *Assistant to the Chief Busybody*, and *Step and Fetch It.* I mean, I've volunteered for jobs in the church that I didn't want, don't get me wrong. Every Christian must do that from time to time, but let's be frank. Those are not the highly sought after jobs that the church has led us to believe. Am I right, Ish?"

"Well, yes, you've captured it, Cherry. They were the officials in the church who investigated when a believer had sinned. For example, if a man was found laying with a virgin, he'd be investigated by them, and if the charge were true, the man caught with the virgin would be asked by the Bishop to declare her to be his wife to the father of the girl. If he would not do that, he would be brought before the church by the Bishop where the Elder would lay out the charges. If the man caught laying with the virgin still refused to marry her, he would be excommunicated by the entire congregation. All this was set into motion by the Bishop's investigation and the Elder's prosecution."

"Exactly what I thought!" Cherry exclaimed. "Can you imagine such jobs? They're not exactly the types of jobs that win popularity contests. That's why I just don't believe that men with more than one wife were prohibited from those offices, *as if they would even want them*. In fact, before Paul explains who can take the office of Bishop, he talks it up, as if it's something nobody would want and he's got to sell. In the very verse that precedes it, 1 Timothy 3:1, Paul says, *If a man desires the office of a Bishop, he desires a good work.* That sounds like something you'd say before asking someone to clean the church toilets, like, *If a man desires the office of chief toilet cleaner, he desires a good work.*"

"Cherry's right!" Asina joined in. "If the job of Bishop were desired by so many, I really don't think Paul would have to talk it up. So what do you think Paul really meant in 1 Timothy 3:2, Cherry?"

"It's simple. He's just saying that men with more than one wife are exempt from appointed offices, not prohibited. Deuteronomy 24:5 exempts men from serving in the military or any *business* when they've taken a new wife.[14] Business, of course, refers to civic or church business. How many more exemptions would a man who'd married much and had many children deserve?"

I was dumbstruck. Cherry had discovered *The Key to Understanding the Husband of One Wife*. A key that many, including myself, had sought for years but in vain.

"Sam," I asked, "Have you ever heard what Cherry just explained?"

"Never."

John couldn't believe what he was hearing. "What?" His voice bellowed. "You've never heard what Cherry just said? What about the rest of you, anyone?"

John looked around the room at us. We answered with silence. Cherry's idea was completely new to us.

"Ish, you've been through seminary, correct?"

"Yes John, and I've never heard Cherry's explanation before today; not in seminary, not anywhere."

"Then your professors truly are the liars and tyrants that I feared they were. Tyrants first kill those who dissent, as in the case of Bernardino Ochino who they exiled to a certain death along with his children in the middle of winter.[15] Next, they wipe out the traces of the dissenter, or they replace the truth with lies.[16] Worse yet, they will even erase an entire section of history just to cover up the existence of a prominent dissenter, as in the case of Martin Madan; one of the best known and greatest defenders of the Christian faith. How could any *Christian Historian* bear the title *Historian* without knowing about the Lex Papia Poppaea!"[17]

"The Lex what?" I said.

"The Lex Papia Poppaea; the marriage laws of Rome at the time of Paul! Any professor of Christian history would certainly be familiar with those laws. The Lex Papia Poppaea punished celibacy and rewarded fruitfulness. A man with many children was rewarded with an exemption from troublesome civil duties and unwanted offices. Paul knew this. That's why he exempted men with many children from the office of Bishop, Elder, and Deacon.[18] The fact that your history *professors* failed to teach you this shows me that they are liars and co-conspirators or ignorant buffoons!"

"I'll vote for the latter!" Suni raised her hand.

John was fuming. "Till this day, I thought it was only Christians in old theology books who thought 1 Timothy 3:2 was a prohibition and not an exemption. Your teachers have kept you in darkness! It makes me wonder what else your teachers have covered up. I thought every modern Christian knew the meaning of Husband of One Wife. I've been familiar with that expression since I was a child. The first time I heard it, I was in the market with my uncle. One of the vendors had a stunningly beautiful daughter and my uncle said to him, 'If the rest of your daughters are as beautiful as this one, you'll become rich with dowries.' The vendor replied, 'I'll have to be satisfied with the profits I make from selling my goods for she is my only child.' My uncle then leaned over to me and whispered, 'Surely he is the husband of one wife.' 'Without a doubt.' I replied, considering it an entirely logical conclusion. Since that day, I've heard the expression Husband of One Wife many times in that same context. It's a common expression in my kingdom for a man with few children."

It was clear that in John's home, sermons weren't set aside for a certain hour on a certain day. They could come at anytime and John wasn't finished with his.

"Any historian who had truly studied first century Rome, would have read much of the Lex Papia Poppaea, the Roman marriage law which included rewards for having many children and penalties for remaining single. It's also clear that this is why Paul defended celibacy, not to promote celibacy as a permanent state, but in reaction to certain of the regulations in the Lex Papia Poppaea. If a single man between the age of puberty and sixty was to receive an inheritance, he would lose it if he didn't get married within one hundred and twenty days. The same applied to single women between the age of puberty and fifty. Paul simply wanted to make sure that no man would marry out of compulsion from the government but would marry only out of a compulsion from God to be fruitful and multiply. We certainly know that Paul never meant for any woman to be without a husband. He clearly stated, *I will, therefore, that the younger women marry, bear children, guide the house, give none occasion to the adversary to speak reproachfully*.13 Paul's command that younger women must marry put a huge responsibility upon the men of the church to make sure that all the younger women were married and since the inception of Christianity there have always been more women in the church than men. The men who refused to marry them, quite logically, were given the troublesome church offices. They weren't busy doing anything else and the offices of Elder, Bishop, and Deacon were certainly troublesome offices. As Cherry wisely pointed out; those who were not the Husband of One Wife were given an exemption from those offices."

Sam and I looked at each other, clueless.

"So it's really true?" John was incredulous. "Your seminaries have removed the history books from their libraries that would have easily explained this to you? You're telling me that every single student of Christianity is still taught that 1 Timothy 3:2 is a prohibition?"

Sam and I nodded.

John shook his head in disbelief. "I'm sorry. I didn't know. It's not your fault. You've had these things hidden from you. *And no marvel; for Satan himself is transformed into an angel of light. Therefore it is no great thing if his ministers also be transformed as the ministers of righteousness; whose end shall be according to their works*19 and we can only pray that your professors will repent before they meet their end."

John's words went way over Mary's head and she wasn't ashamed to say it, "Look, you guys are the theologians, not me. I just think it's sad when a woman has to share her husband with other wives."

John's wives were so delighted to actually have Christian visitors, that they didn't mind that Mary was talking about them. In fact, it was energizing them. John nodded his approval as his wife, Peesha, now took a softer approach.

"Mary, when you were a toddler, if you had an ice cream cone, would you share it? Probably not, I wouldn't have either. But what if you had ten gallons of ice cream and no freezer? I think even a toddler would share the ten gallons, and if she didn't, what a shame, for what was left over would just spoil. John is like that ten gallons of ice cream and it would break my heart to put him on ice. It's just not natural. Men are different."

"My Ish is *not like that.*"

I wasn't sure if it was John or myself who was being insulted but it was clear that Mary was worn out from our discussion. Even so, she had enough energy to take one last jab.

"What were you thinking, Ish, writing a book on polygamy!"

I was silent. Mary had seen me writing every day in my office. She'd seen what I'd written about keeping polygamous families together after they'd been saved. Even before we'd married, she'd been a staunch advocate for that aspect of polygamy. Sam answered for me.

"Mary, not to intrude, but Ish's books on Christian chastity are mandatory reading at most of our Bible colleges and Ish *is* the most respected Christian writer on that subject in the Philippines. As for the subject of polygamy, a writer as prolific as your husband couldn't possibly be expected to write over a thousand pages on the topic of chastity, courtship, and biblical marriage without including a few chapters on the subject of polygamy. And, your husband has done a fantastic job of presenting all sides of the issue, as evidenced by your mission board's confidence in him."

Mary's face brightened when Sam added that I'd presented all sides of the issue but her emotions were raw. Peesha, gracious host that she was, took this as her cue.

"Mary, wouldn't you like to see the rest of our place? Our children have been asking over and over if I'd let them show you the playground their daddy built for them."

"They're not theologians, are they?" Mary quipped.

We all laughed. At least Mary had retained her sense of humor. I gave her a kiss on the cheek as I whispered in her ear, "See you later, love of my life." Mary headed off with John's wives, little

Tisay in tow. Of their family, only John, and his daughter, Ruth, remained at the table with us.

The moment the door shut, Asina sobbed.

"Why haven't you told us this before, Sam! All these single women and a church full of potential husbands!"

"It's a hard teaching, Asina. It's a hard teaching." That was all Sam could utter.

Chapter 10 Footnotes

1. Proverbs 10:19 In the multitude of words there wanteth not sin: but he that refraineth his lips is wise. [KJV]

2. Missionaries who ask men to forsake their Christian wives and family so that their own personal interpretation of scripture will not be upset are like the men Jesus speaks of in Matthew 23:4

"For they bind heavy burdens and grievous to be borne, and lay them on men's shoulders; but they themselves will not move them with one of their fingers."

3. Proverbs 31:30 Favour is deceitful, and beauty is vain: but a woman that feareth the LORD, she shall be praised.

4. Proverbs 31:31 Give her of the fruit of her hands; and let her own works praise her in the gates.

5. Proverbs 31:26 She openeth her mouth with wisdom; and in her tongue is the law of kindness.

6. Proverbs 31:19 She layeth her hands to the spindle, and her hands hold the distaff. [A distaff is a rod used for spinning thread.]

7. Thomas Haweis is mentioned in the Who's Who in Christian History as *assistant to Martin Madan, chaplain of the Lock Hospital* and yet Madan, the most famous preacher among Evangelicals after George Whitefield is left out.

Who's Who in Christian History

Douglas, J. D. ; Comfort, Philip Wesley ; Mitchell, Donald: Who's Who in Christian History. Wheaton, Ill. : Tyndale House, 1997, c1992

8. "The Gospel hath neither recalled nor forbid what was permitted in the law of Moses with respect to marriage."

As part of a notarized letter signed by Martin Luther, Philip Melancthon, Martin Bucer, Antony Corvin, Adam, John Leningue, Justus Wintferte, Denis Melanther.

The History of the Variations of the Protestant Churches by

Jacques Bénigne Bossuet - Bishop of Meaux, "One of his most Christian Majesty's Honorable Privy Council, Heretofore Preceptor to the Dauphin, and Chief Almoner to the Dauphiness." In Two Volumes - Translated from the last French Edition. VOLUME I Published 1836

"The husband must be certified in his own conscience, and by the word of God, that polygamy is permitted to him. As for me, I avow that I cannot set myself in opposition to men marrying several wives, or assert that such a course is repugnant to the holy Scripture." Written 1524

The Life of Luther Written By Himself - Collected and Arranged by M. Michelet and Translated by William Hazlitt - London - George Bell and Sons 1904

9. Concerning Bishops and other overseers Paul says:

1 Timothy 3:2 A bishop then must be blameless, the husband of one wife, vigilant, sober, of good behaviour, given to hospitality, apt to teach.

Titus 1:6 If any be blameless, the husband of one wife, having faithful children not accused of riot or unruly.

1 Timothy 5:9 Let not a widow be taken into the number under threescore years old, having been the wife of one man.

Different denominations have interpreted these verses differently over the years. The Baptists have traditionally considered the first two to be a ban against divorced men becoming overseers because to interpret it as a ban on polygamy would mean that 1 Timothy 5:9 would need to be interpreted as a ban on polyandry and in Judaism, the reference point from which Paul spoke, polyandry is not possible for by definition a woman who has another man in addition to her husband is an adulteress, not a polygamist.

The denominations which ban divorced men from the ministry have reaped some unpleasant effects, for this policy has given the wives of their ministers an inordinate amount of leverage over their husbands. Not only can the minister's wife take away the children if there is a divorce but she will surely take away his livelihood. ***If a minister's wife is not a dedicated Christian, she is the most powerful ally that Satan has to destroy a ministry.*** Such being the case, every Christian should include the wives of ministers in their daily prayers.

10. "Power in the Blood" Author & Composer: Lewis E. Jones

11. Colossians 4:6 Let your speech [be] alway with grace, seasoned with salt, that ye may know how ye ought to answer every man.
12. Tares is the Old English word for weeds. Below is the parable of the tares as told by Jesus.
Matthew 13:24-30 Another parable put he forth unto them, saying, The kingdom of heaven is likened unto a man which sowed good seed in his field: But while men slept, his enemy came and sowed tares among the wheat, and went his way. But when the blade was sprung up, and brought forth fruit, then appeared the tares also. So the servants of the householder came and said unto him, Sir, didst not thou sow good seed in thy field? from whence then hath it tares? He said unto them, An enemy hath done this. The servants said unto him, Wilt thou then that we go and gather them up? But he said, Nay; lest while ye gather up the tares, ye root up also the wheat with them. Let both grow together until the harvest: and in the time of harvest I will say to the reapers, Gather ye together first the tares, and bind them in bundles to burn them: but gather the wheat into my barn.
13. 1 Timothy 5:9 "Let not a widow be taken into the number {placed on the widow's list} under threescore years old, having been the wife of one man, {having been a widow indeed, in other words, the deceased man was actually her husband} Well reported of for good works; if she have brought up children, if she have lodged strangers, if she have washed the saints' feet, if she have relieved the afflicted, if she have diligently followed every good work. But the younger **widows** refuse: {refuse to place on the widows' list} for when they have begun to wax wanton against Christ, they will marry; {not that remarrying is wrong but that it would have been a shame to waste resources on a woman by placing her on the widow's list in the first place if she were going to remarry anyway} Having damnation, because they have cast off their first faith. And withal they learn to be idle, wandering about from house to house; and not only idle, but tattlers also and busybodies, speaking things which they ought not. **I will** therefore **that the younger** women **marry**, bear children, guide the house, give none occasion to the adversary to speak reproachfully." Here, Paul clarifies that the younger widows are not to be placed on the

widow's list because if they remain widows they will cause problems and also because they are not likely to remain unmarried. He therefore "wills it" that the widows remarry and that any other young women marry as well.

14. Deuteronomy 24:5 When a man hath taken a new wife, he shall not go out to war, neither shall he be charged with any business: but he shall be free at home one year, and shall cheer up his wife which he hath taken.

15. "So for the last time Ochino went into exile. On the way he was struck down by the plague at Pinczow. It carried off three of his children; he himself remained alive. Wearied to death, he bade his friends and companions in the faith a last farewell on Advent Sunday. There we lose every trace of him. At the close of the year 1564, he died in solitude at Schlackan, in Moravia. This man, once so highly honored, shared the fate of those who dared to advance beyond the narrow limits of the age they live in, and to take their own path."
Bernardino Ochino, of Siena: A Contribution Towards the History of the Reformation
By Karl Benrath, Helen Zimmern
Translated by Helen Zimmern
Published by J. Nisbet & Co., 1876 - Page 297

16. There are hundreds of articles in journals, dictionaries, and biographies that repeat the lie that Madan composed only one or two hymns. I don't wish to give publicity to liars so I will not cite them. I will, however, cite the first man with the courage to give the evidence of Madan's genius in composition; Nicholas Temperley, through his Hymn Tune Index, has methodically detailed the evidence that proves Madan composed more Christian music, for general use in the church, than any other Eighteenth Century composer. Handel is the only Eighteenth Century composer of sacred hymn tunes who was more prolific than Madan but the majority of his music is too difficult to be classified *for general use in the church*. To this day, most of Handel's hymns are reserved for special performances. Handel's Messiah is one such hymn.

17. Jus Trium Liberorum is the term frequently used to describe what is more accurately called the Lex Papia Poppaea, A.D. 9, which granted special privileges to men with many children and

punished celibacy by limiting the rights of single men. This can account for Paul's discussions on celibacy which should not be taken as encouraging celibacy but as defending the right of a man or woman to voluntarily choose marriage instead of feeling compelled to marry by government decree. The Lex Papia Poppaea decreed punishments such as the loss of inheritance rights for those who remained single after having attained puberty up to the age of fifty for women and sixty for men. A man or woman was given one hundred days to get married upon finding out they were the beneficiary of an inheritance or forfeit the inheritance.
A Systematic and Historical Exposition - ROMAN LAW - In the Order of a Code by W. A.Hunter EMBODYING THE INSTITUTES OF GAIUS AND THE INSTITUTES OF JUSTINIAN, TRANSLATED INTO ENGLISH BY J. ASHTON CROSS, B.A. of Balliol College, Oxford, BARRISTER-AT-LAW, Fourth Edition 1803

18. Deacon: A servant, attendant, domestic, one who serves or waits upon. Obviously the original Greek definition given here is much different from the definition in many churches where a deacon is improperly assigned much authority.

19. 2 Corinthians 11:14-15 "And no marvel; for Satan himself is transformed into an angel of light. Therefore it is no great thing if his ministers also be transformed as the ministers of righteousness; whose end shall be according to their works."

Chapter 11

ZEALOUS WOMEN

Asina and the other girls were quietly sobbing now. I felt like a heel. I felt like all married Christians were heels. We took our marriages for granted. These ladies would gladly have traded their careers, their independence, everything but their love for the Lord, to be the wife of a Christian man and give birth to the next generation of Christians.

We now faced, for the first time, what we'd only suspected before; that Western Christianity had forsaken its single women. The single women in the churches would get along well enough until years of youth activities began to remind them that their own youth had vanished. After that, they'd suffer lives of loneliness, or for those who couldn't contain themselves, marriage with members of the Roman church or one of the many other churches that didn't preach salvation by grace. I'd seen such marriages in my own church and it disgusted me. The pastor would accept a fake profession of faith from an unbelieving man, counsel the couple two or three times, and then preside over their marriage. They'd attend church for a few weeks, sometimes a few months, then fall away. The majority of the old maids remained virgins but some surrendered themselves to whoredom as their God given desires found no suitable outlet.[1] As I considered the mistreatment of these ladies, my emotions welled up within me.

"Not one of you will be left without a Christian husband!" I blurted. "The Lord *will* provide."

I must have sounded silly, declaring that we would find the solution to a problem that hadn't been properly dealt with in the thousands of years since Rome first corrupted the Christian church. Suni responded to my outburst in a soft but confident tone as she wiped away her tears.

"I know you're a good man, Ish. The girls and I know that you would do anything for us, but we're going to have to fix this problem ourselves, and we can do it, with God's help. None of us want to become old maids. We understand there's no *gift of singleness*. The teaching that there is a *gift of singleness* is heresy.[2] If anything, singleness is a curse. Being childless is certainly a reproach. We've learned this from the books you've written, Ish. You pointed out that the first verse in the Bible where the word reproach is used concerns the birth of Joseph to Rachael. It says, *And she conceived, and bare a son; and said, God hath taken away my reproach*: You also pointed out that the first usage of the word reproach in the New Testament concerns the birth of John the Baptist where his mother, Elisabeth says, *Thus hath the Lord dealt with me in the days wherein he looked on me, to take away my reproach among men*.[3] I don't take the Bible lightly, Ish. *To every thing there is a season, and a time to every purpose under heaven: a time to bear children* and so forth.[4] We certainly can't wait much longer. *The time is now and the harvest is ready*. Hinug na kami. (We're ripe.) But don't worry about us, Ish, we'll find a harvester."[5]

"Amen." Asina said. "So you've got those verses memorized too!" Having regained her composure and independence Asina was enthusiastically expressing herself. "We *are* going to fix this! This isn't simply wishful thinking on our part. I can't believe that it's the Lord's will that we should have such a thirst for the *bone of our bones, flesh of our flesh*, a husband, and that the Lord wouldn't provide one.[6] We've seen generation after generation of unhappy old maids in our churches and the others who've fallen away due to unbearable temptation and loneliness. That's not God's will and we're not about to find some lost tribe of single Christian men. They're just not going to arrive. It's time for action and the Lord is on our side concerning this.[7] This isn't just about us, it's about future generations of Christians. I can only imagine how many millions if not billions more Christians there would be today if the last two thousand years had witnessed Christian men taking many wives."

"So Asina, where do we start?" Suni asked.

"We need to be prepared for our husband when he arrives and we need to be able to say to anyone who asks, *Sure, if the right Christian man proposes, I'll marry him whether he already has a wife or not!*"

I knew Asina was feisty but hadn't expected that she'd be

emboldened to take on all Christendom on the issue of polygamy. Yes, I'd preached that every Christian woman should be married but not by becoming a wife to a polygamist.

Now Modelisa added her support for Asina's idea.

"And we need to be able to answer with confidence and back it up with Scripture. People are going to attack us in all sorts of ways. Don't think for a moment that they won't call us sluts, whores, you name it, anything to scare us away from doing what's right. Remember Paul's words, *All scripture is given by inspiration of God, and is profitable for doctrine, for reproof, for correction, for instruction in righteousness*."[8]

I still couldn't believe what I was hearing. The girls were advocating polygamous marriage as the answer to their plight![9]

Sam sensed a need for prayer.

"Ladies, men, let's pray. This is a serious matter and we need the Lord's guidance. Could you please pray." John asked me.

"Sure, John." I said.

"*Lord, the time that we spend on earth is so short when compared with eternity but we do have needs. As Your word says, 'Better is open rebuke than hidden love.'*[10] *Let us never hide our love. We pray that the married women in our churches will stop shunning the single ladies and that instead they'll raise them up in prayer and treat them as their own daughters. Help the men also to act in all holiness regarding the single ladies. Lord, we pray that each one of these ladies will find a husband. Quench their thirst; the thirst that you have in your infinite knowledge placed within them to be married and to have children. Lord, may everything we discuss today have as its ultimate goal to fulfill Your purpose and Your will. Amen.*"

The girls wasted no time in getting back to the subject. I figured my best course of action was to keep quiet. After a few minutes of discussion they were sure to realize the impracticality of their idea. Ruth went first.

"Let's think up every objection that anyone could have to a man's taking more than one wife, beginning with the easiest. After we've gotten warmed up, we can move on to the more difficult objections."

"Great idea," Suni agreed, "How about you start first, Ruth?"

"Okay, Suni, here's the easiest objection I've heard.

If God had intended men to have more than one wife, he would have created more than one woman for Adam."

"Go on." Suni urged.

"Well it's just plain silly. God made billions of women, the descendents of Eve. Furthermore, if men can only have what Adam had then they can't have any wives at all, unless their wives are taken from their own rib. That's the type of wife Adam had."[11]

"You've got a point there." Suni said.

"But what really irks me is the totally illogical premise of their argument;" Ruth said, "that Adam had no other wives."

"What do you mean?" Suni asked, "Adam had other wives?"

"Well, who was the oldest mother in the Bible?" Ruth asked.

"Sarah." Suni answered, "At least that's what all of our pastors have told us."

"Okay, so if Sarah was the oldest mother in the Bible at age ninety, and she was surprised when the Lord told her that she'd have a child, how much more surprised would Eve have been at bearing a child at the age of a hundred and thirty years?"[12]

"That is odd, now that you mention it." Suni replied. "But wait a minute, Ruth, where do you get a hundred and thirty years old?"

"Well, Adam was a hundred and thirty years old at the time of Seth's birth, and that's why I believe that Eve would have been a hundred and thirty years old when she had Seth, if she was Seth's mother, which I think is nonsense."[13]

Ruth wasn't hiding her contempt for what she considered fuzzy theology about man's beginnings. Now she read from her Bible.

"'And Adam gave names to all cattle, and to the fowl of the air, and to every beast of the field; but for Adam there was not found a help meet for him. And the LORD God caused a deep sleep to fall upon Adam, and he slept: and He took one of his ribs, and closed the flesh over it; And from the rib, which the LORD God had taken from man, He made a woman, and brought her to the man.'[14]

Now I think it's *extremely* unlikely that God allowed Adam to suffer in loneliness for very long, let alone the forty one years he would have suffered in isolation if Eve was younger than Sarah at the time Seth was born. Are we to believe that Adam happily spent forty one years naming all the animals? Oh, how exciting. Come on! Any person, including Adam, would go crazy living without contact with other people. How long could Adam have maintained his sanity? The Garden of Eden would have been more like a prison than a paradise if he were tormented with loneliness that long."

"It makes sense to me that the Lord would have created Eve pretty much right away," Suni agreed, "at least as soon as the animals were named, which couldn't have taken more than a few weeks. I don't think anyone here would believe that God had Adam naming animals and waiting in loneliness, year after year."

Modelisa concurred, "What Ruth is saying makes sense. That puts Eve at the same age as Adam and that certainly *would* make her a hundred and thirty years old at the time of Seth's birth."

"If she were still living, that is." Ruth's reply revealed her thoroughness in examining the text.

"What do you mean if she were still living?" Cherry asked.

"Well, the Bible rarely tells us the time of a woman's death. Rachael is one of those rare exceptions and I'm certain that's because of the fact that she died giving birth, but in the case of Eve, after the birth of Cain and Abel, we don't hear a word about her."[15]

"You're going way to fast for me." Modelisa objected. "Let me read about Seth's birth and you explain how it wasn't Eve." She opened her bible and read Genesis 4:25

"*And Adam knew his wife again; and she bare a son, and called his name Seth: For God, said she, hath appointed me another seed instead of Abel, whom Cain slew.*

See? If God appointed another seed for a woman instead of Abel then that woman must have been Eve since she was Abel's mother. Plus, it sounds to me like Adam had sex with Eve *again* because it says *Adam knew his wife again.*"

"Sounds like it, doesn't it, but you have to admit that it doesn't mention Eve by name." Ruth now pulled out her notes. "Listen to what the Hebrew literally says, in the order it would be spoken, word for word, in English.

And Adam made love with his wife a good while and she begat a son and she called his name Seth for God appointed to me another seed instead of Abel because Cain slew him.

Now one could argue that this sentence is very ambiguous. Listen to how a slight emphasis on *to me* forces the conclusion that the woman was other than Eve.

for God appointed, *to me,* another seed instead of Abel

You see? *to me,* instead of *to Eve.* Now I'm not saying that it was positively someone other than Eve, but you can see how it very well could have been, and if it were, then Adam was a polygamist or at the very least he had another wife after Eve's death. But don't forget, people had very long life spans back then and even though it's unlikely Eve would have given birth to a son at the age of a hundred and thirty years, it's also very unlikely that she would have been dead by that time."

"Impressive!" I couldn't keep my mouth shut any longer. "*What did you use to parse this verse, Ruth?*"

"Well, most of my exegesis was done with the help of the AFPMA, the Anderson-Forbes Phrase Marker Analysis of the Hebrew Bible."

"You have that book? That's what we used at seminary in our advanced level linguistics classes."

"Well, Ish, I have to admit that living on a kibbutz in Israel for two years helped my Hebrew as well."

What a pleasure to see Ruth's dedication. Not only was she a woman with a heart for the Lord but she'd dedicated herself to a verse by verse study of marriage. Now she asked the girls,

"Turn to Genesis 46:29. Notice the phrase *a good while*?"

"Yes, I see that." Suni answered.

"That's the exact same word that's translated *again* in Genesis 4:25. Instead of translating it *Adam made love to his wife again* it makes sense to translate it, *Adam made love to his wife a good while.* After all, it sometimes takes *a good while* before a wife gets pregnant. But before we do that, let's look at Genesis 46:29 and read *a good while* as *again* and see what happens. Try reading it that way, Suni."

"Okay, Ruth,

And Joseph made ready his chariot, and went up to meet Israel his father, to Goshen, and presented himself unto him; and he fell on his neck, and wept on his neck again.

Wow, you're right. It sounds just like Joseph had wept on his father's neck on some earlier occasion when you read it that way. The change of one word can sure change the way we understand verses. Hey Ruth, do you think the translators of the verse concerning Seth's birth, Genesis 4:25, set out to mislead us?"

"No, no, I don't think so, but it's clear to me that when you read Genesis 4:25 the way the King James translator has written it, with the word *again* instead of *a good while*, that it tricks your sensibilities into thinking that it was Eve who Adam made love to when the Hebrew doesn't specify anything of the sort. In fact, the word used in Genesis 4:2 for *again* when Eve certainly did bear a son *again*, namely, Abel, is an entirely different word than the one used here. A good translator never forces a conclusion that isn't forced in the original text. When you use *a good while* it could be Eve or it may not be but the conclusion isn't forced. But when you use *again* it really does force a conclusion or at the very least strongly implies the conclusion that Eve was the mother. That conclusion isn't even slightly implied in the Hebrew. We also need to remember that just because two events are found within the same chapter that it doesn't mean that they concern the same person, or in this case, the same wife."

"What else?" Suni was leaning forward on the edge of her seat, excited to hear more.

"Well, you see where it says, *she said*? The words, *she said* are probably written in italics in your Bible and that's because they're not in the Hebrew at all. Those words were added in the English translation. Leaving them out changes it only a little, but to be accurate, let's read it without them, now that I've explained.

And Adam made love with his wife a good while, and she begat a son and she called his name Seth, for God appointed to me another seed instead of Abel because Cain slew him."

"That is amazing." Modelisa said. "It doesn't sound like the woman had to be Eve at all. It could have been any woman.

Someone might even argue that another woman was given the honor of giving birth to Seth because Eve gave birth to the man who murdered Abel."

"I hadn't even thought of that," Ruth said, "but you're right. Now to sum up, we know that when Adam was a hundred and thirty years old that he had another son and that if Eve were still living she would also be a hundred and thirty. We also know that our pastors continue to say that Sarah was the oldest mother in the Bible. That means that they either have to stop calling Sarah the oldest mother in the Bible or they've got to stop saying that Adam had only one wife. They're mutually exclusive."

"Well then, who do you *propose* that Adam married?" I *had* to ask.

"Well, Mr. Punster," Ruth retorted, "He could have married his daughter, his granddaughter, his great granddaughter or any of his various progeny because father/daughter/granddaughter marriage wasn't banned until Moses received the law on Mount Sinai."[16]

"There's nothing wrong with your logic." I admitted "The Bible never claimed that Adam had one and *only* one wife.[17] It simply names Eve as the wife who was taken from his side and when the mother of Seth was mentioned, as you've rightly pointed out, that woman, whether she was Eve or someone else, wasn't named."

Ruth had more to say, "And the argument that a man could have only one wife, because Adam had only one wife, wouldn't have applied to Adam since there was no previous Adam to set such a precedent."

"Touché!" Modelisa declared. "You really are bright! Isn't she, Cherry?"

"Without a doubt. I'm soooo impressed!"

The girls were now giggling in delight.

"Thanks for your compliments." Ruth said. "Now another thing concerning Adam. He was kicked out of the garden of Eden because he hearkened to the voice of his wife.[18] In other words, his life in the Garden of Eden was cut short. We can't know whether God would have taken more wives from Adam's side in that perfect state, before the fall. We don't even know whether Eve bore him daughters before the fall, at a time when it was absolutely certain that there was just one command, not to eat from the Tree of Knowledge of Good and Evil. He could have taken dozens of his own daughters as wives before Eve had eaten from that tree and certainly that would not have been a sin *for where there is no law, there is no transgression.*[19] This point brings up some other claims that pastors make, that Adam made a law in the Garden of Eden. Hah! Adam was not the lawmaker. God *was*, and *is* the lawmaker and God gave one law in the Garden of Eden: *Of every tree of the garden you may freely eat: but of the tree of the knowledge of good and evil, you shall not eat: for in the day that you eat of it you shall surely die.* Now think of this again. Pastors claim that after God created Eve, Adam made a law by saying, *Therefore shall a man leave his father and his mother, and shall cleave unto his wife: and they shall be one flesh.* Could this *law* that they attribute to Adam have been applied to him in the Garden of Eden? Could Adam overrule God's own command that there was but one law and add new laws just like today's popish ministers do? Even more incredible, now listen; their claim is that Adam made a law before he even had the knowledge of good and evil! The truth is, the words were simply a statement of fact, that men and women are heterosexual; that a man shall cleave to his wife, not to a man; for the *woman* was taken out of man. It certainly does not apply in the way that our popish ministers have tried to apply it, that a man can have only one wife just because it says in the English cleave to his wife, *singular.* God also says love thy neighbor, *singular*, but God isn't saying that we're obedient to that command by loving the neighbor to the left of us and hating the one to the right of us, or in front of us, or behind us. The singular word neighbor specifies the type of person you are to love, not the number of persons you are to love, and the singular word wife specifies the gender of the person or persons that a man is to cleave to, not the number of persons he is to cleave to. Neither of them specify the number, unless, as I've pointed out, God is telling us that we may love just one neighbor and hate the rest."

"This is all so fantastic," I said, "the way you're explaining how Adam could have actually had more than one wife before the fall, but what about Adam's life after the fall?"

"We're asked by our pastors to accept the notion that Adam had only one wife before the fall, as well as after the fall, but this ignores reality. On top of this, we're asked to believe that God created only one woman. Ladies, you and I were created by God! Aren't we women? It's true that we weren't created side by side along with Eve but it was God, not our parents, who created us in the womb. Isaiah 44:2 declares that we are created by the Lord. *Thus saith the LORD that made thee, and formed thee from the womb...*

Now, let's consider this, Adam and Eve must have been the most fertile specimens of humanity in history, that is without a doubt. They were created before the fall. So are we to believe that prior to conceiving Cain and Abel and after their births, that Eve was barren? Are we to believe that during the one hundred and thirty years prior to the birth of Seth, that other than the delivery of two sons and one daughter who became Cain's wife, Eve was barren?

Now that I've cleared away the nonsense, let's make some logical assumptions. If Eve was the mother of Seth, as many pastors claim, then she certainly must be considered the most fertile woman in history to have given birth at the age of one hundred and thirty. Now if Eve was the most fertile woman in history then she would have gotten pregnant shortly after weaning each child. Since the average child is weaned by the age of two, she would have given birth every three years. This is if we also assume that she didn't get pregnant while nursing. Now divide one hundred and thirty by three and you come up with forty three births. Subtract out Seth, Abel, Cain, and Cain's wife, and you have thirty nine daughters born to Eve in those one hundred and thirty years. Before Seth was born, Adam would have had his pick of dozens of beautiful women."

"Not to mention the daughters of those women." Suni added. "But why daughters only?"

"Because no sons are mentioned other than Cain and Abel prior to Seth's birth. Now, speaking of Seth, who had no son till he was one hundred and five years old. Are we to believe that in the one hundred and four years before his wife conceived Enos, that Seth had no relations with her or that she was barren? Such an assumption is not just silly, it's out*rageous*. These so-called pastors require us to pretend that an extremely healthy man, Seth, who lived till the age of nine hundred and twelve, would be happy without a wife till the age of one hundred and four! That is the most ludicrous thought that ever crossed the mind of a theologian, and I admit, there have been some whoppers."

Laughter filled the room at Ruth's words. She had brought up something so unique but so obvious that even a kindergartner could have pointed it out. I couldn't imagine why we hadn't thought of it, unless, in cultlike fashion, our churches had literally brain washed us. Ruth continued to open our eyes.

"Now some pastors will object, saying, 'No, no, we didn't say that Eve bore no children for all those years or that Seth had no relations with a wife but only that any births would have been to daughters.' to which I would reply, 'So God allowed the births of dozens of women with no intent of providing them a husband? Sounds like the lie you're still telling the young women in your churches!"

"Let's go beat up a pastor!" Asina yelled. "Just kidding Sam, Ish. Hope you don't mind."

We didn't just laugh this time. We were falling off our chairs giddy. The combination of discovering such obvious truths *and* lies gave us only two choices; laugh or cry. We chose to laugh. After we'd regained our composure, Ruth continued her explanation.

"So if Eve was the mother of Seth and she was not barren, it's abundantly clear that she must have had dozens of daughters during the years before Seth. Susana Wesley, the mother of the founders of Methodism, had twenty-five children in little more than twenty five years, how much more the mother of mankind in one hundred and thirty years!"

Now a rush of clarity came over me. I felt like a child again. Had my eyes been shut that long? How long had I only believed what I'd been told to believe. How much had my church twisted God's word so that my mind could be made to ignore the most obvious of facts; that Eve, the most perfect specimen of womanhood, would have continued to bare children year after year, prior to the birth of Seth, if she was indeed his mother. I listened all the more closely to what Ruth was saying.

"Prior to the birth of Seth, God likely created dozens, if not hundreds, of women through Adam and his female progeny.[20] After all, the pastors always say that Cain and Seth must have married their own sisters. Why do they make that conclusion with such ease but can't consider the possibility that Adam married his own daughters."

At this Modelisa interrupted Ruth. "A friend of mine once said that God would not have allowed Adam to commit a sin that is considered so heinous as to be punishable by burning, and that is the punishment for having sex with both a mother and her daughter, but that God would have allowed Adam's sons to marry their sister, a sin punishable by exile. She claimed that a sin is a sin even before the law."

"Even if your friend wants to ignore the Scripture that says, *where there is no law, there is no transgression*, she can't ignore this: Abel or Cain could have married a sister and then their daughters could have married Adam. Burning is not the punishment for marriage with a granddaughter. Although marrying a granddaughter has been absolutely forbidden since the law of God was given by Moses, there is no specific punishment for it, while the punishment given for sex with a sister is exile. If judged by the punishment, as your friend wishes it to be, her argument is now the losing one. But still, we must not forget that Adam lived far before the law and this woman who told you that Adam would be liable to a law he was not given is simply ignoring God's word."

Now Asina took her turn at biblical analysis.

"Another thing that most people don't even realize, Ruth, is that in the Bible, except for women who were of the unbelieving nations, if a woman had only daughters, she was not mentioned! There's not a mention of even one from Genesis through Revelation. So just because Adam is not said to have other wives doesn't mean that he didn't. They absolutely would not have been mentioned if they bore him no sons, and just like you said, are we to believe that the most perfect specimen of manhood that has ever existed, the first man, Adam, was not impregnating his wife or wives on a regular basis during the hundred and thirty years between Eve's being taken from his rib and Seth's birth? But not to forget, Adam is said to have fathered both sons and daughters *after* the birth of Seth. Now tell me, if Adam had only one wife as nearly all pastors claim, then it was Eve, after her one hundred and thirtieth birthday, who gave birth to at least four more children, *sons and daughters*.[21] Why do pastors so conveniently fail to address this issue?"

Now Suni showed her biblical acumen.

"In addition, Adam's daughters probably begged him to give them children, since they were born many years before any male children were born. We see in the story of Lot's daughters, when they were confronted with what appeared to be a world without men, that they took their father as their husband and they bore children, Moab and Ammon."

"And it only took Lot's daughters a few days to take action." Modelisa added, "How much faster would Adam's daughters have chosen him as a husband knowing *for a fact* that he was the only man on earth?"

"That's a good point," Ruth said, "and there was no condemnation of Lot's daughters making love with their father because their union took place before such relations were forbidden and they understood that by making love with him they were becoming his wives. In fact, the Lord set aside a portion for the children of Lot; the land of Ar. The Bible quotes Lot's daughters like this:

And the firstborn said unto the younger, 'Our father is old, and there is not a man in the earth to come in unto us after the manner of all the earth.' Genesis 19:31

They go on to say:

'We will lie with him, that we may preserve seed of our father.' Genesis 19:32b

Let's keep in mind that when the Bible speaks of *seed* that it's referring to male progeny. Lot's daughters laid with him in order to produce male offspring and if Adam's daughters were born before the birth of Cain and Abel, which is not inconsistent with the Bible, then they too would have had the same rationale as Lot's daughters for laying with their father, to produce male offspring, since Adam was the only man on earth. One might object, 'why would Adam's daughters have thought it necessary to produce offspring for him if they knew he already had their mother, Eve, as his wife. Well, in the case of Lot that didn't seem to make a difference. It wasn't just one of them who laid with their father but both of them."

Cherry now got into the discussion. "And it would also make sense that any daughter that Eve bore after Cain was banished would want to bear sons to Adam as well. They would have assumed that Cain had been exiled to his death and certainly they would not have followed after a murderer. Of course they'd think their father was the last man on earth and he still had no seed, no male heir, until he reached the age of one hundred and thirty. He just kept poppin out daughters, or should I say, wives!"

Ruth now brought up another common fallacy. "Here's one nutty objection that's been brought up so often that many people don't even recognize it as nutty, but it's this; 'If Adam had more than one wife then the Bible surely would have mentioned it.'"

"Why is that nutty?" Suni asked.

"Well, there's not one mention of even one wife of Ibzan of Bethlehem who judged Israel and he had thirty sons, and thirty daughters. Likewise, there's no mention of any wife for Abdon who was also a judge of Israel and he had forty sons![22] Are we to believe that because no wives were mentioned for either of these men that their children were born without mothers? A kind of immaculate conception in reverse? Even more incredible, so-called theologians don't even list Ibzan and Abdon on their list of the Bible's polygamists.[23] Do they seriously believe that it's possible that a man with sixty children didn't have more than one wife at the same time?"

Ruth surely had the gift of Biblical exegesis. The girls were wide eyed as if hearing some hidden truth for the very first time, and I have to admit, so was I.

Chapter 11 Footnotes

1. Old Maid - The age after which a woman has little chance of finding a husband, historically this age has been around twenty five.

Whoredom - a woman's loss of virginity without the benefit of marriage.

2. Gift of Singleness - The heretical teaching that some people are given a gift for being single. It does not derive from Paul's teachings but from a twisting of his teachings.

3. Reproach - shame. There are three cases in the Bible where a woman describes her getting pregnant as the Lord taking away her reproach. The first is the case of Rachel in Genesis 30:23. The second is the case of Elizabeth in Luke 1:25. And the third, historically speaking since it is usually considered to be an *End Times* prophecy, is the case of the seven women in Isaiah.

Isaiah 4:1,2 "And in that day seven women shall take hold of one man, saying, We will eat our own bread, and wear our own apparel: only let us be called by thy Name, to take away our reproach. 2 In that day shall the branch of the LORD be beautiful and glorious, and the fruit of the earth shall be excellent and comely for them that are escaped of Israel."

The "branch of the LORD," literally the branch of YHWH, refers to Jesus.

Zephaniah 6:12 "And speak unto him, saying, Thus speaketh the LORD of hosts, saying, Behold the man whose Name is The BRANCH; and he shall grow up out of his place, and he shall build the temple of the LORD: 13 Even he shall build the temple of the LORD; and he shall bear the glory, and shall sit and rule upon his throne; and he shall be a priest upon his throne: and the counsel of peace shall be between them both."

The son of Rachel, Joseph, was ordained by God to prepare a place for Israel to grow as a people and establish itself. Joseph tells his brothers:

Genesis 45:7 "And God sent me before you to preserve you a posterity in the earth, and to save your lives by a great deliverance."

The son of Elizabeth, John the Baptist, was sent also by God, preparing again the way of the Lord:

Matthew 3:3b "The voice of one crying in the wilderness, Prepare ye the way of the Lord, make his paths straight."

We can only wonder if the seven women spoken of in Isaiah 4:1 will also give birth to men who will prepare the way of the Lord's return particularly since the very verse that follows this prophecy describes Christ's return.

4. Ecclesiastes 3:1,2a To every thing there is a season, and a time to every purpose under the heaven: A time to be bear children...

5. Matthew 9:37,38 "Then saith he unto his disciples, The harvest truly is plenteous, but the labourers are few; Pray ye therefore

the Lord of the harvest, that he will send forth labourers into his harvest."

6. Bone of my bone - Spouse

Genesis 2:23 And Adam said, This is now bone of my bones, and flesh of my flesh: she shall be called Woman, because she was taken out of Man.

My bone and my flesh - A close relative, for example, Laban was Jacob's uncle.

Genesis 29:14 And Laban said to him, Surely thou art my bone and my flesh.

All marital relationships are incestuous to some degree for we are all descended from one man who, in effect, married himself for Eve was taken from Adam's side. After the law (when Moses presented God's law to the Israelites on Mount Sinai) a certain portion of relatives were put off limits in regards to marriage. This did not include marriages that had already taken place. For example, Moses himself was the son of a marriage that after the law, was forbidden. Amram married Jochebed, Jochebed was Amram's own aunt. The law that Moses received on Mount Sinai forbid such relationships but since their marriage took place before the law had been presented it was not imputed as sin.

Romans 5:13 For until the law sin was in the world: but sin is not imputed when there is no law.

Exodus 6:20 And Amram took him Jochebed his father's sister to wife; and she bare him Aaron and Moses: and the years of the life of Amram were an hundred and thirty and seven years.

7. Paul commanded that young women be married.

1 Timothy 5:14 I will therefore that the younger women marry, bear children, guide the house, give none occasion to the adversary to speak reproachfully.

Asina's presumption that she must choose her husband from among the already married is based on this command of Paul. It has been argued that since it has always been the case that there were more single women of child bearing age in the church than single men of all ages that it would be impossible to carry out Paul's command without polygamous marriages. Furthermore, it has been argued that Paul must have known this when he gave this command so that by the very giving of the command he was commanding that polygamous marriage take place.

8. 2 Timothy 3:16 All scripture is given by inspiration of God, and is profitable for doctrine, for reproof, for correction, for instruction in righteousness

9. Jewish tradition considers Boaz to be the same person as Ibzan. Elwell, W. A., & Comfort, P. W. (2001). Tyndale Bible dictionary. Tyndale reference library (623). Wheaton, Ill.: Tyndale House Publishers.

The treasury of scripture knowledge : Five hundred thousand scripture references and parallel passages. 1995. Introduction by R. A. Torrey. (Ruth 2:1).

If it's true that Boaz is the same person as Ibzan then the girls are seeking the same answer to their dilemma as Ruth sought for hers; marriage with a polygamist. Ruth wished to produce godly offspring. She succeeded and this resulted in the line of kings that culminated in the King of kings, Jesus, our Savior. The girls wish to marry polygamously and produce godly offspring who will share the gospel with the unsaved. Dare we discourage them?

10. Proverbs 27:5 Open rebuke is better than secret love.

11. Genesis 2:22 And the rib, which the LORD God had taken from man, made he a woman, and brought her unto the man.

12. Genesis 17:17 Then Abraham fell upon his face, and laughed, and said in his heart, Shall a child be born unto him that is an hundred years old? and shall Sarah, that is ninety years old, bear?

13. Genesis 5:3 And Adam lived an hundred and thirty years, and begat a son in his own likeness, after his image; and called his name Seth.

14. Genesis 2:20-22

15. Genesis 35:18-20 18 And it came to pass, as her soul was in departing, (for she died) that she called his name Benoni but his father called him Benjamin. 19 And Rachel died, and was buried in the way to Ephrath, which is Bethlehem. 20 And Jacob set a pillar upon her grave: that is the pillar of Rachel's grave unto this day.

16. Leviticus 18:17 Thou shalt not uncover the nakedness of a woman and her daughter, neither shalt thou take her son's daughter, or her daughter's daughter, to uncover her nakedness; for they are her near kinswomen: it is wickedness.

17. Uriah is the only man in the Bible about whom it is written he had one and only one wife.

18. Genesis 3:17-19 And unto Adam he said, Because thou hast hearkened unto the voice of thy wife, and hast eaten of the tree, of which I commanded thee, saying, Thou shalt not eat of it: cursed is the ground for thy sake; in sorrow shalt thou eat of it all the days of thy life; Thorns also and thistles shall it bring forth to thee; and thou shalt eat the herb of the field; In the sweat of thy face shalt thou eat bread, till thou return unto the ground; for out of it wast thou taken: for dust thou art, and unto dust shalt thou return.

19. Romans 5:13 For until the law sin was in the world: but sin is not imputed when there is no law.

20. Genesis 5:2 Male and female created he them; and blessed them, and called their name Adam, in the day when they were created.

This verse can also be said only to describe the creation of Adam since at his creation, Adam contained both male and female since Eve was taken out of Adam.

21. Genesis 5:4 And the days of Adam after he had begotten Seth were eight hundred years: and he begat sons and daughters.

22. Judges 12:8-9 8 And after him Ibzan of Bethlehem judged Israel. 9 And he had thirty sons, and thirty daughters, whom he sent abroad, and took in thirty daughters from abroad for his sons. And he judged Israel seven years.

Judges 12:13-14 13 And after him Abdon the son of Hillel, a Pirathonite, judged Israel. 14 And he had forty sons and thirty nephews that rode on threescore and ten ass colts: and he judged Israel eight years.

23. Neither Ibzan nor Abdon are mentioned in the list of the polygamists of the Bible that are contained in Willmington's Book of Bible Lists. Wheaton, Ill. : Tyndale House, 1987

MARTIN MADAN
A MEMORY OF LOVE

Ruth's genius was revealed through her method of Bible study but now she opened up to expose the tenderest of hearts. She set aside her notes, as her voice softened and she delivered a long overdue eulogy for the now forgotten Reverend Martin Madan.

"You remember how Sam said that there's a long list of eminent theologians who've been forgotten simply because they supported polygamy?"

"Yes, I remember." Suni answered, "I was wondering who those might be."

"Well Suni, the Reverend Martin Madan for one. Martin Madan was the most famous preacher in England during the late Eighteenth Century. He's also considered to be the most prolific and talented composer of Christian Church Music for all time.[1] Late in his career, he wrote a book titled: *Thelyphthora; Or, a Treatise on Female Ruin, Its Causes, Effects, Consequences, Prevention, and Remedy*. Part of the prevention against the ruination of women which Madan proposed was polygamy.[2] He put forth in his book that the ban on polygamy, that was originally put in force by the Roman Catholic popes, had been the cause of widespread prostitution and fornication. Nor did he agree with the Church of England's ban against *taking more than one wife*, since nowhere in the Bible is polygamy criticized. In fact, Jesus used such a marriage to describe His own relationship with believers."

Cherry recalled the parable of the Ten Virgins:

"Yes, Ruth, Jesus praised the five brides who kept plenty of oil in their lamps while they waited for their polygamous husband."[3]

"That's a great example, Cherry. Now can any of you tell me what song the following lines come from?

'With th' Angelic Hosts proclaim,

Christ is born in Bethlehem!'"

"Are you telling us that Reverend Madan wrote Hark the Herald Angels Sing?" Suni asked.

"No, Suni, that was primarily written by a very close friend of Martin Madan, Charles Wesley, one of the founders of Methodism, but in 1760, Martin Madan did introduce those two lines along with other changes which Charles approved, and which helped popularize the hymn. Those changes are still in the hymn as we sing it today."[4]

"So he was a well respected Christian of that time, considering he was within the circle of Charles Wesley." Asina said.

"Well, to be accurate, we'd have to say it was Charles who was within the circle of Madan's friends. Madan was the more famous of the two during their lifetimes.[5] Charles so respected Madan that he named him godfather to his own son, Samuel Wesley.[6] Madan was somewhat of an antagonist to Charles' brother, John Wesley, since Madan was an eminent Calvinist of that era while John was the Arminian.[7] Another famous friend of Martin Madan was the great composer, Handel. Lady Huntingdon, a famous Christian philanthropist of that era, who built numerous chapels to further the gospel, said that during Handel's last days Madan was 'with him often, and he [Handel] seemed much attached to him.' Handel, of course, is famous for his masterpiece; The Messiah.[8]."

"That's astounding!" Sam said, "I had never even heard of this guy before your dad mentioned him a half hour ago and you're telling us that he was every bit as famous as the Wesleys?"

"If not more." Ruth replied. "In fact, when the details are made known, Madan will be recognized not only as the Father of the Evangelical Hymnal but as the preeminent defender of Eighteenth Century Evangelicalism.[9]

"When the details are made known?" I asked.

"Yes, Ish. Daddy and I have received some correspondence from a professor at a Christian university in the United Kingdom who is writing a book about Madan. Since we have the largest collection of books by and about Madan, it only made sense that he'd track us down."

"So tell us more about this mystery man, this Reverend Madan." Modelisa said.

"Well, in 1746, thirty four years before Madan wrote his book upholding biblical polygamy, he founded the London Lock Hospital. London Lock was the first voluntary hospital that treated venereal disease.[10] It was during his ministerial duties there that he gained a great deal of first hand knowledge about the consequences of fornication and prostitution."[11]

Cherry was wide eyed, listening to Ruth's story of a man from another century who cared enough for those caught in the bondage of prostitution to open a hospital for them.

Ruth continued, "Shortly after Madan founded the Lock Hospital, the institution opened a new building and it became known as *The Female Hospital.* At first he held services in areas of the hospital *that afforded him the ability to preach as well as to lead the congregation in the singing of hymns* but soon it became crowded, so he set out to build a chapel. With donations from rich patrons he was able to build a chapel which could seat up to eight hundred people.[12] This may not seem large compared with today's mega-churches but it's still a very large fellowship and it was one of the largest of his day. The wonderful thing about Madan's chapel was that it received enough in tithes to become a strong source of support for the hospital[13] and get this, it was there that the singing of hymns first took hold as part of Christian worship.[14] The members of Lock Chapel sang from a hymnal that Madan, himself, had published. He published the hymnal as a benefit to future generations as well as to raise money for the hospital.[15] From the Chapel at the Lock, Hymn singing spread quickly throughout the English speaking world with Madan's hymnal the standard. His mastery of musical worship brought thousands to the Chapel at the Lock and his hymns have brought many more thousands to a saving knowledge of our Lord.[16] In less than thirty short years from the first printing of Madan's hymnal, fully two thirds of the hymns sung, even in the parishes of the Church of England, had been lifted; *word for word, note for note, from Madan's own hymnal.* Madan's hymnal had in fact become the core of the Church of England's hymnal.[17] The Baptists' hymnal came out twenty five years after Madan's.[18] Here is the very hymnal that Madan published. My father let me take the original from his library to show you."

Ruth handed Cherry the hymnal, 'A Collection of Psalm and

Hymn Tunes, Never Published Before by the Reverend Martin Madan'. Cherry held the well preserved hymnal carefully, then reflected.

"So the loving man who published this hymnal was cast aside because of his pity for the women who came under the bondage of harlotry?[19] For wanting the men who knew them only as their mistresses to take them as wives? That was his sin? That's not a sin!" Cherry erupted in tears but was able to pull herself together long enough to complete her sentence. "That's a badge of honor! I would love to have known that man!"

"Cherry, I think there are some men just like the Reverend Martin Madan who are sitting in this room right now."

"I agree. It's wonderful." Cherry wiped her tears. She seemed shy to consider herself one who a Christian might desire. I didn't doubt that she understood her eternal value to the Lord but forgetting her past, let alone believing that any potential husband could forget it, was still beyond her grasp. Cherry wanted to know more.

"So what happened to the Reverend Martin Madan, Ruth?"

"If you believe some histories, you'll think that after he published his book defending biblical polygamy in 1780, that he was forced to resign from the London Lock Hospital, but I've discovered that he *never* resigned. In fact, it wasn't until 1785 that the Board of Governors at the London Lock Hospital appointed what they referred to as the morning and evening preachers. The fact is that the Reverend Martin Madan retained his position as Chaplain of the Lock till the day he died. Some have tried to claim that the morning and evening preachers shared a joint chaplainship prior to Madan's death, but the morning preacher himself, the Reverend Thomas Scott, in his own autobiography, acknowledges that Madan served as the sole Chaplain at the Lock during his lifetime, and Scott further states that after Madan's death, though he shared a joint chaplainship with the Reverend Charles De Coetlogon, the 'joint chaplainship was in name only.' Neither men could fill the shoes of the late Reverend Martin Madan.[20] Of course we want all Christians to find their calling, and both of the chaplains who came after him did, just not at the Lock."

Ruth handed a Webster's Dictionary to Cherry.

"Look up the word, *Lock hospital*."

"Okay, hang on." Cherry opened the dictionary and read the citation. "*Lock hospital: a hospital for the treatment of venereal diseases.*[21] Wait a minute, Ruth, you're telling us that a new word entered the English language because of the Reverend Martin Madan?"

"Yes, Cherry. The Lock Hospital was the first hospital of its kind in the world! Every hospital like it is now referred to as a Lock hospital. To this day, the administrators of such hospitals can only pray that they'll have a fraction of the success that the Reverend Martin Madan had during his years at the Lock."

"I'm afraid to know the rest of what happened to the Reverend Martin Madan but I've got to know."

"Well, Cherry, despite the vicious attacks against him by those religionists who wanted to continue the culture of monogamy and fornication in England, Reverend Madan's love for the Lord and his love for life were not diminished. He retained his wit and good sense of humor through all of it *and* as I've already stated, he retained his position as Chaplain at the Lock till the day he died. This was partly due to the fact that he eclipsed all of his contemporaries in promoting, as well as defending, the faith. It was Madan who defended Whitefield and the Methodists against the vicious satire of playwright, Samuel Foote, in 1760, so it was not surprising that he continued to defend the faith and biblical morality till the day he went to be with the Lord."[22]

"Please tell us more!" Asina said with excitement.

"Yes, don't stop there." Suni pleaded.

"Well, the late Eighteenth Century witnessed a new advocate for the false teachings of Unitarianism. His name was Joseph Priestley, a famous chemist. Among other blasphemies, Priestley's brand of Unitarianism denied the deity of Jesus. As you and I both know, Jesus called Himself the Great I Am by saying, "Before Abraham was, I am."[23] The Reverend Martin Madan's contemporaries were therefore delighted to see him rise to the challenge of Joseph Priestley's false religion when Madan published his *Letters to Joseph Priestley*[24] outlining in great detail Priestley's errors. It was to Madan that Joseph Priestley principally replied in his own book, *Familiar Letters*, published in 1790, the year of Madan's death."[24]

"So the Reverend Madan kept himself busy with Christian and

civic matters even after he was attacked in the press for his book defending biblical polygamy?" Cherry asked.

"Absolutely! Madan's translation of Juvenal and Persius from Latin to English, which he published in 1789, contained copious explanatory notes and till today, is unmatched in thoroughness.[25] On occasion he still preached at the Lock Chapel and he wrote dozens of letters excoriating those who would gamble on the horse races.[26]

In 1785 he excoriated another group of rascals, the judges of England, for their inconsistency in rendering justice. In his seminal work, Executive Justice, he outlined the need for sure and swift punishment of criminals. After his death he was falsely accused of having favored hanging for theft, but he stated in the very book that they quoted out of context against him, that he agreed with the maxim that '*a less punishment, which is certain, will do more good than a greater [punishment], which is uncertain.*'[27] Despite all these accomplishments, not to mention his many published sermons, Christian historians have done their best to erase him from their accounts of the great evangelists of the Eighteenth Century, not to mention the great legal minds of the Eighteenth Century. Because of their hatred for one man who dared to disagree with their notions of marriage, they've erased an important part of Church history; the transition from singing Psalms to singing hymns. And it was that transition that the Lord used to spark the great revivals of the hundred years that followed Madan's ministry!"

"Yes, and I remember wondering how that shift occurred and why there were no books to be found on the subject." Modelisa said. "Now I know why. It's because no thorough book could be written on the subject without bringing up the fact that the most famous Evangelist of the Eighteenth Century endorsed polygamy, and that would destroy their false argument that no famous Christian in history ever favored it."

"Now let me get this straight," Cherry asked, "before Martin Madan promoted the concept, the members of the Church of England didn't sing hymns?"

"Well of course there were random cases of hymn singing." Ruth said, "A church here, or a church there would allow hymn singing, and Christians at non-church venues as well as at dissenting churches sang hymns. However, it took the success of the Reverend Martin Madan's chapel and his music to make it acceptable."[14]

"I don't get it." Cherry said, "What exactly is the difference between singing Psalms and singing hymns?"

"Well, Cherry, singing Psalms is simply that, singing Psalms set to music, while a hymn paraphrases biblical concepts and calls us to repentance and worship. A hymn can be likened to a bible study set to poetry and sung. If one says there's no need for hymns then one must also say there's no need for Bible studies or for pastors. The hymn provides a way for biblical concepts to be presented in poetry set to music. Many lost souls have been deaf to all other forms of preaching, but have been converted by the hearing of a single hymn."

"You really have told me something new today, Ruth!" Cherry broke down in tears. "I'll certainly remember the Reverend Martin Madan the next time I sing a hymn! That precious man. So that man," Cherry was barely able to get out the words through her crying but she managed to complete her thought, "the man who polished some of the most famous words in today's hymnals, the man who composed and arranged the music behind many of those hymns, the man who cared for and counseled those cast aside women of his time, was himself thrown aside; all for the golden calf of monogamy."

"Cherry," Ruth declared, "Society will go to any length to continue the bondage of monogamy and the fornication it causes. Men whose wives are their masters can't have God for their master too. They're fornicators; men who put false gods, *their wives*, in place of our Lord and Savior. Do they do this to defend anything of God? No! They do it to defend their income, their households, and their businesses.[28] There, I've said it."

I hadn't expected to meet such a zealous advocate for polygamy this early in my mission but it was understandable; Ruth's own father had four wives. What was not understandable was how a simple girl who lived atop a mountain in the jungle could have put together such a treasure trove of information about a man I'd hardly known before this day. I too would remember the Reverend Martin Madan, but today I was in awe of Ruth. Her discoveries were ground breaking.

"What happened to the Reverend Martin Madan is really sad." Asina was sobbing too. "Is that what's going to happen to Sam and Ish? Will their churches attack them for telling the truth?"

Now I was perplexed. Today was the first day that I'd even heard women promoting polygamy and Asina was talking as if Sam and I were the force behind their new found plan.

John had been quiet up till this moment but now he read from his Bible.

"*The righteous are bold as a lion.*[29]

I can see from your conversation that each of you ladies has the courage of a lion. I have no doubt that you'll follow the word of God as Jesus quoted:

Man shall not live by bread alone, but by ***every word*** *that proceeds out of the mouth of God.*[30]

Notice that the verse says, *every word*. Tell me, how can we preach repentance if those we're preaching to don't know right from wrong? Does God speak nonsense? Does God speak merely to tickle the ears? No, God speaks and we are to listen to *every* word, and why listen if we're not to teach what we hear? Wouldn't that be a foolish waste of time? So preaching repentance doesn't mean ignoring everything else in the Bible but it means teaching *all* of God's word so that those hearing will find at least one word, one precept of God, so that they will see with their eyes, and hear with their ears, and understand with their heart, and be converted, yes, and the Lord *will* heal them.[31] If *by their example* our Christian brothers and sisters set rules that are not found in the Bible and we don't correct them, and if our teachers teach the traditions of men and we don't object, won't we by our acquiescence be as guilty as they of laying aside the commandment of God? Won't we have become like those Pharisees accused by Jesus, transgressing the commandment of God by our tradition.[32] In fact, won't we be more guilty than those we are called upon to correct by allowing them to stumble. Who are we to say that they won't turn from their sins?

When a righteous man doth turn from his righteousness, and commit iniquity, and I lay a stumbling block before him,' says the Lord, 'he shall die: because thou hast not given him warning, he shall die in his sin, and his righteousness which he hath done shall not be remembered; but his blood will I require at thine hand."33

John repeated the words, "*At thine hand!*" then looked around the room at each of us.

"*Nevertheless if thou warn the righteous man, that the righteous sin not, and he doth not sin, he shall surely live, because he is warned; also thou hast delivered thy soul.*34

Ladies, Sam, Ish, we have a duty; a duty to explain what the Bible says on marriage so that those teaching false doctrine can have a choice; the choice to continue in their sin or to repent. If they repent, these ladies will have plenty of husbands to choose from. It will set in motion changes that will easily double the birthrate in Christian households, but if the men of the churches don't repent," John paused. A huge smile now dominated his face, "*well that will leave all the more women for you to choose from, won't it Ish!*" John slapped me on the back and chuckled. I was at a loss for the appropriate response so I just kept my mouth shut.

John continued, "China still has a one child policy yet the Christian churches here in the Philippines have a no child policy for the millions of believing Christian women who would readily become wives to the already married men in their congregations. These women would have husbands and children except for one thing; tradition, man's tradition. The entire Christian church is in apostasy. Apostasy, that's what it is."35

John threw up his hands in disgust and breathed a great sigh.

"Sorry, ladies." He apologized. "I've never voiced these words before. I guess I'm getting a bit carried away."

Suni countered, "Oh no, John, I'm sure that I'm speaking for all the girls when I say we agree with everything you've just said."

"'Yes, yes!" Each of the girls assured him.

"I think I've said enough for now. I'll let my daughter take up where she left off about the Reverend Martin Madan."

"Thanks Daddy. Well, one night, prior to Martin Madan's

getting saved, he was out having fun with his friends in a London coffee house when they challenged him. Since Martin was a great impersonator, just like my daddy." Ruth looked lovingly at her father. "His buddies challenged him to go to one of John Wesley's sermons so that he could study Wesley's voice and mannerisms and then come back to entertain them with a comical impersonation. They thought it would be great fun to see their impersonator extraordinaire imitate the evangelist extraordinaire. When Madan took up their challenge he had no idea that it was the Lord who had set in motion what was about to happen, for upon entering the church, John Wesley announced the sermon he would preach; *Prepare to meet thy God* and that is in fact what Martin Madan did that very night. His encounter with God was so powerful that he quickly went from reading the Bible night and day to preaching mornings and evenings. He was soon so famous for his preaching that like others who have achieved great fame, he was no longer called by his own name but was known simply as *the Counsellor.*[36] There was not a person in the kingdom who didn't know who you were talking about when you mentioned the *Counsellor.* This referred to Madan's ability to present the gospel in the same way that he had presented cases before a jury as a young attorney. However, these jurors were made up of the many truth seekers who attended his grand revivals and it was they who were on trial. Madan effectively presented God's case against them as follows:

'I have long been accustomed to plead at the bar the cause of man; I stand here to plead the cause of God, and to beseech sinners to be reconciled to him.'[37]

Those who were lost now walked in fellowship with the Lord knowing they had been forgiven of their sins, cleansed by the blood of Jesus!"[38]

"Hallelujah!" Modelisa shouted, tears streaming down her face.

There may be joy in heaven over one sinner who repents but the girls weren't going to wait for heaven. Ruth's story started them rejoicing.[39]

Suni was now shaking a tambourine and Asina was strumming an autoharp that she'd found among John's family instruments.

Ruth handed out some sheets of music and John took his place at the piano. It seemed that the range of emotions my new found friends could experience in a single day was more than I was capable of in a month. I was getting to know each of them so well and yet our entire day had been spent worshipping the Lord through prayer, song, and study. I had not truly known the meaning of the phrase *on fire for the Lord* till this day. The room was like a tinder box that the Holy Ghost had just ignited.[40]

We began to sing from the sheets of music Ruth handed out. I recognized the tune as one that Madan had composed:

"Lo He comes with clouds descending
Once for favored sinners slain
Thousand thousand saints attending
Swell the triumph of his train
Hallelujah, Hallelujah
Hallelujah, Hallelujah! Amen!"

We sang each stanza through to the last.

"Yea, Amen; Let all adore thee
High on Thine eternal throne
Savior, take the power and glory
Claim the kingdom for Thine own
O come quickly
Hallelujah, come, Lord, come."[41]

After the hymn, the girls continued singing to Jesus. Their sweet voices of praise slowly faded as each of them sang or hummed one more loving note to their Savior. They certainly weren't alone when they sang, for they were at one with the Holy Spirit. The glow of a bride on her wedding day shone on their faces as they lifted their hands and looked upward.[42] When the girls had finished, Suni was the first to get back to the discussion.

"So basically, what we've learned here today is that the most notable men of the Protestant reformation, the man who preached God's word in the language of the people: Bernardino Ochino, and the man who wrote the greatest Christian poem of all time; John Milton, and the man whose hymns were the first to be widely sung across the English speaking world; Martin Madan, *all* taught that polygamy is not only acceptable according to the Bible but in many cases it is commendable, for it takes care of a man's and a woman's passions within the context of marriage, steering them clear of fornication and making wives of women who would otherwise have no godly outlet; helping Christians multiply in accordance with God's command. But is it true that our pastors have deliberately set out to deceive us on this issue for fear that telling us the truth would mean an end to their pastoral income?"

"Yes!" Sam fell down on his knees, his head bowed in shame. "I'm guilty. I've done this!" Sam looked around the room at each of the girls as he confessed, "I was the leader of a group of pastors who wanted to keep Ish's books out of the schools. Even though Ish's books didn't promote polygamy, his discussion of the subject was too neutral for our liking. We knew that his books might touch off a renewed interest in polygamy that has been dormant in the churches for hundreds of years. All it would take would be one church that practiced polygamy and we'd lose half our members."

Asina's face reddened.

"So you put your own well being above the well being of your flock!"

"Yes, yes." Sam sobbed. "That is, until I prayed that the Lord would guide me on this. The day after my prayer I contacted some other pastors who were all for Ish's books on chastity and we got his books into as many schools as we could."

Asina quoted a bible passage.

"'If we confess our sins, He is faithful and just to forgive us our sins, and to cleanse us from all unrighteousness.'[43] Of course, we know the Lord has forgiven you Sam, but for what it's worth." Asina's expression turned to gentleness. "I forgive you too."

"Me too." The girls were once again teary eyed as each of them let Sam know they held nothing against him.

"We can discuss theology all day," I interrupted, "but we have a real life polygamist sitting right next to us. John, isn't it about time we hear your story?"

"Story! Story! Story!" The girls chanted.

Their discussion, our praise session, and Sam's confession had done wonders to release their pent up energy and they were back to their cheery selves.

"Okay, okay." John gave in, but before he could start, there was a knock at the door. Ruth opened it. Her mother rolled in a cart with several trays of freshly baked goodies, and as always, a fresh pot of mountain grown coffee.

"Hi mama. You didn't have to do that. I was just about to get the snacks and coffee myself."

"I didn't want my little girl to have to leave her new friends."

"Thanks mama."

Ruth and her mother hugged. John and his wife looked warmly at each other. You could tell how happy they were that their daughter had finally been able to fellowship with Christian friends in her own home. It was clear from her deep knowledge of Christian history and the Bible that she spent endless hours studying in solitude.

"I'll leave you and your friends. Just let me know if you need anything else."

"I will mama." Ruth gave her a kiss on the cheek.

After she'd left the room, John began his story.

"I was born a prince, a young and fortunate prince, a first born prince. As such, I was brought up royal heir to the throne; Prince John, the future king. Spoiled by my mother and her attendants and trained in hunting by my father and my uncles; I was to have both wealth and fame."

I expected John's tale to be as rich and full as the coffee I now sipped. The girls' warm and simple smiles reminded me of Mary when we first met; full of hope and love for the Lord. There is no woman more beautiful than one on fire for the Lord and here I was surrounded by the most dazzling women on earth. I prayed quietly that the Lord would guide their steps, *and mine.*

Chapter 12 Footnotes

1. **Madan's Preaching:** "He (Madan) delivered his first sermon [in the year 1750 at the age of 24] at Allhallows, London, to a large assembly, attracted mostly by the novelty of the fact that a lawyer had turned preacher. But his power as a pulpit orator was immediately revealed, and thenceforward could not fail to secure him crowds of hearers. Wesley had scarcely made a more notable convert, and had never given to his Calvinistic brethren a more

important trophy. Such was Rev. Martin Madan. He was prominent in the Methodistic movement. He traversed much of the country with Romaine, Venn, Lady Huntingdon, and Wesley, proclaiming the truth with great effect. He continued to labor as an evangelist, and as chaplain to the celebrated Lock Hospital."

The History of the Religious Movement of the Eighteenth Century, Called Methodism by Abel Stevens, LL.D. Copyright 1858

Dictionary of National Biography - Edited by Sidney Lee - McMillan and Co.1893

"Vast numbers crowd Blackfriars church *and the chapel at the Lock*" The Chapel at the Lock was the chapel Madan opened in association with the London Lock hospital which he founded.

John Wesley in a letter to Samuel Sparrow - December 28, 1773.

Concerning the Eighteenth Century Calvinistic Methodists, *"the names Berridge, Romaine, Madan, and Venn are consecrated in its annals."* The History of the Religious Movement of the Eighteenth Century, Called Methodism. Volume 1 By Abel Stevens, LL.D. - Page 382

"Wesley had scarcely made a more notable convert, and had never given to his Calvinistic brethren a more important trophy. Such was Rev. Martin Madan. During the present decade of our narrative he was prominent in the Methodistic movement. He traversed much of the country with Romaine, Venn, Lady Huntingdon, and Wesley, proclaiming the truth with great effect."

The History of the Religious Movement of the Eighteenth Century, Called Methodism. Volume 1 By Abel Stevens, LL.D. - Page 388 (Dictionary of National Biography, above, cites this.)

"Possessing a thorough knowledge of the Scriptures in the original languages, and having embraced those evangelical views of Gospel truth, of which he afterwards was so zealous a defender, Mr. Madan was desirous of diffusing amongst his fellow-men the savor of that Name which he loved. Master of an independent fortune, he entered the ministry without any mercenary views: and though his brother, Dr. Spencer Madan, was successively bishop of Bristol and Peterborough, he never accepted any benefice or emolument in the Church. In consequence of his religious sentiments, and the open avowal he made of the faith once delivered to the saints, he experienced some difficulty in obtaining

orders; ["obtaining orders" refers to being officially ordained by the Anglican Church] but, through the perseverance and interest of Lady Huntingdon and some others, he was at length successful. Alluding to this circumstance, George Whitefield, [the leading figure in the Eighteenth Century American revival known as the Great Awakening] says:--'I am glad Mr. Madan is ordained.' Soon after his ordination, Mr. Madan was called to preach his first sermon in the church of All-hallows, Lombard-street. The lawyer turning divine was novel--curiosity prevailed among the million of the metropolis. The manly eloquence of the preacher drew general attention and excited applause. The poor heard the Gospel with gladness, and the rich were not sent empty away. Many were filled with wonder. The croaking cry of prejudice was silenced--her raven voice sunk amidst the loud acclaims of the friends of religion who heard the doctrines of the Reformation nobly defended by an able advocate, whose knowledge was equal to his zeal. Like Boanerges, a son of thunder, he proclaimed the law from the flaming mountain; and from the summit of Zion's hill he appeared a Barnabas, a son of consolation: his countenance was majestic, open, and engaging, and his looks commanding veneration; his delivery is said to have been peculiarly graceful. He preached without notes; his voice was musical, well modulated, full and powerful; his language plain, nervous, pleasing, and memorable; and his arguments strong, bold, rational, and conclusive: his doctrines were drawn from the sacred fountain: he was mighty in the Scriptures; a workman that needed not be ashamed of his labours, rightly dividing the word of truth."
The Life and Times of Selina, Countess of Huntingdon By Aaron Crossley Hobart Seymour, Jacob Kirkman Foster Published 1840 - Pages 165-167

Historian Abel Stevens lists Madan as one of nine *"chief Calvinistic writers"* of the Eighteenth Century.
Preface - The History of the Religious Movement of the Eighteenth Century, Called Methodism. Volume 1 By Abel Stevens, LL.D. Preface.

Madan's Music: "Mr. Madan was cousin to the poet Cowper. He was passionately fond of music, and a respectable composer. The music of 'Before Jehovah's awful throne,' 'From all that dwell below the skies,' 'Salvation! O the joyful sound!' -- 'To God, the only wise,' and many others which were composed by him, are well known and deservedly popular...His first sermon was preached to an overflowing congregation at Allhallows Church, London, the same in which Mr. Wesley preached his first extemporaneous sermon."

ANECDOTES OF THE WESLEYS Illustrative Of Their Character And Personal History By Joseph Beaumont Wakeley
With An Introduction By Rev. J. McClintock Tenth Edition
Hodder And Stoughton 27, Paternoster Row
Butler & Tanner, The Selwood Printing Works Frome And London
Printed 1878

2. Thelyphthora; Or, a Treatise on Female Ruin, Its Causes, Effects, Consequences, Prevention, and Remedy. By the Reverend Martin Madan Published in 1780

3. Matthew 25:1-13 1 Then shall the kingdom of heaven be likened unto ten virgins, which took their lamps, and went forth to meet the bridegroom. And five of them were wise, and five were foolish. They that were foolish took their lamps, and took no oil with them: But the wise took oil in their vessels with their lamps. While the bridegroom tarried, they all slumbered and slept. And at midnight there was a cry made, Behold, the bridegroom cometh; go ye out to meet him. Then all those virgins arose, and trimmed their lamps. And the foolish said unto the wise, Give us of your oil; for our lamps are gone out. But the wise answered, saying, Not so; lest there be not enough for us and you: but go ye rather to them that sell, and buy for yourselves. And while they went to buy, the bridegroom came; and they that were ready went in with him to the marriage: and the door was shut. Afterward came also the other virgins, saying, Lord, Lord, open to us. But he answered and said, Verily I say unto you, I know you not. Watch therefore, for ye know neither the day nor the hour wherein the Son of man cometh.

4. Dictionary of National Biography - Page 288

5. "Madan preached, and was attended by listening multitudes...at the Lock Hospital."

"Charles Wesley...then occupied only a very subordinate place among public men."

The Life of the Reverend Charles Wesley

By Thomas Jackson, Charles Wesley
1841 Volume II - Page 376
"Charles Wesley's hymns would never have influenced the Church, as they certainly have done, but for the intervention of Martin Madan... Chaplain of the Lock."
The Edinburgh Review or Critical Journal
January-April Edition 1894 - Page 320
6. Mr. Madan, his godfather, finding him [Samuel Wesley] one day so belabouring the chair, told him he should have a better instrument by and by.
Journal, Etc: To which are Appended Selections from His Correspondence and Poetry - Page 153
by Charles Wesley - 1849
7. "He was a most popular preacher at the Lock Hospital, and was eminent among the Calvinists in the Church of England."
An Ecclesiastical Biography, containing the Lives of Ancient Fathers and Modern Divines by Walter Farquhar Hook, D.D. Vicar of Leeds Volume VII 1851 - Page 207
8. Shortly before the his death, the Lady Huntingdon had the pleasure of visiting Handel, the great composer of "The Messiah." After her visit she had this to say:
"I have had a most pleasing interview with Handel; an interview which I shall not soon forget. He is now old, and at the close of his long career; yet he is not dismayed at the prospect before him. Blessed be God for the comforts and consolations which the Gospel affords in every situation, and in every time of our need! Mr. Madan has been with him often, and he seems much attached to him."
The Life and Times of Selina, Countess of Huntingdon By Aaron Crossley Hobart Seymour, Jacob Kirkman Foster Published 1840 - Page 229
9. The weight of citations above and below prove that Martin Madan was indeed the preeminent defender of Eighteenth Century Evangelicalism. The fact that he has been deliberately erased from the pages of Christian history cannot change that.
10. "The first special hospital was the Lock Hospital near Hyde Park Corner, founded in 1746 by Martin Madan, who became its first chaplain."
A History of English Philanthropy

By Benjamin Kirkman Gray
London - P.S. King & Son, Orchard House, Westminster - 1905
11. "There are merit-mongers, among the most abandoned sinners. Two women were, some time since, admitted into the Lock Hospital, in order to be cured of a very criminal disease. Mr. Madan, who visited them during their confinement, laboured to convince them of their sin and spiritual danger, 'Truly,' said one of them, 'I am by no means so bad as some of my profession are : for I never picked any man's pocket, in my life.' The other said, 'I cannot affirm that I never picked a man's pocket; but I have this in my favour, that I never admitted any man in my company, on a Sunday, until after nine at night.'
The Works of Augustus M. Toplady page 168. You will remember Toplady as the writer of that famous hymn, Rock of Ages. He was a very close friend and admirer of the Reverend Martin Madan, having also preached at the Lock Chapel.
Good News from Heaven; or, the Gospel a Joyful Sound. At the Lock Chapel, near Hyde Park Corner, June 19, 1774. By the Reverend Augustus Toplady.
Recorded on page 375 of The Monthly Review Volume 52 1775
Madan wrote a tract concerning the sequence of events that led to the conversion of one such prostitute. Despite her conversion and new way of living, she soon died of the illnesses she acquired as a prostitute. This is chronicled in: *A Remarkable and surprising account of the abandoned life, happy conversion, and comfortable death of Fanny Sidney, a young gentlewoman, who died in London in April, 1763, aged 26 years*. By the Reverend Martin Madan
12. "The Lock Chapel was (officially) opened March 28, 1762" but the Reverend Martin Madan conducted services prior to that in other areas of the institution that afforded him the ability to preach as well as to lead the congregation in the singing of hymns.
Dictionary of National Biography - Edited by Sidney Lee - McMillan and Co.1893 - Page 288
Through Martin's exertions a new chapel, capable of seating 800 persons, was erected in the garden of the hospital, he himself contributing 100 pounds.[100 pounds converts to $20,000 in today's U.S. dollars. University of Michigan conversion table.] It was opened on March 28, 1762 and by 1765 was entirely free of

debt.
The Madan Family and Maddens in Ireland and England By Falconer Madan 1933 - Page 112

13. "In the case of the Lock Hospital, the musical movement coincided with the Evangelical. Its chapel was used not only by its inmates, but by a strongly contrasting *West End Evangelical congregation who rented sittings."*
These rented pews helped pay for the expenses of the hospital.
The Princeton Theological Review - Volume XII - 1914
The Princeton University Press - Princeton, N.J. - Page 87

14. "He (William Romaine) held the extreme Calvinistic position as to the exclusive use of inspired words in Praise, and was able to impose his views upon his own congregation. But he could not stay the rising tide of Hymn singing or make a breach between the Gospel and the Hymns of the Revival. *In Martin Madan the new Hymn singing found an effective sponsor.* The humorous and sturdy John Berridge was as early on the field as Madan, but less effective."
The Princeton Theological Review - Volume XII - 1914
The Princeton University Press - Princeton, N.J. - Page 73,74

15. In the preface to the Hymnal that the Reverend Martin Madan published, "The Collection of Psalm and Hymn Tunes sung at the Chapel of the Lock Hospital" Mr. Madan writes:
"I have at last, with no small care and trouble, completed this Book of Tunes for the use of the Chapel; and as the publication of them may be of service to the Charity, I must desire your acceptance of the Entire Copy, hoping that, by the sale of this Music, some addition may be made to your fund for maintaining and promoting the charitable work which you have undertaken."

16. The Church of England's hymnal began with Martin Madan's Collection of Psalms and Hymns (1760).
The New Schaff-Herzog Encyclopedia of Religious Knowledge by Johann Jakob Herzog, Philip Schaff, and others. Copyright 1909

17. In 1788, the publisher of the fifth edition of the Church of England hymnal, "appropriated fully two thirds of the contents of Madan's Collection."
The Princeton Theological Review - Volume XII - 1914
The Princeton University Press - Princeton, N.J. - Page 76

18. The first Baptist hymn-book was Rippon's (1787).
The New Schaff-Herzog Encyclopedia of Religious Knowledge by Johann Jakob Herzog, Philip Schaff, and others. Copyright 1909
19. Harlot - a woman who has engaged in sexual relations without the benefit of marriage. Harlots are in bondage to sin, in bondage to the men they have relations with and draw men into bondage with them. The harlot takes the place of God as head of the man. A wife who takes the position of head over her husband is behaving as a harlot even if she has but one husband.
20. In the words of Reverend Thomas Scott, himself:
"But the affairs at the Lock seemed at last to draw to a crisis.--When the Rev. Martin Madan, who had alone borne the title of chaplain, died, Mr. De Coetlogon and myself were appointed chaplains, instead of evening and morning preachers; but without any other alteration than that of the name."
21. Lock hospital: A hospital for the treatment of venereal diseases. [Eng.] Webster's Revised Unabridged Dictionary, © 1996, 1998 MICRA, Inc.
22. It was Martin Madan who defended Whitefield and the Methodists against the vicious satire of playwright, Samuel Foote in his Exhortatory address to the brethren in the faith of Christ published in 1760. Republished in 2010 by Don Milton.
23. John 8:58 "Jesus said unto them, 'Verily, verily, I say unto you, Before Abraham was, I am.'"
24. Letters to Joseph Priestley. By Martin Madan. Republished in 2009 by Don Milton. Familiar Letters [to Rev. Madan et al] By Joseph Priestley. Republished in 2010 by Don Milton.
25. A New and Literal Translation of Juvenal and Persius; with Copious Explanatory Notes .In Two Volumes. By the Rev. M. Madan -Printed for the Editor, at Mr. Lewis's, No 157, Swallow-Street, Near Piccadilly MDCCLXXXIX (1789) Republished in 2010 by Don Milton.
26. "It was formerly the abode of the celebrated [famous] Dr. Madan [Martin Madan], of whom we have given an account. During his residence here, [Birmingham, England] he interposed his authority as a magistrate, to prevent the introduction of illegal games into the town during the race week; he gave notice to those persons, who were in the habit of letting [renting] their houses for

this purpose, that it was contrary to the laws of their country, and if they persisted in doing it, they must take consequences. Several tradespeople, who disregarded this notice, were sent to prison, which so exasperated the inhabitants, that they burnt his effigy, near the spot where the pump now stands."
Some Particulars Relating to the History of Epsom by Henry Pownall 1825
"I possess twenty-three letters from him to George Hardinge, Esq., M.P., July 9, 1789-March 14, 1790, [Against illegal gaming] written in good spirits and with some wit."
The Madan Family by Falconer Madan 1933
"Mr. Madan, however, the most respectable clergyman in the town, [Birmingham] preaching [1787-1789 - Nine Years after the publication of Madan's pro-polygamy Thelyphthora] and publishing... [against Priestley's Unitarianism] ...I addressed a number of "Familiar Letters to the Inhabitants of Birmingham," in our defence."
An Appeal to the Serious and Candid Professors of Christianity By Joseph Priestley - Page 105
27. Thoughts on Executive Justice with respect to our Criminal Laws 1785 - Page 63 Republished in 2009 by Don Milton
28. "Master of an independent fortune, he entered the ministry without any mercenary views: and though his brother, Dr. Spencer Madan, was successively bishop of Bristol and Peterborough, he never accepted any benefice or emolument in the Church."
The Life and Times of Selina, Countess of Huntingdon By Aaron Crossley Hobart Seymour and Jacob Kirkman
Foster Published 1840 - Page 165
29. Proverbs 28:1 The wicked flee when no man pursueth: but the righteous are bold as a lion.
30. Deuteronomy 8:3 And he humbled thee, and suffered thee to hunger, and fed thee with manna, which thou knewest not, neither did thy fathers know; that he might make thee know that man doth not live by bread only, but by every word that proceedeth out of the mouth of the LORD doth man live.
31. Matthew 13:5 For this people's heart is waxed gross, and [their] ears are dull of hearing, and their eyes they have closed; lest at any time they should see with [their] eyes, and hear with [their] ears, and should understand with [their] heart, and should be

converted, and I should heal them.

32. Matthew 15:3 But he answered and said unto them, Why do ye also transgress the commandment of God by your tradition?

33. Our character, John, quotes Ezekiel 3:20 in regards to warning the righteous but the same principle applies to warning the wicked and it's found in Ezekiel 33:8 "When I say unto the wicked, O wicked man, thou shalt surely die; if thou dost not speak to warn the wicked from his way, that wicked man shall die in his iniquity; but his blood will I require at thine hand."

It's clear from this verse that Christians are not just "supposed to" witness to non-Christians but they are required to witness to them or the blood of those non-Christians will be on their hands.

34. Ezekiel 3:21

35. 1 Timothy 4:3 Forbidding to marry, and commanding to abstain from meats, which God hath created to be received with thanksgiving of them which believe and know the truth.

Polygamy advocates say that "Forbidding to marry" can only refer to the Christian Church's anti-polygamy stance since no other type of marriage is permitted in the Bible but forbidden by the church.

36. Dictionary of National Biography - Edited by Sidney Lee - McMillan and Co.1893 - Page 288

37. "Mr. Madan delivered a very memorable sermon from Zachariah 10:12. One Sentence in that sermon was retained in the memory of an aged disciple, who died many years after: *'I have long been accustomed to plead at the bar the cause of man; I stand here to plead the cause of God, and to beseech sinners to be reconciled to him.'*"

The Life and Times of Selina, Countess of Huntingdon By Aaron Crossley Hobart Seymour, Jacob Kirkman Foster Published 1840 - Page 388

38. 1 John 1:7 But if we walk in the light, as he is in the light, we have fellowship one with another, and the blood of Jesus Christ his Son cleanseth us from all sin.

39. Luke 15:7 I say unto you, that likewise joy shall be in heaven over one sinner that repenteth, more than over ninety and nine just persons, which need no repentance.

40. Matthew 3:11 I indeed baptize you with water unto repentance: but he that cometh after me is mightier than I, whose shoes I am not worthy to bear: he shall baptize you with the Holy

Ghost, and with fire.
41. The Poets of the Church: A Series of Biographical Sketches of Hymn-writers with Notes on Their Hymns By Edwin Francis Hatfield D.D. Copyright 1884
42. Isaiah 61:10 I will greatly rejoice in the LORD, my soul shall be joyful in my God; for he hath *clothed me with the garments of salvation*, he hath covered me with the robe of righteousness, as a bridegroom decketh himself with ornaments, and *as a bride adorneth herself with her jewels.*
43. 1 John 1:9 If we confess our sins, he is faithful and just to forgive us our sins, and to cleanse us from all unrighteousness.

Final Note to this Chapter

Those who claim bias concerning the high praises given to the Reverend Martin Madan from *The Life and Times of Selina, Countess of Huntingdon* should consider that the same men who heaped such high praises upon him also wrote the following.
"The publication of this singular work [Thelyphthora] caused Mr. Madan to sink into *deserved oblivion*."

Certainly if they believed he deserved to sink into oblivion, their high praises cannot be taken lightly for they would not have passed up any opportunity to condemn him. The fact is, they could find nothing in him to condemn. Even their claim that he sank into oblivion is not a condemnation of him but a condemnation of themselves for it is a lie. The Reverend Martin Madan continued to be the primary mover in Evangelicalism till his death in 1790, ten years after the publication of Thelyphthora. Furthermore, from the age of just twenty-one, when he founded the Lock Hospital, till his death at age sixty-five, he dedicated himself to bringing God's word and God's comfort to the cast aside women of that noble institution. *No man before, nor since Madan, has given his life so completely to end the bondage and suffering of prostitutes.*

It's appropriate to close this chapter with another quote taken from the 1840 edition of The Life and Times of Selina, Countess of Huntingdon. On page 464 the authors write concerning Madan:

"*He was mighty in the Scriptures; a workman that needed not be ashamed of his labours, rightly dividing the word of truth.*"

Chapter 13

RITES OF MANHOOD

John now sipped from his own cup of coffee, breathing deeply to savor the fresh aroma. He sighed loudly as he exhaled as if revisiting his past would be painful.

"John was not always my name. I've gone by the name John for many years to protect the identity of my family. To that end, I've also changed the names of some of the characters in my story; for there are places where family would turn against family before the Lord would have it.[1] The Lord is preparing those places and families for the time that His message of peace *as well as division* must be delivered. There are powerful forces of both a spiritual and earthly nature that do not want the Lord's message to reach the entire world, yet through prayer and godly example we can reach those lost souls who as yet are in darkness.[2] As the Lord shall choose the day, it is for us to call upon Him and search for His will. His Holy Scriptures will reveal new treasures to those of us approved worthy in that day.[3] Would that today were that day!"

John's serious demeanor was now replaced with a look of joy and anticipation. His eyes shone with emotion.

"I'm thankful that all of you here will be able to pass this story on at the appropriate time and I'm praying for the blessings of our Lord and Savior, Jesus, upon you. Wherever the hearer be when you tell this story, may it be told to bring glory to the Lord and to accomplish His will. It's a story of many blessings and many trials. May my story help you to know the Lord better and may you follow Him in everything. May you give thanks to the Lord for your blessings and depend on Him to deliver you through every trial.[4]

When I was a child I played with the children in the market, suffering little more punishment than an occasional whipping for coming home dirty. But I never resented the whippings. It was a small price to pay for having spent the whole day tasting my favorite peasant dishes. I had, as you'll remember from your own childhood, a knack for getting dirty as if it were a talent to be improved upon. This talent, my mother admired no more than yours. Though she knew I must be punished, she took heart that her son, a prince with royal blood, was able to have friends beyond the palace gates.

The reason my clothes appeared so dirty was that they were not my clothes at all. I was in the habit of trading my royal garments for one of my friends' peasant garb as soon as I left the palace. This way I'd have the whole day to play with my friends and not a soul would suspect my real identity.

If you could have seen what my poor nannies went through trying to change that peasant garb back into clothes befitting a prince. My nannies couldn't figure out how I could have gotten my elegant clothes so utterly filthy. They'd try soaps, dyes, a snip here, a snip there. They would even add pieces of lace and colored material to the outfit. Each night it seemed I would burst from holding back my laughter at their tortured manipulations when right on schedule, they would leave for their evening prayer meeting. Before leaving they would hang the clothes in my royal wardrobe muttering that they'd have to keep trying later.

With uncanny timing, the mother of the friend I'd traded clothes with would show up the moment my nannies had gone. She would switch my real clothes, which she'd neatly pressed and brushed, with the clothes my nannies had so hopelessly tried to repair. When my nannies came home they'd pat each other on the back saying how this or that cleaning method must have been the one that returned my clothes to their original state. Sometimes they would get into shouting matches about whose remedy had actually worked.

'It's the drying, the drying that did it. Notice how properly I hung them up to dry?' To which the other would counter, 'Oh no, without my secret cleaning fluid, none of this would have been possible.'

Oh, those delightful nights I spent watching them. I thought I had such secret knowledge. All the while, my loving nannies had been putting on a show for me. It was their job. As I got older I found out that the nannies my mother had hired were formerly court jesters, or is it jesteresses? It was their comic genius that gave me an appreciation for the power of illusion both for good and evil. Men who we think are great peace makers, may be nothing more than illusionists performing an act; transforming their beastly selves into little lambs.[5]

My mother was the king's first wife. For my mother this was both a blessing and a curse. A blessing, in that she had given birth to the king's firstborn and was treated with all the pomp of a mother destined to see her son ascend to the throne. A curse, in that she didn't have the luxury of picking her husband's other wives. A second wife knows the identity of at least one of the wives she'll share her husband with. A third wife knows the identity of two. And the fourth wife knows the identity of all three wives before she weds. Of course, a king's wife rarely has the luxury of choosing her husband. Her parents would never stand for her turning down a royal offer of marriage and denying them the honor of becoming part of the royal family, but my father's wives did choose him and they loved him very much. Neither did his wives have enmity between them. My father wasn't wicked in his ways like his grandfather but spent most of his days romancing his different wives. He'd built his estate in such a way that he could meet with his advisors between visits to wives. His days were half love making and half business."

"Like you, daddy?"

"Yes, Ruth, like me."

Ruth couldn't hide her deep love and respect for her father. Why would she? Her parents were open in showing their own love for her.

"As my father's children increased in number, his time with his wives diminished, but each of his wives still got more attention than any wife in the kingdom. After all, no laundry to do, no cleaning, and the children all had private nannies to watch over them. Even with my father's busy schedule, he still had time for poetry writing. I have volumes of his poetry that he wrote to each of his wives."

At this, the girls demanded that John share some of the poetry with them.

"Poetry! Poetry! Poetry!" They chanted.

"All right, girls. My father wrote this poem for my mother.

'Many fools I've met, always waiting.

But do I wait, to open my heart
And ask you in to share it's secret treasures
No, 'twould be better to be robbed by thieves
Than to let treasures, forever, go unseen.
Yet you, a maiden of many fascinations
Resemble not a thief
And there is no treasure within my heart
No secret that I would not impart
In hopes that you might love me.'"

"Uh!" The girls hummed what was their standard response to anything romantic.

"Of course, my mother was already madly in love with my father by the time he'd written this poem. All wise men know it's the woman who chooses. *Only a fool chases a woman whose heart is not already his.*

My childhood moments with my mother took place mostly in the palace courtyard. She would hold me on her lap and whisper in my ear,

'You have a great destiny ahead of you. You must walk toward your destiny and never be afraid.[6] Do not lean on your own understanding but depend on the Lord[7] for it is the Lord who will deliver you out of harms way.[8] The Lord is calling you. Will you follow Him?'

To which I was expected to reply,

'Yes, and may the Lord use me to deliver His followers from the hands of the infidels.'[9]

My mother was the one who taught me to pray. She said,

'You must know there is one true God and He alone you must follow. Pray to Him no matter where you are and He will lead you to the truth.[10] Do not fear the infidels for there are some among them who you will lead and there are those among them who shall lead you to the water that takes away all thirst.'[11]

Only many years later would I know the meaning of her prophetic words. To this day parts of her prophesy are yet to be fulfilled.

As I grew to be a man I became weary of the ever increasing security measures taken to protect me from kidnappers. I felt I was already a prisoner of the palace guards who never let me out of their sight. The kingdom had grown much since my childhood and the king now had many enemies. The precautions were prudent but the lack of freedom wore heavy on me.

Now a young prince, recognized wherever I went; I longed for anonymity. I'd been able to disguise myself as a child so I returned to my former ways, only more elaborately. My father's court magicians taught me so that I became not only a master of disguise but a magician."

John now pointed to the hymnal that Cherry had been holding. It disappeared as quickly as our eyes had fixed on it but before we had a chance to comment it reappeared.

"Ang galing! (So skillful!)" Suni exclaimed. The rest of us were just as astonished. John went back to his story telling.

"When word got out that I was disguising myself, the merchants became wary that anyone from a rich man to a beggar could be the prince, so a standard response evolved when a customer asked, 'Is that your best price?' The merchant would lower the price again, then reply, 'There, I could not give it to you for less if you were Prince John, himself. *You're not, are you?*' At which they'd both laugh and the merchant would wrap up the purchase. I know, because sometimes the buyer *was* the prince.

The public also became more generous to the poor. I know this to be the case for when I when I sat in the market disguised as a beggar I would receive a day's wage in an hour. Now before you judge me and say that I was taking advantage of the people's generosity, I want you to understand that I presented all of the alms collected in this manner to charities that I established for the families of slain and disabled police officers. To that, I added an equal amount from my own account. There are many things for which I could have been judged unrighteous but the way I handled money wasn't one of them.

My father heard of all this and was concerned that those who were able to work would take up begging, and indeed, some counterfeit beggars had begun to appear. The king, therefore, made a proclamation; that all who could work but chose to beg would receive ten lashes.[12] In addition, he proclaimed that anyone who mistreated the prince by accident, while the prince was in disguise, would not be punished.

Even with my father's proclamation, the shopkeepers remained generous to the poor. Quite by accident, I had taught them the joy of giving and the benefits of offering a fair price; business was good. Shopkeeper and peasant alike believed I'd set out from the start to teach this lesson. They thought me both kind and wise. They would open their shops by shouting,

'Who teaches charity and equity?'

To which the people retorted,

'Prince John for he is wise!'

They claimed that I had even made the kingdom safer for women; reasoning that the criminals feared that any beggar on the street might be the prince himself, and that I might come out of the shadows to dispatch them should they attempt to defile a woman. However, their reasoning was flawed; women didn't go about unescorted on our streets, and certainly not at night. Despite this, the tales of my exploits grew as the story tellers embellished each new version.

During the telling of one such tale, I sat leaning against a wall in the market, disguised as a sleepy old man. Just as the storyteller got to the part about my jumping out of the shadows, I leapt to my feet, sword in hand, and played the part myself. I disappeared just as quickly into the crowd. As you can imagine, this added no small amount of material for the storyteller's next rendition, and the myths about me have continued to grow in my absence.

I loved the attention I was getting, earned or not. What young man wouldn't? Had it not been for my departure, vanity surely would have destroyed me."

John now turned to Ruth.

"Could you please read what Princess Kasmina wrote in the memoirs she gave to Peesha?"

"Sure daddy."

John took out the now well worn papers from his pocket and handed them to Ruth.

"'Prince John did more than warm the hearts of his admirers. He knew well the spell he could cast with a smile and I, Princess Kasmina, was not immune to his charms. I treasure still the small gifts he gave me as a child. Ever since I was a little girl my heart beat faster when the prince approached. I dreamed of Prince John at night and when I awoke my daydreams of him would begin. I dreamed of riding off into the sunset on royal stallions, the prince escorting me through his island paradise. I dreamed of ascending mountain peaks, John at my side, to gaze at distant islands embraced by the sea's warm blue waters. Would that I were one of those islands and John were the sea. Tall and strong, John should be mine! However this could not be. All the palace princesses knew John was first in line to the throne. As such, he was expected to take many foreign princess brides to strengthen the now delicate alliance. Yet Prince John was all my little heart desired. Only the year before John's Manly Voyage, I, Princess Kasmina, was a little girl. Now I was thirteen and required to wear a veil since I was of marriageable age. Though a princess rarely marries that young, the veil was our custom and I looked forward to wearing it as an indication that I was a maiden. I was convinced Prince John was secretly in love with me and I prayed five times daily that he would defy custom and take me as a wife. I wished I could run away to return secretly behind my veil as one of his *foreign* brides. I knew he could easily keep me in his harem without anyone's knowing my true identity. After all, it would be better to have one tenth of John then one hundred percent of any other man. Alas, poor Kasmina, I knew only too well that I could never bring up such a plan to the prince for the mere doing so would be scandalous, and would lower me in his eyes. It was my lot to keep my love for John as secret as my dreams. I wondered if he could see the loving looks I gave him from behind my sheer veil as I looked at him adoringly each time we spoke. I wanted to shout out my love for him but destiny had other plans. There would be a husband for me, that one and only, who had truly been selected by the hand of our Lord. I still pray five times a day for John, not that I may have him but that he would continue on his pursuit of the destiny that the Lord has placed before him. The Lord has already led him to many destinies. *I have met some of them*.'"

As Ruth read these last words of Princess Kasmina's memoirs, a loud crashing came from the hallway. John's four wives along with Mary, fell through the door and into the room. Apparently they'd all been leaning against it, listening. They got up giggling and John's wife, Peesha, feigned a swoon.

"Wow, I'm a destiny!"

At this, we all broke into a fit of laughter. The tension that had been building in John's story, the women falling through the door, and Peesha's comment, had all combined into a funny bone elixir more potent than John's mountain grown coffee. After each of us had thoroughly discovered the others' particular way of giggling, moaning, chuckling, and guffawing, we gained our composure.

Mary and John's wives now joined us and John took a break from story telling to lead us in prayer. As he prayed, he included names, places, needs, and blessings; no unspoken prayers here. John would break from his prayer to ask the name, age, marital status, occupation, and children of those we prayed for. He wanted to know the circumstances surrounding our special friend's need for prayer as well as our relationship to them. I could sense the Lord walking among us, ministering to those we prayed for.[13] I hid this in my heart to remember during my prayer sessions for the women Sam had assigned to me.

After John had finished his prayer, we ate snacks and sipped coffee, patiently waiting for him to tell us the rest of his story. John's wives huddled closely around Mary on their expansive sofa, like school girls around a campfire. They were combing her hair and putting ribbons in it and just when they'd finished embellishing it they would start all over again. Mary hadn't experienced such sisterhood since she was involved in one of the campus ministries in college. She got up from the primping just long enough to pour herself a cup of coffee from the pot that sat on the cart in front of me. Suni, who'd been doing her best to lean against me without making it look deliberate, sat up quickly when Mary approached.

"Oh don't mind me," Mary assured her, "you look so cozy. Just so I get him back later. What's a shoulder anyhow, he's got *two* of them." Mary then turned to Ruth. "You have such a wonderful family. I'll just go back and sit with your mom and the others."

Ruth took Mary's comment about my having two shoulders as her cue. If Suni could have one then she was going to have the other. She sat down and leaned against me, then took it a step further, sliding her fingers between mine, clasping my hand. Mary rolled her eyes as she turned and walked back to her new friends. I'd seen nieces in the Philippines give their uncle the same affection they might give to their dad so I thought nothing of it.

"Tell them about your Manly Voyage now." Ruth prompted her

father.

"Sure baby." John looked lovingly at his daughter.

"On my 21st birthday I left on my Manly Voyage. In my kingdom, no man was given the title of knight or noblemen... king, for that matter, if he hadn't taken his Manly Voyage, and I was no exception."

John paused to answer the question that he knew all of us had.

"Yes, I said knights and noblemen. Believe it or not, there are still kingdoms in the Celebes sea where National Geographic has not been.

We departed boys on our Manly Voyage and if we were fortunate enough to return, we were given the privileges and responsibilities of manhood. Some of us came back rich men. Others considered themselves lucky to have returned with their lives. Still others were lost at sea, murdered by pirates, or eaten by cannibals, the latter were not necessarily killed first.

Despite the tales I'd heard, I was not frightened, nor were most boys who left on their Manly Voyage. We all believed that we would be the next man whose exploits would spawn a new generation of legends and myths.

For those lucky enough to be sailing on one of my father's ships, it would be our first voyage on a *Flying Fish*. Sure we'd been on boats both large and small but never on a *Flying Fish*. My father's ships were called *Flying Fish* because during monsoon season the king's fleet never lost an island princess race. Witnesses claimed father's ships could hop from wave top to wave top. Whether they were able to perform these fantastic maneuvers because of the monsoon winds or in spite of them, the captains would never tell. Sailing secrets were passed on from generation to generation but never sold. Some said black magic was used so that the king's ships could take bites out of the other ships' hulls. Others said that because the captains of my father's fleet were descendants of mountain people, they were able to jump their ships from one mountainous wave to another. There is truth to this in that the winner of the princess race always received a mountain princess for his wife. Many of the other ships would break to pieces upon these gargantuan waves as all the sea's fury was being released. Others yet, were swallowed whole by the relentless seas and vomited out when they came crashing down on coral reefs. The fresh firewood washed up on the beaches after such races was evidence enough that the sea had gotten its fill. Now it was the sea villagers' turn as they scavenged the wreckage for a hinge, a mast, or some rope. Some of the houses that were built over the water had masts recovered from these wrecks and if not for their stilts, looked like they could have sailed into the sunset. A closer look revealed that the masts were sporting the latest in peasant underwear, and with the help of an equatorial breeze could dry clothing as well as any modern appliance. The Princess Races provided the winning captains with a dowry and a mountain princess for a wife. Though the princess was the daughter of a mountain chieftain she was indeed of royal blood and quite beautiful.

As long as the captain kept the princess for his wife he had diplomatic immunity, since his wife was considered an ambassador from her tribe. This kept the Princess Races highly competitive. Captain Stephen, the captain of my ship, had three such wives. He had composed a poem which he was fond of reciting. It went like this:

'The man who lays a hand on me
Deals not with one but one plus three
Each wife I have has a father too
A cannibal chief to avenge me
A cannibal chief to avenge me'

These captains were free to use their skills and wisdom as they saw fit because of their diplomatic immunity. The king preferred such captains, knowing that their skills were well tested. Most had not only saved members of the royal family from the hands of pirates, but also from the jaws of unforgiving monsoons. It had been a long time since such a captain had done other than the best for his king. It was such an honor to be the husband of a princess that they sought to keep their standing in the community unstained. It was, therefore, with not too much concern that my father chose Captain Stephen to pilot the ship which took me on my Manly Voyage.

This rite of passage, the Manly Voyage, involved sailing to various islands, hiking into the hills, discovering what tribes were there and trading with them. The object was to avoid trading lives for treasures. The treasures would be for a future bride and in my case, brides. By this custom a boy would become a man simply by setting foot on foreign soil. I consider myself fortunate to have survived my Manly Voyage.

My father had chartered Captain Stephen's ship exclusively for me. He made sure that the ship, its crew, and captain were dedicated to one thing; my setting foot on foreign soil and returning home safely. My father loved me very much, which goes without saying, I was his first born. He chose Captain Stephen because he didn't want a captain whose loyalties might be split between performing a merchant function and my getting back in one piece. Captain Stephen was known for his loyalty and was richer than any of the king's subjects. Still, he wasn't above achieving greater wealth and I'm sure my father paid him many times more than he would have received for transporting any ordinary cargo. Even so, my family and my servants were there at the dock praying for my safe return.

A safe return for my companions however, was not so assured. The fiercest tribes required that a crew member be left behind as evidence of friendly intentions. After all, if their visitors were truly friends, would they not return again? When the crew member's family did return to look for their loved one, they would find no trace of their beloved nor of the tribe. At best they would find the scorched bones of their dear relative around a fire pit. Worse yet, they may very well find the tribe and be eaten as well. I had no intention of leaving any of our crew behind. They were the fathers of my childhood friends. Their wives had been kind enough to cook up native dishes for me and return my unsoiled clothing pressed and brushed. No, I could never leave one of these men behind. Better that I be left behind than to sacrifice one of these men of humble heritage. Little did I know how prophetic my thoughts would be.

We sailed three weeks without sighting any islands large enough to explore. Then as quickly as the last little island disappeared behind us, the wind stopped. There was nothing we could do but drift. We tried rowing back in the direction of the last island we'd seen but the current had its own mind. We did all we could with no wind and no land in sight. We fished, we rationed the water and we waited. As we waited the current moved us. The black sky turned to daylight once again and an island appeared. Like a magnet our ship was pulled toward it. We were unmistakably being moved in the direction of the island. Captain Stephen assured the crew that it was just the current moving us, not some evil force pulling us to our doom. Just before sundown, we anchored in a small harbor. There was no sign of life anywhere. Anxious to set foot on my first foreign soil, I had one of the crew members take me to shore in a dinghy. The captain was concerned about the current so he tied one of the ropes to our little craft as we rowed ashore. Amazingly, there wasn't a current at all, just the waves gently lapping against the sides. The very moment I stepped out of the dinghy onto the white sand, my oarsman shouted:

'You're a man! Now let's get out of here!'

I don't think he intended to startle me, but he did. The sun was setting in absolute silence behind our ship and his voice shot past me like a spear. Had it been, he could easily have penetrated the lush tropical growth that began where the sand ended. One thin strand of beach separated sea from jungle. I stood between these two powers of nature. Would they wield their power recklessly against me or would the Lord use them to bless me as my mother had said He would. My oarsman didn't appreciate my silence nor that I hadn't gotten back into the dinghy with him. I could see he was getting a little edgy so before he could utter another protest, I shouted:

'I'm a man! Let's get out of here!'

Getting his head lopped off for a brat prince wasn't on his itinerary so he was relieved when I jumped back into the dinghy. One of the crew pulled us back to the ship with the lifeline. Indeed, I was a man, treasure or not.

The celebration of my manhood was simple. The Captain said a prayer over me and that was that. I didn't feel any different. But I *was* a man. It was written, and so it came to be. I needn't feel any different, for the law declared me a man. The crew members now lined up to shake my hand. This was likely the only chance they'd have to shake the hand of a prince and it was something they could tell their grandchildren about. I could see they were sizing me up as each one grasped my hand, looked me in the eye, and said: 'Lalaki ka na!' (You're a man!) They knew I could become great, or follow in the footsteps of my long deceased great grandfather, corrupt and cruel.

The crew spent the next day restocking the ship with fruit and fresh water so that by evening they were ready for some entertainment. They took turns telling each other tales and were a boisterous bunch until one of them started reciting the sea gypsies' nursery rhyme about Sumba.

'Dream a dream of pirates plunder
Dream a dream of life at sea
Drop a gift and not the anchor
When Sumba sailors you have seen
When Sumba sailors you have seen

Dream a dream of pirates plunder
Forget your family
Just don't forget your mama loves you
When Sumba sailors you have seen
When Sumba sailors you have seen

Don't dream of pirates plunder now
Don't dream at all tonight
For you may be the sacrifice
When Sumba sailors you have seen
When Sumba sailors you have seen'

The crew's appetite for stories ended as they remembered how far from home they were. Anchored in a jungle harbor isn't the best place for scary tales, especially since mutinies had their beginnings in fear and superstition. I welcomed their loud snores as each of the crew dropped off to sleep. At least they'd keep till morning, *if Sumba sailors didn't get them first.* I slept soundly. Tomorrow would take care of itself."[14]

Chapter 13 Footnotes

1. Micah 7:6 For the son dishonoureth the father, the daughter riseth up against her mother, the daughter in law against her mother in law; a man's enemies are the men of his own house.
Luke 12:52,53 For from henceforth there shall be five in one house divided, three against two, and two against three. The father shall be divided against the son, and the son against the father; the mother against the daughter, and the daughter against the mother; the mother in law against her daughter in law, and the daughter in law against her mother in law.
2. Ephesians 6:12 For we wrestle not against flesh and blood, but against principalities, against powers, against the rulers of the darkness of this world, against spiritual wickedness in high places.
3. Colossians 2:3 In whom [God the Father and Christ] are hid all the treasures of wisdom and knowledge.
4. 1 Peter 1:7 That the trial of your faith, being much more precious than of gold that perisheth, though it be tried with fire, might be found unto praise and honour and glory at the appearing of Jesus Christ.
5. 2 Corinthians 11:14-15 And no marvel; for Satan himself is transformed into an angel of light. Therefore it is no great thing if his ministers also be transformed as the ministers of righteousness; whose end shall be according to their works.
6. Luke 12:22 And he said unto his disciples, *Therefore I say unto you, Take no thought for your life, what ye shall eat; neither for the body, what ye shall put on. The life is more than meat, and the body is more than raiment. Consider the ravens: for they neither sow nor reap; which neither have storehouse nor barn; and God feedeth them: how much more are ye better than the fowls? And which of you with taking thought can add to his stature one cubit? If ye then be not able to do that thing which is least, why take ye thought for the rest? Consider the lilies how they grow: they toil not, they spin not; and yet I say unto you, that Solomon in all his glory was not arrayed like one of these. If then God so clothe the grass, which is to day in the field, and to morrow is cast into the oven; how much more will he clothe you, O ye of little faith? And seek not ye what ye shall eat, or what ye shall drink, neither be ye of doubtful mind. For all these things do the nations of the world seek after: and your Father knoweth that ye have need of these*

things. But rather seek ye the kingdom of God; and all these things shall be added unto you. Fear not, little flock; for it is your Father's good pleasure to give you the kingdom.

7. Proverbs 3:5 Trust in the LORD with all thine heart; and lean not unto thine own understanding.
8. 2 Chronicles 20:17 Ye shall not need to fight in this battle: set yourselves, stand ye still, and see the salvation of the LORD with you, O Judah and Jerusalem: fear not, nor be dismayed; to morrow go out against them: for the LORD will be with you.
9. Proverbs 11:21 Though hand join in hand, the wicked shall not be unpunished: but *the seed of the righteous shall be delivered.*
10. John 14:6 Jesus saith unto him, I am the way, the truth, and the life: no man cometh unto the Father, but by me.
11. John 6:35 And Jesus said unto them, I am the bread of life: he that cometh to me shall never hunger; and he that believeth on me shall never thirst.
12. 2 Thessalonians 3:10 For even when we were with you, this we commanded you, that if any would not work, neither should he eat.
13. Matthew 20:28 Even as the Son of man came not to be ministered unto, but to minister, and to give his life a ransom for many.
14. Matthew 6:34 Take therefore no thought for the morrow: for the morrow shall take thought for the things of itself. Sufficient unto the day is the evil thereof.

Chapter 14

TREASURES OR TROUBLES
PRINCE JOHN'S STORY CONTINUES

"Today I would learn my first lesson as a man; that the rising and the setting of the sun is the only thing we can be sure of in this life.[1] As wise king Solomon said, *When your day brings treasures, be happy, and when your day brings troubles, remember; The Lord has made all the days and it is not for man to know what a day will bring.*[2]

I woke up early enough to see the sun rising over this island of mystery as surely as I'd seen it set behind the sails of Captain Stephen's ship the night before. I greeted the day with anticipation for I sensed we weren't far from the treasures we sought. I knew the crew didn't share my enthusiasm for exploration but Captain Stephen wasn't going to let me, a prince, return from my Manly Voyage empty handed, so after a hearty breakfast we set out with determination.

The mountain men my father had hired to carry our supplies into the hills, and our treasures back, were glad to get off the boat despite the heavy loads the crew had placed across their shoulders. Their bouts of seasickness had been the only form of entertainment we'd had on our long voyage. Now it was the mountain men's turn to be entertained by the members of Captain Stephen's crew. The mountain men had immediately regained their land legs but the crew walked wobbly legged, struggling to keep from sliding down the muddy trail. Upon reaching the first leg of the trail, each member of Captain Stephen's crew would smile the same proud smile then in like manner as those who'd preceded him, lose his balance, then his footing, and finally that look of pride as he slid down the side of the trail into the growing pile of crewmen at the bottom of the ravine.

The morale of the mountain men, having been elevated far above the crew's, and their humiliation at getting seasick long forgotten, I ordered them to tie ropes along the side of the dangerous slope. It would have been bad enough had one of the men been injured on his slide to humility, but to risk the life of a man for the entertainment of others, is blasphemy; for we are created in the image of God, Himself.[3]

After the men who'd slid down the side of the trail made their way back up, they continued on with more care. Hours later we reached the top of a ridge overlooking the harbor. I pulled out my telescope and looked down at the ship. Captain Stephen was looking back at me through his own telescope. We waved to each other. I was relieved to see that the men who'd remained behind with him hadn't mutinied. In fact, I was elated, but my elation vanished the moment I saw we were surrounded by a tribe of well armed natives. So this was the fate of my Manly Voyage? I felt more foolish than manly. Thoughts rushed through my head; why hadn't there been another way to support my future brides? After all, I was a prince. What could I possibly need from these islands that I couldn't buy at our local market? Then I heard the eerie whirring; the voices on the wind; Sumba! We were on Sumba! I'd heard the tales of the island ghosts. Now in unison with the ghastly voices on the wind, the tribe was chanting. The bones that they wore as bracelets and headdresses rattled as they danced.[4] I wondered if they were human bones. At this point I was beginning to wonder if the *tribe* were human. I knew I had to do something fast to keep my men from panicking. If I had fears, what fears must they be having, fed by years of superstitious tales.

Suddenly, a song from my childhood came to mind. I'd found the song in a book I'd taken from a pirate ship. This was the song I burst out with that moment on Sumba. I sang it to one of my oldest bodyguards, Elkanah, for best effect. He was Hadassah's father. Hadassah was a delightful little servant girl who was ever at my mother's side. Had I not been a prince, that sweet peasant girl would have been my first choice for a wife. Hadassah; strong but delicate. I thought of her as I sang and danced such a ridiculous dance with her father. One of his legs was shorter than the other which made him appear to be hopping each time he took a step. While singing I exaggerated the words to the song as I looked into this shriveled up old man's eyes.

'Little brown jug how I love thee.
Little brown jug how I love thee.'

Then, as if on cue, the old man cracked a smile, showing off his one and only, that's right, solitary tooth. Neither my men nor the tribe could contain themselves any longer. They were laughing so hard that they forgot we might be enemies. The rest of the tribe now came out from behind the trees. Little children, old women, young women, and warriors. After they'd wiped the last of their tears from laughing, Elkanah and I ended our dance. It was then that the warriors stepped aside to reveal their leader. His countenance was unmistakably that of a king. This was my opportunity to present the gift I'd brought.

The ghostly voices continued like the rustle of leaves in the wind but the tribe had stopped their chant. I spoke to my crew in our dialect, telling them not to be afraid for the sounds must be a magicians trick. This calmed them a bit.

Now everyone was watching to see how the king would receive my gift. The gift was a book from one of the many pirate ships that sank off our shores. We called any foreign vessel a pirate ship. After all, for what other reason than to steal would men from a distant kingdom come to our shores. With that in mind, I wondered what our island hosts must be thinking of us.

The king's response dispelled my apprehensions. His eyes lit up as if he'd seen a book like it before. He took my hand and shook it with such vigor that I wondered what the book contained, or was it just his pleasure at receiving a gift instead of a knife through the ribs. Then he spoke excitedly to his tribe:

'Mananampalataya! Mananampalataya!' [Believers! Believers!]

His tribe gathered around him to get a closer look at the book. Again, the king spoke.

'Ang magandang balita!' [The good news!][5]

At his words they began shouting thanks to their God, calling Him by a Name I had not heard before. I'd never witnessed such open and joyous praises for God. Had it not been for my relief that they were thanking God instead of cursing me, I might have been offended by such a personal way of addressing God. I'd always seen God as far off. One Who could only be prayed to in a very formal way.

What good fortune that we'd delivered something of such great significance to them. From their reaction, a chest full of priceless gems could have gotten no better reception. None of my people had ever been able to translate the book but it was apparent that some of the members of his tribe could not only read the book but were finding new religious insights within its pages.

The king saw it as nothing but the hand of God that brought us to his shores and invited me and Elkanah to stay the night. Of course we accepted. This would provide us with a chance to establish a trading relationship. Besides, we had no alternative. It's the custom on the islands of the Celebes Sea that a man must accept hospitality. It's taken as a great insult if he declines. Wars have been fought over less. We were the king's guests till he bid us goodbye, or if necessary, till we escaped.

My men couldn't hide their relief when I ordered them to put down my supplies and return to the ship. I handed one of them a note for Captain Stephen with orders to set sail for a safer harbor that we'd seen on our ascent.

The king led me and Elkanah to a clearing near the edge of the bluff where we could watch our shipmates hike back down the trail. It was apparent the tribe had seen us hours before we'd arrived for we could see each twist of the path as it made its way down to the shore.

'Please, rest. There will be time for introductions later.' The king said, pointing to some hammocks that had bird's eye views of the trail and the harbor. 'We'll take you to my place after you've seen your men arrive safely to your ship.'

Elkanah and I laid down on our hammocks and watched the men descend. I was excited at having met my first *uncivilized* tribe but I was exhausted after the climb. I tried to keep my eyes open as I watched the men struggle down the trail but was soon asleep. After what had to be hours, I woke just long enough to see my men climb aboard and set sail, then I closed my eyes again, this time to dream. I dreamed of wondrous gifts and the wives with whom I might share them. From what my father and uncles had told me, gifts would never satisfy them. In my dream I found myself praying that my wives would be different. It was the first of two times while on Sumba that I found myself praying in a dream. In this dream I felt for the first time that I knew Who I was praying to. It was as if a spirit deep within me was praying to the Spirit of the Almighty.[6]

Suddenly I was awakened. The ghostly voices of Sumba had become louder, more like screams, but it hadn't been these sounds that woke me. It was the uproar that was going on near the edge of the bluff. Some members of the tribe were frantically shouting over the edge. Forgetting anything I'd dreamed, I jumped to my feet and ran to see what the shouting was about. From the bluff I could see my crew fighting to raise the sails in an effort to keep the ship from dashing against the coral reef. The storm had apparently blown them back into the harbor. Then one of the sails went up. It caught wind, moving them away from the reef and back out of the harbor. Just as quickly, Captain Stephen lowered the sails. He took a moment to signal me that he'd return after the storm. Again the sail went up and just as quickly he lowered it. Each time the captain raised the sail the wind mysteriously took them closer to the opening of the harbor. Of course it wasn't mysterious to Captain Stephen. He knew through years of experience how to catch these gale winds as they whirled off the cliffs of island harbors. Captain Stephen had all the sails hoisted when his ship finally reached open waters. I watched her disappear over the horizon. It was then that I realized it might be days before the winds made it possible for Captain Stephen to return, if ever. I was reminded again that no one had ever been to Sumba and lived to tell of it. I wondered what the probability of his safe return to this harbor could be, not to mention the odds of our safe return home.

As I was gazing over the harbor I felt something breathing so closely behind me that I feared my throat was about to be torn by a wild beast. Turning suddenly, I came face to face with a leopard, close enough to bite off my nose or slash my face with its claws. To my relief, it was the headdress of the island's tiny princess, Sarapita.[7] She looked up at me. At six feet tall I must have seemed a giant to her, but the tiny princess was unafraid; her father was king. I felt fortunate to see her before she came of age for they followed the custom of veiling women. Indeed, I was baffled why she hadn't been covered already for despite her size, she was all woman. And her face? It combined all those things a man desires. Had I not been raised to know that a man is master, it would have been easy to take orders from this little princess.

Our languages were similar enough so that Sarapita and I had no problem introducing ourselves. It was only after the introduction that the differences became apparent. She began laughing so hard that I realized what meant one thing in my language must have meant something entirely different in hers, so to avoid saying the wrong thing, I continued our conversation in sign language. This only changed her laughter to hysteria. So contagious was it that when her cousin joined us she fell into a fit of laughter herself though she had no clue as to what was so funny. Not wanting her cousin to miss anything, Sarapita began imitating my sign language with such exaggerated hand movements that I too was laughing. For the next ten minutes, the three of us tried unsuccessfully to regain our composure. Lack of oxygen finally forced us into silence. This was the most I'd ever laughed with total strangers. In fact, I hadn't laughed so hard since my nannies had entertained me as a child.

Sarapita now became the diplomat as she introduced her cousin, Zuah, in a flowery speech.

'May I introduce to you my uncle's daughter, Zuah, the available, the mature and the graceful; *a maiden, ripe for the picking.*'

I was sure Sarapita was unaware that her introduction was every bit as funny as my sign language, but since she said it in all seriousness, I responded in kind.

'It is my pleasure to make your acquaintance, oh graceful one.' At this, I took Zuah's hand and bowed.

Now I heard something that I'd heard often in my own kingdom. Starting from a low tone and then rising, 'Uh!' Sarapita hummed. The teenage girls at home did this in the same manner when teasing one of their friends who had a crush on someone. It didn't surprise me that they followed the same custom. My uncles had me convinced that women all over the world were the same. I had no reason to believe these two would be any different.

Zuah was so embarrassed by Sarapita's flowery introduction, and my response, that her delicate veil could not hide the crimson glow that flushed her cheeks, giving her mahogany skin a rosy hue. Despite her shyness, her almond shaped eyes seemed to beckon me. I wondered if her lips, hidden behind that veil of hers, were as inviting. I was enjoying their company, maybe a little too much.

We hiked up a nearby hill that overlooked the sea. It was there that I first learned the secret of Sumba. Sarapita pointed to the bushes that covered the hills and explained.

'Zuah is named after the briars that line these ridges. We call the briars Zuahmba. We use its coarse fiber to make rope and nets.'

Zuah now took my hand and placed it on one of the bushes. The sound halted. Startled, I pulled my hand back from the bush. The sound began again. Zuah's eyes lit up with delight as she saw my surprise. She spoke for the first time, bubbling, as if this were the first secret she'd shared with anyone.

'This bush, with its bladelike brambles, whirs as the wind blows through its flat sinewy vines. The many Zuahmba bushes along the ridges of this island harmonically interact with each other, heightening the effect. Depending on the wind speed and direction it can at times be deafening. Not surprisingly, no ships come close to our island. Now that you know the nature of the ghostly voices, you must promise not to betray us.'

'I promise, I will never forsake you.'

'What! What is this you have said?' Sarapita asked.

I wondered if I'd used a word that meant something different in their language. I said it again, this time more slowly so that there would be no mistake.

'I promise, I will never forsake you.'

They both giggled. Sarapita elbowed Zuah and whispered something in her ear.

'I see.' Sarapita said. 'You are a prophet then. So be it.' They laughed all the more. I didn't get the joke but was to learn later that I'd uttered the very words that a groom on Sumba recites to his bride before consummating their marriage.

'So why were you named after these bushes?' I asked Zuah.

'My mother told me that when I was a baby, I was always making noises, crying, or babbling till she would quiet me with her touch. So she named me Zuah for the briars that can only be silenced with a touch.'

As we walked, Zuah was, in fact, humming. It was the same tune that the tribe had been chanting when we'd first arrived, only Zuah hummed it so melodiously. It was hypnotic. Sarapita noticed that I was gazing intently into Zuah's eyes so she said,

'Zuah is a woman now and not so much like the briars. If you were to hold her she might sing all the more.'

This time Zuah didn't blush. I could see the outline of a smile behind her veil. Her eyes sparkled as she fixed her gaze on mine. Her stare was intense and unguarded, like the moment before a kiss. Suddenly the commotion that woke me earlier started again. Could Captain Stephen be returning so soon? From the ridge where we stood, we watched as the ship made its way back into the now calm harbor. It had sustained some damage in the storm. The mast was twisted and the ship was listing. Just then the wind surged again, impaling the craft against the coral reef. The ship was sucked beneath the crashing of the surf. The strong undertow left little hope for survivors. The treacherous sea that had taken the ship would be no less cruel to a rescue vessel. We were helpless to do anything. Even so, Sarapita's father, the king, sent his fastest runners to scout out the beaches for any signs of the crew. It was a kind gesture but I knew it was in vain. None could have survived those waters.

Now, it seemed from behind every bush, the members of the tribe who'd witnessed the ship wreck came out to meet me. They were offering their condolences and assuring me I would have a place in their tribe. I was wondering where Sarapita and Zuah had gone till I realized they'd been at my sides all along, their eyes now filled with tears. I couldn't understand how total strangers could shed tears for me. This wasn't what I'd expected. I'd been warned about the ferocity of the island tribes and now these people were showing genuine empathy for my loss. They knew more than I how unlikely it was that I would ever return to my kingdom. I learned soon after that the only other ship that had reached their shores experienced the same fate as mine."

Chapter 14 Footnotes

1.Ecclesiastes 1:5 The sun also ariseth, and the sun goeth down, and hasteth to his place where he arose.

2. Ecclesiastes 8:17 Then I beheld all the work of God, that a man cannot find out the work that is done under the sun: because though a man labour to seek it out, yet he shall not find it; yea further; though a wise man think to know it, yet shall he not be able to find it.

3. Genesis 9:6 "Whoso sheddeth man's blood, by man shall his blood be shed: for in the image of God made he man."
4. The tribe wore bracelets on their wrists and had bands stretched across their foreheads with scriptures written on them. They had made them from deer antlers so they appeared to be bones.
Deuteronomy 11:18-23 Therefore shall ye lay up these my words in your heart and in your soul, and bind them for a sign upon your hand, that they may be as frontlets between your eyes. And ye shall teach them your children, speaking of them when thou sittest in thine house, and when thou walkest by the way, when thou liest down, and when thou risest up. And thou shalt write them upon the door posts of thine house, and upon thy gates: That your days may be multiplied, and the days of your children, in the land which the LORD sware unto your fathers to give them, as the days of heaven upon the earth. For if ye shall diligently keep all these commandments which I command you, to do them, to love the LORD your God, to walk in all his ways, and to cleave unto him; Then will the LORD drive out all these nations from before you, and ye shall possess greater nations and mightier than yourselves.
5. Good News: Another term for the promise of salvation found in the Bible, also called the *gospel.* Frequently used to refer to the New Testament.
6. Romans 8:26 Likewise the Spirit also helpeth our infirmities: for we know not what we should pray for as we ought: *but the Spirit itself maketh intercession for us with groanings which cannot be uttered.*
7. Sarapita: A combination of two Tagalog root words:
[sarap - delicious] [ita - small and of female gender]
In other words: Delicious Little Woman.

Chapter 15

DREAMS AND VISIONS
PRINCE JOHN'S STORY CONTINUES

"So much had happened that afternoon that I would have forgotten Elkanah had Sarapita not reminded me that he was still asleep in his hammock. She and Zuah accompanied me back to him with their entourage of bodyguards.

He'd slept through everything. He didn't know that the ship had left nor that it had returned. Neither did he know that upon its return it had been swallowed by the sea.

'Elkanah, Elkanah. It's time to get up.' I said.

He sat up, a far away look in his eyes. He must be drowsy from his long nap, I thought. Then he jumped to his feet. His eyes were alert and he spoke with a voice full of authority:

'Your wives will not be like other wives. They will not be of this world though they will be in this world.'[1]

I remembered my dream, how I'd prayed that my wives would be different. Now Elkanah was giving me an answer to my prayer as if he were a prophet. Then I realized he didn't even know my prayer. How strange that Elkanah, a man who'd never spoken a religious word to me, would prophesy. How much *more* strange that *I*, who'd been known more for playing pranks than playing hymns, would make a prayer and hear its answer on the very same day.

Elkanah spoke again. 'Your friends' fathers, our shipmates, they're alive.'

Now this was too much. I'd seen the ship go down with my own eyes yet Elkanah was speaking as though he'd had a vision, a vision that contradicted what I and the whole tribe had witnessed first hand. Despite Elkanah's knowledge of my dream, I didn't want to consider the possibility that Elkanah could be blessed with visions.

'We can talk about that later.' I said. 'This is Sarapita, the king's daughter and her cousin, Zuah. They'll take us back to their camp.'

Elkanah bowed. Then followed us.

Sarapita's body guards flanked us on all sides as they guided us through the jungle to their camp, at least that's where I thought we were headed. Instead, the jungle path led to a park and then to a stone highway lined with beautiful homes. The trees on both sides of the highway and the setting sun framed a mountaintop castle in the distance.

'See you at the top!' Sarapita said as she stepped inside a carriage drawn by two white stallions.

After she'd left, another coach pulled up. The driver got down and opened the door for us.

'To the top?' He said.

'Where else!' I answered. Where else indeed? Such a fantastic kingdom! Horse drawn carriages and a castle that dwarfed any I'd ever seen. Elkanah and I got in. If we had any fear before, it was now replaced with awe.

What at first appeared to be no more than a few miles turned out to be a two hour journey by coach. I was stunned that the beautiful homes lining the highway continued all the way to the king's palace. We'd expected to find a primitive tribe but now I was feeling the more primitive; surrounded by great wealth and about to enter the gates of the king's castle. There were gas lamps below every window making it literally sparkle. Now that the sun had set, I could only imagine what a dazzling site it must be from below.

We entered the gates and found Sarapita and Zuah waiting for us at the foot of the steps leading to the castle.

'Please, come with us.' Sarapita said.

She and Zuah led us to a courtyard behind the king's quarters where there was a great feast in the makings.

'I hope you won't think me rude for taking so long to begin introductions. My father thought it would be better that you come here first. The jungle might be a nice place to picnic but a man's home is his castle.'

Her tipping upside down that old adage brought a smile to my face, her father's... *home?*

'There, I knew I could make you smile.' She said warmly.

Sarapita and Zuah now introduced each of their little brothers and sisters to me. There were about twenty of them. The children were much easier to speak with than Sarapita and Zuah. They spoke more slowly and understood me perfectly well. At least they didn't giggle at every other word, not that I hadn't enjoyed the company of Sarapita and Zuah. I loved their company and was really looking forward to spending more time with them.

The kids all wanted to know about the place I'd come from. As I described my kingdom, Sarapita and Zuah listened every bit as intently as the children.

'So he is a prince!' Zuah shouted. She jumped as she said it. 'I knew it!'

Sarapita dutifully began grilling me.

'You say you're a prince but you couldn't read the book you gave my father? How can we believe that an illiterate is a prince? All princes can read!'

I loved Sarapita's frankness but remembered her exaggerated introduction of Zuah. Everything Sarapita did was intended for effect. I knew to one degree or another that this was true of all women but Sarapita was an especially talented and delightful actress.

'I can write in my own language.' I replied to this little detective, 'I've even composed some poems that I'll give to my wives one day.'

This time it was Zuah making the school girl *uh* sound as she teased Sarapita about the love poems I'd written for my wives.

'So you are married?' Sarapita asked.

Again Zuah made the *uh* sound.

'No, I can only marry princesses and you're the first eligible princess I've met since becoming a man.'

Zuah was doing all she could to keep back her laughter. She could see that Sarapita had finally met someone who had every bit the talent for getting attention that she had.

'Surely you've met other princesses.' Sarapita quizzed me.

'As surely as we speak, not an eligible one. I'm forbidden from marrying princesses from my own island.[2] I must marry foreign princesses to strengthen our alliances. Nor could I have married prior to setting foot on this island for until then, I hadn't passed our test of manhood.'

'Silly, your test of manhood shall be passed when one of your wives bears your first son. Such strange customs you have; test of manhood!'

I ignored Sarapita's rudeness. It was her right. She was a princess. In fact, my father had told me that the delight of man is not only many wives[3], but wives who could light up a room with their fire. Sarapita surely had that fire and I wanted to know her more.

'I'm so glad that you, a princess, so close to becoming a woman, are so concerned with my status. You must invite me to your coming of age party.'

At this, Sarapita became quite serious.

'I will most certainly invite you, and you shall be the first prince I greet upon becoming a woman.'

I could no longer tell whether Sarapita was saying this for effect or from her heart. I don't think she knew either.

A princess is trained from an early age to wrap a man around her finger. An important part of this training involves learning to behave in such a way as to divert a man's attention from the true intent of her behavior. For example, it's not uncommon to see a little princess, no older than the age of four, walk into a room where her father is entertaining a guest and say,

'Oh kind sir, please tell me when the great Datu (Prince) from across the sea arrives for I have heard many wonderful things about him. I wouldn't want to lose the opportunity to be in his presence, even if just for a moment. Maybe someday my father will be so grand as to marry me off to such a man as he.'

Of course the man her father was entertaining would indeed be that great Datu and he would respond;

'Such a delightful little princess you are, let me see that pretty little face of yours for you're not far from taking on the veil. Have a cookie.'

At this, the little princess would say; 'Why thank you kind sir!' Then she would run away, having obtained her cookie for that was all she'd really wanted.

As the years passed, the princess would learn to be more subtle in her methods. She would learn how to find out the wealth of her suitors without their knowing. I don't say this to be critical of the training that princesses receive. Their training is very important for they must know how to deal with powerful men. I admire their abilities for without them, they might become no more than destitute trophies.

I wondered how many cookies Sarapita might require of the man who would take her in marriage. I also wondered whether by that time she would have learned her part so well that she could no longer tell the difference between her performance and her true feelings. Would she lose sight of what she really wanted? Could a princess really know? Maybe she would simply let her father choose the man she'd marry, rather than take a chance on her own fickle feelings.

This practice of choosing a husband for one's daughter has been much maligned in the West. Why should it be unusual for a young and innocent girl, having never ventured into the world of deceit and corruption, to trust her father's judgment on these matters? I assure you Ish, that my eldest, Ruth, fully understands that I've chosen a man for her."

John placed his hand on Ruth's, the hand which was already holding mine. Patting her hand before withdrawing his, he leaned back, now thoughtful.

"There's another thing that upsets, or rather *entertains* me. It's the hard headed, or should I say, *dense* man. Although he knows that princess and maiden alike are taught to pretend in order to get what they want, he believes everything his beloved wife tells him. Few of these men can control their emotions, let alone their women, yet most of their women have no problem controlling them. Who is the helper in this relationship? Let's read Genesis 2:18 to see who God says it must be:

And the LORD God said, It's not good that the man should be alone; I will make him a helper for him.

Hmm, make him a helper for him. It's clear that woman was not only made *for* man but she was made for a *specific purpose*, as *man's helper*. Yet men in the West continue to slave away for their wives. This is beyond my grasp.

Now, listen to the last words of the book of Proverbs. They're found in Proverbs 31:31

Give her of the fruit of her hands; and let her own works praise her in the gates.

Give her of the fruit of her hands? not of the fruit of her husband's hands? What a novel idea, and it came right out of the Bible!"

John let out a belly laugh then continued his discourse with a huge smile.

"Of all the words that Solomon could have chosen to complete his Book of Proverbs, he chose words that declared that *a wife must support herself* and that she must *not look to her husband's work to obtain her identity*. Reread Proverbs 31:31 at your leisure and you'll see that I'm right.

When a man has such wives he will certainly become wealthy, and so it should be; for his wife was given *to him as a helper for him*. Now just because she's a helper doesn't mean she's not wonderful. Solomon writes in Proverbs 18:22

Whoso finds a wife, finds a good thing, and obtains favor of the LORD.

Whether a man finds a first wife, a second wife or any number of wives, he finds a good thing, and certainly does obtain favor of the LORD. But the Western mind has twisted things so that the husband has become the helper to the wife, which is the exact opposite of the order that God has established. This is why they cannot conceive of a man having more than one wife, after all, if the wife is the master, and by his labors he must serve that master, he can have only one. Maybe this accounts for your use of the unbiblical word, matrimony. Take the word apart and it means mother support, money to be paid to a mother. It's not a coincidence that the Roman Temple of Juno was erected to worship a blasphemous *mother god* whose name, often called Juno Moneta, is where you get your word *money* as well as your word *matrimony*.

Another fact that those in the West don't seem to understand is that a woman who does not retain her honor, dishonors herself.[4] Only by refusing to rid himself of such a wife can a husband be defiled by her, yet I've heard that your preachers tell you to stay married to women who speak nothing but fornication. Worse yet, I've heard that some of your preachers tell you to stay married to an adulteress![5] The Lord forbids a man who has divorced his wife to remarry her after she has married another and been divorced again or has become a widow.[65] How much more is that man forbidden from staying in a marriage with a woman who has defiled herself with adultery? A man must rid himself of such a wretch.

Now if we claim to be believers then we must accept God's word and it states that a man is; to his wife, as Christ is to the church.[7] Does Christ lose face if a member of the church dishonors Him? Certainly not! To Jesus, our Savior, be all honor and glory. God offers love and it does not diminish Him nor His offer of salvation if someone refuses to accept it. It only shows that they were never worthy of it in the first place; that they were not one of his elect. So it's the unbeliever's problem if he refuses to accept God's authority, and it's the fornicating wife's problem if her husband throws her aside because she refuses to accept *his* authority. The man bears no stain for an impudent wife *unless he keeps her*. Weak men don't understand the nature of the relationship between a man and wife. These are the mama's boys and misfits that you find in places where honorable men don't go. They blaspheme God by idolizing women or worse yet, by imitating them.

I listened closely to my father's instructions[8] for I knew that one day I would have many wives and an understanding of marriage is crucial to a well functioning household. He pointed out that I had a choice; having wives that would be staunch allies in all difficulties or having wives who would become enemies within my own household. A lukewarm[9] wife, he pointed out, was no better than an enemy. He further explained that there is such a woman who is true and who willingly accepts her man's love but even to such a woman, I must never give power over my wealth, nor mock God by putting her on a pedestal.[4]

The Lord has ordained that a husband shall rule over his wife[10] but a woman who rules her husband *leads him to err*."[11]

The girls applauded as John finished his impromptu sermon, then he returned to his story telling.

"By the time Sarapita had sufficiently quizzed me, everyone in the courtyard was listening. I told the story of my Manly Voyage and the tales I'd been told about Sumba, then as I finished my story, one of the children spouted,

'If I'd heard your stories about Sumba before I was born I would not have come out!'

His comment was met with laughter that reminded me of my own family's get-togethers.

I hadn't noticed that the king had been present till he got up from a lounge where he'd been resting. He walked over to the dining table at the center of the courtyard and sat down, then one of his attendants announced;

'*Dinner is served.*'

Everyone who had been sitting informally around the courtyard now stood up and quietly took their seats around the table. I sat myself as far away from the king and as close to the servants as I could. This was part of the court etiquette that my father had taught me when I was a boy. The king now spoke.

'I must apologize to you, John. Your words were so many, that at first, I took you for a tale bearer but now I must say that I'm moved to believe your entire story. *Come up closer*, take your place next to me.'

'Thank you, your highness.' I bowed, then sat in the chair he'd designated.

'Now, Prince John,' he addressed me, 'let me read for the benefit of my family what I'm sure your father, the king, must have taught you well. This is from our great book.

Do not put yourself forward in the presence of the king, and do not stand in the place of great men: For better it is that it be said to you, Come up closer; than you should be put lower in the presence of the prince whose eyes you have seen.[12]

Can you tell me, John. Is it true that you've heard these words before?'

I was flabbergasted. The king had read the identical words that my father had read to me from my mother's book of the great men.

'That's quite astounding, sire. I'm brought low by someone who has knowledge from the great book. I'd be blessed to learn at your side.'

'So be it. Let your first lesson be this.' The king took my hand in his and put his other hand on my shoulder. He looked into my eyes yet deeper, as if speaking to my soul itself.

'The fear of the Lord is the beginning of knowledge. Fear not them which kill the body, but are not able to kill the soul: but rather, fear him which is able to destroy both soul and body in hell; The Lord God Almighty'[13]

'This is a wise thing you've said, sire. I look forward to your teaching me from the great book.'

'And I look forward to teaching you. Now as for what you've heard about our island that you call Sumba, some of what your legend says is true, as I'm sure some of what we've been told about you and your people is true, but we can discuss such things later. Let's eat.'

The king's table was more elegant than any I'd seen. It was even more elegant than the table in the great hall of my father. It spanned sixty feet in length. Its top appeared to be made of a single cut of an enormous mahogany tree. The intricate designs along the edges were inlaid with shells that I knew to be rare. The finish shone like polished marble but indeed it was wood behind a sparkling glaze. It's surface was so hard that it resisted even the assault of the children sitting across from me. Their faces reflected as clearly as if it were a mirror. Sarapita's father noticed that I was admiring it and said,

'A gift from a superstitious bunch of pirates.' He laughed. 'I can't imagine why they would part with such a table. It shall be a wedding gift to my daughter, Sarapita, and the prince who marries her.'"

John's youngest son now interrupted his story telling.

"Daddy, daddy. That's our table now, isn't it? Grandpa gave it to us, right?"

"Solomon, please don't spoil the story for the others." John said, chuckling at his son's exuberance.

"Well, I guess they would have figured it out anyway. Yes, Solomon, Grandpa gave that to us. Now I'm sure you'd like to hear how your Grandpa prayed that first day I met him; when I ate at this very table with him, wouldn't you?"

"Oh yes!" A few of John's children chimed.

"All right, this is what he prayed. When all his family saw that Grandpa, the king, that is, was about to pray, the room became very silent in respect. Just like you're silent when daddy prays."

"That's right!" One of John's more boisterous children shouted.
"Okay, so this is what your Grandpa prayed that day:

'Almighty, Lord over all. You know all things. You know our hearts for through You all things were created. You spoke and we came into being. Your Perfect Love has made our passage through the Narrow Gate that leads into Your kingdom easy. We thank You that You have accepted us into Your kingdom and that You assure us even now that when we leave this life You have a place prepared for us in heaven. We can't imagine ever being able to forget Your love for us in that You loved us while we were yet in rebellion against You. We pray now that You would strengthen us in weakness so that we will never dishonor Your Name. We thank You that You have blessed us with the presence of John. We know that You have sent him here for a special reason. We pray Your blessings upon John right now. We pray that his eyes now and forever would be fixed on You, Your will, and Your kingdom. We pray also that You would stir the spirits of John's family so that they would know he is safe and that they also would now and forever seek Your will and Your kingdom. We pray that John will not have long to wait before he is blessed with a wonderful family of his own. We pray also, Lord, that we will follow Your will and seek Your guidance in all our dealings with John. With praises for Your Almighty Name we pray this, in the Name of Jesus. Let it be so.'[14]

Then all at the table repeated;

'Let it be so!'

When the king prayed that I would soon have a wife and family, there hadn't been one giggle from the girls. It wasn't that they were overly somber. I would more describe them as reverently joyous. Their eyes looked up to the heavens as they prayed. It was as if they expected the Almighty to visit them at that very moment. I'd never heard the word Jesus before so I simply assumed it was another Name for God but I was curious at what seemed to be a more personal and spontaneous prayer than the repetitious prayers I'd witnessed in my own kingdom."[15]

John's youngest son interrupted his story telling again, "You didn't know about Jesus, Daddy?"

"No, not yet, Solomon."

"That's very sad, Daddy. What would have become of you had you died without Jesus?"

"Well, we don't need to worry about that now because the Lord took my rebellion and turned it to my own good, having secured my salvation by showing me my own weakness, having planted that seed of faith in me, without which I would have been doomed. Praise the Lord that He sees fit to bless us who have no faith with that faith which is not of ourselves!"[16]

John's sermonette was met with praises to the Lord and Alleluias throughout the room.

"Now, as I was saying, Sarapita's father, the king..."

"King Tatang!" Solomon spouted.

"Yes, Solomon. Now the king had a great love for the Lord. He prayed eloquently and with conviction. He prayed as a man certain that he was accepted of God. His prayer was not the slightest bit arrogant *but*, unsaved that I was, I thought it a bit presumptuous that he could believe he had such assurance before God. I couldn't understand what gave him the right to approach the throne of the Almighty so boldly.[17]

'Excuse me your highness,' I said to the king, 'I hear your family calling you Tatang but what shall I call you?'

'I'm called Jochan, King Jochan. However, according to your servant, Elkanah, you will be on our island for quite some time so you may be more informal with me. Just call me Tatang (dad or daddy) as do my family members and the children here on ... Sumba, yes, Sumba. I like your name for our kingdom.'

'Thank you Tatang, I'm very fortunate to be visiting such a friendly island. Forgive my hopeful attitude. Call it youthful exuberance if you like, but I do believe that I'll find my way back home.'

'Oh, you'll find your way back home. Lord willing, in more ways than one.'[18]

I could tell that Tatang and I would get along well. He radiated confidence. Sarapita showed her love and admiration for her father as she doted on him. The servants kept out of her way as she made sure to keep his cup full and a platter full of choice food within his reach. This was one of the many things my mother told me that she loved about my own father. She said father could get what he wanted with a look or a gesture. People sought to please him. He didn't have to shout orders. He used this charismatic power wisely. It was as if he could send out thoughts and people acted upon them. My father was generous with praise.[19] I'd been blessed to have such a loving father.

When Tatang and I had first met, when he'd accepted my gift of the old book, he reminded me of my father. He looked on me with such love, simply for doing what I considered a matter of diplomacy. I could see how my father's subjects had been motivated to please him. Thanks given heartily is a gift, in and of itself. I hadn't really taken the time to thank my parents for the blessings they'd bestowed on me and wished there were some way they could know my thoughts across the sea.

Despite these momentary lapses into self pity and longings for my family, I couldn't help but feel blessed once again; an island full of friendly natives and a princess near coming of age. Of all the places I could have been shipwrecked, this wasn't bad.

'We understand that you know little of the book you gave us,' Tatang said, 'but we know that you've had a long journey and are in need of rejuvenation so we won't trouble you with a discussion of our beliefs at this time.'

I'd been longing to find out what the book contained but had been reluctant to ask about it for fear of breaking taboos. Tatang's mention of the book gave me an opening to the subject, so I replied.

'Oh no, it's no trouble at all. I'd like to know the significance of that book and to have you tell me about all your beliefs. Part of my education as a prince has been religious. I've already studied all the holy books as a requirement prior to my Manly Voyage, all of them, that is, except the one I gave you. It was a holy book, wasn't it?'

'Yes,' Tatang answered. 'If a book can be holy, it certainly is. My most gifted men have read through its entire contents this very afternoon and I myself have read no small part of it.'

Tatang's retort was more knowing than I would have expected from someone on such a remote island. Only someone with religious training would have recognized, as he had, that *no book* can be looked to as an *idol* though its writings may be perfect and true.

'This book is so precious to us. It tells us many things which our own books have told us yet from a different perspective. It doesn't contradict the former holy books we've used and so you see, we're quite amazed.[20] You've most certainly blessed us by coming here with such a gift. We'll be up late into the night reading from this new book and praying. Will you join us?'

'Yes, I'd love to.' I said.

The little children clapped their hands together. They'd been sitting at my sides inspecting my different style of clothing and admiring the signet ring my father had given me. Though beautiful, the signet ring was not much use for making purchases on my father's account. Nobody here had even heard of him.

Elkanah was getting his share of the children's' attention too. They were clamoring to sit on his lap. He didn't have to do anything more than act like the grandpa that he was, to make them happy.

Tatang's eyes were fixed on my signet ring.

'Our book has a story about a young man who was given a ring such as yours. I've never seen one before. Isn't it true, that with such a ring, you may stamp a contract and your debtors will know that if payment isn't forthcoming, your father will make good on your behalf?'

'Yes, that is true in my kingdom.'

'And so shall it be true in my kingdom; up to the dowry of seven princess brides.'

Sarapita took my hand and lifted it close to her face so she could get a good look at my ring.

'It has very delicate and tiny inscriptions on it.' She said.

'Yes,' I answered, 'and those inscriptions were made by my father's chief artisan in such a way that no one else could duplicate the mark made with this ring.'

'So it is indeed like the ring in this story.' Tatang said, lifting the prized book I had given him.

'Oh Tatang!' the children shouted, 'Please tell us the story of the ring.'

Tatang gave them a stern but gentle look and they quieted down.

'Of course. I can't deny you a good story,' he said. 'and it comes from the very book that Prince John gave us. The Prophet in this book told a story of two sons.'

Tatang translated as he read the book which was written in a different language than his own.

'A certain man had two sons and the younger son said to his father, Father, give me the portion of goods that I will inherit; So the father divided his wealth between his two sons. A few days later, the younger son gathered all of his wealth together and left on a journey that took him to a far kingdom. There he wasted all his wealth with unrighteous living. When he had spent everything, a great famine came on that land; and he became needy. He became a servant to a citizen of that kingdom; and was sent into the fields to feed the pigs. He wished he could eat the husks that the pigs were given and no one had pity on him. When he came to his senses, he said, How many hired servants of my father's have bread enough to spare, and I am dying with hunger! I'll get up and go to my father, and will say to him, *Father, I have sinned against heaven, and against you and I'm no more worthy to be called your son: make me one of your servants,* and that's exactly what he did. Now when he was still a long way off, his father saw him, and had compassion, and ran, and fell on his neck, and kissed him and the son said to him, *Father, I have sinned against heaven, and in your sight, and I'm no more worthy to be called your son.* But the father said to his servants, *Bring out the best robe, and put it on him; and put a ring on his hand, and shoes on his feet. And bring out the fatted calf, and kill it; and let us eat, and be merry: For this, my son was dead, and is alive again; he was lost, and is found.* And they began to be merry. Now his elder son was in the field: and as he came and drew nigh to the house, he heard music and dancing. And he called one of the servants, and asked what these things meant. And he said unto him, *your brother has come; and your father has killed the fatted calf, because he has come home safe and sound.* And he was angry, and would not go in: therefore his father came out, and spoke with him. And he answered his father, *These many years I've served you and haven't disobeyed anything which you have asked and yet you never gave me a baby goat, that I might make merry with my friends: But as soon as this son of yours came, which has devoured your living with harlots, you have killed the fatted calf for him.* And the father said to him, *Son, you are always with me, and all that I have is yours. It was right that we should make merry, and be glad: for this, your brother was dead, and is alive again; and was lost, and is found.*'[21]

'*Praise God! Alleluia! The Lord is wonderful!*' The table erupted with shouts. I'd never heard such a joyous commotion.

'Excuse us!' Sarapita shouted as she danced, shaking a tambourine. 'We've never heard this story before. It's so wonderful. God has blessed us so much that you brought this book. We were told of its existence but only now do we know its wonder!' She continued dancing and shaking the tambourine as she laughed, then she sang.

Sarapita's voice was like nothing I'd ever heard. Her melody and words sang praises to an Almighty that I had known far too little. She sang with joy of His love and of His forgiveness. She danced as if He Himself were holding her in His hand, and truly, it were as if, suspended in air, she moved about.[22]

I was trying to figure out the meaning of the story that they felt was so wondrous. They couldn't all be crazy. There must be something grand in the story that I had missed. How could they see it so clearly and yet I saw nothing but an ungrateful son.[23] I even wondered if Tatang were insinuating with the story that I had left home in some improper manner, but he had already anticipated what I was thinking.

'John, I know that you left home to please your parents and to become a man. Your ring just reminded me of the story. Please don't take offense.'

'Oh, I don't take offense at all. However, I'd like to hear the meaning of the story. Did the prophet explain it?'

'I believe He did, John, in what He said just before telling the story. He said there is joy in the presence of the angels of God over one sinner that repents.[24] The youngest son represents us.'

I couldn't help but wonder how he could compare those of us who sat around that grand table with the youngest son who'd spent his money with harlots. I was sure that if it weren't for their book none of them would have even known what a harlot was. Certainly someone at the table must be sharing my horror at Tatang's comparison, especially his wives. Again, Tatang read my thoughts.

'We have all put other *gods* in the place of the one true God, and by doing so, we have not only become like the youngest son but like the harlot herself, who has put many men in place of one husband. When we put our own selfish desires ahead of God's desire for our lives, haven't we forsaken our Master?'[25]

'So we who are not holy men are nothing more than harlots?' I asked. The king was ready for my question.

'There is none Holy but the Lord. Even so called holy men do not create themselves and can never repay the debt they owe to God!'[26] Then with a smile and a wink, Tatang politely offered, 'We can change the subject if it offends you.'

Tatang's ominous sermon was tempered by his gentle and personal manner so that it was difficult to remain offended for long.

'Not at all,' I said. 'The truth shall prevail.'

And to that they all shouted,

'Let it be so!'

All the while I'd been talking with Tatang, Sarapita and Zuah had been gazing up at me. The fire danced in their dark eyes like shooting stars in a night sky. Every once in a while one of them would sigh, then they'd whisper something to each other and giggle.

Tatang interrupted their fascination,

'Will you stop whispering about John's eyes and tell him outright that you adore them!'

'Oh, sorry Tang, ' Sarapita admitted, 'I've been rude.'

'John,' she addressed me, 'you have the most beautiful eyes and I do adore them.' She cocked her head slightly to the side and gazed deeper. 'Do all the men in your kingdom have such eyes?'

I was taken aback by the directness of Sarapita's compliment and inquiry. She spoke from the heart.

'W...well thank you very much,' I don't think I'd ever stuttered before that moment. 'My eyes are uncommon in my kingdom as well. They are the eyes of my mother.'

Zuah now blurted out,

'I'm sure she could have attracted any prince with those eyes!'

Then Zuah put her hand over her mouth, embarrassed by the spontaneity of her own words. She hadn't gotten used to the fact that her mouth was already covered by her veil. I could see her childlike directness would never leave her; a blessing for her future husband.

'Now your face has changed to such a beautiful rosy hue.'

Sarapita touched my face as she spoke. 'It's so warm, and your eyes now, I don't believe it! Look Zuah, his eyes now change, you see? They weren't that color before! His eyes have changed from one beautiful mosaic to another.'

Zuah got up so close to my face that, for a moment, I thought she was going to kiss me. She looked deep into my eyes.

'We call the kind of eyes that I have, hazel.' I said, 'My mother's eyes would change their color every time my father touched her.'

I hadn't realized the significance of what I'd said till the words left my mouth; that Sarapita could affect the color of my eyes by the mere touch of her hand. Were my eyes revealing a destiny that Sarapita and I shared?

'Enough with the eyes for now!' Tatang chided the girls. 'There'll be plenty of time for that later. Now John, we're just very glad to have you as our guest. I only hope that my family doesn't so spoil you with compliments that your good nature will be changed to vanity.'

'I'll do my best to avoid that pitfall.' I said, 'All would do well to avoid conceit.'[27]

Again, they shouted, 'Let it be so!'

They surely loved saying *let it be so.* It seemed to be a habit associated with their beliefs. When they heard something that seemed wise they would say, *let it be so.*

'On behalf of Elkanah and myself,' I told them, 'I want you to know that we're so glad that you're watching over us.'

'It's the Lord who watches over you.' Tatang replied, 'We're only his tools. He's blessed us by using us for this purpose. We're sure that he has a reason for putting a prince into our midst.'

'Of course it may simply have been to deliver the great book. In which case, a beast may tear you apart as you sleep!' Sarapita quipped.

'In that case, maybe you girls had better keep close watch over John tonight.' Tatang advised.

'We will. We will.' They said dutifully, not realizing he'd been teasing.

I was beginning to feel very much a part of Tatang's family. They prayed with me and they kidded me. The young women made clear their interest in me and the children curiously asked questions.

We finished eating our dinner and it was time for dessert. There were all kinds of special dishes. One of them was a plate of betel nuts delicately wrapped in spiced samat leaves. I'd chewed betel nuts before but didn't care for their bitter taste. I was relieved when Zuah poured me a cup of coffee which gave me an excuse to decline the betel. Chewing betel nuts colors the teeth an amber red within minutes and the stain lasts for days. Bachelor prince that I was, I didn't want anything so disgusting on my teeth. I gave in, however, noticing that most of the young ladies were chewing it.

Sarapita kidded, 'What a shame; if you'd eaten the betel nut earlier, it would have matched your face!'

They all laughed. Would they ever tire of kidding! I didn't mind, though. Their laughing let me know that they weren't afraid of me.

Tatang was a forthright man. I intuitively trusted that he was sincere and would do nothing to dishonor God. Even though I'd been trained to defend the faith with great fervor and had even been taught questionable methods for tearing down religions that didn't agree with mine; I'd grown too fond of Tatang to do that. Besides, I was certain he could have held his own.

I'd heard of pagans who knelt down before dumb statues made by man and I pitied them.[28] Now I envied Tatang who seemed able to see his God more clearly by lifting up his hands to heaven than the pagans could see Him in the little figures they prayed to. The pagan's god was so small that they could place it on the hearth. The God my mother prayed to held the heavens in His hands. I was sure this was Tatang's God as well.

I had a premonition that the Lord was going to use Tatang to deliver a special message to me that evening. First a dream, now a premonition? Odd combination for a prince who'd given little thought to religious matters before finding himself shipwrecked on an island with strangers. Right on cue, Tatang interrupted my thoughts.

'John, I have been holding Sarapita back for too many years. If I delay further she will no longer be suitable for marriage. She's having her coming of age party a week from today. It will be her eighteenth birthday. You are invited.'

The king's words astonished me. I could never have guessed that Sarapita had been a woman for so many years. Maybe it was the fact that she was so tiny, or that her childlike femininity had not been marred with excessive pride, but she didn't appear a day over twelve. I gave the king no delay in answering.

'As we sit here tonight, so shall I be there!'

The now familiar 'Let it be so!' resounded around the table.

Yesterday, I became a man. By next week, a husband?"

Chapter 15 Footnotes

1. John 17:14-16 I have given them thy word; and the world hath hated them, because they are not of the world, even as I am not of the world. I pray not that thou shouldest take them out of the world, but that thou shouldest keep them from the evil. They are not of the world, even as I am not of the world.

2. Solomon's sin was not that he married many wives but that he married wives of unbelieving nations who practiced idolatry.
Nehemiah 13:26-27 Did not Solomon king of Israel sin by these things? yet among many nations was there no king like him, who was beloved of his God, and God made him king over all Israel: nevertheless even him did outlandish women cause to sin. Shall we then hearken unto you to do all this great evil, to transgress against our God in marrying strange wives?

3. Ecclesiastes 2:8 I also gathered for myself silver and gold and the treasure of kings and provinces; I got singers, both men and women, and many concubines, man's delight. RSV Bible

4. Proverbs 11:16 A gracious woman retains honor: and strong men retain riches.

5. Isaiah 5:20 Woe unto them that call evil good, and good evil; that put darkness for light, and light for darkness; that put bitter for sweet, and sweet for bitter.

6. A man may not marry a wife that he has divorced if she has been with any other man after the divorce. Deuteronomy 24:3,4 And [if] the latter husband hate her, and write her a bill of divorcement, and giveth [it] in her hand, and sendeth her out of his house; or if the latter husband die, which took her [to be] his wife; Her former husband, which sent her away, may not take her again to be his wife, after that she is defiled; for that [is] abomination before the LORD: and thou shalt not cause the land to sin, which the LORD thy God giveth thee [for] an inheritance.

7. Ephesians 5:23 For the husband is the head of the wife, even as Christ is the Head of the Church: and he is the saviour of the

body.
Now in Romans 12:4-5 Paul also said,
"For as we have many members in one body, and all members have not the same office: So we, [being] many, are one body in Christ, and every one members one of another."
Let's consider; Believers have one head and that is Christ and He has one body which has many members, each of them a believer. If this metaphor is taken plainly as it was written in the Bible then a woman who is married has one head but that head (the husband) has one body which has many members, each of them one of his wives. There is no hocus pocus here, no twisting, the metaphor is plain since we are not using it to overturn a command.
8. Proverbs 13:1 A wise son heareth his father's instruction: but a scorner heareth not rebuke.
Proverbs 15:5 A fool despiseth his father's instruction: but he that regardeth reproof is prudent.
9. Revelation 3:15-16 I know thy works, that thou art neither cold nor hot: I would thou wert cold or hot. So then because thou art lukewarm, and neither cold nor hot, I will spue thee out of my mouth.
10. Genesis 3:16 Unto the woman he said, I will greatly multiply thy sorrow and thy conception; in sorrow thou shalt bring forth children; *and thy desire shall be to thy husband*, and **he shall rule over thee.**
In addition to this verse telling us that the man has authority over the woman, it tells us that the woman's desire shall be to have control over her husband. The Hebrew that is translated here as *desire shall be to* actually means *to have control over*. The same form is used in God's warning to Cain that sin's desire shall be for him (Cain) but that Cain must rule over him (sin.)
Genesis 4:7 If thou doest well, shalt thou not be accepted? and if thou doest not well, sin lieth at the door. And *unto thee shall be his desire*, and thou shalt rule over him.
We can gather from this verse that we are not only forbidden from allowing sin to rule over us but we are also forbidden from allowing our wives to rule over us. In addition, as we are to rule over sin, to prevent it from causing us to err, we are every bit as much commanded to rule over our wives so that we do not allow them to cause us to err.

1 Timothy 6:1 Let as many servants as are under the yoke count their own masters worthy of all honour, that the name of God and his doctrine be not blasphemed.

11. Isaiah 3:12 As for my people, children are their oppressors, and **women rule over them**. O my people, they which lead thee **cause thee to err**, and destroy the way of thy paths.

12. Proverbs 25:6 Do not put yourself forward in the presence of the king, and do not stand in the place of great men: For better it is that it be said to you, Come up closer; than you should be put lower in the presence of the prince whose eyes you have seen.

Luke 14:7-11 And he put forth a parable to those which were bidden, when he marked how they chose out the chief rooms; saying unto them, When thou art bidden of any man to a wedding, sit not down in the highest room; lest a more honourable man than thou be bidden of him; And he that bade thee and him come and say to thee, Give this man place; and thou begin with shame to take the lowest room. But when thou art bidden, go and sit down in the lowest room; that when he that bade thee cometh, he may say unto thee, Friend, go up higher: then shalt thou have worship in the presence of them that sit at meat with thee. For whosoever exalteth himself shall be abased; and he that humbleth himself shall be exalted.

13. Proverbs 1:7a The fear of the LORD is the beginning of knowledge.

Matthew 10:28 And fear not them which kill the body, but are not able to kill the soul: but rather fear him which is able to destroy both soul and body in hell.

14. Romans 10:12 For there is no difference between the Jew and the Greek: for the same *Lord over all* is rich unto all that call upon him.

1 Kings 8:39 Then hear Thou in heaven Thy dwelling place, and forgive, and do, and give to every man according to his ways, whose heart Thou knowest; (for Thou, even *Thou only, knowest the hearts of all the children of men;*)

John 1:3 All things were made by him; and without him was not any thing made that was made.

1 John 4:18 There is no fear in love; but *perfect love casteth out fear*: because fear hath torment. He that feareth is not made perfect in love.

Matthew 7:13-14 Enter ye in at the strait gate: for wide is the gate, and broad is the way, that leadeth to destruction, and many there be which go in thereat: 14 Because strait is the gate, and *narrow is the way, which leadeth unto life*, and few there be that find it. ."

Hebrews 10:21-22 And having a high priest {Jesus} over the house of God; Let us draw near with a true heart in *full assurance* of faith, having our hearts sprinkled from an evil conscience, and our bodies washed with pure water.

Matthew 25:34 Then shall the King say unto them on his right hand, Come, ye blessed of my Father, inherit the kingdom prepared for you from the foundation of the world.

Romans 5:8 But God commendeth his love toward us, in that, *while we were yet sinners, Christ died for us.*

Psalm 112:6-7 Surely he shall not be moved for ever: the righteous shall be in everlasting remembrance. He shall not be afraid of evil tidings: *his heart is fixed, trusting in the LORD.*

The Lord stirs even the spirits of unbelievers as King Jochan had prayed:

Ezra 1:1b-2 The LORD stirred up the spirit of Cyrus king of Persia, that he made a proclamation throughout all his kingdom, and put it also in writing, saying, Thus saith Cyrus king of Persia, The LORD God of heaven hath given me all the kingdoms of the earth; and he hath charged me to build him an house at Jerusalem, which is in Judah.

15. Jesus referred to himself as God by using the Name God used for Himself when speaking with Moses.

Exodus 3:14b Thus shalt thou say unto the children of Israel, I AM hath sent me unto you.

John 8:58-59 Jesus said unto them, Verily, verily, I say unto you, Before Abraham was, *I am*. Then took they up stones to cast at him: but Jesus hid himself, and went out of the temple, going through the midst of them, and so passed by.

It's clear that the Jews understood Jesus to be calling Himself God since they picked up stones to cast at him after he referred to Himself as "*I am*," the Name that God called Himself to Moses.

16. Romans 8:28 And we know that all things work together for good to them that love God, *to them who are the called according to [his] purpose.*

2Corinthians 12:9 And he said unto me, *My grace is sufficient for*

thee: for my *strength is made perfect in weakness*. Most gladly therefore will I rather glory in my infirmities, that the power of Christ may rest upon me.
Matthew 17:20 And Jesus said unto them, Because of your unbelief: for verily I say unto you, *If ye have faith as a grain of mustard seed,* ye shall say unto this mountain, Remove hence to yonder place; and it shall remove; and nothing shall be impossible unto you.
Ephesians 2:8-9 For by grace are ye saved through faith; and that not of yourselves: [it is] the gift of God: Not of works, lest any man should boast.
2 Thessalonians 1:8-9 In flaming fire taking vengeance on them that know not God, and that obey not the gospel of our Lord Jesus Christ: Who shall be punished with everlasting destruction from the presence of the Lord, and from the glory of his power.
17. Acts 17:31 Because he hath appointed a day, in the which he will judge the world in righteousness by [that] man whom he hath ordained; [whereof] he hath given assurance unto all [men], in that he hath raised him from the dead.
Hebrews 4:16 Let us therefore come boldly unto the throne of grace, that we may obtain mercy, and find grace to help in time of need.
Hebrews 13:5-6 [Let your] conversation [be] without covetousness; [and be] content with such things as ye have: for he hath said, I will never leave thee, nor forsake thee. So that we may boldly say, The Lord [is] my helper, and I will not fear what man shall do unto me.
18. Luke 15:6 And when he cometh home, he calleth together [his] friends and neighbours, saying unto them, Rejoice with me; for I have found my sheep which was lost.
19. Proverbs 16:24 Pleasant words [are as] an honeycomb, sweet to the soul, and health to the bones.
20. 1 Corinthians 14:32-33 And the spirits of the prophets are subject to the prophets. For God is not [the author] of confusion, but of peace, as in all churches of the saints.
21. Luke 15:11-32 Parable of the prodigal son.
22. Psalm 139:10 Even there shall thy hand lead me, and thy right hand shall hold me.
23. Isaiah 44:18 They have not known nor understood: for he hath

shut their eyes, that they cannot see; [and] their hearts, that they cannot understand.
24. Luke 15:10 Likewise, I say unto you, there is joy in the presence of the angels of God over one sinner that repenteth.
25. James 4:4 Ye adulteresses, know ye not that the friendship of the world is enmity with God? whosoever therefore will be a friend of the world is the enemy of God.
26. 1Samuel 2:2 [There is] none holy as the LORD: for [there is] none beside thee: neither [is there] any rock like our God.
Romans 4:4-8 Now to him that worketh is the reward not reckoned of grace, but of debt. But to him that worketh not, but believeth on him that justifieth the ungodly, his faith is counted for righteousness. Even as David also describeth the blessedness of the man, unto whom God imputeth righteousness without works, [Saying], Blessed [are] they whose iniquities are forgiven, and whose sins are covered. Blessed [is] the man to whom the Lord will not impute sin.
27. Proverbs 26:12 Seest thou a man wise in his own conceit? [there is] more hope of a fool than of him.
28. 1 Corinthians 12:2 Ye know that ye were Gentiles, carried away unto these dumb idols, even as ye were led.
Revelation 9:20 And the rest of the men which were not killed by these plagues yet repented not of the works of their hands, that they should not worship devils, and idols of gold, and silver, and brass, and stone, and of wood: which neither can see, nor hear, nor walk.

Chapter 16

COMING OF AGE
PRINCE JOHN'S STORY CONTINUES

"It had only been a week since Tatang had announced the Coming of Age party for his daughter, Princess Sarapita, yet it seemed it had been months. Studying under King Jochan had brought time to a standstill. He so filled my days with study of the Scriptures that a day under his tutelage was like weeks spent engaging in pastimes. He did little editorializing. He had a method of cross referencing Scripture. He would teach me the proverb and then show me every other verse that shared the same principle. However, I felt a growing tension such as I'd never experienced before; a tension between a dark evil hidden deep within me and the light of the gospel that Tatang was teaching. The more that the king taught me, the more I felt I could never bridge that gap. We'd completed all the proverbs of King Solomon as well as Ecclesiastes, a book I'd not heard of before my studies under the king. Today we'd begin our study of Isaiah 53. I looked forward to this day passing. It was Sarapita's birthday and tonight would be her coming of age party.

I sat down for my lessons with Tatang. Unlike the teachers I was accustomed to, he was teaching me that I was to know the truth directly from the Scriptures. The Scriptures, not his opinions, would form the basis for my beliefs. He taught me that by learning the Scriptures in the historical order of their writing, I could more fully understand what followed and that I could also test men to see if they were false prophets.[1] Today Tatang entered the room nervously. He seemed distracted about something.

'Your Elkanah, he is... full of prophesies. Time will tell.'

'What has he prophesied today?' I asked.

'We can save any talk of Elkanah till after your lessons. I want to make some serious progress today.'

'Sure, where will we begin, Tatang?'

'We'll start as planned.'

'Okay,' I said, 'I have the Scripture you gave me, Isaiah 53.'[2]

'Please read it.' He said.

I read the entire chapter out loud and after I was finished, Tatang asked me to read verse ten again.

Yet it pleased the LORD to bruise him; he hath put Him to grief: when thou shalt make his soul an offering for sin, he shall see his seed, he shall prolong his days, and the pleasure of the LORD shall prosper in his hand.

Who is this man, Tatang, and what is this prophesy?'

'He is what the Scriptures have referred to as the Messiah. The messenger of God, the Son of God. Coming from the Father in heaven to us, as a man.[3]'

'A man offered for sin? A God man? This is what you believe?'

'Yes, but let me first give you some background on the verses you're reading. The chapter you're reading was written over twenty seven hundred years ago. That's over seven hundred years before the Messiah died for our sins. You're right that it is a prophesy. Many times prophesies are written as if the event has already occurred.'

'Yes, it did sound like it was something that had already happened at the time it was written.'

'Well, there is a reason for that, John. God sees events well before they happen. Do you believe that?'

'Of course! God is all knowing. All includes the future, right?'

'Well said, John. Now at the time this verse was written, the sacrifice for sins was a burnt offering and other types of sin offerings, but as you can read, this verse says the Man, elsewhere referred to as the Messiah, will have His soul made an offering for sin.'

'So it is really true that you believe that this man, Jesus, died for our sins?'

'May I answer that question by telling you about the man who brought my ancestors the Bible we are reading today?'

Tatang had broken from his traditional way of teaching and was about to tell me something I'd longed to hear, how he'd come by all his books and his Bibles and how he'd learned to read such strange languages.

'Well of course! I've been waiting to hear about that.'

'Over three hundred years ago,' Tatang began, 'a badly battered ship arrived in the very same harbor where you arrived. Only a handful of the crew survived. Within weeks they went mad, killing each other. Only one remained. His name was Jochan Jansen. He was a visionary and a very rich man. He'd brought with him his entire library which was made up of hundreds of titles. For each title there were eight copies. He explained to my ancestors that he'd planned to establish seven libraries across the seven seas and that the eighth copy of each title was for his personal library. When my ancestors first helped Brother Jansen, he had a bad case of humidity fever. Because of this they placed him in one of our low humidity huts. These are huts that have a mixture of salts placed in trays beneath the floorboards. The mixture of salts absorbs the water from the air. At the end of each day, the mixture is thrown out along with the water it has absorbed and replenished with fresh salts. The mixture is not the type of salt we eat but looks like salt and serves the purpose of reducing humidity wonderfully. We have endless supplies of it in our caverns. When Brother Jansen came out of his fever we helped him to build a library out of Ironwood and built special dehumidifying trays in the floorboards throughout the library so that his books would be well preserved. Furthermore, the shelves of the library were made of mahogany to keep away bugs. His library is in perfect condition as we speak, just as if it were built yesterday.[4] I'll show it to you later. I'm sure you'll find the library an amazing part of my kingdom's history. If you wish, we'll teach you German and English so that you may read his books.'

'I'd love that, Tatang.'

'Now Brother Jansen met with much difficulty in bringing my people to accept what the Bible taught so he stopped teaching and began praying. Everyday, he'd shut himself up in his library and do nothing but study and pray. It was our custom not to mistreat the insane so my ancestors fed him and provided him with refreshment. They were convinced he was quite mad just as his shipmates had been. After some time though, my ancestors were brought to a saving knowledge of the Messiah.'

'I had a dream last night about your God, or should I say, my God.'

'What do you mean your God?'

'I don't know if you'd call it a dream or a vision. I could feel it pushing in on me.'

'What do you mean pushing in on you!'

Tatang seemed irritated, as if I was talking about some taboo subject.

'Well, there were voices of people praying for me. It wasn't our language but even so, I understood the meaning as if I spoke their tongue. They were praying,

Dear God, reach out to those lost souls who have never heard the gospel. Touch them in dreams and visions. Pray that they will know your salvation. Reach the hardest of hearts and melt that hardness and replace it with love and thanksgiving. Give them the time and place for all the rest of your word to be explained to them and do not let them backslide.'[5]

'Who told you this? Who told you the rest of the story of our ancestors so that you might take it for your own! Who told you that it was through visions that we came to know the Lord? Who?'

I stepped back. I wanted no trouble. I knew nothing of the story he referred to. Last night, before the dream, I would have loved a confrontation with Tatang. Before my dream, the warm feelings that I had for him on that first night of our arrival had disappeared. I'd grown to hate him for what I considered his blasphemies. I'd planned to kill him this very morning but last night's dream changed everything. After the dream I was different. I was a new creation. I was no longer a man with murderous thoughts who hated anyone who dared speak directly to our Lord. I myself was speaking directly to the Lord and He was answering. I was different, no longer the prince, but servant to a Prince. The kingdom I now sought was not my own but my Lord's. As I stepped back from Tatang, I took off my coat which contained a noose and other deadly weapons, the weapons I'd been taught to use since childhood by my father and my uncles. I handed the coat to him. I removed my belt with my daggers and sword in their sheaths and dropped them at his feet.

'I'd planned to kill you this morning but after my vision I could never do it. Your teachings angered me, but when the Lord touched me in my dream, I knew that even the sins that lay at my door[6] had no power to destroy me, for Christ had triumphed over them, nailing them to his cross.'[7]

I knelt down at Tatang's feet.

'Forgive me for having planned your execution. Baptize me now!'

Tatang's eyes showed his confusion. He knew when I landed on this island that I was not saved but had not seen how black my heart was. I'd fooled myself also with my princely upbringing and my *charity*, but all my righteous deeds were as filthy rags[8]. *I* was the infidel. *I* put ritual above a true relationship with the Lord. *I* admired those who performed their memorized prayers in public, more than those who showed a godly example in their deeds.[9] This was why Tatang's personal relationship with the Lord had so angered me. Who was he to think that he could speak directly with God as a forgiven one? Who was he to think he could be certain of his own salvation before he'd died and stood before the Lord Himself? He didn't go to prayers at set times each day. He hadn't even built a house of worship. Those were my thoughts before I slept the night before. Tatang never had a chance of reaching me. This is why the prayers of the saved that went out for the lost souls in distant lands had found me. My heart was so hard that there could have been no other way to reach me but through the prayers of the saved, and that, only while I slept.

'Baptize me now!' I shouted again.

My eyes were now filled with tears. King Jochan's family and other members of the royal family came out to see what was going on. Sarapita, Zuah, and the children were there. Elkanah was also there. Then something quite amazing happened. I shouted,

'Baptize me in the Name of the Father, and of the Son, and of the Holy Spirit.'[10]

Then one of the tribe exclaimed.

'He speaks German! Did you hear that.'

Another said.

'What are you talking about, it was English he spoke. That was straight out of the King James Bible.'

Then Sarapita spoke.

'No, he now speaks our language. He speaks it clearly now. Who's been teaching him?'

'Prophesy again John!' Tatang pulled my arm. Words now

tumbled out of my mouth.

'So we, being many, are one body in Christ, and every one members one of another. Having then gifts differing according to the grace that is given to us, whether prophecy, let us prophesy according to the proportion of faith.'[11]

Sarapita now said, 'You are right, It was German.'

Another said, 'What? I heard our language.'

I spoke again involuntarily.

'Now when this was noised abroad, the multitude came together, and were confounded, because that every man heard them speak in his own language.'[12]

'Praise God!'

'Alleluia!'

The king's court was now filled with praise for God but Tatang quickly brought order.

'John has in fact spoken in many tongues. We have all heard! This will surely strengthen our faith, and more. Let us be thankful for these two saved souls, Prince John and Elkanah.' But before the king had finished his sentence, some in the courtyard and others pouring in from the streets were crying and shouting.

'I've not known the Lord till this moment. Baptize me again.'

'Me too.' Another cried and others shouted similar things.

The king, now preacher, took me to a trough behind the courtyard that was used for watering the livestock and plunged me under the water.

'I baptize you in the Name of the Father, and of the Son, and of the Holy Spirit.'

'Let it be so!' Roared those who watched.

'Baptize me also.' Elkanah said as he approached the king.

Now King Jochan plunged Elkanah beneath the water and repeated:

'I baptize you in the Name of the Father, and of the Son, and of the Holy Spirit.'

'Let it be so!' The onlookers roared.

The king now announced.

'I will continue baptizing until everyone who wants to be rebaptized has had their chance. It looks like we've had many hypocrites among us. Let's rejoice that the power of God has been seen today and may these new believers now accept their place not only in this kingdom but in the Lord's kingdom. Let it also be known that we have a prophet among us. That prophet is Elkanah. This morning, Elkanah prophesied that Prince John would kneel before me and ask to be baptized. This prophecy has been fulfilled! Let us now have Elkanah tell us the rest of the prophecy.'

Elkanah stood next to Tatang.

'I saw Prince John kneel before the king as he has already told you but my vision did not end there. In my vision I also saw Princess Sarapita kneel before Prince John and accept his offer of marriage and I saw her enter the marriage chamber with King Jochan's blessing.'

'Let it be so!' Decreed Tatang.

'Let it be so!' The rest shouted, *except for Sarapita* who quickly disappeared into her quarters.

Zuah took this opportunity to lead me to a hillside just outside the palace walls. She sat me down on a bench that had a view of the king's highway and took her spot next to me. From where we sat we could see tens of thousands of King Jochan's subjects riding in coaches, on horseback, and walking along the sidewalks, to meet the groom who would marry Princess Sarapita. They'd also heard of my conversion through the drum beats that had been echoing from the palace walls. As they approached they closed in around me, not out of curiosity but to greet me. They wanted to welcome me, not just to their kingdom but to the kingdom of God.

I said to Zuah, 'I'm just a new believer. I don't deserve the respect I'm receiving from these people.'

'*You may be a new believer but you'll soon be heir to the throne of Sumba.* From death's door to Prince of Sumba, that's quite a jump.'

'Death's door?'

'You don't think the king has body guards?[13] They were watching your every move. What man wears a coat as heavy as the one you were wearing in this heat? It was clear that you were heavily armed and well trained in killing as any prince would be. You don't think that the king saw the anger growing in your eyes? We saw it, all of us. I'm so glad you've found the Lord.' Zuah now touched my hand. She was sobbing as she put her head on my shoulder. 'You'll learn. Christians are the fiercest soldiers. Every one of them will fight to the death for their freedom and for their king whether earthly or in heaven. I'm so glad the Lord preserved you for this day. We were afraid that we'd lose you.'

'Why is it that Christians are such fierce fighters, Zuah?'

'It's because our faith is the only faith that teaches that you will not enter the kingdom of heaven without accepting its God. We would die rather than place a ruler above our God.'[14]

'Wait, my former religion was like that.'

'No, John, your religion required that people *say* that they agreed with it. That religion is more concerned with conformity and what a man *says* than what's in his heart. True Christianity says that each man finds his path to the Lord voluntarily. Without this voluntary acceptance of the Lord, the churches are destroyed. Even when conversion is voluntary, there are hypocrites enough. If it were mandatory, nearly all converts would be hypocrites.'

'I guess that's why one hundred percent of the people in my kingdom claim to agree with its religion. If they said otherwise, they'd be put to death for blasphemy, but my mother was spared that.'

'Your mother?'

'Yes, she didn't read holy books the way the so called holy men did. She spoke of forgiveness and repentance. We just thought it was her weakness, and because my father was the king she was able to say what she liked inside the palace. I suppose that's why my father would never let her leave the palace grounds without him.'

'So you believe that your mother may even be a Christian?'

'I think so. She used to whisper in my ear when I was a child, saying,

The Lord is calling you. Will you follow Him?

To which I was expected to reply,

Yes, and may the Lord use me to deliver His followers from the hands of the infidels.[15]

She was the one who taught me to pray. She said,

You must know there is one true God and He alone you must follow. Pray to Him no matter where you are and He will lead you to the truth. Do not fear the infidels for there are some among them who you shall lead and there are those among them who will lead you to the water that takes away all thirst.

Have I found this water that takes away all thirst? Is Jesus that living water, Zuah?'

'For a new Christian, the Lord has surely blessed you with wisdom, John. Absolutely, that's what it means. Jesus said,

Whosoever drinks of the water that I shall give him shall never thirst; but the water that I shall give him shall be in him a well of water springing up into everlasting life.'[16]

'Then my mother was a Christian. I wish there were some way that she could know I have accepted her Lord as my Lord.'

'She already knows, John. As you were prophesying today I had a vision. I saw her thanking the Lord for your salvation.'[17]

'I believe you, Zuah. I believe you. I never imagined that I could be here like this when I left home. I was sure that I would die. I had a vision, even then. I was being drowned in water over and over but I kept coming up for air. It was only after last night's dream that I knew the meaning of my vision; that I would die to sin so that I might live a new life in Jesus.'[18]

Zuah now began to look at me differently. I'd seen that look before. It was the look that Princess Kasmina gave me.

'You're a Christian now. Do you know what that means, John?'

'Well, of course. It means that I'm not alone; that what strength I do not have I can ask from the Lord and He will never leave me nor forsake me.'[19]

Zuah smiled and looked me directly in the eyes.

'Yes, John, it means that, but it also means that you are no longer limited to a certain number of wives, that you are no longer limited to marrying princesses, and that you may marry any maiden who is a Christian.'

'But in my kingdom, the niece of the king is a princess. I could have married you even if I'd not become a Christian.'

'Ah, but I could not have married you.' Zuah said, 'A Christian may only marry another Christian.'[20]

'So you're glad that you can marry me now?'

'Oh no, I am only glad that you have come to know the Lord. You may marry whoever has eyes for you.' Then Zuah spoke frankly. 'Of course! What girl in the kingdom wouldn't want a tall handsome prince for her husband. You think I'm crazy or something?'

'One of a kind would be the word. You're Zuah, the available, the mature and the graceful, a maiden, ripe for the picking.'

'Such a memory!' Zuah giggled. 'You're forgetting. You'll be wed tonight. It's been prophesied by your... What is Elkanah to you anyway?'

'He's the father of my mother's delightful little servant girl, Hadassah; strong but delicate.'

'We must ask your Elkanah if he's had any visions concerning your Hadassah. Maybe she's had a dream too.'

'Hadassah has been at my mother's side for many years. They're inseparable. Hadassah is... she's a Christian! I remember a hymn that she and my mother would sing when my father would shush them and make them return to their quarters. The words were,

He dwells in the high and holy place, with Him also that is of a contrite and humble spirit,

This is speaking of Jesus!

to revive the spirit of the humble, and to revive the heart of the contrite ones.

That's us by God's grace!'

'They made a song of that? How wonderful!' Zuah pulled out her Bible. 'Here it is, Isaiah 57:15. I'll read it. 'I dwell in the high and holy place, with him also that is of a contrite and humble spirit, to revive the spirit of the humble, and to revive the heart of the contrite ones.''[21]

'This is astounding! How is it that my people can read this verse and not know what it's about. What's even more astounding is that I've never found much to talk about with a woman and now I'm talking about everything with you.'

I could hear music now coming from the palace. Sarapita's Coming of Age party had begun. I was sorry that my conversation with Zuah had to end so soon but I was looking forward to greeting Sarapita on her first day as a woman.

'We must go now, John. Your bride awaits you.'

I walked back inside the king's gate both confused and clear of mind. In many ways I now had answers. In many other ways I had all the more questions. One thing for sure. My desire for a woman would be met tonight. A desire that now had more meaning. I would be siring warriors for Christ, not just another generation of men out for vain glory, but men put here by the hand of God to usher in His kingdom, the kingdom of Jesus the Messiah!

Tatang was waiting for me at the gate and brought me to the marriage suite where Sarapita and I would consummate our marriage. Zuah was to be one of my attendants. Tatang put Zuah's hand in mine.

'You'll have Zuah also, after you have finished the week with Sarapita.'

How could I refuse? There was no longer a limit to the number of wives I could have, and besides, Zuah seemed the perfect choice. Sarapita loved her cousin Zuah as her best friend. I only hoped that it would please Sarapita as it pleased me.

Tatang, as usual, knew my thoughts. Maybe his intuitive understanding of what I was thinking was because he too was once a young prince.

'John, Sarapita was the one who suggested to me that you take Zuah as your bride. She knew that one day you'd be voyaging far from here and didn't want to be away from *all* of her family. This way, if you return home, Sarapita will have her beloved cousin Zuah to keep her from becoming too homesick.'

'I shall treasure her!' I thanked Tatang as he left me alone with Zuah.

I now felt comfortable looking at Zuah with all the desire that had been unmet within me for so many years. She led me to where I would be bathed.

'John, Sarapita and I have another surprise for you. Call it a wedding gift, or should I say, call *her* a wedding gift. She'll be your handmaid and your wife. She's an orphan and has no guardian, so she has authority to give herself in marriage and she's already agreed, that is, if you want her. She'll help me prepare you for this evening. Some women sing, some women dance, and some women do what Saldexa does. I'm sure you'll agree she does it well.'

Whatever could she mean, I wondered, till I experienced Saldexa. Saldexa was behind a curtain waiting to bathe me. When Zuah pulled it open, Saldexa was coming up out of the water, her long head of hair was full of lather and the sudsy water soaked me when she swung around to greet me. She made a barely perceptible moan. Her thin clothing stuck to her skin like frosting. She was nearly my height and every part of her perfectly sculpted body reminded me of God's glorious power to create. No exercise or regimen could have produced this beauty. The soapy water was now running down her cheeks. She touched a drop that had made it to the side of her mouth, then giggled and turned away, offering my eyes a feast of her perfect silhouette. They say that the effect a woman has on a man is fifty percent imagination and fifty percent beauty, but in Saldexa's case, I couldn't tell where the beauty ended and where her feminine charms began. She was stunning. God left no feature out of place. I could even smell Saldexa. Not a perfume, but the scent of woman. A scent that begged my attention. Saldexa now whispered to Zuah who in turn whispered to me.

'Saldexa is a bit shy and has a few questions she'd like me to ask for her. She's not a princess, except in the kingdom of God where we're all given robes of righteousness.[22] As you've already experienced, Saldexa has a rare ability to direct the desire of man.'

'That is apparent.' I answered. 'So what are her questions?'

'Here's what she wants to hear from your lips, John. Do you love the Lord?'

'Yes, I love the Lord. He's given me a new life.'

'Saldexa also wants to know; will you always dispense your love first to Sarapita, second to me, and third to Saldexa?'

'Certainly, for the Bible says:

If a man takes him another wife; her food, her raiment, and her duty of marriage, he shall not diminish.'[23]

'Finally, she asks, can you promise never to put her on a pedestal, no matter how strong your desire to please her?'

I turned to Saldexa to answer this question:

'Your beauty is rare and you are deserving the attention that any woman of God deserves, but as one created, not as an idol, for it is the husband who is to be raised up, as lord unto his wife. It is written:

For the husband is the head of the wife, even as Christ is the head of the church: and he is the saviour of the body.[24]

So ought men to love their wives as their own bodies.[25]

As my body, you will be one of my beloved help meets, one who serves me, not as a trophy that I might be tempted to put up on a pedestal, but as part of me, covered with my own garment as a protection.'

Saldexa's shyness to speak disappeared as she quoted Scripture, substituting her name for Ruth's.

'I am Saldexa, your handmaid: spread therefore your garment over your handmaid.'[26]

I embraced Saldexa tightly as she fell upon my neck, kissing it. After amply anointing my neck with kisses she led me to the bathroom on the other side of the marriage suite.

'Go, relieve yourself, and shower, but don't be long. Zuah and I must prepare you for Sarapita. We'll be waiting for you in the bath.'

After showering I came out and stepped down into the bath. It was the bath of a prince, deep and long. Zuah and Saldexa were waiting. They were both wide eyed and smiling as they prepared me for my wedding night. Each of them were betrothed[27] to me, as good as married except for the consummation which would take place on our wedding nights. Both were *NBSB* (No Boyfriend Since Birth) and neither had touched a man till they bathed me that evening. They scrubbed me as thoroughly as a mother scrubs a child who's been caught playing in the mud, then they applied lotions and colognes. They finished their preparation by placing an elegant robe upon me. Candles had already been lit for it was nearly the Sabbath and I could hear the musicians in the courtyard playing in honor of our marriage. There was an elegant tent[28] set up within our suite with many curtains. This would serve as our marriage chamber. Zuah and Saldexa seated me on a couch in the middle of the tent. As they sat at my sides a veiled woman rolled a cart into the chamber which had trays full of exotic native dishes and delicacies on it. She picked up a note that was left on top of it, handing it to Zuah before exiting.

Zuah read it, 'Tatang proclaims:

My daughter is yours. May the Lord bless you and keep you...safe from those who wish to harm you. May your wives bless you with many children and may their arguments be over you, not with you. The maidens Zuah and Saldexa shall be your only guests at Sarapita's Coming of Age party for Sarapita is already yours. Love her and love your other wives for that is the command of the Lord. I am a happy father this night. May you and your wives live to see each one of your many children celebrate such an evening as this.'

Now Zuah and Saldexa checked their work.

'Quickly, make sure there's no dirt on him. He must be spotless for the princess.' Zuah said with a serious tone.

They each looked over my face as if I were a child going to his first day of instruction. They were searching for the tiniest imperfection, a misplaced hair, a piece of dandruff. They even sniffed me.

'Umm!' Saldexa said, as she pinched my cheek. 'He looks good!'

'Num!' Zuah said, 'Ang sarap!' (tasty)

What was I? A man or a boy... or a piece of food? I felt like all of that, but when Sarapita entered the room, singing as she danced, I was a groom on fire for my bride!

I'd only seen such artistry in the hand crafted music boxes that my mother kept. Sarapita missed not one beat, nor was any note untrue as she sang and danced around me. Her performance lasted hours but I can tell you no more or I'll surely cause the men here to sin by coveting her."

John now broke from his storytelling and turned to someone I'd thought was one of his daughters.

"Sarapita, there are no words but one; tonight!"

I felt like I was looking at two newlyweds. Sarapita's face showed no wear from her twenty-five years spent as mother and wife. John's face showed the excitement of a college boy on a first date when he said that one word, *Tonight*.

"Wow! How beautiful your story is!" Suni said. "If my man could take me as you've taken your wives I'd be everything to him." Suni squeezed my hand.

"There is no other way to have a man. To have a man who is not worthy to be shared is to have no man at all!" Ruth added, lightly caressing my other hand.

John now turned to another who I'd thought was his daughter.

"Saldexa, isn't dinner ready now?"

"Yes, John. Let's go eat." Saldexa stood. She was the tallest woman I'd seen on Mindanao. "Come, join us. We've prepared an entirely new banquet and there will be some surprises."

John's description of Saldexa had reminded me of Modelisa. Each could present whatever face she wished. Tonight Saldexa presented the face of a gracious wife serving her guests.

Modelisa looked at me just as I was musing on their similarities. She'd never looked at me like that before. Desire filled me. Mary's voice brought me back from my dreamlike state.

"Ish, dinner is ready. Let's go eat. Take your two buddies and join us."

Mary winked. She could see I was enjoying the attention of Suni and Ruth and didn't suspect for a moment that it could lead to anything other than fond memories.

Ruth and Suni strolled at my sides, leaning against my shoulders. They seemed in a dreamlike state. I certainly was.

Modelisa, not to be left out, cut in.

"Suni, you've had him long enough. Now it's my turn."

Suni graciously consented. Modelisa, who was still using her skill at filling me with desire, took my hand and entwined her fingers in mine. She knew how to stroll, saunter, move her hips and pout her lips, all the while keeping her eyes on mine, or should I say, keeping my eyes on her. Realizing the effect she could have, Modelisa made sure to remind me that I had to step up into the dining hall. Had she not done so, I might have tripped over my hanging jaw.

Chapter 16 Footnotes

1. 2 Timothy 3:16 All scripture is given by inspiration of God, and is profitable for doctrine, for reproof, for correction, for instruction in righteousness.

Test new prophets by old prophets and new books by old books. When a religion sprouts from Judaism or Christianity then its writings must not contradict the Bible for the Bible is the earliest book of those two religions. To the date of this writing there still has not been one religion to come up with any new book which they claim to be Scripture that does not contradict the Bible. Look to the Bible for answers on salvation. Do not look toward faiths claiming to be from the God of the Bible if their own books and so called prophets contradict the Bible.

Romans 10:17 So then faith cometh by hearing, and hearing by the word of God.

2. Isaiah 53 was written 700 years before Jesus walked the earth and yet it perfectly described the Roman crucifixion of Jesus, the Messiah. Jews accept Isaiah as an authentic book of the Bible.
3. John 3:14 And the Word was made flesh, and dwelt among us, (and we beheld his glory, the glory as of the only begotten of the Father,) full of grace and truth.
4. Dehumidifiers that use replaceable salts are common, even today. I have used them in my Philippine home to keep the clothes in the closet from rotting.
5. There are Christian organizations today whose sole, or should I say, soul purpose is to pray for what they call the "Unreached Peoples Groups."
6. Genesis 4:7 If thou doest well, shalt thou not be accepted? and if thou doest not well, sin lieth at the door. And *unto thee shall be his desire*, and thou shalt rule over him.
7. Colossians 2:13-14 13 And you, being dead in your sins and the uncircumcision of your flesh, hath he quickened together with him, having forgiven you all trespasses; Blotting out the handwriting of ordinances that was against us, which was contrary to us, and took it out of the way, nailing it to his cross.
8. Isaiah 64:6 But we are all as an unclean thing, and all our righteousnesses are as filthy rags; and we all do fade as a leaf; and our iniquities, like the wind, have taken us away.
9. Mark 7:13 Making the word of God of none effect through your tradition, which ye have delivered: and many such like things do ye.
10. Matthew 28:19-20 Go ye therefore, and teach all nations, baptizing them in the name of the Father, and of the Son, and of the Holy Ghost: Teaching them to observe all things whatsoever I have commanded you: and, lo, I am with you alway, even unto the end of the world. Amen.
11. Romans 12:5-6 So we, being many, are one body in Christ, and every one members one of another. Having then gifts differing according to the grace that is given to us, whether prophecy, let us prophesy according to the proportion of faith.
12. Acts 2:6 Now when this was noised abroad, the multitude came together, and were confounded, because that every man heard them speak in his own language.
Joel 2:28 And it shall come to pass afterward, that I will pour out

my spirit upon all flesh; and your sons and your daughters shall prophesy, your old men shall dream dreams, your young men shall see visions.

13. Proverbs 30:29-31 There be three things which go well, yea, *four are comely in going*: A lion which is strongest among beasts, and turneth not away for any; A greyhound, an he goat also; and *a king, against whom there is no rising up.*

14. Matthew 7:21-23 Not every one that saith unto me, Lord, Lord, shall enter into the kingdom of heaven; **but he that doeth the will of my Father which is in heaven**. Many will say to me in that day, Lord, Lord, have we not prophesied in thy name? and in thy name have cast out devils? and in thy name done many wonderful works? And then will I profess unto them, I never knew you: depart from me, ye that work iniquity.

15. Proverbs 11:21 Though hand join in hand, the wicked shall not be unpunished: but the seed of the righteous shall be delivered.

16. John 4:14 But whosoever drinketh of the water that I shall give him shall never thirst; but the water that I shall give him shall be in him a well of water springing up into everlasting life.

17. Joel 2:28 And it shall come to pass afterward, that I will pour out my spirit upon all flesh; and your sons and your daughters shall prophesy, your old men shall dream dreams, your young men shall see visions.

18. 1 Peter 2:24 Who his own self bare our sins in his own body on the tree, that we, being dead to sins, should live unto righteousness: [Jesus] by whose stripes ye were healed.

19. Hebrews 13:5 Let your conversation be without covetousness; and be content with such things as ye have: for he [Jesus] hath said, I will never leave thee, nor forsake thee.

20. 2 Corinthians 6:14 Be ye not unequally yoked together with unbelievers: for what fellowship hath righteousness with unrighteousness? and what communion hath light with darkness?

21. Isaiah 57:15 For thus saith the high and lofty One that inhabiteth eternity, whose name is Holy; I dwell in the high and holy place, with him also that is of a contrite and humble spirit, to revive the spirit of the humble, and to revive the heart of the contrite ones.

This is a Messianic verse. The One spoken about here who is "of a contrite and humble spirit" is the Messiah, Jesus.

22. Isaiah 61:10 I will greatly rejoice in the LORD, my soul shall be joyful in my God; for he hath clothed me with the garments of salvation, he hath covered me with the robe of righteousness, as a bridegroom decketh himself with ornaments, and as a bride adorneth herself with her jewels.
23. Exodus 21:10 If he take him another wife; her food, her raiment, and her duty of marriage, shall he not diminish.
This verse is a command. It absolutely forbids a man from diminishing the first wife's food, clothing, or time for love making, even if the first wife says it's okay. Those who say that wives should be treated equally are opposing this Scripture.
24. Ephesians 5:23-24 For the husband is the head of the wife, even as Christ is the head of the church: and he is the saviour of the body. Therefore as the church is subject unto Christ, so let the wives be to their own husbands in every thing.
25. Ephesians 5:28-30 So ought men to love their wives as their own bodies. He that loveth his wife loveth himself. For no man ever yet hated his own flesh; but nourisheth and cherisheth it, even as the Lord the church: 30 For we are members of his body, of his flesh, and of his bones.
Genesis 2:23 And Adam said, This is now bone of my bones, and flesh of my flesh: she shall be called Woman, because she was taken out of Man.
So we see clearly here that it is the woman who is a member of her husband's body, not the reverse. A man who is the member of a woman's body is the man visiting a harlot.
1 Corinthians 6:15 Know ye not that your bodies are the members of Christ? shall I then take the members of Christ, and make them the members of an harlot? God forbid.
26. Ruth 3:9 And he said, Who art thou? And she answered, I am Ruth thine handmaid: spread therefore thy skirt over thine handmaid; for thou art a near kinsman.
27. Betrothal is an exchange of authority from the woman (or from the woman's guardian) to her husband to be. It changes from a betrothal to a marriage as soon as it is consummated.
28. The first marriage *tent* mentioned in the Bible
Genesis 24:67 And Isaac brought her into his mother Sarah's tent, and took Rebekah, and she became his wife; and he loved her: and Isaac was comforted after his mother's death.

NO OTHER WAY TO HAVE A MAN
PRINCE JOHN'S STORY CONTINUES

The huge banquet table in John's dining hall now had new meaning for us. It was not simply a beautiful creation, but evidence of John's adventure. After we'd all been seated, Sarisa handed out prayer shawls to the women.

"What are these?" Mary asked.

"Sam and I have been discussing this for some time, Mary. We've come to the realization that there's no way to interpret 1 Corinthians 11:6 other than the way it reads. Women must cover their heads when they worship, pray, or sing to the Lord."

"How is that?" Mary objected. "Most churches teach the covering simply refers to long hair, which all of us have."

"Sam and I have researched this," Sarisa said, "and we discovered that up until the wild Sixties, all women wore hats in churches. Part of the reason they stopped doing that was because their ministers had forgotten the real reason the custom had begun. That reason was that the Bible requires it. Two thousand years of bonnets, shawls, and hats can't be overlooked, but as you and I know; none of that matters if the Bible doesn't teach it. Let's read the verse.

'For if the woman be not covered, let her also be shorn: but if it be a shame for a woman to be shorn or shaven, let her be covered.'[1]

That's clear enough. You see, Paul says she must be shorn if she is not covered but if *not covered* meant she had no hair then how could she be shorn? She's already shorn. So when Paul says *not covered*, he's clearly referring to some article of clothing, a veil, a bonnet, or a hat."

"Well, I'll agree to disagree." Mary pouted.

"Okay, Mary, It's between you and the Lord. Your High Priest is Jesus.[2] Do as you wish as long as your conscience is right with Him."

Sarisa continued to hand out the prayer shawls. The girls quickly snatched them up.

"John's wives made them. They're yours to keep." Sarisa told them.

"In that case, I don't want to be rude." Mary backtracked. "Let me have that one with the pink ribbon and beautiful embroidery."

Mary smiled her thanks to John's wives from one side of her mouth while scowling at me from the other. This was just one of Mary's many talents for hiding from the world what she was feeling toward me. I hadn't suggested the prayer shawls to Sam and Sarisa but Mary had a way of blaming me for anything she didn't like.

"You'll be blessed!" Suni assured Mary. "Whenever we discover a new way to please God, He blesses us."

Even though Mary had put on her prayer shawl, she didn't appear convinced.

John, cleared his throat and we quieted down for his prayer. After he'd prayed, he made an announcement.

"First, I'd like to welcome you to our church. It's the only church my family and I have and we are grateful for it. We are to always be prayerful[3] and yet, there are times when we want to dedicate ourselves to prayer, worship, and praise. This is such a time. Our Almighty is good, isn't He?"

Praise erupted around the room. The girls shouted praises to the Lord as if their prayer shawls had given them a new boldness.

"Praise be to the Lord. Alleluia."

"Glory to God who is highest."

"He is a wondrous God!

The calls of praise now became a song and Asina danced, shaking a tambourine. I remembered John's story of Sarapita. Until now I hadn't known how thrilling it could be to watch a maiden dance to the Lord. Asina danced, untouched beauty that she was, flying through the air as if lifted on the breath of the Lord[4] as indeed she was, for God's Spirit was moving among us as we joined in song.

Mary now relaxed and took Ruth's place at my side. She sang

with us as we had begun to sing a familiar hymn. It was wonderful to see her hard demeanor melt in praises to the Lord. Now *that* was the sweet girl I had married. I couldn't help myself. I turned to Mary and whispered in her ear.

"Now what was it that John said to Sarapita? Oh yes, *Tonight.*"

The twinkle in Mary's eyes at that moment was enough to make the lights in the room appear dim.

"And tomorrow as well." She replied.

We dined between worship and praise. By the time every one of us had gotten a chance to sing our favorite hymn and to give praises to the Lord, we'd finished eating the main course. John closed in prayer and we all sat down to dessert. Our eyes should have been fixed on the table which had been set with the most delectable assortment of pastries and fruits but instead all eyes were on John. Suni was the first to break the silence. She stood up, crossed her arms, and peered at John through squinted eyes.

"You're not going to just leave us hanging, are you Princikins?"

The room erupted in laughter. John had a habit of being very formal but he was by no means a prude. Of all of us, it was John who laughed the loudest at Suni's well timed quip. The only thing powerful enough to take us away from John's story had been the worship service, that being complete, we wanted to know the rest of his tale.

"I'll tell you the rest of what happened as long as you promise to eat your desserts while I'm telling it."

To that, one of his daughters jested.

"Not that, please, anything but that. Don't make me eat scrumptious desserts while listening to a wonderful tale."

"Hey, that was supposed to be my line." Asina retorted.

These corny exchanges continued for a few minutes as we got our silly bones exercised, then we regained our composure in anticipation of John's story.

"Let's see, where did we leave off?" John asked.

"You were describing Sarapita's dance." Mary said, "You said you'd only seen such artistry in the hand crafted music boxes that your mother kept."

"Oh yes. Thank you Mary. Now before Zuah and Saldexa retired themselves to their beds, they pronounced their blessings upon Sarapita and me. Zuah began first.

'Oh, Sarapita, both great and small, your most delicate beauty is far above that of the butterflies. May you never be mistaken for a fairy and may your husband not squash you like a caterpillar when he turns in his sleep.

And blessings upon you, Prince John. May Sarapita's lips be as the dew on autumn leaves at the suns first rays; moist with kisses, and may she be like the flowers of spring, always opening for you.'

Saldexa would not be outdone. She stood and did a mime of Sarapita and me embracing. To see it you would think that I were a giant and Princess Sarapita but a mouse. As Saldexa mimed my embrace of the tiniest of princesses, she used her finger tips, not her arms, to imitate my embrace of Sarapita, and when she showed how I might kiss the princess, she pretended that I had choked on her and had to cough her back up again. Her acting exceeded anything that I could describe here.

The love of Zuah and Saldexa for Sarapita, their good friend and sister in Christ, was apparent. My love for all of them was growing each moment, but tonight belonged to Sarapita, so Zuah and Saldexa left us as they kissed me and their Princess goodnight.

For a moment, there was silence, then Sarapita, my precious bride, spoke.

'My prince, may I be as a shadow when there is light and as a dream at night, ever with you. May you know that I love you even when I don't say it, and may you know that you are as the Lord to me. May you know that your greatest hopes are mine as I pray that our Lord shall guide you. I am yours. The cloth for the tokens of my virginity has been laid upon our bed of love. Take me now.'

If a man can still live without breathing, I am proof. As I looked upon Sarapita that first night of love, there was no room left within me for anything but her. She immersed me in a most splendid suffocation. Her scent filled my lungs, her kisses stopped my breathing, and her love beat within my heart. May every man who loves the Lord experience such a love as this.

A week after I'd taken Sarapita as my bride I took Zuah. A week more and I took Saldexa. One month later I was shocked to find all three of my wives sick and vomiting. I ran up to Zuah who was retching over the toilet.

'Who has poisoned you?'

'If it is poison, you have done it! I'm pregnant and so are Sarapita and Saldexa.'

I wasn't happy that they were suffering but I was overjoyed that children would soon be a part of our family. After a few weeks, the joy turned to frustration. None of my wives wanted me near them. Their moods went from angry to maniacal with little respite. Sarapita took the lead in making sure I dealt with my situation.

'We are this way when we are pregnant. This is true of most women in our kingdom. You must get yourself a fourth wife or you'll go mad. A man with your stamina cannot allow himself to be chained. Find a love, a tender voice among the maidens; a handmaid to the Lord and she will be your handmaid as well.'[5]

The Lord had blessed me with three wonderful wives and, despite their reaction to pregnancy, I wasn't anxious to add anyone new. Furthermore, Tatang's blessing was being fulfilled; they were taking out their bad moods on each other, not me. Even so, *with three wives telling me to get a fourth, who was I to argue?* After giving it some thought, I decided on a plan of action, then I visited Tatang for advice.

'Tatang, I need your help.'

'Whatever it is you need, I'll do my best.' He said.

'I've been thinking about what the Lord would want me to do and have come to a decision on the best way to proceed. Can you bring three of your most promising lady students to share in our Bible studies; maidens who love the Lord and can quote Bible verses on any subject; ones who could not go an hour without picking up their Bibles, let alone a day?'

'I would, if only I could find three of them. What you're asking for is not just three ladies who love the Lord but three ladies who cannot get enough of studying His word. This is a rare thing, even in a man.'

Had my intuition misled me? I'd felt that Tatang would be my help in this mission, then Tatang finished his thought.

'Yet there is *one* such woman. There is none like her in the kingdom; who seeks the truth in Scripture and never gives up. She is waiting for me in my library as we speak. She has so advanced in her studies that I learn more from her than she from me.'

'Let's go!' I jumped up the steps to his library in anticipation.

Upon entering, a young woman looked up from a reference

book she'd been reading. She was smiling like a girl who has been dreaming of far away places.

'You can't believe what I've been reading, Tatang!' She lowered her eyes when she noticed that I was with him.

'Please, share what you've discovered with Prince John. He loves the Lord and has begun studying the Bible with vigor. I won't be studying with you today. Please excuse me, Sulpicia, John.'

Tatang left before Sulpicia could object to her being left alone with me. I sat down across the table from her. She had books opened and spread across the table, overlapping each other. Had she been anyone else, I'm sure she would have sought a way to leave the room. After all, I was a new convert and my only credentials were worldly, but Sulpicia looked at me politely and smiled.[6]

'Tell me what you've discovered.' I asked Sulpicia.

She was scribbling her notes quickly but deliberately. Occasionally she would pause and turn her head to the side as if trying to remember some nuance of what she'd just discovered in her studies. Finally, her face lit up in a self congratulatory smile and she looked up at me.

'I couldn't possibly have remembered all that. Thanks for being patient.'

'Why do you study so?' I asked her.

'The Lord has laid it upon my heart. It is mine to do and so I do it with all my might.'[7]

'So tell me about this discovery that you wanted to tell Tatang.'

Sulpicia then began expositing verses, referencing one to another in ways far beyond what Tatang had done. After each exposition she would quiz me and ask if I understood. Sulpicia and I were both astonished that I was not only able to explain what she'd discovered but to add to it. When Tatang came back in the room, Sulpicia and I spoke as one.

'Back so soon?'

'Soon? I've been gone all day! The sun is nearly set. Your wives are worried about you, John. Didn't you think to tell them you'd be late?' Tatang was irritated at first then began to smile as if he were first to be privy to some new snippet of gossip.

'So how long did you think I'd been gone?'

Again, Sulpicia and I answered as one.

'An hour?'

Sulpicia and I immediately turned to face each other. We were meeting again in a new way. She looked at me differently now, and I her. She had accompanied me through the hallways of the knowledge of the Lord. We had shared the depths of the Scriptures and learned each from the other. What most scholars would take weeks to discover, even months, we had found in a day, yet it seemed as minutes to us. We added, each to the other and were as one in studying God's word.

'I never suspected that a man of such noble rank would be a scholar and a theologian too, and after how many years of study?'

Tatang couldn't believe what he was hearing.

'What are you talking about, Sulpicia? John is a new convert and has only studied the Scriptures for a couple of months.'

'I can only tell you what I've seen today. There is no match in the kingdom for John's ability to analyze, cross reference, and find a deeper meaning in Scripture. He has obviously been blessed, once again, through a fortunate birth, this time, of a heavenly nature. These gifts that the Lord poured out on him when he was born again shall be a blessing to many.'[8]

'Sulpicia is right, John. My ability to teach you ended on the day you were born again. What you have been posing as questions since then were in fact insights, and when you had a real question, the question would be so deep that I had no answer. The Lord has blessed you with a love and understanding of Scripture that godly men will fear[9] and which proud men shall envy.'[10]

After that day, Sulpicia and I studied the Scriptures together every day. The days quickly turned to months. As I was waiting one afternoon for Sulpicia to get back to the library from having lunch with her family, I looked up to see Tatang frowning at me.

'John,' he said, 'what is it you want of Sulpicia? She trembles at your name. She wants to end this.'

'End what we have? None but Sulpicia can walk with me through familiar Scriptures and like a ripe field, pick new fruit from trees already gleaned many times over? She must never leave me.'

'And you would want such a woman to spend her life studying without regard to her own person?[11] Sulpicia is waiting outside.

She is yours if you want her. I'll send her in. Be kind, whatever you do.'

The moment Sulpicia walked in, she kneeled before me.

'Forgive me John, but I would have burst had I not told Tatang of my love for you. I am tortured that we walk together through each page of the Bible as through God's own estate but as we walk I cannot take your hand. The Lord lifts us to great heights on the wings of His Spirit yet I cannot hold onto you as we sail through His kingdom. His Word tells us of great pleasures, we speak of them, and the words that flow from your tongue are completed by mine yet I am not able to taste your lips. Forgive me.'[12]

'If there were anything to forgive, I would, but it is I who have sinned for failing to tell you of my love for you. Forgive *me*, Sulpicia. See this coin? It represents my offer of marriage. I have nearly rubbed off its inscription from holding it in my hand as we studied God's Word. I did not want to offend someone who so loved the Scripture by making her think that my intentions were of the flesh.'

Sulpicia responded. 'Is it the flesh that calls out to you, *take away my reproach.*[13] Is it the flesh that calls out to you, *subdue me in all holiness and let me know what it is to have a lord here on earth?*'[14]

'As always, we two are one when we speak. This coin represents my offer of marriage. Here, you hold it now. Will you be mine?'

Sulpicia clung to my leg crying.

'My master. Take me now.'

I lifted Sulpicia to my arms and set off for my estate. I had built a suite at the corner of the roof;[15] a getaway, where I could escape my wives whose pregnancies had affected their moods. Sulpicia and I would spend our nuptials there.

'For a moment, John.' She whispered.

Then I realized how impetuous I'd been. No honorable man takes a wife without her parents knowledge.

'Of course, I must meet your parents first.'

Sulpicia's father and mother had been trailing us in a panic, afraid to speak because I was a prince, afraid to turn back because of the treasure I carried in my arms. I addressed them.

'I dishonor you kind friends. You have a wonderful daughter. I wish to marry her.'

'She is yours.'[16] Her father answered.

Her mother added, 'Maybe now she'll put down her books long enough to look in the mirror. Here is the cloth for the tokens of your virginity, Sulpicia. Come visit us after your week, and bring Prince John if he's willing.'

'To be guest to the gracious parents of my bride would be my pleasure.' I said, 'Pardon us.'

I set off now, even more determined, to my private quarters, Sulpicia holding on more tightly than before. I sprang up the steps like a boy on an adventure and nearly flew across the terrace to my quarters, then I slid the last few yards across the marble floor. I turned the lever with my knee and shut the door behind us with my foot. I laid Sulpicia down on the couch but before I could lean over to kiss her, she leapt back into my arms, pressing her lips on mine. I felt a dizziness like that which comes when roused from a deep sleep. Embracing her tightly, I kissed her, then laid her down once again.

'Time is ours." I said. "We must prepare.'

I sent my maids in to attend to Sulpicia's needs and left the room. After they'd finished bathing her, I could hear her pleading with them to leave.

'Please go, I'm just a simple girl. John loves me as I am. What? What's this? Mm, delightful, and this? Ah.'

I chuckled to myself. They'd presented her with my gifts; colognes and lotions of the kind found only on the dressing tables of rich men's wives. Amazing what the right gifts can do to a simple girl. One moment a girl, the next a princess. As they applied the lotion to my Sulpicia's ticklish back, I could hear her giggling. She inhaled deeply as they anointed her arms and ankles with cologne, then I heard her shout.

'Am I to be in chains!' I continued listening at the door to see what could possibly be the matter.

'No, no princess. You must not be naked as a peasant on your wedding night.' One of the maids said. 'You must wear these.'

'They're heavy. Too heavy, what is this?'

'It is gold, pure gold. If you do not want them we cannot force you.'

'Oh no, please. Put them on me. Oh, they're so heavy!'

'Your lord's love is heavy for you. We do not know where he got these but there are no such chains of gold in the kingdom. Surely he loves you dearly.'

The maids amused me. They had told Sulpicia that she must wear her bank around her wrists, ankles, and neck. The reason they believed there were none like them in the kingdom was because my other wives kept theirs safely locked away. Seventy pounds of gold is a bit much to wear, even for a princess. Certain that all was well with Sulpicia, I bathed and prepared myself for our marriage. When I came out of my washroom I could hear Sulpicia's voice calling to me.

'Make haste, my beloved, and be like a roe or a young stag upon the mountains of spice.'[17]

Even now, Sulpicia's beauty lay in her appetite for Scripture. Would that her appetite for love could be as great. Did I just pray? If the Lord agreed, I would drink deeply of love this night.

Sulpicia could take a verse and make it her own, an epic tale, and put us at its center. This, was the great love we shared, to live by and walk in the Scriptures. I returned her call for me in verse.

'I will go up to the palm tree, I will take hold of the boughs thereof: now also thy breasts shall be as clusters of the vine, and the smell of thy nose like apples; And the roof of thy mouth like the best wine that goes down sweet, causing the lips of those that are asleep to speak.'[18]

Now entering Sulpicia's room, I saw her laying upon the bed, the cloth for the tokens of her virginity beneath her. I removed the gold chains which weighted her down and laid them on the floor. The sheer material of the bride's robe she wore was all that separated maiden from wife. A few more steps and...

Isn't it time for you kids to go to bed?" John broke off his story telling.

"Ah," Moaned one of the kids. "Aren't you going to tell us how it ends?"

"She's your mother, Sitay, you know the rest of the story. Now go on, get to bed. All of you kids, go to bed and don't be asking your mothers for any more bedtime stories tonight."

"Ah, c'mon!" They all moaned.

Another said, "The ending can't take that much time for you to tell."

"Okay, here's the ending. So Sulpicia and I smooched real good, so long in fact, that we had to brush our teeth because our breath started smelling bad, well, okay, daddy's breath started smelling bad, and we lived happily ever after. The end."

"That's what I meant," Sitay said. "No *happily ever after* and the story isn't over. Silly daddy."

"Silly daddy or not, I've got to have my good night kisses."

Each of John's children now gave him a goodnight kiss and said their *I love you*s, then his entire family said their goodbyes to us for the night. His kids were snickering as if this had been a ploy to distract us from what was really about to happen.

"I think we ought to call it a night, don't you?" John said.

"Not exactly." Mary objected, "You can't make us go to sleep without telling us how you got off that island."

"And telling us what happened to your mother." Suni added.

"And who that man at the market was; the man who sold you those guns." Asina *would* have to be the first to mention that.

At this, John roared a laugh so loud that his dogs began barking. After regaining his composure he said, "The old man at the market was Elkanah."

"So that's why he knew our special word." Asina said. "He called those machine guns NBSB. I wanted to hit him over the head with one of them when I heard him say that. I'll stack up what I've been saving for my husband against those stupid guns any day. Oh, you know what I mean."

"Yes, and I'll make sure to tell Elkanah that we must find a more appropriate term when speaking of guns."

"Speaking of guns," Modelisa said, "you nearly ran over them when you backed up your jeepney. How come you were driving so recklessly?"

"Modelisa, I might not be the best driver on Mindanao, but that was deliberate. I had to make it look like an accident to get close enough to the box. The box you saw was just a facade with trap doors. Before Elkanah slid the crate with machine guns into it, I smuggled some special guests into my jeepney through it. One of them was a sweet young peasant girl, strong but delicate."

"Hadassah? Hadassah is here?" Mary's eyes lit up, reminded by John's description of Hadassah.

"Yes, when Elkanah said NBSB, he was referring to his daughter, Hadassah. Some other guests were hiding inside Elkanah's stall too. He drove them all the way from Iligan to the market before dawn. That's the real reason we went down to Marawi this morning. We smuggled them in on one of our ships last night. There are those who would do them harm if they knew their whereabouts."

"Do who harm?" Suni asked.

"My mother and Kasmina, of course."

"They're here too? Why haven't you introduced them to us!" She protested.

"I've kept them busy cleaning and polishing my new machine guns, of course." John couldn't help kidding the girls. "Oh, c'mon! They've been asleep! I just told you they got up before dawn to meet us at Elkanah's stall. Now, you wouldn't expect me to wake up three princesses from their sleep, would you?"

"Well Prince Charming did, didn't he?" Suni couldn't help it. John had set himself up.

"Okay, you got me there, Suni."

"Wait, a minute!" Mary said. "Hadassah... Hadassah is now a princess?"

"Well, not technically, but you're all invited to our wedding tonight."

"So that's what you meant when you said to Sarapita, *tonight.*" Mary was intrigued by the unfolding mystery.

"Yes, our wedding will be tonight. Sam will clue you in on our customs, which shouldn't be that difficult to get used to, they're exactly the same as the customs found in the Bible."

"You mean you're not going to just drag her up to your rooftop like you did Sulpicia?" The way Asina's eyes lit up when she said it, I got the feeling that she would like her future husband to do the same.

"Just wait and see." John said, "But for now, you can all get some rest. I'll see you back here in an hour and a half."

Chapter 17 Footnotes

1. 1 Corinthians 11:6 For if the woman be not covered, let her also be shorn: but if it be a shame for a woman to be shorn or shaven, let her be covered.

It's astounding how today's Christians are able to ignore the most simple sentence in the world and make it complicated. If the penalty for violating this command is to cut off the hair then the woman in violation of this command certainly has hair! Since a woman with hair can be in violation of this command then the hair is obviously not what is being referred to by cover. A cover is a hat or a shawl. If you're a typical Christian woman, you probably violate this command every day. Repent.

2. Hebrews 2:16-17 For verily he [Jesus] took not on him the nature of angels; but he took on him the seed of Abraham. Wherefore in all things it behooved him to be made like unto his brethren, that he might be a merciful and faithful high priest in things pertaining to God, to make reconciliation for the sins of the people.

3. Ephesians 6:18 Praying always with all prayer and supplication in the Spirit, and watching thereunto with all perseverance and supplication for all saints.

4. John 20:22 And when he had said this, he breathed on them, and saith unto them, Receive ye the Holy Ghost.

5. Ruth 2:13 Then she said, Let me find favour in thy sight, my lord; for that thou hast comforted me, and for that thou hast spoken friendly unto thine handmaid, though I be not like unto one of thine handmaidens.

6. 1 Timothy 4:12 Let no man despise thy youth; but be thou an example of the believers, in word, in conversation, in charity, in spirit, in faith, in purity.

7. Ecclesiastes 9:10 Whatsoever thy hand findeth to do, do it with thy might; for there is no work, nor device, nor knowledge, nor wisdom, in the grave, whither thou goest.

8. 1Peter 1:23 Being born again, not of corruptible seed, but of incorruptible, by the word of God, which liveth and abideth for ever.

Romans 12:6 Having then gifts differing according to the grace that is given to us, whether prophecy, let us prophesy according to the proportion of faith.

9. Hebrews 12:28 Wherefore we receiving a kingdom which cannot be moved, let us have grace, whereby we may serve God acceptably with reverence and godly fear.

10. Acts 13:45 But when the Jews saw the multitudes, they were

filled with envy, and spake against those things which were spoken by Paul, contradicting and blaspheming.

11. Young women are to get married, in fact, The Apostle Paul commanded it,

1 Timothy 5:14 I will, therefore, that the younger women marry, bear children, guide the house, give none occasion to the adversary to speak reproachfully.

And again Paul states,

1 Timothy 2:15 She shall be saved in childbearing, if they continue in faith and charity and holiness with sobriety.

Saved from what? -- saved from a life of fornication so that the adversary (Satan or anyone else who opposes righteousness) may not have any reason to attack the virtue of the young women. The Greek word translated as *younger women* is *neos* which means recently come into being, young, youthful, new, and in the context of marriage Paul is speaking of women who have recently become women, in other words, recently had their first menstrual cycle. So Paul not only commands that the younger women marry but he defines those young women much younger than the last hundred years of history has considered appropriate for marriage. Is it any wonder that fornication is so common today considering marriage is delayed far beyond the age at which a woman becomes a woman. Paul wrote scripture, these were not the mere words of a man, and unlike today, the Roman law of that day was actually in accordance with Scripture for Roman law required that upon reaching puberty every citizen must marry or lose many rights and privileges. The Lex Papia Poppaea, A.D. 9, decreed punishments such as the loss of inheritance rights for those who remained single after having attained puberty. A man or woman was given one hundred days to get married upon finding out they were the beneficiary of an inheritance or forfeit the inheritance. Information on the Lex Papia Poppaea can be found in:

A Systematic and Historical Exposition - ROMAN LAW - In the Order of a Code by W. A. Hunter EMBODYING THE INSTITUTES OF GAIUS AND THE INSTITUTES OF JUSTINIAN, TRANSLATED INTO ENGLISH BY J. ASHTON CROSS, B.A. of Balliol College, Oxford, BARRISTER-AT-LAW, Fourth Edition 1803

12. Proverbs 27:5 Open rebuke is better than secret love.

13. Genesis 30:23 And she conceived, and bare a son; and said, God hath taken away my reproach.
This is the first usage in the Bible of the word reproach. It concerns a woman's bearing a son to her husband. A man who is asked to take away a woman's reproach is being asked to take her as a wife and give her sons.
14. 1 Corinthians 11:3 But I would have you know, that the head of every man is Christ; and the head of the woman is the man; and the head of Christ is God.
15. Proverbs 25:24 It is better to dwell in the corner of the housetop, than with a brawling woman and in a wide house.
16. A marriage consists of a transfer of authority by the father or the woman followed by consummation. Samuel Wesley, the polygamist son of Charles Wesley, the famous hymn writer said the following concerning his first wife:
"She is truly and properly my wife by all the laws of God and nature. She never can be made more so by the mercenary tricks of divine jugglers but yet, if a million of ceremonies, repeated myriads of times, by as many successors and imitators of Simon Magus, can serve to make her more happy, or more honourable, I am ready to pay them for their hocus pocus, for I am told that in this evangelical age, the gift of God is not to be purchased without money." Samuel Wesley to his mother - November 7, 1792 Rylands DDWF 15/5 The Letters of Samuel Wesley: Professional and Social Correspondence, 1797-1837
By Samuel Wesley, Philip Olleson - 2001 - Page xxxiii
17. Song of Solomon 8:14 Make haste, my beloved, and be thou like to a roe or to a young hart upon the mountains of spices.
18. Song of Solomon 7:8-9 I said, I will go up to the palm tree, I will take hold of the boughs thereof: now also thy breasts shall be as clusters of the vine, and the smell of thy nose like apples; And the roof of thy mouth like the best wine for my beloved, that goeth down sweetly, causing the lips of those that are asleep to speak.

Chapter 18

HADASSAH'S WEDDING

Mary had already unpacked and given our suite her own special touch, including scented candles, but I wasn't expecting what happened next. The moment we got inside she grabbed me. I hadn't felt that much passion in her embrace since our honeymoon. I returned the passion and more. I lifted her to the bed where we lost ourselves in love making. After what seemed like only a few minutes we heard someone knocking. I walked over to the door and slid open the peep hole. It was Suni.

"What's taking you so long. You've had over an hour to get ready. It's just twenty-five minutes more till the wedding." She said.

"We'll be down in a few minutes." I assured her. "We've been resting up a bit."

"Well you can rest up a bit later. We've all got a wedding to attend." She said.

"Oh, absolutely, Suni. We'll *rest up* a bit later." Mary shouted from the bed. I could see now that this would become our new code phrase for love making; *rest up*.

Mary grabbed me again and pressed her lips, still full from an hour of passionate love making, against mine.

"Mm, are we resting up a bit?" I responded.

"Yes, but we'll have to rest up later. We have to hurry."

Before Mary let me go she squeezed my butt. She hadn't done that since we were newlyweds. She then half walked, half danced to the bathroom. Before entering, she turned back, intuitively knowing that my eyes would be following her scantily clad body. On cue, she dropped what few articles of clothing she was still wearing to the floor and stepped into the shower.

The passion that had taken us so many years of marriage to lose had miraculously returned, as if it had never left. Some might claim that John's story telling had sparked a primal chord in Mary but I'd been married far too long to believe that. A story, regardless of content, couldn't have caused such real passion to return with such fervor. No, I was certain it was the prayers of the forty nine single ladies over whom Sam had given me headship. Sam had told me that he'd instructed them long before I'd taken headship over them to start praying for the man he would appoint, and I was that man. They had been praying for my needs long before I'd even known that I would be praying for theirs.

Mary and I got down to John's dining hall with only a few minutes to spare. A stage now covered the area where the dining table had been and there was a large tent that adjoined it. The words *Marriage Chamber* were embroidered above the door. The tent, the stage, and everything on it, was white.

Elkanah was seated with John's family and there was an older gentleman sitting next to him.

"Could that be King Jochan?" I whispered to Mary.

"It must be." She said. "He has features just like Sarapita."

As the dining hall lights dimmed, John's sons began playing instruments and his daughters sang. I'd never heard such music before but there was something familiar about it. Then I realized that it was the sound John had described in his tale, the song of Sumba. A spotlight now lit the center of the stage. Ten women, all dressed in white, were holding lamps. Their flames burned brightly. The Song of Sumba increased in volume till I was sure I would have to cover my ears. Suddenly the sounds stopped and at the same moment five of the flames went out. John was apparently using the parable of the ten virgins as the backdrop for his wedding. Now the stage was filled with chatter. The brides whose lamps had gone out were begging the other five to give them oil. Finally, with no flames for their lamps, the foolish virgins left,[1] shouting to each other. "Hurry, we must find oil for our lamps." As soon as they'd gone, John opened the door from inside the marriage chamber and the five remaining brides entered. I was barely able to make out that it was John's four wives followed by Hadassah. After the door had shut, the five foolish virgins who had left for more oil returned to discover they'd been locked out of the marriage chamber.

"Lord, Lord, open to us![1]" They cried.

Now we heard John's bellowing voice from inside the marriage chamber reply.

"Verily I say unto you, I know you not.[1]"

The five foolish virgins left the stage playing their part, eyes downcast and sobbing what appeared to be real tears.

John's sons began to play a hymn as his four wives made their way back to their seats with their family. The girls, who had been playing the part of the five foolish virgins, took their seats as well.

The music faded and Elkanah stood up.

"John has asked for my daughter, Hadassah, as his wife. Not only have I gladly given her in marriage to him but she has joyously accepted John's offer of marriage. Let us dine while they taste the first fruits of their love."

The music began again, this time more upbeat like the sounds of a parade. Some of John's sons rolled the marriage chamber, John and Hadassah still inside, to the far end of the dining hall. Then they rolled the stage away to reveal John's banquet table, more glorious than ever. The abundance and variety of dishes made it clear that the delicacies we'd eaten earlier were no more than appetizers to ready us for this grander feast. I wondered who would feed me this time.

With uncanny timing, John's mother invited Mary to sit with her and her daughters-in-law. As she excused herself, Mary whispered in my ear as she gave it a nibble.

"Enjoy yourself. I know you're anxious to have some of your pretties make over you."

I kissed her on the cheek and she made off with her new found friends. She'd tell me later what common ground she had found with John's wives. I was sure they must have considered Mary and Sarisa a lonely pair; no wives in their households to share the joy of family with.

The moment Mary had left, Ruth grabbed her spot, like a child waiting her turn to grab a seat in musical chairs. She'd brought another girl with her who she managed to squeeze in between us.

"I think it's wise that my mother, Sarapita, offered her cousin, Zuah, in marriage to my father." She said. "That way she'd never be without at least one of her family members when she left Sumba. Ish, I'd like to introduce you to my cousin. She's been so anxious to meet you. Her name is Tamisa. It means perfection."

Ruth had a way of taking everything one step further. There was no taking two steps forward and one step back for her. Everything was full throttle and straight ahead.

"She is... perfection," I said, "I mean, her name means perfection. That is, Tamisa means perfection in Hebrew. Well of course, that's what you said."

Ruth tilted her head to one side and looked deeply into my eyes. Then she reached out with both hands and squeezed my cheeks.

"Mm! You're so cute when you have a crush."

I guess I was losing it. I didn't seem to be able to conceal what I was thinking anymore when it came to the single ladies.

"Was it that obvious?" I said.

"Ish, you're how old?" Ruth asked. "Never mind. When it comes to girls, you're like a school boy. I love you."

Tamisa reached out and shook my hand. She had the softest hands I'd ever touched. Ruth could tell I'd noticed.

"Even her hands are perfect, huh? My aunt never lets her clean or do chores without gloves and my uncle has wrapped her legs in a pillow case every night since the day she was born. You must touch her feet and feel how soft they are."

Ruth nodded in the direction of Tamisa's feet which she had folded underneath her where she sat nestled between us. Tamisa smiled and nodded, giving me the go ahead.

They *were* delicate and I couldn't resist. I planned to reposition myself in my seat and touch them as if it were an accident but once my hand felt their softness I had to let it linger a bit. Abruptly, I put my hands back on the table, forcing myself to focus on something, anything else.

Ruth winked at Tamisa as if signaling their plan had worked, or was it a signal for her to take my hand.

"Ruth tells me that your Mary doesn't mind that the girls have been giving you so much attention." Tamisa lightly stroked the hairs on the back of my hand as she spoke. "Ruth says you're a man with many destinies. Do you think she's right?"

"I'd much rather hear about you, Tamisa. Since Ruth has given you such an introduction, may I assume that you're born again?"

"Yes, but you're not going to change the subject that easily. What would you do if you had many wives, Ish? Would you treat them all the same?"

"Certainly not!" I said a little more forcefully than I'd intended.

"So he has thought about taking other wives!" Tamisa snapped her fingers, gleefully announcing what she thought she'd uncovered.

Ruth's face was now serious, like an interrogator.

"Why did you answer so quickly when Tamisa asked that question, Ish?"

I remembered John's story of Sarapita when she was seeking more information about him, how she'd taken the role of interrogator.

"You're forgetting that I'm in the habit of witnessing to people of many faiths. I like to bring out the differences between what the Bible teaches and what other religions teach. As your own father explained in his story, the Lord commands in Exodus 21:10 that if a man takes additional wives he may not diminish the food, the clothing, or the time he spends love making with his current wives.'2 I've written about this in depth. I've even referred to this verse as the establishment of the *first wives* club. A wife can hit her husband over the head with this verse like a club if he stops giving her what the Bible says is her due."

"Ruth is right, Ish. You are one of a kind." Tamisa squeezed my hand. "But let's be serious. You really have thought about what it would be like to have more than one wife, haven't you?"

"Tamisa, I haven't. But let me tell you a story."

"Go ahead, Ish." Tamisa continued to stroke the back of my hand, fascinated with the small hairs that stood at attention to her touch.

"When I was courting Mary, I still had some ideas that were certainly not Christian. I'd misled myself into believing that I would be happier if I didn't have any children."

"That's horrible, Ish. What ever gave you that idea?"

"I guess it was the lifelong indoctrination that goes on in every American school."

"So what did Mary have to say about your weird idea of having no children?" Tamisa asked.

"As our relationship grew, we arrived at a crossroads. I realized that it would be wrong of me to deny children to a wife who wanted them, so I prayed to the Lord for an answer and I did something that I thought would help me to understand Mary better. I tried to imagine what it would be like to want children but to be denied them. I tried to imagine what a woman would gain by having children and what she would miss by not having them. As I did this I couldn't help but realize all the things that I myself would miss out on by not having children. Having many children is part of that epic adventure that the Lord has made available to us. Why would I be so stupid as to refuse it. At that moment of epiphany, I penned a letter and sent it to Mary who was away visiting her mother. In it, I told her that I'd realized I wanted her to be the mother of my children, not just a few children but a dozen children. At the same time that my letter was making its way to her, she was sending a letter to me. In her letter she said that she wouldn't be happy without me and if it meant not having children then she would adjust."

"Wow! It's so wonderful to hear a story about a man with his maiden. Can I ask you to do something for Ruth and me?"

"Sure." I said.

"I want you to consider what it's like to be a woman who is ready to marry but can't, because the man who God has appointed for her doesn't want to marry her. This is the case for women such as Ruth and myself who have no hope of a husband unless we choose our husband from the already married. Who would want a single man anyway, no track record, and obviously not enough passion to drive him to get even one wife. We're like Mary was to you, only this concerns wives and not children. You wanted a wife but no children. You prayed about it and tried to empathize with Mary and came to the realization that having children was part of that epic drama that the Lord had put you here to enjoy. Well, now you want a wife but don't want additional wives. Furthermore, you have no reason whatsoever for not wanting the additional wives. You yourself have said that you have never seriously considered it."

"Well, I have to admit, you're right about that."

"Having more than one wife could surely be part of that epic drama that the Lord has put you here to enjoy. We ask only that you pray about it and try to empathize with Ruth and me, for we truly believe that you are our beshert, that one and only man who the Lord has chosen for us."

"I don't know what to say. I'm honored at what you're saying."

"Just say, you will."

"As in *I will.*"

Ruth and Tamisa politely smiled but they were no longer in the mood for flirtation. Ruth persevered.

"Please, Ish, we're serious. Don't make fun. My father and Tamisa's father have given their blessings to the union already. We could be wed tonight if it were your will. We're only asking that you'll pray with us about this and that you will do your best to imagine what blessings the Lord would bestow on you if you were married to us. You and Mary have not even had one of the dozen children you yourself have said you want. Having more wives may very well be the answer."

Had it not been for the loud music we would have been the center of attention but there was not one person in that room who heard what went on between Ruth, Tamisa, and myself. I was now overtaken with shame. I'd been using the girls' interest in me as a way to get attention, never realizing that they were not flirting. They were serious. The feeling of dread that comes upon a man when he knows he has sinned to the hurt of others caused my heart to sink. I thought of Suni. Just then I looked up and noticed she was observing us. I smiled warmly and nodded my head.

I answered Ruth and Tamisa, "I'll pray as you have asked. Please pray for me also, that I will be led of the Lord in all things."

"We will." Tamisa touched me again with her softest of hands. "Just remember, Ish, we are virgins and our fathers have agreed with us that you are our perfect match. You're a free man. A man need not have a calling from the Lord to get married. It is his decision which and how many help meets to accept. The Lord gave to Adam based on Adam's need, not based on Adam's calling. We will pray also that you will know that God has delivered us into your care as a blessing."

"Tamisa, your face is so perfect, no blemishes or wrinkles. It hides your wisdom." Tamisa looked down as was customary when complimented, then replied.

"There are so few men, Ish, that I *must* be wise. Solomon himself said that there is but one sincere man among a thousand. Ruth and I know that you are one of those. Solomon also said that there is not one such woman among a thousand but may the Lord grant that Ruth and I be such women among ten thousand as well as any other wives you may acquire."

"Amen." The three of us concurred.

We bowed our heads and held each others' hands while I prayed.

"Lord, I have never seriously considered having more than one wife. Help me to seriously consider this today. Guide me as I seek to understand this matter. Help me to understand the challenges and the blessings. Help me to know if this is something I should seriously pursue and help Mary to understand if I proceed. If I fear praying for Your wisdom on this matter, give me courage. If I fail to seriously consider this matter, give me the strength to rightly consider."

"Amen."

I looked up and saw that Suni, Modelisa, and Asina had joined us in prayer. They had tears in their eyes, then Suni spoke.

"We've been praying for a way to tell you Ish, but Ruth and Tamisa have done it already. I'm sure you know that Modelisa, Asina, and, I believe that the Lord has prepared you for us as well. There's no reason that you can't take all of us as wives."

"That's right." Ruth said.

The girls were all smiles now. I remembered wise King Solomon's words;

"Open rebuke is better than secret love."[3]

I was glad their love was no longer secret even though I was utterly confused as to what the Lord would want of me.

Before our happy little group had time to discuss anything further, the music stopped. An ornate box had been pushed out from a trap door of the marriage chamber. Elkanah ran over to get it. He opened it up.

"The tokens of Hadassah's virginity!" He shouted.

Elkanah walked back to his seat proudly carrying the box which held the blood stained cloth, the tokens of Hadassah's virginity.[4] The music began to play again, this time more quietly, in anticipation of the groom and his bride exiting the marriage chamber, now man and wife. All eyes were on the marriage chamber and we were not disappointed. John threw open the door.

"Ladies and gentlemen! My wife; Princess Hadassah."

John bowed and Hadassah curtsied. The lovely couple then proceeded to dance as John's sons played a waltz. The scene reminded me of the waltz scene in the *King and I* except that John had a full head of hair and Hadassah's gown looked like it came out of the pages of a fashion magazine.

John waltzed as you would expect a prince to waltz and Hadassah; Hadassah could have been Esther herself.[5] John had musicians, singers, dancers, great chefs and more, and they were all part of his happy family. He even had a biblical scholar in Ruth, not to mention Sulpicia and himself. After the waltz, John and Hadassah took their seats across the table from me.

"I suppose Ruth and Tamisa have had a chance to chat with you?" John asked.

"Yes, they have. Suni, Modelisa, and Asina have spoken with me as well, same subject."

"Well I approve, and so does Edward, Tamisa's father. Suni, Modelisa, and Asina can speak for themselves. What have you decided?"

"I haven't decided anything. I told them I would pray about it and that I would try to imagine things from their point of view."

"Try imagining it from your point of view too, old chap. You could do worse."

"That's true. I certainly don't know how I could do any better!"

"Honestly, Ish, I don't know either!"

John laughed that belly laugh we'd all grown so fond of. Now his mother brought Mary back to my side.

"John's wives have nearly convinced me that marrying you off to more wives would lengthen my life, restore my youth, and grow hair on a tortoise shell. And what have you been discussing with the girls, Ish?"

John answered for me.

"The girls have informed Ish that he'd better put up or shut up. If he doesn't marry them there's to be no more flirting or holding hands."

Mary thought John was kidding so she played along.

"Yes, I warned him about that. He's still trying to figure out which of the girls to marry first. That would make a difference in the pecking order."

"Indeed it would." Sarapita entered the conversation. "But in our case, that's never been a problem. *Many waters cannot quench love*[6] and John's love for us is great. We were so happy for Hadassah when we found out John was taking her for his wife. She'll never lack the love and attention that every wife deserves."

"Sarapita," Mary replied, "I think John was just kidding about Ish and the girls, but even so, I'm willing to listen to anything you have to say as long as John doesn't keep us waiting too much longer to hear the rest of his story."

"Well, Mary." John stood as he spoke. "Then you shall have the rest of the story. But first, let me introduce you to my betrothed, Princess Kasmina."

From the look on Mary's face, she was just as astounded as I was at John's words. No sooner had he taken a new wife than he'd announced his betrothal to another!

John walked over to where Princess Kasmina had been sitting and escorted her to us.

"I'd like to introduce you to some friends." He said. "This is Ish, the missionary I've been telling you about, and Mary, his wife."

"It gives me great pleasure to make your acquaintance." She said.

Mountaintop fortress or not, Princess Kasmina retained all the formality of her royal station. It was easy to imagine a band playing *God Save the Queen* every time she walked into a room.

"Princess Kasmina and I shall be wed seven days from tonight." John said.

"Congratulations!" Mary replied.

Although Mary had meant her congratulations for John, it was Princess Kasmina who thanked her. Even a princess was considered fortunate to have gotten a man in John's world, a world where a strong man could have all he wants. I wondered what it took to get such strength. Could all this have come from the material? He had five wives and now Princess Kasmina. He had a fortress on a hill, a book collection worth millions and surely tens of millions more in the bank. Anyone hearing his tale would not be able to resist calculating the value of the gold he gave his wives on their wedding nights, at least I couldn't. I figured it at over a million dollars each, and that was just sliding under the dresser money. I wondered what could be the source of John's power. Then I remembered Ruth, and the other girls. Here I was wondering where John got his power, and I had five beautiful virgins anxious to hear whether I would take them as wives! What took John twenty-five years to acquire had fallen into my lap in a matter of days. Where indeed did such power come from? Was I just finding out what happens when you throw a few good men among an abundance of chaste and God fearing women? Mary tugged my arm, pulling me back to reality... reality?

"Ish, maybe Princess Kasmina could tell us the rest of John's story."

Without realizing it, Mary had just forced Princess Kasmina to agree. Court etiquette doesn't allow a princess to appear cold or inhospitable to her guests. Princess Kasmina's response revealed that she was either a fantastic actress or genuinely interested in telling John's story. I was sure that both were true as she replied.

"That's a wonderful idea, Mary. That is, if my Prince agrees." Princess Kasmina looked at Prince John.

John's mother answered for him.

"Oh this will be fun. I'd like to share some of what I know as well."

"Then it's settled, mom." John said, "Hadassah and I will see all of you at breakfast time, well, brunchish."

We now heard John's new bride, Hadassah, speak for the first time.

"Yes, Brunch it shall be." Her voice was melodious, both strong and delicate. Now I knew what John meant in describing her as Hadassah, *strong but delicate*. Mary and I looked at each other, sharing our pleasure at discovering this tidbit of John's tale together.

"I've been rude." John said, "Let me introduce my mother, Princess Karima; the generous, the noble." John's mother smiled and nodded her head with royal bearing as she was introduced.

"Now that I've been introduced," she said, "let me offer a toast." She stood and raised her glass high. "May the marriage bed be blessed in all.[7] Be fruitful and multiply!"[8]

So many of us repeated her toast that it was like a shout, "Be fruitful and multiply!"

After the groom and his bride had left, John's mother took her seat, and began to speak.

"Now I can tell you things that only a mother could know. And Kasmina, the stories she can tell!"

According to John's story, Kasmina must have been about fourteen years older than his eldest child, but she appeared no older than the young ladies in Sam's church. The royal air about her disappeared as she took on the role of favorite niece to John's mother, even laying down on the bench to rest her head in her lap. John's mother stroked Kasmina's hair as she continued John's tale.

"Kasmina is wildly in love with my son, as you all know by now. Ruth told me how John let her read Kasmina's private memoirs to you as if it were a trite little love poem. If I'd been in the room, well, I wasn't, and what's done is done but let me tell you about Kasmina, her loyalty to me and Hadassah nearly got her killed and surely would have if Captain Stephen hadn't arrived when he did. She'd have lost her head for sure."

"Captain Stephen is alive?" Mary couldn't keep back her excitement.

"Alive? That man is alive enough for all his princess brides and then some, and a more loyal man I've never met. He saved Princess Kasmina, Hadassah, *and me* from the clutches of the worst kind of haters; those who demand tolerance for every kind of abomination but persecute those who worship the Lord. Praise the Lord we've made it here alive."

"So Elkanah's prophesy was true!" Mary said, "Captain Stephen didn't go down with the ship on Sumba!"

"Yes, Mary, the ship that went down on Sumba didn't even belong to Captain Stephen. What heavenly coincidence caused that wreckage to enter the harbor just when it did, is just that, heavenly, for it convinced my son, John, that he was indeed alone. That isolation along with the prayers of so many distant believers was what the Lord used to open up his heart to the gospel. Speaking of Elkanah's prophesies; you ought to hear what he's prophesied about your Ish, but you'll hear that soon enough. You asked for a tale of adventure and you'll have it."

"Grandma, could we pray before your story?" Ruth said.

"My granddaughter, Ruth, is wise. I must apologize. We barely made it out with our lives and my anger is still hot on my tongue. Can you forgive me, Ruth?"

"Of course, who wouldn't be upset after having just escaped from such horrible people. Maybe Sam can begin with a prayer for them."

John's mother nodded her head and then put on her prayer shawl. Sam prayed.

"*Lord, You know the hearts of all men and women. You know*

that without Your grace and leading9 that not one of us in this room could have the faith to believe that You sent Your Son for us, and that He died for our sins. Thank You for this. We pray now for the people of Princess Karima's kingdom. Lead their hearts and if necessary, use dreams and visions, so that they'll see that You are the One Holy God. Bless them to shame and bring them to a saving knowledge of You and Your Son, Our Lord and Savior Jesus the Messiah. In His Name we pray."

"*Amen.*" We agreed as one.

"Thank you Sam." John's mother tearfully whimpered. "I think I'll let Kasmina begin the story. I have lost so much of my zeal in all this. I know you must think me horrible. I've just been saved out of the hand of murderers. I should be grateful, but I'm so tired, so very tired."

"We understand, grandma, of course you're tired." Ruth comforted her grandmother then she spoke to Princess Kasmina. "Will you forgive me that I read your memoirs, Kasmina?"

Kasmina sat up from where she'd been laying in John's mother's lap.

"Yes, of course. You're so dear. I see the love you have for the Lord and you cannot hide your great love for Ish."

Mary turned to me and then looked at Ruth, realizing for the first time that John had not been kidding. The girls wanted me for their husband.

Chapter 18 Footnotes

1. Matthew 25:1-13 Then shall the kingdom of heaven be likened unto ten virgins, which took their lamps, and went forth to meet the bridegroom. And five of them were wise, and five were foolish. They that were foolish took their lamps, and took no oil with them: But the wise took oil in their vessels with their lamps. While the bridegroom tarried, they all slumbered and slept. And at midnight there was a cry made, Behold, the bridegroom cometh; go ye out to meet him. Then all those virgins arose, and trimmed their lamps. And the foolish said unto the wise, Give us of your oil; for our lamps are gone out. But the wise answered, saying, Not so; lest there be not enough for us and you: but go ye rather to them that sell, and buy for yourselves. And while they went to buy, the bridegroom came; and they that were ready went in with

him to the marriage: and the door was shut. Afterward came also the other virgins, saying, Lord, Lord, open to us. But he answered and said, Verily I say unto you, I know you not. Watch therefore, for ye know neither the day nor the hour wherein the Son of man cometh.

2. Exodus 21:10 If he take him another wife; her food, her raiment, and her duty of marriage, shall he not diminish.

This verse is a command. It absolutely forbids a man from diminishing the first wife's food, clothing, or time for love making, even if the first wife says it's okay. Those who say that wives should be treated equally are opposing this Scripture.

3. Proverbs 27:5 Open rebuke is better than secret love.

The following verse also applies to anyone waiting for love:

Proverbs 13:12 Hope deferred maketh the heart sick: but when the desire cometh, it is a tree of life.

4. Deuteronomy 22:15 Then shall the father of the damsel, and her mother, take and bring forth the tokens of the damsel's virginity unto the elders of the city in the gate.

5. The Esther of the Bible was called Hadassah before she became a princess.

Esther 2:7 And he brought up Hadassah, that is, Esther, his uncle's daughter: for she had neither father nor mother, and the maid was fair and beautiful; whom Mordecai, when her father and mother were dead, took for his own daughter.

6. Song of Solomon 8:7 Many waters cannot quench love, neither can the floods drown it: if a man would give all the substance of his house for love, it would utterly be contemned.

7. Hebrews 13:4 Marriage is honourable in all, and the bed undefiled: but whoremongers and adulterers God will judge.

8. Genesis 28:3 And God Almighty bless thee, and make thee fruitful, and multiply thee, that thou mayest be a multitude of people.

9. Psalm 25:5 Lead me in thy truth, and teach me: for thou art the God of my salvation; on thee do I wait all the day.

Psalm 84:11 For the LORD God is a sun and shield: the LORD will give grace and glory: no good thing will he withhold from them that walk uprightly.

HYMNS THAT CONVERT THE SOUL

Asina broke the tension.

"Princess Kasmina, we're so anxious to hear what happened next with your prince."

"Of course, I'll start by telling you what happened when Captain Stephen returned home without Prince John."

Kasmina hesitated.

"Mary, are you all right?"

The Princess reached out and felt Mary's forehead.

"I think this mountain air has given you a fever. We've got to get you some medicine and put you to bed."

Modelisa rushed over to Mary and opened up a black bag. She took out a stethoscope and a blood pressure cuff.

"You don't need to do all this for me." Mary moaned.

Modelisa simply continued to check Mary's vital signs.

"Her blood pressure is fine and she couldn't have a stronger heart, Ish."

Modelisa slipped a thermometer under Mary's tongue before she could object.

"You've got a slight temperature, Mary. How does your stomach feel?"

Mary cracked a smile as she looked down at her normally thin waistline, her tummy protruding against her belt.

"I have to admit, I haven't stuffed myself this much since I was a kid at thanksgiving dinner."

"Try loosening your belt a notch." Modelisa advised.

"Ah, oops. Excuse me." Mary belched loudly as she finished loosening her belt. "Much better." She sighed. "I'm okay now. I'm ready to hear the story."

Asina whispered to Mary, "Please, let me get you some tea for your stomach first."

"No thanks, Asina, but you could get me some of Ruth's wonderful mountain grown coffee, grown right here on this mountain, *just like Ruth*."

Mary exaggerated the phrase, *just like Ruth,* to let everyone know that my flirtations with Ruth had not gone unnoticed. Just as exaggerated was the position of Mary's head as she spoke, which she carefully kept turned in any direction but mine. This so delighted Asina that she had to turn her own head away from Mary's and bite her lip to hold back a giggle.

Just then Ruth's little sister pushed a cart with coffee and pastries into the room.

"Wonderful!" Asina spouted, shifting all of the energy from her held back giggle into a huge grin. "Just what you wanted Mary, coffee, *and more pastries*!"

Asina pushed out her own tummy now, demonstrating to Mary that she wasn't the only one to have over indulged. She was able to push that tiny belly of hers out so far that she looked five months pregnant. As Mary cracked up, so did the rest of us, grateful that the tension had left the room.

These girls were so fun to be with. I felt so at home. I remembered the girl at the church coffee as everyone filled their cups, mostly with cream.

"Do you take coffee in your cream, or do you drink it white?" One of them had said.

"Black," I replied.

"Black cream?" She giggled. "Whoever heard of such a thing."

Asina brought me back from my daydream, grasping my hand to pour coffee in my cup. Talk about chemistry, I hadn't felt a burst of sensuality like that since Modelisa introduced herself. Had she been giving Asina lessons? At first Asina's hand was graceful and warm, then as quickly as she'd startled me with her sensuality I felt her pull back. I looked up. Her eyes were misty. Since no one had ventured to take the seat next to mine after Mary's comment, I motioned to Asina.

"Please, sit here. Princess Kasmina is about to begin her story."

I wondered if Asina's affections would speak as loudly as she did. I wasn't disappointed. The Asina I'd learned to love and respect plopped herself down on the chair territorially, making sure to command the side of it closest me, her leg pressed firmly against mine.

We were all seated now; Mary to my right, Asina to my left,

Sam, Sarisa, and the girls had taken their places around the table, and the Princess with her soon to be mother-in-law sat across from us. John's wives had left to put the younger kids to bed and to supervise their other children who were busy cleaning up after the banquet.

I was glad that someone other than myself would again be the focus of attention. Certainly I didn't believe that a story, no matter how well Princess Kasmina might tell it, would make Mary forget the predicament I'd put us in. Nonetheless, it would allow me to relax and lose myself in someone else's adventure.

Asina was silent now, in contrast to her normally boisterous self. Her words had been replaced with what felt like an electro-magnetic current passing from her body to mine. I wondered if she felt it too.

"Bet you didn't know Modelisa was a doctor." Asina whispered to me.

"Well, judging from Modelisa's talents, I'm not surprised." I whispered back. "Why doesn't she use her title?"

"She made us promise not to. She thought it might scare you away."

Now I wondered even more whether Modelisa had orchestrated this mountain retreat for the sole purpose of getting me to marry her and the rest of the girls. Who better than Modelisa to conduct such a symphony of seduction. The fact that she was a doctor would have been the last thing about Modelisa that would have made me timid. I laughed to myself. If I did marry Modelisa and the rest of the girls, just think of the money my wives would save on gynecologists. Not to mention that if anyone ever gave us legal trouble they'd have Asina, our feisty attorney, to deal with, and that is a challenge no man in his right mind would welcome. It was now Asina's gaze that brought me back to the moment. Her inquisitive eyes were inspecting every aspect of my face, first my eyes, then my lips, now my cheeks.

"Ahem." Princess Kasmina alerted us that she was about to begin.

"The life of a princess in my kingdom is not happy. Her life is filled with more perils than that of a peasant girl. At the whim of the king, a princess may be given as chattel in a treaty with heathens or abused inside the palace and the crime covered up.

Peasants can always appeal for justice to the king, but if the king's own household is dealt with treacherously, where shall they appeal? I count myself especially blessed that the Lord has used Princess Karima to watch over me."

Princess Kasmina now grasped Karima's hand.

"She has taught me and she has guided me. It was through her secret books that I was able to come to a saving knowledge of our Lord and Savior, Jesus, the Messiah."

The room echoed with praises.

"Praise God, Alleluia, That's wonderful."

"Secret books?" Mary asked.

"Yes, secret books. In In my kingdom, if you are caught studying any book that teaches that Jesus is the Messiah, you will be taken to the neighborhood basketball court where you'll be publicly executed. Their favorite method is to saw your head off slowly with a dull blade. The religious leaders teach that theirs is a religion of peace but it is a religion of destruction, even hate. Princess Karima taught me from the gospel of John and a few hymns. That's how I learned English. She had miraculously come into the possession of versions in both our language and in English. I was fascinated to learn a foreign tongue and it was this fascination that kept my attention long enough to realize that it is not by works of righteousness which we might do, but according to His mercy that God has saved us, by the washing of regeneration, and renewing of the Holy Ghost."[1]

The praises to God from around the room began again. The inspiration of Princess Kasmina's testimony caused the girls to begin silently praying and worshipping the Lord. Occasionally the worship would be vocalized with a *Praise the Lord* or *Praise His Name*, all in a low enough tone so that Kasmina could continue her story.

"Oh, wonderful." The Princess said, "This is how the joy of our Lord is shared where we have no fear of reprisals? I'm glowing!" Kasmina fanned herself. "I think I've got a little bit of Mary's fever. So this is what my John meant when he said you were all on fire for the Lord. Praise God Alleluia! Oh, this is invigorating."

"*Amen!*" Suni piped.

"*Alleluia!*" Asina followed suit.

"This is joyous." Princess Kasmina continued in a more

animated voice now. "Before today, my salvation was shared only with Princess Karima, Captain Stephen, and Hadassah. Excuse me, I should be saying *Princess* Hadassah. But we did find joy in singing, even though we sang in whispers for fear of the religious leaders. In fact, I came to know the Lord through a song that I was reading in order to learn English. You may have heard it. I memorized it. I'll sing it for you if you like?"

"Please do, please do." The girls pleaded in unison.

"O Jesus, our Lord
Thy Name be adored,
For all the rich blessings,
conveyed through thy word.

In spirit we trace
The wonders of grace,
And Cheerfully join,
in a concert of praise.

Princess Karima could no longer be sad and joined her soon to be daughter-in-law with a melodious harmony.

The Ancient of Days
His Glory displays,
And shines on his chosen,
with cherishing rays."

The song that the two princesses sang moved Mary such that she forgot her pouting and whispered in my ear.

"I've never heard that song. It's so lovely and moving. Where on earth did they find that?"

I was at a loss. I hadn't heard the song either.

"I don't know, Mary. It's quite angelic, isn't it?"

"That's the word, Ish, angelic."

Mary sat back, satisfied that she was hearing something quite unusual and heavenly.

Asina was now up, and again, like an angel herself, the feet of a ballerina, she floated across the room. Her tambourine accented the song in perfect timing. The girls hummed melodiously till the part where the verse repeated itself, and then they sang along. No one had to give them permission to praise God in song. Formality had no place when they expressed their love for the Lord.

"The trumpet of God
Is sounding abroad,
The language of mercy,
salvation through blood.

Thrice happy are they
Who hear and obey,
And share in the blessings,
of this gospel day.

The people who know
The Saviour below,
With burning affection,
to worship him glow."

Mary was singing every bit as much as the girls now. The hardness in her face had left as tears rolled down her cheeks. Still, she sang along, having been handed a hymnal from Prince John's collection. Ruth had opened it to the song Kasmina had begun.

"Their anguish and smart,
And Sorrows depart,
Who find his salvation,
inscribed on their heart.

This blessing is mine,
Through favour divine;
But O my Redeemer,
the glory be thine.

The work is of grace;
Thine, thine be the praise;
And mine to adore thee,
and tell of thy ways."

We were all clapping now, both to the Lord and for our joy to have found such a song. How could this song have remained hidden for so many years. Having never heard it, it sounded new and fresh. What could it have been that caused such a heartfelt song to be lost, I asked myself. Mary was asking the same question, only to Ruth.

"Ruth, Ruth, what is this hymnal?"

Ruth shyly looked down.

"It's, it's the hymnal that Martin Madan put together." Ruth now raised her eyes and looked directly at Mary. "He donated this hymnal to the London Lock Hospital for Women in hopes that the proceeds from its sale would help to maintain and promote the charitable cause of that institution."

"I, well you know I hate the idea of polygamy, but this song, I can't think of any reason that anyone would want to cover up such a song to the Lord, unless they had something against the author and didn't want to give him credit. Did, Martin Madan write this song?"

Ruth lost her shyness now as she spoke of the man who she considered persecuted for righteousness sake.

"As far as I know, he wrote the words to the song.[2] At least I haven't found any record in history of anyone else taking credit for it and he's certainly credited with composing the music for it. It first showed up in his hymnal. The tune is called Winwick. It's wonderful, isn't it?"

"Of course Ruth, especially since its words brought Kasmina to a saving knowledge of our Lord."

"But if there's any doubt as to his authorship of this song," Ruth said, "it's undisputed that he wrote the words to *Now Begin the Heav'nly Theme*. Most people know it as *Redeeming Love*."[3]

"He wrote *Redeeming Love*!" Cherry shouted. "That's the song that Sarisa had playing in the background when I first came to know the Lord! I'll never forget the words,

Ye, alas! who long have been
Willing slaves to death and sin,
Now from bliss no longer rove,
Stop and taste redeeming love."

"That's wonderful Cherry!" Ruth bubbled. "But you know, Martin Madan's legacy didn't end with his own music."

Ruth now spoke to everyone present, delivering a much needed lesson in church history.

"Martin Madan's good friend Charles Wesley, who we know as the greatest hymn writer of the Eighteenth Century, had a son named Samuel. Now Charles Wesley respected Martin Madan so much that he made him the godfather of this son, and during the many days that Samuel Wesley spent with his beloved godfather, he learned from the Bible that a man doesn't need a public ceremony to be married. He also learned that the Bible allows polygamy."

Ruth handed Mary a book, pointing to a paragraph she'd circled.

"Read what Samuel Wesley had to say about his first wife. This is a book that contains all of his letters."[4]

Mary put on her reading glasses, then peered over them at Ruth.

"First wife? Okay, okay. I'll read it. Just don't look at me like that. I'm supposed to be the angry housewife." Mary winked. "Here's what Samuel Wesley wrote concerning his, ahem, *first wife*, Charlotte Louisa Martin.

She is truly and properly my wife by all the laws of God and nature. She never can be made more so by the mercenary tricks of divine jugglers but yet, if a million of ceremonies, repeated myriads of times, by as many successors and imitators of Simon Magus, can serve to make her more happy, or more honourable, I am ready to pay them for their hocus pocus, for I am told that in this evangelical age, the gift of God is not to be purchased without money."

Mary handed the book back to Ruth, then commented.

"I agree with what he's written here, Ruth. No pastor or pope needs to preside over any marriage to make it valid."

Ruth was determined to build on this momentum.

"I'm happy to hear that Mary. Then you'll agree that when Samuel Wesley betrothed his fifteen year old maid to himself and consummated the marriage in the same house where he was still living with his first wife, that the marriage was valid?"[5]

"Wait a minute, Ruth. You're telling me that Charles Wesley's son, Samuel, was a polygamist?"

"Yes, Mary, and if Samuel hadn't taken Sarah Suter as his

second wife, *Pexy* as he was fond of calling her, they wouldn't have given birth to the man known as..."

Mary finished the sentence.

"Don't tell me! *Samuel Sebastian Wesley*? the premier organist and most famous church musician of the 19th century?"[6]

"That's right Mary. You know him as the grandson of Charles Wesley but the church has covered up the fact that Charles Wesley was the father of a polygamist. The greatest hymn writer of the Eighteenth Century; father to a polygamist. The greatest church musician of the 19th century, son of a polygamist. The Lord was watching over him though for Samuel Sebastian Wesley was never denied the legitimacy of the son of a first wife even though he was the progeny of a polygamist's second wife. By the end of his illustrious life he had reached such heights that he was offered a knighthood in recognition of his great contributions to music.[7] We would not have such tunes as ..."

Mary couldn't help finishing Ruth's sentence again.

"*The Church's One Foundation is Jesus Christ her Lord!*"

"Amen!" The room shouted.

"But my point," Ruth continued, "is that if Samuel's father had feared what others might think, to be specific, what confused Christians might think, he might not have taken Pexy as a second wife; Samuel Sebastian Wesley would not have been born, and we wouldn't have all those hymn tunes that have brought millions closer to the Lord."

Mary loved the older hymns and by now she was in tears.

"I don't know what you're doing to me, this is all so... shocking!" She sobbed, "But I love these men, Charles Wesley, then Martin Madan who put it all together in that hymnal that sparked the great 19th century revivals,[8] and finally, the grandson of the great Charles Wesley, Samuel Sebastian Wesley, son of a polygamist, who continued the legacy of his family's ministry through music. Now you tell me that the evangelism of the last two hundred years would not be what it's been except for the appearance on the scene of the Reverend Martin Madan, a dear Christian man..." Mary was nearly overcome with her sobbing now. The girls huddled around her, comforting her. She stopped sobbing long enough to finish her thought, "a dear Christian man who just happened to write a book favoring what I am loathe to accept, but must, that the Bible clearly teaches a man can have more than one wife."

Chapter 19 Footnotes

1. Titus 3:5 Not by works of righteousness which we have done, but according to his mercy he saved us, by the washing of regeneration, and renewing of the Holy Ghost.

2. Martin Madan is credited with having composed "Winwick" which is the tune for this Hymn. This hymn first showed up in Madan's 1765 printing of A Collection of PSALM and HYMN TUNES Never Published before.

References: Hymn Tune Index - Nicholas Temperley

Since there is no record of any author for the words and the hymn first turned up in Madan's own hymnal, it is very likely that Madan also wrote the words.

3. The Reverend John Langford has wrongly been credited with writing Redeeming Love. Although it appeared in his hymnal of 1776, he did not mark it with an asterisk as was his custom for his own hymns. Furthermore, Redeeming Love first appeared in Madan's hymnal *thirteen years earlier.* See Annotations Upon Popular Hymns By Charles Seymour Robinson 1893 - Page 322.

4. Samuel Wesley to his mother - November 7, 1792 Rylands DDWF 15/5 The Letters of Samuel Wesley: Professional and Social Correspondence, 1797-1837

By Samuel Wesley, Philip Olleson - 2001 - Page xxxiii

5. The Dictionary of National Biography Edited by Sidney Lee Volume XX Ubaldini----Whewell Published 1909 - Pages 1231-1233

A Family Tree of the Wesleys can be seen on page 908 of the Cyclopaedia of Biblical, Theological, and Ecclesiastical Literature by M'Clintock and Strong Volume X.--SU-Z 1891

6. Samuel Sebastian Wesley: A Life by Peter Horton Hardcover - 2004 - Page 5

7. Samuel Sebastian Wesley: A Life by Peter Horton Hardcover - 2004 - Page 1

8. "He (William Romaine) held the extreme Calvinistic position as to the exclusive use of inspired words in Praise, and was able to impose his views upon his own congregation. But he could not stay the rising tide of Hymn singing or make a breach between the

Gospel and the Hymns of the Revival. *In Martin Madan the new Hymn singing found an effective sponsor.* The humorous and sturdy John Berridge was as early on the field as Madan, but less effective."
The Princeton Theological Review - Volume XII - 1914
The Princeton University Press - Princeton, N.J. - Page 73,74

Who could have guessed that the most popular Christian concerts of the 18th century would take place in a chapel attached to a hospital for the treatment of venereal disease? Such was the miraculous beginning of the ministry of Reverend Martin Madan.

Lock Chapel as it stood in Madan's day.

Chapter 20

GOOD TIDINGS

Mary was no longer crying. She looked up at all the girls who'd been huddled around her and said,

"You are such a wonderful group of godly women. I'm so sorry that it's only now that I'm willing to get to know each one of you."

"Oh no, Mary, don't talk like that." Modelisa objected, "Everyone has their own comfort level. We knew you'd warm up to us. After all, you've just arrived. You're suffering from a bit of culture shock."

"Yeah, just a bit of culture shock." Mary sniffled, then broke into the giggles.

The girls giggled along with her as each one of them repeated the understatement of the evening: *Just a bit of culture shock.*

Mary, however, was more shy than they realized. It hadn't been so much the culture shock that kept her separated from them but her sense of being an outsider. Mary never reached her comfort level until she felt part of a group. She now felt as fully part of their group as if she'd attended college with them. As she relaxed, she opened up.

"Ruth," Mary confided, "how can I blame you for wanting my husband. Pleasing him is all I think about."

I caught myself thinking, "Yeah sure, pleasing me? Is that why you complained about our going to Mindanao?" Then I repented. Here I was; an imperfect man, judging Mary; *who by every word she spoke was proving that she did want to please me. I prayed that I could be as willing to please the Lord as Mary had been willing to please me.*

Ruth responded to Mary, "I also think only of pleasing your husband. It seems I can think of little else. Since you arrived I've been struck with some kind of ..."

Mary stopped Ruth mid-sentence,

"Okay, okay, I got your point. You don't have to rub it in."

Ruth finished the sentence anyway, "...mania."

Mary shook her head in disbelief that Ruth could respond so matter-of-factly to the wife of the man she wanted.

"You're so innocent, Ruth, and your faith that the Lord is going to change my heart about this matter is even more endearing, but I can't believe I'm even talking with you."

"I'm glad that you are, Mary."

"I have to admit it, Ruth, I am too."

Mary and Ruth hugged like long separated best cousins, then Ruth added,

"The Lord has His own plans. We'll just have to see what those are."

"Yes, we will, Ruth." Mary now turned to me. "You're not off the hook yet, Ish, but I just can't blame these innocent girls for falling for you. It really *does* seem like the best men are taken, at least among Christians."

"I'm not off the hook yet?" I replied. "I wasn't aware a husband could ever be off the hook."

"Hooks." Suni corrected me, then she made a hook with her index finger and teasingly shook it at me. The other girls did the same.

Mary rolled her eyes but couldn't help smiling at their silliness.

"I've been corrected," I responded. "*Hooks.* Now let's take a moment to pray before Princess Kasmina continues her story.

Lord, you know the hearts of these women. You know my heart. You know Mary's heart. Guide me. Guide Mary and guide these women. Princess Kasmina has been telling us her story, a story of Your great grace. May her story continue to remind each one of us that we are saved by Your grace, not by works lest anyone should boast.[1] In the Name of Your Precious Son, Our Lord Jesus, we pray. Amen.'"

Mary squeezed my hand in agreement that the Lord's will be done. Asina was now more relaxed and caressed my hand openly.

"We're ready for your story, Princess." Mary coaxed Kasmina.

"Thank you, this is all so new. As I was saying, I came to know the Lord through the Reverend Martin Madan's song. It was this verse:

The language of mercy,
salvation through blood.

I had never encountered any teaching that spoke of mercy and blood. As each of you knows, before coming to a saving knowledge of our Lord, we can be taught many things, but there is a moment for most of us where some odd sequence of words or events strikes us in such a way that the salvation of our soul presents itself as a choice.[3] Princess Karima had taught me long and well about the blood of Jesus but it meant nothing till these words parted my own lips; first in song, then in ecstatic praise.

'The language of mercy,
salvation through blood.'

My voice kept getting louder as I nearly shouted it,

'The language of mercy,
salvation through blood!'

Then Princess Karima struck me from behind, knocking me to the ground, and covered my mouth.

'Kasmina!' She whispered through clenched teeth. 'Those outside the gates will hear us!'

I wondered why she could be so angry with me for praising the Lord.

'Please,' Karima continued. 'We love the Lord too but there is a time to die. Let it not be today. It is true that my husband is the king but he is surrounded by wretched men who swear allegiance to *tolerance*, a tolerance for anyone who is *not* Christian.'

'She's right.' Hadassah chided me. 'We're overjoyed that you now know the Lord but let's wait for the time and place where we may publicly share our love of Him. Let us not die today.'

I realized they were right and at once became aware of how strange and brutal was the kingdom in which I lived."

Princess Kasmina broke from story telling and now enthusiastically asked the girls.

"When will you take me to the street corners, the sidewalks, the anywhere that we may shout our love for the Lord!"

"Why not here and now?" Asina asked.

Then Princess Kasmina ran to the window, and threw it open.

"I love the Lord of Abraham, Isaac, and Jacob![2] I praise you Jesus! Alleluia! Praises to the One and Only Lord of all. Thank You Jesus! May my voice never be silenced for fear of persecution again!"

As Kasmina said *again* her expression turned from joy to sorrow.

"Captain Stephen came to know the Lord too," Kasmina explained, "but in the process of freeing us, he was captured."

At that very moment, the door burst open.

"Captain!" Princess Kasmina shouted.

Captain Stephen's years at sea could be counted in the furrows of his face; parched by the salt air and equatorial sun, he looked old and worn, till he smiled, then his face lit up from his jowls to his temples. I'd never seen a man who had that many wrinkles but more hair than a teenager. His three wives huddled closely around him while their quiver full of kids were huddling just as closely around them. His bodyguards had stationed themselves just outside the door.

"Captain Stephen!" Kasmina broke into a flood of tears. She could barely speak. The joy that had flushed her cheeks earlier returned, and then some.

"Do you forget so quickly?" Captain Stephen said,

"*The man who lays a hand on me*
Deals not with one but one plus three
Each wife I have has a father too
A cannibal chief to avenge me
A cannibal chief to avenge me"

"I always thought that song was a bit silly," Kasmina responded, "but now I know you weren't kidding."

"Well, I did make up the part about them being cannibals but the rest is true."

Captain Stephen's eyes twinkled expressively. He was wearing a grin like a school boy who'd just played a practical joke.

"Josiah, you're going to take care of this, right?" Captain Stephen was speaking to John's eldest son as he motioned toward his children.

"Yes, yes, Captain. We'll take care of them."

Some of John's teenage kids who'd been helping in the kitchen were now scooping up Captain Stephen's kids like they were carry on luggage.

"Whoa there." Captain Stephen said, "I've got to give them their good night kisses."

As the Captain bent down to say good night to his kids, I heard him whisper to them,

"We're safe now. We have five kings to protect us. Jesus who is The King of kings, your three grandfathers, and King John."

Captain Stephen then said a prayer as he held his hands over his children, then he kissed each one of them before sending them off with Josiah.

"We'll get them fed right away and make sure they're cleaned up before bed." Josiah assured the Captain.

"I know you will, Josiah. Thank you brother."

"It's nothing Uncle." Josiah addressed Captain Stephen like family.

"Princess," Captain Stephen apologized, "I'm sorry for interrupting your gathering but just when John's sons were letting us in the gates I heard you shouting out the window. I couldn't let you think I was rotting in a dungeon, or worse. Now that you know we're safe, my wives and I will be getting some sleep."

"Captain Stephen," Sam interrupted, "before you leave us, please be seated. We have a custom when visitors arrive. It will just take a few minutes. Besides, your rooms are still being readied."

Some of John's children had brought basins with warm water into the room. Sam began washing Captain Stephen's feet3 and the rest of John's sons washed the feet of the men we'd mistaken for bodyguards. They were actually Captain Stephen's three fathers-in-law, themselves kings. Princess Kasmina set about washing the feet of one of Stephen's wives and Princess Karima another. Sarisa was about to start washing the feet of the other of Captain Stephen's wives when Mary jumped up.

"No, let me, Sarisa."

I hadn't seen Mary wash feet since she'd taken care of her grandmother. It wasn't that Mary didn't know how to serve. Her ability to serve made me look like a selfish brat. It was that Mary resisted service that was commanded by Scripture, as if it made her less of a person, but Mary was behaving very differently now. She seemed more connected, as if she finally felt part of an extended family of Christians.

Sam apologized that we hadn't gotten the same reception;

"Ish, you and Mary weren't welcomed with a foot washing because we weren't sure how you'd react. We thought you might think we were a bunch of kooks. I guess we were wrong."

"No Sam, you weren't wrong," Mary said, "I'm sure I would have thought you were nuts but a lot has happened today. I'm not the person I was this morning and I owe that to the girls."

"Oh Mary, don't give us credit for something we did for selfish motives." Modelisa objected.

"Selfish or not," Mary said, pouring the water out of her basin and washing her hands in the sink. "the Lord used you girls to soften my heart, especially toward my dear husband, Ish. Ish, you're a good man. I'm sorry that I haven't said that enough and if it brings one of those adorable tears to your eyes for my saying so, then I'll just have to kiss it away."

Mary sat back down next to me, taking my hand again then continued. "But just as you are so emotional on one level, you are far too analytical on another. I know you've been praying that the Lord will let you know whether it's His will that you make wives of Suni, Ruth, Modelisa, Asina, and Tamisa but what I've got to say about this is; *Are you nuts?* The Bible permits you to marry who you will so why wouldn't you? Sorry Ish, I want to explain this to you in all submission, especially since I know you as my lord today more than I could *ever* have imagined, but I must speak. We've been married many years and there are lots of things you are; stubborn, arrogant, even condescending at times, but stupid? Never! Stop praying for an answer when you need none. Accept your blessings! Not to mention, *Go and multiply*."[4] Then she winked!

I couldn't believe my eyes, or my ears. It was as if they were on fire. Mary now looked at the girls, "Now I'm the one being selfish, Modelisa. No matter how great a husband he is, life can be monotonous. Having you girls as wives for Ish would mean a home full of godly people, and your children, *how beautiful they will be*!"[5]

All of us were so shocked at Mary's change of heart that not one of us had noticed that Princess Karima was crying, then she spoke.

"My husband is dead, isn't he, Captain?"

"Dead? Dead to sin. He's more fit than I am and you don't have to take my word for it. You can take it up with him yourself. He'll be up here in the morning."

Princess Karima paused to wipe her tears away.

"Then why have you referred to my son John, as king?"

"It's like this, princess. The king, well, the former king, your husband that is, has put together some papers, and in them he says that he's given the crown to your son, John. Simple as that."

Captain Stephen's sinewy muscles strained as he picked up a cube shaped case, big enough for a large bowling ball. He reached inside and pulled out a crown. It was huge. I could see that when Captain Stephen said the crown was John's he mean it, literally.

"Here's King John's crown and here are the papers."

Captain Stephen handed the papers to Karima. I couldn't resist gawking, and sure enough, there it was, a stamp made with the king's signet ring exactly as John had described it in his story.

Captain Stephen placed the crown in the middle of the table in front of us. It was dazzling. It was made of layer upon layer of diamonds woven together with gold. It cast a brilliant rainbow of light around the room. My first thought was; where's the security? Then I remembered Captain Stephen's fathers-in-law and John's armory. If there were a safer place in all the Philippines for such riches, I knew of none. Captain Stephen then explained the reason for giving the crown to John.

"Your husband has decided that it will take a younger man to retake the kingdom and make it free for Christians. It's your son, King John, who will have that honor. Lord willing, John will bring freedom to your kingdom so that you can return soon. Oh yes, there's the matter of Josiah's sons."

"Josiah's sons?" Grandma Karima scowled. "Josiah knows better than to keep secrets."

Captain Stephen clarified himself;

"Excuse me, Princess Karima, it isn't that Josiah has been keeping secrets, but that your husband has grown weary of waiting for his grandson to take a wife, so he sent three princess brides for him. Josiah will have sons soon enough. May I introduce the betrotheds of Prince Josiah."

Three tall and attractive women stepped into the room. Just then, Josiah returned, so instead of introducing the princesses to us, Captain Stephen let the princesses introduce themselves to Josiah.

"Your intended, Prince Josiah." Captain Stephen said to the women.

Each of them gracefully knelt before Prince Josiah, their husband to be.

"I am Princess Carmel."[6] The first said. She took Prince Josiah's hand and kissed it. "May the Lord always be praised in our home."

"Amen." Prince Josiah responded.

The second said,

"I am Princess Carshena."[7] She kissed Josiah's hand, then added.

"May our family pray in humility and may the Lord gently guide us when we fail him."

"Amen." Prince Josiah responded again.

Before the third spoke, Josiah whispered to Princess Karima.

"What happened to Grandpa, is he...?"

"Your grandpa's fine. He'll be here in the morning. Don't worry."

Prince Josiah's face now shone brightly. He was proclaimed a prince sooner than he'd expected and he couldn't have picked better wives if he'd done it himself.

The third princess now took Josiah's hand, holding on to it. A tear rolled down her face, falling onto the back of his hand.

"I am Princess Casiphia. I can add little to what the others have said, but to tell you that my name means 'longing for the LORD' and that my prayer is this; Just as the LORD has put a longing and a love for Him in my heart, even in my name, that He will also put a longing and a love for you in my heart as you take away my reproach, and as I am called by your name."

Prince Josiah looked upon Casiphia kindly. It seemed as if the vainglory he'd momentarily enjoyed had left him and he now reminded me of his father, King John, stately and full of love.

"May all my wives learn to love me and may I be as the Lord in my love for each of them, ever giving. May the Lord answer all their prayers. Amen."

In an instant, Casiphia's face lit up, as if her prayer to long for and to love Prince Josiah had just been answered. She looked up at him adoringly. Stooping down, Josiah helped each of them to their feet, then declared.

"I present to you my princesses, Carmel, Carshena, and Casiphia! May I adorn their lives with family and fullness, as they adorn this room with their beauty, and may they always love the Lord more than they love me. Amen!"

A chorus of *Amen*s and applause followed.

I whispered in Ruth's ear. "Three brides and just a few minutes ago he didn't even have a girlfriend!"

"I've got to admit it," Ruth whispered back, "even though I'm the daughter of a polygamist, three brides in three minutes must be some sort of record."

Josiah now asked Captain Stephen, "Am I right that these princess brides are gifts from my grandfather?"

"Yes, Prince Josiah."

"And did Grandfather command that I take one before the other?"

Before Captain Stephen had a chance to answer, Josiah's grandfather walked in the door, a bit earlier than expected. He exchanged smiles with his wife, Karima, then answered Josiah's question himself.

"Casiphia is your bride tonight. Go now. See that you please her."

His grandfather pointed to the tent which had been set up by Josiah's brothers and sisters while he'd been distracted by his brides. The musicians began playing and it was a wedding all over again, this time Josiah's.

Casiphia's God given desire to be with her new husband was apparent in the flush on her face, by her smile, and by her hands which held tightly to the bridegroom's arm. This was her night.

The other two princesses appeared unbothered by the fact that another bride was preceding them into the marriage chamber and that their weddings would be on another night. If anything, they appeared thrilled to have become part of the family as they sat cheerfully chatting with Karima and Kasmina.

Princess Casiphia was consumed with the moment. She nearly skipped by Josiah's side as they entered the marriage chamber. The veil closed behind them, signaling the beginning of something grand.

"Prince Josiah! May he live long!" His brothers shouted.

Mary couldn't help herself, shouting her own blessing.

"And may he find pleasure, solace, support, and wombs full of children all his days."

The room erupted with laughter at Mary's unintended pun. When she caught it herself she smiled proudly as if she'd intended it all along, and maybe she had.

The music that we'd heard during Prince John's and Princess Hadassah's entrance into the marriage chamber began again, this time for Prince Josiah and his own bride, Casiphia. The trays of sumptuous food rolled in as well, filled with delicacies I'd not seen earlier. This time it was the hand of my Mary feeding me.

"I have no idea what this is." Mary smiled as she shoved something delicious into my mouth. Even more delicious was the knowledge that it was now Mary who was sitting next to me, loving me, and encouraging me to accept the love of Suni, Ruth, Modelisa, Asina, and Tamisa; even urging me to take them as my wives.

It was well past midnight and despite the excitement of the evening, both Mary and I were having trouble keeping our eyes open so we excused ourselves and went back to our room. Exhausted, we barely had enough energy left to brush our teeth and say our prayers. Despite Mary's scolding, I continued to pray for the Lord's will concerning the girls. Could the Lord really want me, an American missionary, to marry the very girls he'd sent me to minister to? I prayed out loud as Mary prayed with me, her head covered with her newly acquired prayer shawl. Never before had I felt such spiritual oneness with my beloved wife, Mary. My prayer closed with, "May it *not* be my will, *nor* Mary's will, *nor* the girls' will, but *Thy* will be done. Amen." Within moments, we were asleep.

Chapter 20 Footnotes

1. Ephesians 2:8-9 For by grace are ye saved through faith; and that not of yourselves: it is the gift of God: Not of works, lest any man should boast.

2. Exodus 3:5-6 And he said, Draw not nigh hither: put off thy shoes from off thy feet, for the place whereon thou standest is holy

ground. Moreover he said, I am the God of thy father, the God of Abraham, the God of Isaac, and the God of Jacob.

3. John 13:14 If I then, your Lord and Master, have washed your feet; ye also ought to wash one another's feet.

4. Genesis 28:3 And God Almighty bless thee, and make thee fruitful, and multiply thee, that thou mayest be a multitude of people.

5. Psalm 127:3 Lo, children are an heritage of the LORD: and the fruit of the womb is his reward.

6. Carmel means *fruitful field.*

7. Carshena means *a lamb* or *slender*.

Chapter 21

THE BETROTHAL

Mary and I were awakened by a pounding at the door. I got up and looked through the peep hole. It was Ruth. I put on my robe, then opened the door and stepped outside. She grabbed hold of both of my hands and lifted them to her lips, kissing them, over and over.

The normally intellectual Ruth now spoke in soft tones, her intonations songlike. "You are my beloved. My first love. Forgive me. I can't hold back my words nor my affections any longer."

There's nothing that can empty a man's head of other thoughts like the kisses of a maiden in love, and Ruth's kisses had emptied my mind of all but her.

"But the reason I woke you, Ish, is because Sam's been arrested."

"Arrested?" I nearly shouted. "The police came up here?"

"No, no, Ish. We let you and Mary sleep all morning. It's nearly noon. Sam and Sarisa went back to their place at sunup and a few hours later they arrested him."

"For what?"

"We don't have time to go over the details now because you've got to get back to Sam's place right away. A mob has gathered outside their house and we're afraid they're going to burn the house down with everyone inside! Get your stuff together, quickly. I'll be outside."

Mary had overheard the entire conversation and was already packing our bags when I went back inside our room. By the time I'd finished my morning shower, John's entire family was waiting outside. Mary, Ruth, and the girls were seated comfortably in a brand new luxury SUV. John handed me the keys.

"I was going to wait to give this to you as a wedding gift but Ruth convinced me that I wouldn't be making a mistake by giving it to you now. We'll be praying for all of you. Drive safely. Now get going." John shook my hand, then added, "Consider your offer of marriage accepted in advance. When you lay with Ruth, she will indeed become your wife."

My wife? I was about to object, but then I remembered Mary's scolding from the night before and my own prayer to which I still had no answer.

"I'll abide by that." I replied, but before I could get into the driver's seat, Tamisa's father took me aside. Shaking my hand, he introduced himself.

"I'm Edward, Tamisa's father." Then he repeated the same phrase that John had spoken, "Consider your offer of marriage accepted in advance. When you lay with Tamisa she will indeed become your wife."

Again, I answered, "I'll abide by that."

At that, he hugged his daughter and opened the back door of my new SUV to let her in, then he added,

"I'm not a preacher like you, Ish, but even so, I think I can offer you some wise counsel. Make sure Tamisa's legs and arms are covered up well if you go out. If you go for a bike ride, or even for a walk in the park, make sure that her skin is not marred by a fall or scraped by thorns. She's kept them all these years without scars or blemishes for you. Indulge her. Let her maintain this aspect of her beauty. Don't consider it vanity. Consider it a form of love, that she would offer herself, an unblemished lamb, to be yours. Savor her pleasures and see that you please her."

"I'll remember what you've said." I replied.

By now I was sweating profusely, but this time it wasn't because of the heat but because I'd just been officially offered Ruth and Tamisa as wives. I silently prayed that the Lord would give me an answer. "Could such marriages be possible, Lord?"

"Let's go, Ish. Sam needs our help, *now*." Mary coaxed me.

"You're right, Mary. We're outta here." I got into John's *wedding present* and buckled up.

Some wedding present; the three rows of seats easily accommodated all of us. Asina sat comfortably between me and Mary. Tamisa, Suni, and Modelisa were in the second row and Cherry, Tisay, and Ruth were in the back.

One of John's wives hurriedly handed a basket full of food through the window to Mary.

"You and Ish haven't even had a chance to eat. You must be

starving." She said.

"Well, I am a bit hungry. Thanks." Mary answered, "But I don't think I could have eaten before now. I've never gorged myself on so much food as I did last night."

John's wife just smiled and then passed a second basket of food through the window.

Praying first, we waved goodbye and headed out the gates. It seemed unbelievable that just twenty four hours earlier we'd entered in through those very same gates. The gates closed behind me like a chapter of my life to which I could never return. Yes, I was returning to the same world but I could never see it the same way again.

The new SUV John had given me was the type most popular with the ultra rich. The bumps we'd experienced on the way up were gone beneath its smooth suspension and the climate control kept out the exhaust from other vehicles. I couldn't imagine why John was still driving a jeepney when he could have been driving one of these. Ruth read my mind.

"We only take these out for emergencies. Daddy likes to keep a low profile."

"These? How many of *these* do you have?" I chuckled.

"One less than yesterday." Ruth winked as she caught me glimpsing her through the rear view mirror.

"One less, huh?"

"Well, if I must tell you, Ish, we still have seven. For emergencies, you know."

Ruth was tickled to see me, the preacher, dazzled by something other than theology. She looked so much the princess, sitting in the slightly elevated and elegantly upholstered back seat of my new ride.

After the intense discussions at John's place, Mary and I were ready for some light conversation and Ruth and Tamisa kept us busy with stories and folklore about the villages we were passing.

It seemed we'd only been driving a few minutes but we were already passing the brass market. The vendors were just beginning to open their stalls. We drove over the same deep ruts that had caused my teeth to chatter on the way in. The bumps barely caused a ripple on the surface of my coffee which was cradled securely in its heated cup holder. My pride in my new SUV gave me second thoughts about accepting it. If it were a choice between idolatry and riding in a dilapidated vehicle, I'd take the dilapidated vehicle. Guilt overwhelmed me.

It wasn't the least bit hot with the climate control running but I'd begun to sweat again. My demeanor changed from cheerful to worried. Ruth read my mind for the second time in minutes.

"Ish, only a *holy man* would worry that a gift could cause him to stumble. Praise the Lord that you've been blessed and may the Lord see you enjoy this toy for many years. Surely the Lord deserves to see the pleasure of his child enjoying a new toy. He's seen your heart and your concern, not to mention that you will surely have enough wives to keep you humble. This SUV is just a material object, but an object that can do astounding things for you as well as others. Witness yourself, how quickly we were able to get down the mountain. We'll be to Sam's place hours earlier than we could have in a jeepney. Who knows, but those extra hours may change destinies."

Ruth's choice of the word *destinies* brought a smile not only to my face but to Mary's. We could never hear that word again without remembering John's wives falling through the door during his story telling. It was then that I noticed Suni, Modelisa, and Asina weren't smiling. In fact, they hadn't said a word since we'd left John's place.

"You three have been awfully quiet." I said.

That was all it took, and each of them snapped back their response.

"You... you." Asina was at a loss for words for the first time since I'd met her.

"Don't act like you don't know!" Suni pointed her finger accusingly.

"Know *what?*" I replied.

"Look at that. Look at how he acts, like he doesn't know." Modelisa harrumphed then snubbed me, turning her face away from me.

I'd never seen Modelisa loose her composure but now she was fuming.

"What, already?" I said.

"Listen to that. Look! *Look!* He's pretending not to know." Asina squawked.

"Pretending? What are you all talking about?"

"Humph!" They responded in unison, then sat silent.

Tamisa leaned forward and whispered in my ear.

"I think they're upset because you didn't say, *I'll abide by that*, to their daddies."

"Aye, aye, aye!" I shook my head.

Ruth now became advocate for the three pouters.

"Modelisa and Asina were both disowned by their fathers when they became Christians, and Suni is an orphan. If they offered themselves the way our dads offered us, how would you answer them?"

"Exactly as I answered your father, of course; *I'll abide by that.*"

"Oh! Isn't he wonderful. Our man." Suni swooned.

"Yes, the most charming." Asina squeezed my hand and looked into my eyes adoringly.

"And he's so, *Je ne sais quoi.*" Modelisa cranked up her charm as she gazed deeply at me through the rear view mirror.

"Oh yes, he *is* that." Mary couldn't help a bit of light hearted sarcasm as she threw in her two cents.

Now we were all laughing and I, once again, was bewildered. What test was God putting me through that he'd placed the destinies, there's that word again, of five beautiful girls into my hands, and it was only yesterday that I'd met my first Christian polygamist!

We drove up the road that led out of Marawi and were soon at the check point. Ruth handed the vehicle registration to the guard who did his inspection more out of admiration for our SUV than duty.

"You need a body guard to keep you safe on the highway." He warned us.

"No thanks," I answered, "Datu Daransanan assured me that his men would be patrolling the highway today."

This was the exact phrase that John had given me to get out of the customary police escort offered foreigners. Since we were driving a new luxury vehicle, the favorite of local politicians, the soldier didn't question us further. I remembered the line from Fiddler on the Roof; *When you're rich they think you really know.*[1]

"Go ahead." He handed the registration back to Ruth and waved us on. I could see him through my rear view mirror, gazing after our vehicle like a school boy admiring a rich kid's toy.

"Your dad gave us just the right words." Mary said.

"My daddy understands power, and money is a type of power. He says it's really not that difficult to use effectively. The key is to retain it,[2] and he says that simply takes patience. My daddy's very patient."

"I'm sure he is, with all those children." Mary's wistful look told me she was thinking once again of her own barrenness. So many years and still no children.

We passed the same sign pointing to Maria Christina Falls that we'd passed on the way in to Marawi.

"I wonder if my hubby and I will ever get the chance to see the falls." Mary sighed. "Ahhh."

The girls copied her in unison, sighing just the same way. "Ahhh."

We were all giddy now. Sure, we were on our way to deal with a serious matter; Sam's arrest, but what was on all our minds was the possibility of a marriage that would include five new brides.

"My father says Maria Christina Falls is a wonderful place for a honeymoon." Ruth wasn't going to drop the subject of the falls. Through the rear view mirror, her eyes spoke with intense gazes of longing and desire.

"Well, Ruth, Ish and I have been to Disneyland, Yellowstone National Park, and to about every other landmark in the United States, but the closest we've ever come to a second honeymoon was your place. I could never have imagined there was a mountaintop hideaway like yours, where a family of so many talented Christians lives so happily."

"Thank you, Mary. That's the most wonderful compliment I've ever received!" Ruth's eyes grew misty. "I was so afraid you'd hate all of us."

"Well, it's a little late for that, seeing as how I'll be sharing my husband with you."

"It *is* a little late, isn't it." I said, "Yesterday, you were the only woman in my life, Mary. Today, there are five more so I'd better make myself clear. Mary, I will not take any woman as a wife whose love for me depends on your approval. A marriage is lifelong and between one man and one woman. If there is anyone other than the husband who has a say in offering marriage, to any of his brides, then there will be a shadow cast over the man's authority in that marriage. Do you understand this Mary?"

"Yes, I understand, Ish."

"Do you understand girls?"

"Yes." They answered in unison.

"So, even if Mary were opposed to it, you'd marry me over her objections?"

They all nodded in agreement.

"Well, then, it's settled, and the sooner the better."

At this, Cherry began congratulating each one of the girls with what I realized for the first time were customary words, "You got him! You're *so* blessed!" Then she realized I wasn't finished.

"Oh, sorry, Ish. Go ahead."

"Thank you, I will."

To which Suni couldn't help spouting, "*Ahhh*, I love those words, *I will*."'

The girls were all feigning swoons by now but after they'd had their fill of fun they quieted down and let me complete my thought.

"Well, for what it's worth, I really didn't have to pray whether the Lord would have me take more than one wife. I knew from years of study that there wasn't a problem with that. And when the Lord answered, He answered simply, with the same words He put into the mouth of the Psalmist, *Delight thyself also in the LORD; and He shall give thee the desires of thine heart.*[3] Suni, Modelisa, Ruth, Tamisa, Asina, I *desire* you, and of course, I *still* desire my wonderful Mary. Cherry, Tisay, you are our witnesses. Let no man say that my betrothal to any of these women is not in accordance with the Bible. When I lay with each, then each shall indeed become my wife. Amen?"

"Amen!" They agreed.

Cherry had already opened her Bible to pronounce blessings upon us and she paraphrased Ruth 4:11

"*The LORD make the women that have come into your house like Rachel and like Leah, which two did build the house of Israel*!"[4]

Tisay nearly sang her blessing:

"May you be fruitful and may the Lord bless you with your daily bread!"[5]

This was the first time I'd heard Tisay speak but she wasn't through.

"Pastor Ish, Cherry told me that it was your books that gave her just the right Bible verses to reach those lost souls at the barbecue. God has blessed you by using you to strengthen the ministry of so many. I'll be praying that the Lord will continue to bless you and use you, as well as every one of your wives, and your children! Please pray that He will use me too."

"Tisay, I've been praying for you ever since I first saw you at the barbecue and so has Mary. Every one of us here will continue to pray for you too. We'll pray as you've requested, that the Lord will bless you and use you for His glory."[6]

"Amen!" We all shouted.

Mary began singing one of the hymns we'd learned at John's place and before long we were all singing, but by the time we entered the city limits of Iligan the growl of my stomach was nearly as audible as our voices. Seeing the vendors on the side of the road selling roast chicken, rice, and snacks didn't help. The baskets of food that John's wife had given us were empty now so I pulled over. A small boy ran over to us holding up his specialties. Ruth rolled down her window and in less than a minute every one of the vendors was vying for our attention. We departed with a wide assortment of dishes.

"There's a parking stall," Ruth pointed to a parking stall in front of the police station. "We can eat there."

As soon as I'd parked the car a policeman walked over to us. Peering in through the darkly tinted windows, he recognized Ruth. He gave her the thumbs up, then ran up the stairs to the police station.

Ruth explained, "My father called ahead of us to transfer the vehicle title of our wedding gift into your name. Someone will be out with your papers in a few minutes."

Tisay leaned over to whisper something in Ruth's ear then Ruth asked Cherry,

"Can you accompany Tisay, please?"

"Sure, I've got to go too."

Cherry and Tisay got out of the car, apparently to use the restroom in the police station.

Now a middle aged lady came up to Ruth's window and began

exclaiming, "Lord bless you. Lord bless you. Long live Datu John."

Ruth rolled down her window and spoke with her for a few minutes. After the lady had left, Ruth explained, "She's the widow of a police officer who was killed in the line of duty. She was thanking me for the fund my father set up for families of slain and disabled police officers. I was explaining to her that our gift is so small compared with her sacrifice. Besides, we deserve no thanks for that fund. The Lord commands us to provide for the widows, orphans, and strangers among us.[7] Please don't forget me and my family in your prayers. Pray that it will be out of the love that the Lord places within our hearts that we give, not just to avoid curses or to get blessings."

"Pray for your family? Uh, correction." I said. "They're our family now, all of them."

As I was speaking, Ruth had quietly climbed up behind me to pull the lever on my recliner. Dumping me into her lap, she covered my face with kisses. Then she cheerfully sing-songed, "*I got him first. I got him first.*"

Asina, who'd been sitting at my side, simply gave a twist and now she was on top of me. I was amazed at how such a tiny woman could so easily overpower me. I guess I wasn't resisting much. There wasn't any reason to; she was my betrothed, judging from her enthusiasm, had we been alone she would have quickly become my wife.

"Well, I haven't had enough of you yet," Asina said giving me one last kiss, "but there'll be plenty of time for that later." Then she sat back in her seat looking all the more lovely for what I'd just experienced.

Barely had I time to recover from Asina when Suni took me in her arms. "You had me with the first tear that fell from your eyes, back at my place, by the courtyard." Suni said. "I don't know what I would have done if you hadn't loved me too." Suni took a break from talking to cover my neck with her kisses. I was getting drenched by her tears as she wept then moaned. "You look good in tears but I guess I better clean up after myself." Taking out her handkerchief, Suni wiped my neck and face dry of her tears but one last tear fell off her cheek onto my lips. I licked it off and said. "Delicious!"

The girls exclaimed something in their native tongue, then giggled wildly, but not long enough to distract Tamisa from taking her turn.

I'd never experienced such a delightful pillow. That's the easiest way to describe Tamisa. She was soft from head to toe, even her hair seemed softer than any I'd touched. Her lips were like cotton candy and her tongue was like taffy, melting with each kiss. Her whispers, soft, like mist on a morning lake.

Now Modelisa came to me. As I looked at her face it was ever changing, as if she didn't know which of her many faces to put on. Then I saw a Modelisa I had never seen, unbridled, out of control and passionate. When she was done kissing, embracing, and grabbing at me, she shook her head as if to get back her bearings, "Whoa," she said, "I really had not been prepared for that." Then she came at me again. "Mm, mm. I don't want to stop!" She said. "I won't!" Then she grabbed me and threw me back against my recliner, laughing passionately, stopping only long enough to gasp for air. After the longest kiss of my life without breathing she pulled herself back from me, straightened her clothing and said, "You better not believe in long betrothals, that's all I've got to say!"

Asina concurred, "She's right! Did you ever think a missionary could kiss like that?" Asina crossed her eyes and moved her head around like a dashboard bobble.

As the girls were exchanging their comments about how kissable I was, Mary's left cheek began to twitch, then her upper lip began to quiver, and finally she couldn't hold back any longer as her words blasted out at me.

"You are one blessed man! I hope you never, *ever*, forget how much the Lord loves you. Don't you ever!"

It was my turn to grab someone and I gave Mary the most passionate kiss of her lifetime.

"If you think that will ...." Mary paused, dazed. I kissed her again.

"Wow!" Suni exclaimed, "Mary isn't immune despite how long she's been with Ish."

The moment Mary and I ended our passionate embrace, the Lord's spirit descended upon all of us at once. Mary and the girls put on their prayer shawls and they began to pray. They were praying for me. I'd never experienced such an outpouring of love in my life. God was obviously preparing me for something special. *He who finds a wife finds a good thing, and obtains the favor of the LORD.*[8] How wonderful when the Lord looks upon a man with favor! I certainly didn't deserve it. I prayed also, and as I did, I looked into the eyes of every one of my betrotheds as well as Mary.[9] "Such blessed women!" I prayed out loud, "May I bless them as the Lord would have me bless them and may You bless them, Lord, even more. Amen!"

Cherry and Tisay arrived back to the car only moments after we'd finished praying.

"I hope we didn't miss anything," Cherry said. Then she noticed something was different about us. Stomping her feet like a little girl, she moaned, "*Ah, what did we miss!*"

"Just a few private moments between a man and his women." Suni said, "That's all."

"Oh, that's all." Then Cherry did a double take, "What?"

"Oh, nothing you need to know." Suni said.

After Cherry had climbed back into the car Suni began whispering something in her ear and as she whispered Cherry's eyes grew wider and wider. Finally, Cherry covered her ears, and shouted with her eyes closed. "God bless you! God bless you! You've told me enough. Please, my ears are stinging."

We all broke into laughter at Cherry's innocence. Her remarks showed us that she was indeed a new creation, having regained all the innocence of her childhood, but Modelisa couldn't help herself, adding.

"May your ears sting every time we tell you about our beloved and may he forevermore adorn us with kisses."

We hadn't even begun eating the food we'd just purchased so I said the blessing and we ate. A few minutes later the police officer returned with the title and registration to my new SUV.

"It's yours." He said, handing the paperwork to me through the window.

"Thanks for your fast work." I replied.

"You're welcome sir. Have a good day." He stepped back, waving us off.

"Is that it, Ruth? Are we ready to go?" I asked.

"Yes, I'm worried about everyone at Sam's place. We can't

delay."

At that, I pulled out of the driveway and continued the drive to Sam's house.

Chapter 21 Footnotes

1. Even though people might not *always* value a rich man's wisdom, it is a fact that they despise a poor man's wisdom.
Ecclesiastes 9:16 Wisdom is better than strength: nevertheless the poor man's wisdom is despised, and his words are not heard.
2. Proverbs 11:16 A gracious woman retaineth honour: and strong men retain riches.
3. Psalm 37:4 Delight thyself also in the LORD; and he shall give thee the desires of thine heart.
4. Ruth 4:11 And all the people that were in the gate, and the elders, said, We are witnesses. The LORD make the woman that is come into thine house like Rachel and like Leah, which two did build the house of Israel: and do thou worthily in Ephratah, and be famous in Bethlehem.
5. Genesis 1:28-29 And God blessed them, and God said unto them, Be fruitful, and multiply, and replenish the earth, and subdue it: and have dominion over the fish of the sea, and over the fowl of the air, and over every living thing that moveth upon the earth. And God said, Behold, I have given you every herb bearing seed, which is upon the face of all the earth, and every tree, in the which is the fruit of a tree yielding seed; to you it shall be for meat.
6. Ephesians 1:14 Which is the earnest of our inheritance until the redemption of the purchased possession, unto the praise of his glory.
7. Deuteronomy 24:19-21 When thou cuttest down thine harvest in thy field, and hast forgot a sheaf in the field, thou shalt not go again to fetch it: it shall be for the stranger, for the fatherless, and for the widow: that the LORD thy God may bless thee in all the work of thine hands. 20 When thou beatest thine olive tree, thou shalt not go over the boughs again: it shall be for the stranger, for the fatherless, and for the widow. 21 When thou gatherest the grapes of thy vineyard, thou shalt not glean it afterward, it shall be for the stranger, for the fatherless, and for the widow.
2 Thessalonians 3:10 For even when we were with you, this we commanded you, that if any *would not work*, neither should he eat.

would not work, i.e., refuse to work even though able bodied.
8. Proverbs 18:22 Whoso findeth a wife findeth a good thing, and obtaineth favour of the LORD.
9. Mark 10:11 is confusing to many students of the Bible. In that verse, Jesus presents us with a syllogism. A syllogism is a logical argument that has the form; If A and B, then C. Here is the syllogism Jesus presented in Mark 10:11

Whosoever shall put away his wife, and shall marry another,
[A] [B]
committeth adultery against her.{DBY}
[C]

Notice that the Bible **DOES NOT SAY:**

Whosoever shall **not put away** his wife, and shall marry another,
[NOT A] [B]
committeth adultery against her.
[C]

Since this example is **not found anywhere in the Bible**, we lie if we claim that a man who has *not put away his wife*, and marries another, commits adultery. Only when a man marries a new wife, having put away another wife, has he committed "adultery against her." William Tyndale, the first English translator of the Bible, renders it, "breaketh wedlocke to her warde" which is synonymous with "causeth her to commit adultery." Mark 10:11 is simply one of the many examples of *putting away* "for reasons other than fornication." *Putting away*, "saving for the cause of fornication," *is* forbidden. Marrying a new wife, *without putting away another wife*, is *not* forbidden.

Matthew 5:32 But I say unto you, That whosoever shall put away his wife, **saving for the cause of fornication,** causeth her to commit adultery: and whosoever shall marry her that is divorced committeth adultery.

Chapter 22

RIOT AT SAM'S HOUSE

By the time we turned the corner onto the street where Pastor Sam lived, the mob had grown to hundreds. They made way for us as we edged toward Sam's house. I wasn't surprised that they moved out of the way so quickly. A brand new SUV, as expensive as mine, was uncommon even in the most exclusive areas of the country, let alone a provincial barrio such as this. They must have thought some important officials were inside because they let us pass right through the gates and into Sam's driveway. A lone policeman stood in the courtyard. He closed the gates behind us then shouted to be heard above the angry cries of the mob.

"I've been doing my best to calm down the crowd by calling out to them through my bullhorn but, if anything, my words have had the opposite effect."

"Can I borrow that?" I said, pointing to his bullhorn.

"Please, please do! Maybe you can get them to go home."

He handed me the bullhorn and I got out and stood on the back bumper of my SUV, hanging onto the roof rack with one hand and the bullhorn with the other.

"We're all here to put a stop to the immorality that's going on right now in Cagayan de Oro." I called out. "Do I have an Amen?"

Several leaders of the crowd angrily shouted, "*Amen!*"

"And we're not going to stop at anything to make sure this immorality stops!" I shouted even louder.

The leaders again shouted, "*Amen!*"

"In fact, I'm here to tell you right now that *I don't mind going to jail* if it means we can put a stop this immorality today! Amen?" I called out again.

This time only one of their leaders replied, "Amen!"

The rest of the crowd had grown silent, so I spoke into the bullhorn softly for effect.

"In fact, I'm glad that the church installed these security cameras." I pointed to the cameras that were mounted strategically around Sam's house. "These cameras will record everything that takes place here today, so that the City officials can see to it that everyone here gets the reward they deserve."

The crowd was motionless for a moment till they realized the force of my quiet words. Now those who had been pushing against the gates, ready to break through, dispersed so suddenly that the policeman easily handcuffed their ring leader. He put him in the back seat of his squad car, then came over to me.

"You're an answer to my prayers," he said. "and not just my prayers concerning the mob you sent home."

"Really?" I responded, "How's that?"

"My little girl," his voice cracked from emotion, "she..." he gathered himself together and steadied his voice, "she came home last week and forgave me."

"Forgave you?"

"Forgave me for refusing to give her in marriage."

"Well, it's your right."

"It's my right to refuse to give her in marriage while she's still a virgin but it's my duty to obey the Lord in other cases. I didn't obey Him when I refused to give her to the man I found her with, the man who took her virginity, the man she loved.[1] I was so angry with my daughter that I got a friend of mine, the foreman of the jobsite where her boyfriend worked, to fire him. That put my daughter's boyfriend in a hard place. You know how work is here, and he was entirely responsible for his family. His mother is a widow. He had to go to Davao to find work, hundreds of miles from here."[2]

While we were talking, Ruth, Mary, and the rest of the girls had gotten out of the car and were now walking toward us.

"Ruth!" The policeman exclaimed, "What a wondrous day the Lord has given me. He's so worthy to be praised!"[3] The words tumbled naturally out of his mouth. Ruth's face lit up in surprise.

"Mang Ricardo,[4] so nice to know you're here keeping us safe. It really is a wondrous day when I hear you praising the Lord! How has this change come over you?"

Ricardo looked down, his eyes teary. "It's nothing I did. That's for certain."[5] Then he raised up his head and looked directly at

Ruth. "But God is real and when he grabs you, he doesn't let go." I didn't know how literally Ricardo meant those words till I heard his story.

"But please, don't honor these tears as if they mean anything. They don't. Everything that happened to me was a work of God. There was nothing left to me. My heart was that hard." Just then, he noticed Tisay and ran toward her. He grabbed her and swung her up into his arms, cradling her like a baby. "This Tisay, she is very special." He said. "The Lord used her to melt my heart."

I was astounded. It had only been a couple of days since Tisay herself had come out of prostitution. How was it that her witness had already been used of God?

"This little girl." Ricardo spoke with such gentleness. "She came into the police station two days ago, asking if someone could accompany her to the bar where she'd worked so that she could get her stuff. We were all incredulous. We were used to hauling in the underage girls and trying to find an orphanage that would take them in, so when Tisay, this little Tisay, came into the police station saying she'd been arrested many times we didn't believe her. She looked so innocent that we all thought it was a strange joke. Not one of us were able to recognize her. She looked like one of the little angels in those paintings of some heavenly choir. She looked that innocent." Ricardo looked at Tisay. "Still does."

Ricardo rocked her in his arms as she closed her eyes, quite snug and content to let him cuddle her.

"That day in the station," Ricardo began his story, "Tisay was such a darling. We couldn't help but engage her in conversation. Yet nothing she said could shake us of the idea that she'd been sent in to play a joke on us, so we played along."

'Where's the club you worked in?' I asked her.

'Hell's Doorstep.' She answered.

When I heard the name of the club, I was even more skeptical since it had a reputation for the worst types of sex crimes.

'And what's your name?' I asked her.

She lifted her truly innocent eyes and looked into mine.

'Tisay.' She answered.

The mention of that name so disgusted me, that I raised my hand to slap her, but another officer caught my wrist. Angrily, I screamed at Tisay.

'Don't you ever play this game with us again. We know Tisay. She's a whore! I don't know who sent you here but how dare you pretend to be such a filthy thing!'

Then I looked around me and saw that every one of the other officers was quietly sobbing. That made me look a little more closely at this little angel.

'Tisay?' I barely whispered, 'Is that you?'

This time I reached out my hand, not to slap, but in awe, to caress her now innocent face. Realizing it could be taken the wrong way, I pulled back, and as I did I was knocked to my knees. Someone had clubbed me in the back. I was in agony. I was about to curse whoever did it but then realized there was no one there. It was only me and little Tisay in the middle of the station. All the other men were at their desks, holding their heads in their hands, still sobbing.

'What is this?' I gasped, looking up at Tisay's angelic face, but before I could say anything else I felt a hand pushing me to the ground. I was now flat on my face. Tisay was praying over me, and the unseen hand was holding me firmly to the floor.

'Lord You know this man,' she prayed, 'Lord You have taken this man. Lord Jesus we praise Your Name as You take him as Yours. As You blot out his sins. Thank You Jesus!'[6]

Some of the officers had begun praying as well and shouting praises to God.

'What is this nonsense!' I shouted from beneath the hand. 'I've heard every one of you curse to make a whore blush. I should know; I taught you.'

Now it felt like a foot was pressed down on one side of my face pinning my cheek to the floor. I looked up at Tisay and asked, 'What's happening to me?'

'I don't know what's happening to you.' She said, 'I can only tell you what's happened to me. I heard God's word. His word gave me faith. A burden fell from me. I had a new life. I was a new creation.'[7]

Tisay then began singing a hymn while skipping across the floor. Now I was sure I must have passed out and was dreaming, then the other officers began singing with her, which convinced me all the more. By this time, Pastor Sam, who'd been waiting for Tisay in his truck, came in to see what was taking Tisay so long.

'Whoa,' he said to me, 'that's some angel with his foot on your face!' Sam quickly kneeled but stood up just as fast. 'Yep, says he's an angel and I'm not to bow. Says you're the stubborn type so he was sent in ahead of the Holy Ghost to rough you up a bit.'[8]

'You got that right.' I groaned from beneath the angel's enormous foot.

'By the way,' Sam continued, 'after the angel leaves, you get to meet the Holy Ghost.'

'*Oh no!*' I said out loud and as quickly as I'd said it the angel let go of me. I jumped to my feet and looked in every direction, trying to see what Sam had seen, but there wasn't an angel, except for little Tisay of course.

Sam and my fellow officers were singing along with Tisay louder than any church choir I'd ever heard. Then there was the sound of a voice with joyous words that made my heart leap. Though the language was not my own, I knew what the words meant. I was forgiven, right then and there. I hadn't even asked for forgiveness[9] but I've been thanking the Lord every moment since. What the angel said to Sam before the Holy Spirit spoke to me was an understatement. I wasn't just stubborn; my heart was black. I wasn't even capable of knowing that I needed forgiving until I'd already been forgiven.

Tisay knew what had just happened inside my heart and the Bible verse she quoted described it perfectly;

'*When we were God's enemies, we were reconciled to God by the death of His Son, much more, being reconciled, we shall be saved by His life. And not only so, but we also joy in God through our Lord Jesus Christ, by Whom we have now received the atonement.*'[10]

Now I'm not a dancing man, but when those words of Scripture came out of her mouth the Holy Spirit sent me whirling around the room giving praises to God. Praise Him! Let's praise him now!"

Ricardo, having finished his testimony, lifted his hands toward heaven and led us in a praise song right there in Sam's driveway. We had ourselves a choir to be heard that afternoon. We sang praises to God in the driveway till dusk, then Analyn cautiously poked her head out the door of Sam's house and whispered.

"Praise the Lord you're here. Is the mob gone?"

"Yes, they're all gone." Ricardo assured her.

"We've been praying in the basement since last night when the mob gathered." She said.

Mary and the girls exchanged hugs with Analyn.

"Let's go inside." She urged us.

"Yes," Mary answered, "You've got to get some sleep Analyn. Such an ordeal you've been through, poor dear."

"Excuse me, Ish." Ricardo interrupted. "I'll be leaving you now." He shook my hand. "I've got a prisoner in the back of my squad car. This day began a mess but it looks like it's going to end up all right. God bless all of you."

"I'm going too." Cherry said. "Mang Ricardo promised he'd drop me and Tisay back at my apartment."

We said our *goodbye*s then stepped inside. Once inside Mary put her arm around Analyn and led her to a leather recliner by the window that overlooked the harbor.

"You sit down here and rest while we take care of dinner." She said.

"Oh, no, Mary. I can't sit in Pastor Sam's chair, not while he's locked up in jail. Just let me lie on that couch over there for a few minutes."

Analyn laid down on a little couch that was just outside the laundry room and immediately fell asleep.

After a few minutes, Sam's other maid, Rosemary, came out of the kitchen where Sarisa and the girls were preparing dinner.

"Poor Analyn," she said, looking over at her co-worker. "I'm not surprised she conked out. Can you help me take her to her room, Ish?"

"Sure, just tell me where to put her."

I picked Analyn up in my arms and followed Rosemary down the hall. She pointed to a bed in their cozy little maids' quarters. I put Analyn on it and positioned the pillow under her head.

"There," I said, "she looks adorable sleeping so soundly."

"Oh, she'll be angry to hear that," Rosemary scolded, "Only adorable when she's sleeping?" Her eyes twinkled as she fished for compliments for her roommate. "But you'd better hurry up and get back to your beloveds. I'll bet they're drawing straws right now to see who gets to claim her place next to you at the dinner table."

Rosemary was right. As we stepped out of her room, Asina ran up to me. Standing on the footstool just outside of Rosemary's door, she put her arms around my neck and pressed her lips to my ear, whispering, "Tonight, you're mine."

Asina took my hand, playfully folding her fingers in mine as she led me to the dinner table where Mary was assigning seats.

"You sit here, Asina." Mary pulled out a chair for Asina. "And this is for you, Ish." She pointed to the vacant chair between Asina and Tamisa. I'd never seen Mary so pleased. She was at home with the girls and enjoying their fellowship.

"Looks like you're the only man here." Sarisa said. "So I'll ask that you say the blessing."

"Sure," I said,

"*Lord, thank You for this food. Thank You for this day. Thank You for our many loved ones and for the graciousness of our hosts. Thank you also for your Son in Whose precious Name we pray blessings upon this food. Amen.*"

After the rest of those at the table had said their *Amen*s, Sarisa stood up.

"We're so glad that you've come on short notice." She said. "I hope you liked our welcoming committee. I'm sure that Mang Ricardo can arrange a private conference for you with their leader, any time, *in the city jail!*"

Sarisa continued to speak over our laughter. "As you all know, my husband has also been arrested, but don't worry, he'll be out soon enough. You see, in the Philippines, when a legal wife consents to her husband's taking more wives, there's no crime. Sam took seven new brides a little over nine months ago. We had our reasons for keeping it secret, but we can talk about that in the morning. I've got to go help my husband's other wives with their newborns; eight baby boys in all, including a set of twins. All of you please enjoy your private dinner tonight. Rosemary's in the kitchen. She'll make sure you're taken care of."

Before we could object to her leaving, Sarisa was out of the room.

"We're missing *two*." Ruth said in a somber tone.

"Ruth's right." Mary said. "Sam's got seven. Seven new brides."

I realized what they were saying. In fact, the moment Sarisa had told us that Sam had seven new brides, I couldn't help but remember the Bible verse my professors were unable to explain; Isaiah 4:1

"And in that day *seven* women shall take hold of one man, saying, We will eat our own bread, and wear our own clothing: only let us be called by your name; take away our reproach."[11]

As I pondered Isaiah's prophecy, and what it could mean, I heard a scream.

"No! I can't be left behind!"

It was Analyn. She was running down the hall screaming. When she got into the dining room she threw herself at my feet. She was quickly joined by Rosemary, then they spoke as one.

"We will eat our own bread, and wear our own clothing: only let us be called by your name; take away our reproach!"

They were shaking and sweating profusely as they cried out those words over and over.

They held tightly to my legs like children about to be ripped from their parents by jack booted thugs. Then, God's Spirit filled me as I prophesied my answer.

"Bear my name, and I will take away your reproach. Guide our house so that none may speak evil against you nor against our household."[12]

The moment I finished, Mary and my other brides jumped to their feet and began singing the words of Isaiah 4:2-6

In that day shall the branch of the LORD,
Yes the branch of the Lord
Be beautiful and glorious
In that day shall the branch of the LORD,
Yes the branch of the Lord
Be beautiful and glorious

And the fruit of the earth shall be excellent and comely
For them that are escaped of Israel.
Yes, the fruit of the earth shall be excellent and comely
For them that are escaped of Israel.

And it shall come to pass, that those who live in Zion
Yes, those in Jerusalem are called holy, called holy.
Yes, all those written among the living, in Jerusalem.
Shall be called holy.

For the Lord has washed away the filth of the daughters
Washed away the filth of the daughters, of Zion
Yes the Lord has washed away, the filth of the daughters
He's made clean the daughters of Zion

Now the blood of Jerusalem, it shall be purged
It shall be purged by the spirit of judgment
By a spirit of burning and judgment
The blood of Jerusalem shall be purged

And the LORD will protect, yes the Lord will protect
Every dwelling place of mount Zion
And the LORD will protect, yes the Lord will protect
All the assemblies of Zion, of Zion

A cloud of smoke by day, a fiery flame by night
Shall be our defense in Zion
A cloud of smoke by day, a fiery flame by night
Shall be our defense in Zion

The Shekinah of the Lord will protect us
As a shadow from the heat and a cover from rain
The Shekinah of the Lord will protect us
As a cover from the rain and storm

Sarisa spent the next seven weeks trying to get Sam out of jail. *I spent the same seven weeks taking away the reproach of my seven new brides.*

I can't say that I spent much time fretting over the outcome of Sam's predicament. I knew he'd be out soon. In the Philippines it takes a formal complaint signed by the wife to keep a husband in jail for concubinage. So with my mind at ease I spent each wedding week blissfully, in accordance with Scripture. I thought of nothing but the moment and the moment's name changed with each week. First Asina, then Suni, then...

Chapter 22 Footnotes

1. Exodus 22:16 And if a man entice a maid that is not betrothed,

and lie with her, he shall surely endow her to be his wife.
Leviticus 19:29 Do not [cause thy daughter to be defiled,] to cause her to be a whore; lest the land fall to whoredom, and the land become full of wickedness.

The **verb** *prostitute* is what the King James Bible uses in the brackets above. I have replaced it with *cause to be defiled* which is the actual meaning of the Hebrew word *chalal*, the word used in this verse. The problem with using the **verb** *prostitute* in this sentence is that it brings to mind an exchange of money which has nothing to do with this sentence. The Lord is simply saying that when you **cause** your daughter to go with a man other than the first, you are **causing** her to be defiled. This is the same principal as Jesus gives, that if a man divorces his wife for other than fornication, he is the **cause** of her subsequent defilement. The presumption of God's Word in Leviticus 19:29 as well as in Matthew 5:32 is that any woman who has given herself to a man and then forced to depart from him, will inevitably find a another man. That is how she is **caused** to be defiled. In the case of a father standing between the first man and her husband, it is the father who is guilty of **causing** that defilement and he is forbidden from doing so by Leviticus 19:29. In the case of the husband who forces the woman away from himself when she has not fornicated, it is the husband who is guilty of **causing** the defilement. Any land that is full of such women has f*allen to whoredom*. America has fallen to whoredom as well as many other nations. A whore is simply a woman who has allowed herself to be touched sensuously by someone other than her betrothed or husband.

Ezekiel 23:3 And they committed whoredoms in Egypt; they committed whoredoms in their youth: *there were their breasts pressed, and there they bruised the teats of their virginity.*

From this verse we can see that even a *so called virgin* has become a whore when she has *allowed her breasts to be touched.* In addition, there is a significant difference between lying with (shĕkobeth) another man's wife so as to commit adultery and lying with (shakab) an unbetrothed virgin so as to be forced to marry her. The Hebrew word shĕkobeth specifically refers to copulation while the Hebrew word shakab does not force that interpretation. The tense of the verb lying with (shakab) that is found in

Exodus 22:16, the verse requiring a man to marry the unbetrothed virgin he has been found lying with, is QAL. Which is to say, it is the tense which does NOT require us to render it to mean sexual relations, let alone copulation. Had the Lord wanted the requirement of marriage to apply only when a man was found copulating with an unbetrothed virgin, He would certainly have had Moses use the same word used in Leviticus 18:20 that refers specifically to copulation or at least the Lord would have had Moses modify the verb to stipulate copulation as in the story of Dinah. In the account of Dinah, Shechem is not only said to have lain with her but the word lay with was preceded by "took her" and followed by "humbled her."

In conclusion, a shotgun wedding, that is, a forced marriage, for finding a man lying with a virgin who is not betrothed, is biblical, whether copulation has taken place or not.

2. Zechariah 7:10 And oppress not the widow, nor the fatherless, the stranger, nor the poor; and let none of you imagine evil against his brother in your heart.

3. Revelation 4:11 Thou art worthy, O Lord, to receive glory and honour and power: for thou hast created all things, and for thy pleasure they are and were created.

4. Mang is a Filipino title of respect for an older person.

5. Ephesians 2:8 For by grace are ye saved through faith; and that *not of yourselves*: it is the gift of God.

6. Acts 3:19-20 Repent ye therefore, and be converted, that your sins may be blotted out, when the times of refreshing shall come from the presence of the Lord; And he shall send Jesus Christ, which before was preached unto you.

7. Romans 10:17 So then faith cometh by hearing, and hearing by the word of God.

Matthew 11:30 For my yoke is easy, and my burden is light.

Romans 6:4 Therefore we are buried with him by baptism into death: that like as Christ was raised up from the dead by the glory of the Father, even so we also should walk in newness of life.

Corinthians 5:17 Therefore if any man be in Christ, he is a new creature: old things are passed away; behold, all things are become new.

8. Angels have been sent ahead of God on many occasions. The following is just one example.

Numbers 22:31 Then the LORD opened the eyes of Balaam, and he saw the angel of the LORD standing in the way, and his sword drawn in his hand: and he bowed down his head, and fell flat on his face.

9. Romans 5:8 But God commendeth his love toward us, in that, while we were yet sinners, Christ died for us.

10. Romans 5:10-11 For if, when we were enemies, we were reconciled to God by the death of his Son, much more, being reconciled, we shall be saved by his life. And not only so, but we also joy in God through our Lord Jesus Christ, by whom we have now received the atonement.

11. Genesis 30:23 And she conceived, and bare a son; and said, God hath taken away my reproach.

This is the first usage in the Bible of the word reproach. It concerns a woman's bearing a son to her husband. A man who is asked to take away a woman's reproach is being asked to take her as a wife and give her sons.

12. 1 Timothy 5:14 I will therefore that the younger women marry, bear children, guide the house, give none occasion to the adversary to speak reproachfully.

Chapter 23

GRAND ADVENTURE

Prince John had promised us a grand adventure when he came down from his mountaintop villa so when he told us to meet him at the harbor we were expecting to find him waiting on a ship like the ones he'd described in his tale. Instead, John and his entire family were waiting for us aboard his new mega-yacht; *The Grand Adventure*. It was more like a luxury liner than a yacht.

"Good, good. So nice to see you." John greeted us. "You've brought your whole family too. I was afraid some of your wives might have changed their attitude about adventure, *being married and all.*"[1]

To judge from the fire in Asina's eyes, one would think she was about to thrust John through with one of her sharp witticisms, but she knew John's comment was meant to be endearing, a way of saying, "We're family, so I can kid around." Besides, Asina had bridled her tongue since becoming my wife. The fire in her eyes had been there all morning. It was from the excitement of going on her first mission as an evangelist's wife.

"The Lord has opened up paths for us." Asina said, "We don't for a moment think that our marriages, or yours, or Sam's, are coincidental. The Lord is so wonderful! I can't stop singing His praises and loving my husband. Wherever Ish goes, I go.[2] I now know what it is to have a lord here on earth. I'm so blessed to be Ish's wife."

"Me too!" My other wives chimed in, each with their particular variation of the same thought.

"Wonderful, wonderful." John said, "The Lord has blessed us all, and our wives as well. Is it true what I've heard, Ish, that every one of your brides is pregnant?"

"Yes, and what a perfect time for a cruise, they won't know if they've got seasickness or morning sickness."

Asina may not have responded to John's comment with a verbal thrust but mine earned me a thrust to the ribs.

"Hey, be gentle with him." Ruth objected, "He's mine today."

"Oh, sorry." Asina apologized to Ruth.

"So Ruth gets a sorry and I get nothing?"

"Well, hopefully you get a big bruise. I'm sorry, Ish. Just try being nicer." Asina leaned her head against my chest and looked up at me with her dreamiest eyes, then purred, "*I love you.*"

I was still thrown off balance each time Asina said she loved me. In fact, every time that any of my wives told me she loved me I felt like the Lord was speaking through them, saying, *See what I have done for you? Now follow Me as your wives follow you. Offer Me praises as your very own wives do for you. You have your heart's desires, there must be nothing more to distract you from the task I've set before you.*

"Sorry to interrupt you love birds," John said, "but I'm wondering; where's Sam? I would have thought he'd be ready for an adventure by now."

"Oh, he'll be along." I replied, "He's been working on a baby harness."

John's eyes lit up at the possibility of a new invention. He was a rich man and could bank roll any idea he thought worthy.

"So what kind of baby harness is Sam creating?" He asked.

"Well, regular folks can make it with a baby harness that holds one kid, but Sam's got eight newborns to cart around."

"But what about his wives? I don't understand."

"Well, John, there's no problem there, except that Sam's always trying to figure out ways to pick up more of his sons than he has arms. Here he comes now."

Sam was waddling up the gang plank carrying eight kids in a double-decker baby carrier. He had two kids in front, two in back, and two on each side. We roared with laughter on witnessing Sam's attempt to be the perfect daddy. I was relieved when he stepped off the swinging gang plank and onto the deck.

"Okay, I give up." Sam gasped, "This is silly!"

"*No,* silly?" Asina couldn't help herself, "If that thing had wings you might be able to do something with it. It looks like one of those gyrocopters but it's got babies where the blades ought to go. Teach them to flap their arms and see what happens."

Sam spoke above our laughter, "What I want to know is why the Lord gave me so many wives when Asina's still around to keep me humble?"

Asina blushed. "I... I."

Asina was speechless and Sam was incredulous.

"What have you done to that girl!, Ish? You've surely made a wife of her. Will you look at that. I've never seen her blush in all the years she's been a member of my church, and stutter? I've seen the changes in your other wives too; *Modelisa, Analyn, Ruth, Rosemary, Tamisa, Suni, and Mary*. God is wondrous! And the choirs our three households have; can they be matched by any household in the nation?"

John cleared his throat, "Ahem, yes, Sam, I'm sure they can."

"W...what?" Now it was Sam's turn to stutter.

John explained, "An angel visited me last week and told me there are other families like ours. I want everyone to hear about it so let's go into the galley. Have we all boarded?"

We did a head count three times to make sure, then followed John. I couldn't help smiling; John wasn't John without a galley and a galley fit for John would surely be fit for a king. I wasn't let down. The table in John's galley was every bit as elegant as the one at his mountaintop estate. It had ample room for our three families, some sixty of us, more or less. After we'd seated ourselves, John spoke.

"We're about to get under way so I'll be brief. Sam, Ish, and myself are not the only Christian men on Mindanao with eight wives. Moreover, Sam and Ish are certainly not the only Christian men in the world with *seven new brides*. The angel who visited me last week told me that there are one hundred and forty-four thousand Christian men who have *at least seven wives*. Most were already married so that they now have eight.[3] Many, like Sam and Ish, had to be softened up a bit to be willing to accept the possibility of new wives. Others, received theirs in an instant, all seven brides pleading at once. I know nothing more than that. My family will take you to your rooms. We'll meet back here for breakfast in a half hour."

Sam and I looked at each other. I knew we were thinking exactly the same thing; how many more seconds before we could sit down and scour the Scriptures for an explanation of what John had just told us. John's kids showed us to our rooms and when I was sure that all my wives were happily situated, I pulled out my

Bible and read. It seemed no more than a few minutes when Ruth walked in my cabin door.

"Breakfast is ready, are you?"

"Ready?" I asked, distracted.

She looked at the Bible in my hands, "We're all waiting to see what you, Sam, and my dad will have to say about the hundred and forty-four thousand. What does it mean? Have we really entered the *End Times*?"

As usual, Ruth's thoughts were mine when it concerned the Bible.

"Well," I answered, "There are twelve thousand from each of the tribes of Israel who will be sealed in the last days. That adds up to a hundred and forty-four thousand but we might not know who they all are till there's *an angel ascending from the east, having the seal of the living God*."[4]

"Well, I don't think *an angel will ascend from the east* till after we have breakfast so let's go eat, Ish."

"But, it'll only be a few more minutes."

"I know your few minutes, *Ishy*. If your wives were as few as your minutes you'd have hundreds of us."

"You're right, Ruth, I do have a penchant for long Bible studies." I stood up and grabbed her, pulling her close, kissing her. "Mmm, you have wonderfully soft lips." With each of my kisses she took another step back toward the door, till I had her pressed hard against it.

"Stop it now, or I'll think up a reason to be late for breakfast." She scolded.

"Well if that's the case, why stop?" I pressed ever more firmly to her as I began to kiss her shoulders and neck. Her skin still glistened from her morning application of lotions, or was she beginning to perspire?

"No! I'm not going to disappoint my father." Ruth twisted away from my grip. I tripped empty armed against the door, bumping my head.

"Ouch!" I said, rubbing my forehead.

"I'm sorry, Ish. Sometimes I forget that your authority has replaced my father's.[5] You want to skip breakfast, *daddy*?"

Ruth tenderly kissed my head where I'd bumped it, then grabbed me with a new passion and pushed me down onto the bed. She breathed her words through kisses, "We'll skip breakfast. We can just snack later." She pressed her body against mine, kissing her way from my temples down to my neck.

"I've got a better idea." I managed to say from beneath her kisses. "I don't want to disappoint your father either, and I know he's got a lot of stuff to tell us. How about we eat breakfast and then have dessert in your cabin."

"Mmm, dessert after breakfast? In my cabin? I promise there'll be a hot dish waiting for you." By this time Ruth had already made her way down to my chest and was unbuttoning my shirt with her teeth, then just as quickly as she'd become the aggressor, she got up. "Okedoke. Let's go eat breakfast." She straightened her clothing, then opened the door.

We strolled back to the table, gazing at each other. As we walked, our arms swung in rhythm to our hearts. I was glad breakfast was not the biggest meal of the day. I was looking forward to *dessert*. Ruth and I sat down next to each other at the table. I took my eyes off her just long enough to acknowledge my other wives but it was Ruth's day. My other wives would have scolded me later if I hadn't been giving my all to Ruth.

"Let's pray." John said.

"*Lord, you are our Great Provider, our Mighty Protector. Thank You for this food and Thank You for our brethren here with us today. We ask that You strengthen us through Your Holy Spirit. In Jesus' Name we pray, Amen.*"

A room full of *Amen*s accompanied John's, then we were quiet. At that moment, John's eldest, Prince Josiah, entered the galley and took a seat next to his now seven wives.

"We're all here?" John asked him.

"Yes, every one of us."

"And the auto-pilot is on?" John winked at his son.

"Everything's fine, Dad."

"I haven't said much prior to this," John explained, "because we couldn't have known who was listening *for we wrestle not against flesh and blood, but against principalities, against powers, against the rulers of the darkness of this world, against spiritual wickedness in high places.*[6] But now, my son has informed me that we've begun *passing through*. This is the reason I can now explain where we're headed. Satan has no power in this place.

You might call it a tent, albeit, a giant tent and a tent whose fabric only God knows. The world calls it, the Dragon's Triangle; a place where radio waves, radar, and sound cannot pass, and from which few have ever returned. Don't worry though. We have a guide."[7]

John walked over to one of the windows and raised the blinds. I about fell off my chair. An angel was riding in a chariot that was pulling the ship.[8] It was then that I noticed the engines were off but we were still moving. John sat back down.

"Please, let's eat. This will be a long day."

We were speechless upon seeing our first chariot of God, not to mention the angel who held its reigns. The women put on their prayer shawls the moment they realized they were in the presence of an angel.[9] We ate without conversation. When we were finished, John got up and walked to the door.

"Follow me," He said, walking out of the galley to stand on the outer deck. Take a look over the rail. We looked. There was a huge wake trailing the ship as we sped along.

"I know this is hardest for Ish to understand," He pointed to the wake and the chariot that pulled us. "But we in the Philippines know there is another world. A world that we seldom see but which contains spirits who are *not like us*. In fact, on Mindanao, that's what we call the spirits, *not like us*, but please, don't any of you be frightened. Any spirits you see here are the good guys, in that way, they are *like us*. As I said, Satan has no power here. He knows no more about the Dragon's Triangle than the world does. It's kind of funny that the world has chosen to name this place after the one creature who cannot enter, *the dragon, that old serpent, which is the Devil.*[10] But such is the world, *calling evil good, and good evil; putting darkness for light, and light for darkness; putting bitter for sweet, and sweet for bitter.*"[11] John looked at his family lovingly. "These, our families, are good, but the world hates us,[12] especially your countrymen, Ish, and they would steal our children if they could!"

John was referring to the recent placement of over three million home schooled American children into foster homes run by homosexuals, fornicators, and adulteresses. I remembered how the government had first taken more than four hundred children from a small religious group and there was no outcry, then they took thousands of the children of Hasidic Jews in New York City and still no outcry, then methodically the state governments, under the auspices of the CPS,[13] would select one group then another, slandering its members, then painting them as evil in order to justify stealing their precious children.[14] After the state had gotten the children they would put them into homes with drug abusers and teens with STDs.[15] Any home was fit for the state, as long as no Bible could be found. Sadly, nothing could be done about the situation in the United States, short of a heavenly intervention. Ever since the assassinations of the Supreme Court justices, our so called President had a lock on power. Some even dared to call him Messiah. Needless to say, I wouldn't be returning home soon; my eight wives were pregnant with at least eight future home-schoolers.

John continued his sermon. "The world hates us. They hate those who have loving wives; wives who willingly follow them into marriage and submit to them as Sarah submitted to Abraham, calling their husband lord.[16] The world hates fathers who refuse to allow their daughters to make bad choices, and who betroth them early; teaching them to follow the godly precepts stated by the Apostle Paul that *the younger women marry, bear children, guide the house, and give none occasion to the adversary to speak reproachfully*.[17] Yes, they hate us because they hate God's Word, and all of you know that those who refuse to submit to God's Word, refuse to submit to Jesus![18] Let's continue to pray for those whose hearts are hard.

Now, I have a wonderful announcement for all of you. This really is a party, you'll soon see, because you're each going to receive an astounding gift. Every one of us on this ship, as well as millions of believers around the world, will receive the gift at the same moment. The angel who visited me called the gift; *Fond Memories*. He explained it as being a sort of *Holy Ghost Address Book* that contains information about every believer we will ever meet or hear about in our ministries. You may have wondered how believers will know who is a friend and who is an enemy in the last days. *Well, now you know*."

At the moment John finished speaking those words, my mind was filled with new people, places, even thoughts and ideas; concepts that I had not known till that day. It was also revealed to me who the tares[19] among the church were. Most of the members of my very own Mission Board were not only tares but stooges for Satan himself! In spite of the startling revelation about the tares, I was overwhelmed with joy. Anyone who has experienced the death of a loved one knows the empty feeling that lingers long after their departure. But what I was now experiencing was the exact opposite, multiplied by millions; close friendships with living people who I had not know till that moment. I longed to smile at them, to shake their hands, to embrace them and for a moment, I did, in a million encounters that took just a fraction of a second. Dazed, I could barely make out the voice of a man calling for help.

"Can anybody help me over here? Please, grab my rope."

It was Daniel, from my *Fond Memories* in the *Holy Ghost Address Book* that the Lord had just endowed me with. So many of us ran to the rail to meet him that even John's huge ship swayed in the water. The waves nearly swamped Daniel's boat.

"Hey, I know the Lord's watching out for me, but I don't want to be that guy's lunch."

Daniel pointed to a huge shark that was swimming next to his boat. He threw the rope up to Elijah, one of John's sons. Elijah pulled their boat to the back of John's yacht and attached the sling hoist. After it was secure he extended the gang plank for Daniel and his family to get on board.

"Just leave your luggage there." Elijah said, "My brothers and I will get it after I've hoisted your boat out of the water."

Daniel ushered his wives off of his small sail boat and onto the gangplank. "Got to be extra gentlemanly with this many wives or it's eight times the punishment to endure. Ha ha ha!" Daniel's laugh was operatic. I couldn't wait to hear *his* choir.

"Let's have an adventure." I said, welcoming his family aboard.

Daniel looked at the name on the ship, "Yeah, a *Grand Adventure*."

Daniel hadn't even told me his last name, but I knew it. Miller, Daniel Miller. I wondered what stories he'd have to tell. My *Fond Memories* gave me just a sketch of who he was. Well, I'd have to find out later. Ruth and I had a date for *dessert*. I couldn't wait to taste what she'd be serving.

Chapter 23 Footnotes

1. Paul's statements concerning marriage and chastity must never be taken out of the context of what Paul himself has stated elsewhere. In his letter to Timothy Paul wills (commands) that the younger women be married:

1 Timothy 5:4 I *will* therefore that the younger women marry, bear children, guide the house, give none occasion to the adversary to speak reproachfully.

If you're making the claim that Paul argues for celibacy, that claim is proven false by the above verse for *if* Paul were had argued for celibacy he would have been arguing against what he himself has written in Timothy 5:4 above!

It does not take a theologian to know that married women usually behave better than single women and it is a fact that women who behave better will be able to serve the Lord better. Prince John, in this novel, is simply kidding Ish's wives based on the Romish misconception that married women will not be on fire for the Lord as much as single women.

2. Ruth 1:15-16 And Ruth said, Intreat me not to leave thee, or to return from following after thee: for whither thou goest, I will go; and where thou lodgest, I will lodge: thy people shall be my people, and thy God my God.

3. Revelation 14:3-4 And they sung as it were a new song before the throne, and before the four beasts, and the elders: and no man could learn that song but the hundred and forty and four thousand, which were redeemed from the earth. These are they which were not defiled with women; for they are virgins. These are they which follow the Lamb whithersoever he goeth. These were redeemed from among men, being the firstfruits unto God and to the Lamb.

According to Strong's Greek Concordance the word translated here as virgin is *a man who has abstained from all uncleanness and whoredom attendant on idolatry, and so has kept his chastity.* Such a man would not make an idol of his own wife. In fact, he might very well have several wives for he would have *rightly divided the word of truth* concerning marriage.

2 Timothy 2:15 Study to *show thyself approved unto God*, a workman that needeth not to be ashamed, *rightly dividing the word of truth.*

A man who clings to the false teaching that he may have just one wife cannot be said to be chaste for he has rejected God's word and replaced it with custom.

4. And I saw another angel ascending from the east, having the seal of the living God: and he cried with a loud voice to the four angels, to whom it was given to hurt the earth and the sea, 3 Saying, Hurt not the earth, neither the sea, nor the trees, till we have sealed the servants of our God in their foreheads. 4 And I heard the number of them which were sealed: and there were sealed an hundred and forty and four thousand of all the tribes of the children of Israel. Revelation 7:2-4

Twelve Thousand from each of the tribes of Israel.

5. Marriage is an exchange of authority from the woman and/or her father to the husband. Ish's wife, Ruth, understands that Biblical law. That said, it is sad that many of today's marriages are nothing more than licensed harlotry for the woman has never given her husband anything resembling authority over her. In fact, the laws of the United States give a woman the *so called* right to divorce her husband whereas the Bible only gives that right to the husband. Only a harlot moves from one man to another at her own will. See the following verses for clarification:

Numbers 30:13 Every vow, and every binding oath to afflict the soul, her husband may establish it, or her husband may make it void.

Ephesians 5:23 For the husband is the head of the wife, even as Christ is the head of the church: and he is the saviour of the body.

1 Corinthians 7:10-11 And unto the married I command, **yet not I, but the Lord**, Let not the wife depart from her husband: *But and if* ***she depart****, let her remain unmarried*, or be reconciled to her husband: and let not the husband put away his wife.

The verse above is describing a case where the wife has left, not those cases where the husband has sent the wife away with a Bill of Divorcement for valid cause, as described elsewhere in Scripture. Are there cases where a woman can ask her husband to divorce her out of mercy toward her? Of course. Such would be the case of a man who is imprisoned for life for a capital crime of which he is guilty, or who had become infected with an incurable venereal disease through some sin he committed. Jesus often listed mercy as a reason to break laws. The law given through Moses also allowed for exceptions.

6. For we wrestle not against flesh and blood, but against principalities, against powers, against the rulers of the darkness of this world, against spiritual wickedness in high places. Ephesians 6:12

7. Hosea 14:7 They that dwell under his shadow shall return; they shall revive as the corn, and grow as the vine: the scent thereof shall be as the wine of Lebanon. Ephraim shall say, What have I to do any more with idols? I have heard him, and observed him: I am like a green fir tree. From me is thy fruit found. Who is wise, and he shall understand these things? prudent, and he shall know them? for the ways of the LORD are right, and the just shall walk in them: but the transgressors shall fall therein.

8. The chariots of God are twenty thousand, even thousands of angels: the Lord is among them, as in Sinai, in the holy place. Psalm 68:17

9. 1 Corinthians 5-10 But every woman that prayeth or prophesieth with her head uncovered dishonoureth her head: for that is even all one as if she were shaven. For if the woman be not covered, let her also be shorn: but if it be a shame for a woman to be shorn or shaven, let her be covered. For a man indeed ought not to cover his head, forasmuch as he is the image and glory of God: but the woman is the glory of the man. For the man is not of the woman; but the woman of the man. Neither was the man created for the woman; but the woman for the man. **For this cause ought the woman to have power on her head because of the angels.**

10. And the great dragon was cast out, that old serpent, called the Devil, and Satan, which deceiveth the whole world: he was cast out into the earth, and his angels were cast out with him. Revelation 12:9

11. Woe unto them that call evil good, and good evil; that put darkness for light, and light for darkness; that put bitter for sweet, and sweet for bitter! Isaiah 5:20

12. Marvel not, my brethren, if the world hate you. 1 John 3:13

I have given them thy word; and the world hath hated them, because they are not of the world, even as I am not of the world. John 17:14

If the world hate you, ye know that it hated me before it hated you. John 15:18

13. CPS is the oxymoronic acronym for Child Protective Services.
14. Children who are thus stolen by CPS will sometimes conveniently disappear from their records without a trace.
If a man be found stealing any of his brethren of the children of Israel, and maketh merchandise of him, or selleth him; then that thief shall die; and thou shalt put evil away from among you. Deuteronomy 24:7
CPS literally makes a business out of stealing and selling children. As their case load increases their personnel increase and those already working for CPS are promoted with pay raises for their increased theft of children. Their motivation has become to increase the size of their bureaucracy and they take the shortest route to that goal which is to steal more children.
Thou therefore which teachest another, teachest thou not thyself? thou that preachest a man should not steal, dost thou steal? Romans 2:21
15. STD - Sexually Transmitted Disease - STDs are more prevalent among those who are in foster care than among the general public and they are certainly more prevalent among the general public than among homeschoolers.
16. 5 For after this manner in the old time the holy women also, who trusted in God, adorned themselves, being in subjection unto their own husbands: 6 Even as Sara obeyed Abraham, calling him lord: whose daughters ye are, as long as ye do well, and are not afraid with any amazement. 1 Peter 3:5-6
17. Improperly deferring marriage is the cause of much harlotry. Young women are to get married, in fact, The Apostle Paul commanded it,
"I will, therefore, that the younger women marry, bear children, guide the house, give none occasion to the adversary to speak reproachfully." 1Timothy 5:14
And again Paul states,
"She shall be saved in childbearing, if they continue in faith and charity and holiness with sobriety." 1Timothy 2:15
Saved from what? -- saved from a life of fornication so that the adversary (Satan or anyone else who opposes righteousness) may not have any reason to attack the virtue of the young women. The Greek word translated as *younger women* is *neos* which means recently come into being, young, youthful, new, and in the context

of marriage Paul is speaking of women who have *recently become women*, in other words, *recently had their first menstrual cycle*. So Paul not only commands that the younger women marry but he defines those young women much younger than the last hundred years of history has considered appropriate for marriage. Is it any wonder that fornication is so common today considering marriage is delayed far beyond the age at which a woman becomes a woman. Paul wrote scripture, these were not the mere words of a man, and unlike today, the Roman law of Paul's day was actually in accordance with Scripture for Roman law required that upon reaching puberty every citizen must marry or lose many rights and privileges. The Lex Papia Poppaea, A.D. 9, decreed punishments such as the loss of inheritance rights for those who remained single after having attained puberty. A man or woman was given one hundred days to get married upon finding out they were the beneficiary of an inheritance or forfeit the inheritance.
A Systematic and Historical Exposition - ROMAN LAW - In the Order of a Code by W. A. Hunter EMBODYING THE INSTITUTES OF GAIUS AND THE INSTITUTES OF JUSTINIAN, TRANSLATED INTO ENGLISH BY J. ASHTON CROSS, B.A. of Balliol College, Oxford, BARRISTER-AT-LAW, Fourth Edition 1803
18. John 5:46-47 For had ye believed Moses, ye would have believed Me: for he wrote of me. 47 But if ye believe not his writings, how shall ye believe my words?
John 14:15 If ye love me, keep my commandments.
19. *Tare* - Old English word for weed.
Matthew 13:38-43 The field is the world; the good seed are the children of the kingdom; but the tares are the children of the wicked one; The enemy that sowed them is the devil; the harvest is the end of the world; and the reapers are the angels. As therefore the tares are gathered and burned in the fire; so shall it be in the end of this world. The Son of man shall send forth his angels, and they shall gather out of his kingdom all things that offend, and them which do iniquity; And shall cast them into a furnace of fire: there shall be wailing and gnashing of teeth. Then shall the righteous shine forth as the sun in the kingdom of their Father. Who hath ears to hear, let him hear.

Chapter 24

A NEW FRIEND

After dessert with Ruth, I couldn't nap, despite the fact that she was happily snoozing. She lay there like sleeping beauty, except that my kisses couldn't awaken her.

My *Fond Memories* were full of facts about Daniel but I still didn't know how he'd met his brides or the reason the Lord had placed him on John's yacht. I figured he'd be in the galley by now so I scribbled on a notepad, *Went to Galley,* and placed it next to Ruth's toothbrush where she'd find it.

Just as I was stepping out of Ruth's cabin door I caught a glimpse of Daniel entering the galley. By the time I caught up with him, he was sitting at the table with John and Sam. John looked around the table at us.

"Now that we're all here, *let's celebrate.*"

He pushed a buzzer on the table and a few seconds later one of his daughters peered out from behind the kitchen door.

"Yes Daddy?"

"Precious! Please come over here.

This is my daughter, Princess Michaiah. You look so wonderful this morning, as always, and the Lord has blessed you with a warm disposition. Could you be so kind as to bring me and my barkadas[1] some coffee and a tray?"

His daughter nearly skipped across the room to give him a hug as she leaned over his shoulder, kissing him on the cheek.

"Of course, Daddy. I'll bring it right away."

Within moments Princess Michaiah was back, pushing a Dim Sum Cart.[2]

We picked out our favorite dishes, then Michaiah poured our coffee, leaving the pot on the table for us.

Sam prayed. "*Thank You Father for this food and this company. Guide us and strengthen us. In Jesus' Name, we pray. Amen.*"

We concurred with our own *Amen*s.

"So, Sam, how did you get out of jail?" Daniel asked as he

picked up one of the goodies that he'd loaded onto his plate.

"Well, it wasn't so much a matter of *getting out.*" Sam said. "I knew I'd get out, eventually. As for the fact that it took seven weeks, I guess you can blame that on Ish."

"Oh, Sam, how could you say that?" I objected.

Sam now turned to John. "Okay, so it was your fault. You're the one who distracted Ish, enticing him with the prospect of five new brides." Sam wagged his finger in John's face. "You expected him to focus on getting me out of jail with five wannabe brides along for the ride? Not to mention the two you had waiting in ambush for him at my place."

"Me?" John shot back, "Asina was with him that night. So where do you suppose he got her? Not from any church of mine. And those two maids of yours, you're blaming me that *your* maids came after Ish?"

"They're not maids, I'll have you know. Both of them have PhDs in education." Sam said. "They were merely helping Sarisa and me with the kids till the right opportunity came along."

"I'd say they were helping." John said. "Helping themselves to Ish. Is that the right opportunity you're talking about?"

"Hey! You're talking about my wives!" I protested, but I was unable to keep a straight face. I was no match for Sam and John when it came to acting.

"To tell you the truth," Sam said, "if the three of us didn't pretend to be upset with each other, we'd have such boring days. With eight wives running our households, life is so *very boring*."

"Yes, *very boring and difficult!*" John chuckled.

Of course their days and mine were anything but boring *or* difficult. Having more wives gave us freedom from the daily concerns that monogamists have. If eight wives can't handle a household without their husband's help then nobody can. Our daily duties were now limited to the very things we loved; reading the Bible, teaching our families, and teaching our communities. Our nightly duties were none of anyone's business nor were the quiet times our wives had built into our schedules. We were blessed and we were thankful, as was our new guest, Daniel.

Sam continued speaking as we dined.

"To explain how I got out of jail, Daniel, I'll first have to explain how I got thrown in. It wasn't for concubinage[3] as rumored, but a result of treachery. Some members of the church board were so upset that my extra wives had given me the needed children to trigger the transfer of the church properties to my name, that they altered the covenant that specified the terms for the transfer. The covenant *had* read; 'At such time the pastor begets twelve children, the deed for all church properties shall be transferred to his name.' The conspiring board members added an apostrophe *s* after the word pastor and added the word wife. Thus, the *pastor's wife*, singular, would have to give birth to twelve children in order for him to be the beneficiary of the church properties. In addition, they inserted an entire line into the covenant which stated, *If the pastor be found to have sired any children with any woman other than his one wife then he shall immediately be dismissed from his duties as pastor and evicted from any and all church properties.* The judge who issued the warrant for my arrest knew they'd made forgeries to the covenant because prior to becoming a judge he was the attorney for Mr. Tigas, the man who'd donated the church properties in the first place. I was never actually thrown in jail. That was just a rumor we allowed to take hold. I was put under protective custody in the judge's own house to protect me from those who'd forged the covenant. The judge knew that anyone who bears false witness to harm a man has murder in their heart[4] and he wanted to make sure that all those guilty of the forgery were in custody before I was released. It was all done with my consent and the judge gave me one of the best rooms in his mansion. In fact, every night was a second honeymoon, first one of my wives sleeping over, then another of them. My kids would visit every day. To tell you the truth, I kind of miss that mansion."

Daniel had finished his food and now joined our conversation.

"What astounds me is how you were able to keep all those wives hidden." He said. "John, you've been married to four of your wives for over twenty-five years. Could you ever have imagined that Sam could keep seven wives hidden till every one of them gave birth?"

John leaned over the table, and whispered. "As a matter of fact, Daniel, I *did* imagine it." Then he winked and leaned back in his seat. "But it's no secret now. Let me introduce myself; My name is King John... Tigas. I *am* Mr. Tigas."

"So let me get this straight," Daniel said, "You thought with a little coaxing that Sam, here, would grab himself a few *extree* wives and hatch himself a few kids?"

"I wouldn't put it that way, Daniel, but judging from what the Holy Ghost has stuffed into my head about you, that's precisely how you'd put it."

"Well, I would, and I did, but it must have taken a bit more than a *little* coaxing to get his wife on board."

"It was simply a matter of leverage." John explained to Daniel. "With the help of some of the girls in Sam's church we made Sarisa's job of running her household more and more difficult by the day, while increasing the number of girls she could call upon to help out."

"We? I didn't think you were quite welcome in Sam's church, at least not according to my *Fond Memories*."

"Well, I wasn't, Daniel, but Ruth *was*, and she used every match making skill in that huge brain of hers to choose just the right girls. *The easiest part was getting the members of the church board to impose on Sam.*"

At that we all cracked up. John talked through his chuckles to continue his explanation.

"What a bunch of rascals were on that church board! In no time at all, they were having breakfast board meetings, lunch board meetings, and nearly every night they'd have a dinner board meeting. Then it happened."

"What happened?" Daniel asked.

"The leverage I was talking about. The girls who'd been helping Sarisa in the kitchen left for a week long mission trip. Sarisa soon realized she couldn't survive without the girls helping her out around the house, not to mention, she missed the Christian fellowship she'd shared with them. It was then that the thought crossed her mind that if Sam had enough wives he could fill up the house with his own children in less than a year, and that would be that; the church and all its properties would be her husband's. So, Sarisa took the covenant to an attorney, recommended by Ruth, just to make sure."

"Let me guess, John, the same attorney?"

"You guessed right, Daniel, the very same one. My attorney assured her that no matter who the mother of the children was, that the covenant that governed the ownership of the church was absolutely clear; if Sam had twelve of his own kids living under his roof, all the church holdings would become his. Now keep in mind, Sarisa still didn't know I was Mr. Tigas, but she knew from her friendship with Ruth that my family might be able to convince Sam of the benefits of having more than one wife. I'd known all along that Sam would have to think it was his own idea to make it work, and I had a plan ready. In fact, just about a year later, we used the very same plan on Ish and Mary."

"So now Sam's got eight wives, a baker's dozen of kids, and all the church holdings. That's a lot of blessings!" Daniel said.

"Speaking of blessings," John said, "here come some of our own right now."

John walked to the door to greet our families and I hurried to my cabin to get Ruth. She was still sleeping. By the time Ruth and I got back to the galley, everyone aboard the ship was there. John waited for us to seat ourselves, then raised his glass.

"To wives!" He toasted, then scratched his head. "That's T, O, wives. To wives!" he repeated, raising his glass. We couldn't help but laugh at what may or may not have been a deliberate pun on John's part, then he introduced Daniel.

"I've asked Daniel to tell us his love story. It's an incredible love story... even compared to yours, Ish."

John paused for a moment to make sure I was paying attention. I felt like a kid who'd been caught goofing off in class. Could I be blamed? I'd been lost somewhere between Ruth's smile and her large black eyes.

"But before you tell your love story, Daniel, would you please pray blessings upon our table?"

"Sure, John.

Heavenly Father, God of our salvation, we ask that You bless this food. Help us to pray continually. Help us to keep our hearts and minds on You. Help us to remember that blessings and righteousness come only from You. Turn us from worldly lusts so that we will not lift up our souls in vanity.[5] *In Jesus' Name we pray. Amen.*"

"Amen." We responded.

"Thanks so much for asking me to share my love story, our love story, that is." Daniel motioned to his wives. "As I look around the table at each of my new brides, and my Hannah, who has stood by me, I still can't get it out of my head that this may all be a dream. In fact, I keep this safety pin attached to my collar just to remind myself how blessed I am." Daniel rubbed a well worn safety pin between his thumb and forefinger. "Every once in a while, I unhook it, and give myself a poke. Just like this, *ouch*!"

The kids giggled at seeing Daniel jab himself with the pin.

"I can see from the dreamy eyed faces around the table that some of you might do well to have a safety pin too. Well, you're in luck. I brought a whole box of them."

Daniel put the box of safety pins on the table.

"There's enough for everyone, even the kids." He said.

Everyone else took theirs and hooked it on their sleeve or collar. I took mine and immediately jabbed myself.

"Didn't feel a thing." I announced, "I am dreaming." Then I succumbed to gazing in Ruth's eyes again.

Chapter 24 Footnotes

1. Barkada (Tagalog) - a member of a group of very close friends who share a nearly identical code of conduct.

2. Dim Sum Cart - A cart with four or five levels of trays, each having an assortment of Chinese dishes.

3. In the Philippines there is a clear difference stated in law between adultery and concubinage. Their definitions are closer to the Bible than most countries. Adultery always involves a married woman. Concubinage (in Philippine law) always involves a man who is legally married but also has wives that are not legal. The wife who is not legal is usually referred to as a kabit which means hidden. If the legal wife has stated openly or in writing that it is okay for the husband to have extra wives then it cannot be prosecuted. In addition, if the first wife is not legally married she cannot file a complaint of concubinage. Legal marriage (in the Philippines) requires a license. Without a complaint from a legally married wife, the state cannot prosecute for concubinage, i.e., polygamy. In this way, the Philippines is one of the most free countries in the world for men who want more than one wife.

4. In the following verses it is made clear that bearing false witness is the first step toward murder:

Exodus 23:7 Keep thee far from a false matter; and the innocent and righteous slay thou not: for I will not justify the wicked.

Matthew 5:21-22 Ye have heard that it was said by them of old time, Thou shalt not kill; and whosoever shall kill shall be in danger of the judgment: But I say unto you, That whosoever is angry with his brother without a cause shall be in danger of the judgment: and whosoever shall say to his brother, Raca, shall be in danger of the council: but whosoever shall say, Thou fool, shall be in danger of hell fire.

5. Psalm 24:3-4 Who shall ascend into the hill of the LORD? or who shall stand in his holy place? He that hath clean hands, and a pure heart; who hath not lifted up his soul unto vanity, nor sworn deceitfully.

DANIEL'S STORY

"My name is Daniel Miller. I'm a professor on sabbatical from a small Christian college, a few hours drive from London. My ministry was church history and hymnody, still is. Until recently my work had been fairly routine; gather up a few ancient books, remove the superfluous language, then translate them into one volume in modern English. I would then teach my graduate students from these new books. As I said, until recently, my work *had* been fairly routine, that is, until the bookstore where I'd gotten most of my rare books came by a large cache of hymnals and manuscripts from the Eighteenth Century. It was in that trove that I came across one book, then another, describing a man whose talents and ministries were so great and varied that only a calculated cover up could have kept him out of the standard textbooks used in seminaries. I was startled by my discovery, to say the least, but more than that, I was obsessed; obsessed to discover who this man was. He was a philanthropist on the grandest scale.[1] He preached to the high born as well as the low born.[2] He was a composer of sacred hymns and as for those hymns most popular in Christian congregations, his hymns were preeminent.[3] If these avocations were not sufficient to fill one life, he was also a poet and a Greek and Latin scholar, having translated that famous Latin work, Juvenal and Persius into English with copious explanatory notes.[4] He was also an attorney who worked on behalf of the downtrodden.[5] He was quoted by Benjamin Franklin[6] and his hymn tunes were sung by America's Founding Fathers and England's royalty, as well as the flower girl on the corner of Chapel street and Hyde Park. In fact, the famous Chapel Street in London was named after his chapel, the Lock Chapel.[7] This long hidden treasure of a man was none other than the Reverend Martin Madan, the most famous preacher of Eighteenth Century London. His Sunday night concerts at the Lock Chapel, which he founded, delighted listeners with the most exhilarating Christian music the world had ever heard.[8]

Due to what the president of my college referred to as my Madan mania, I was asked to take a long overdue sabbatical. It couldn't have come at a better time; I'd heard rumors that there was a library of Madan's writings and hymnals, in near perfect condition, somewhere near Cagayan de Oro. My wife Hannah and I got on the first plane for Mindanao and I began my search.

Now that you know my scholarly obsession and how I ended up on Mindanao, let me tell you the rest of my obsessions; the Bible of course. It brings me closer to the Lord. Just like Ish, Sam, John, Sulpicia, and Ruth, I can't go more than a few hours without scouring its pages for some new crumbs that might fall from the Master's table.[9] My new family is also an obsession. Who wouldn't be obsessed with such a family? They're so very precious to me. So without further delay, *here is our love story*.

There was a time when Hannah and I weren't exactly getting along. In fact, within weeks of our arrival on Mindanao she had abandoned me and was headed back to the UK. Losing my wife was bad enough but losing her in a far away place, with no friends and no family, was devastating.

I began to take trips around Mindanao to forget. During one such trip I nearly lost track of time, normally nothing to fret about on Mindanao, as you all know, but it was Friday, the day of preparation. There was less than an hour till sunset and my internal alarm clock went off. I was reminded of the Sabbath, that precious gift from the Lord. Now, regardless of how depressed I might have been, I take my Sabbath seriously. It is one gift from God that arrives on time, every week, and without asking for it. I treasure my Sabbath and enjoy the much needed rest it provides me.

Since I had to make the best of my time to prepare for the Sabbath, I hailed a tricycle driver[10] to help me find lodging for the night and food for the following day. It would have been impossible to make it home before sundown and the Sabbath's arrival.[11]

For the first time since Hannah had left me, I was positively glad that she'd gone. It meant she wouldn't have the chance to degrade herself by demanding an explanation for my coming home a day late. *Demanding an explanation*, what kind of drivel was that?

The typical *Christian* woman's desire for dominance, demonstrated in the reverse roles she demands of her husband, had become abhorrent to me. Furthermore, the fact that my own wife had made me the target of such impudence was becoming less sufferable by the day. Anyway, I was relieved that my inattention to time wasn't going to be an opportunity for Hannah to commit positional fornication,[12] grounds for divorce that I, like most other Christian Patriarchs, wasn't anxious to invoke. The rare woman that considered such rebellion sin, kept silent about it in the company of *The Sisters of the Cutting Tongues*, the name that my friends and I had begun to attach to the Christian wives in our congregations who relentlessly tried to dominate their husbands. The sad fact was that *The Sisters of the Cutting Tongues* had come to include nearly all Christian wives. Hannah's particular method of dominance was to argue, and I'd had enough. The tricycle driver I'd flagged down interrupted my retrospection.

'Where can I take you?' The driver asked.

'I'm looking for a hotel that has rooms with refrigerators.' I said.

'Over there.' He pointed to a prestigious looking building a few blocks away. 'They've got a restaurant too.'

'Okay, let's go.' I said.

He signaled me to get in. Once I was seated, he raced up the few blocks to the hotel in less than thirty seconds.

'They have everything you need.' He told me, then sped off.

I ascended the granite steps to a set of enormous mahogany doors. A plaque above the doors read, *The House of Esther*. Together the two doors formed a picture of the Garden of Eden. Adam's hand was etched into a brass plate on one door, palm up, having just accepted the forbidden fruit. As the doorman swung open the door, the brass plate swung with it to reveal another etching; seven women kneeling at the feet of one man.[13]

'You have intriguing artwork.' I said to the doorman.

He smiled proudly then glanced down at my one piece of luggage; my ever present bag. In addition to containing my laptop with all its bible software, it contained a fresh change of clothes and toiletries for just such an emergency as this.

'No other luggage, sir?' He asked.

'No, this is it.' I said.

'And if you don't mind, sir, what is your religion?' A curious question coming from a doorman, I thought, but I answered nonetheless.

'I'm Christian, Christian Patriarch.'

'Ahhh, Christian, Christian Patriarch.' He repeated, 'You've come to the right place. We'll get started right away on your preparation for the Sabbath. We have rooms with mini-refs and private tables in our self serve restaurant. There is no Sabbath breaking here. You'll have the run of the house.'

'That's fabulous, for certain!' I said. 'I've never heard of such lodging, but it's fantastic.'

'Follow me, sir.' He said, then walked inside.

As we entered he whispered something to a concierge who was standing next to a huge curtain. Whatever it was, the concierge greeted it gleefully. Effervescing with hospitality, he spoke:

'It is fortunate that you have arrived before the Sabbath, sir.'

'You're quite right.' I said. 'I've been told that you have food, lodging, and a refrigerator?'

'Etcetera!' He said.

If the one who'd designed *The House of Esther* had set out to invoke mystery, he'd certainly succeeded. The curtain behind the concierge stretched the length of a banquet hall and it was all I could do to keep myself from pulling it aside. As I looked around me I tried to figure out what the name of the place might mean. My thoughts were interrupted when the concierge left me with the receptionist.

'I'm Miss Unabrea Panil. Welcome to *The House of Esther,*' she said, 'and you are?'

'Daniel Miller. My friends call me Danny.' I responded.

'Then I shall call you Danny, if that's okay, and you shall call me Una.'

Una's answer was simple enough but it left me confused, or should I say, *Una* left me confused. She was beyond exotic. Her long lashes framed her oval eyes like lace curtains. Her clothing, though modest, was inadequate to hide her exquisite body. Some might say I noticed these things about her because of lust[14], that frequently misdefined word, but, truly, it was because of what the Lord had put in me when he created me, that part of me that longed to multiply; to fulfill His command. Of course, I don't deny that Una's ample endowment played its part. Nonetheless, some men are made to have but one wife while others are made to have many; wives who will bear them great quivers full of children.[15] During the long weeks of separation from Hannah I'd had much time to think on these things and had come to the conclusion that I was of the latter sort, and Una, Lord willing, might be the first of many wives.

'Now that we're friends,' I said, 'Can I confide in you?'

'Sure, what is it?' She asked.

'Among all my friends, you're the most beautiful.'

Una's dark skin quickly turned a mahogany hue as she blushed at my compliment. I must say that her modesty became her.

'Oh, thank you.' She said. 'I look forward to being your friend. I must be honest with you though. I've been pretending not to know who you are. I knew your face the moment you walked through the door. I recognized you from the back cover of your book. I've read all your books. In fact, everyone that works here has read all your books. You're pretty much of a star around here. When I realized it was you, it was all I could do to gather up my wits and greet you.'

'Now you're trying to make *me* blush, aren't you?' I said.

'Oh no sir, I….' Una stopped mid-sentence when she realized I was jesting.

'Una, you needn't ever call me sir.' I said.

I put on my reading glasses to read the menu she'd placed on the table in front of me. It was more of an order form than a menu.

'You want me to fill out all this just to eat?' I asked her.

'Oh, nobody *just eats* here.' She protested. 'This is not your typical restaurant. We're a club for true Christians only. Please, hurry and fill up the information because the Sabbath is coming.' Then she caught herself. 'I'm sorry Danny. We don't need any of this from you. Have you forgotten what you described in your last book?'

As I looked around me, I realized that *The House of Esther* was identical to the Sabbath keepers lodge I'd proposed in my book.

'How could I have missed it? This is remarkable!' I said.

'You're not offended that we've lifted your idea?' She asked.

'Offended? I'm flattered! Okay, since this place is based on my book,' I said, 'I'll take *Solomon's Quarters*, if it's available.'

'Available?' Una said, 'It has been reserved for you, Mr. Daniel

Miller, ever since, especially for you! Nobody has ever been given *Solomon's Quarters*. It has been kept vacant for that auspicious occasion when you would drop in.'

Unabrea's reaction may have been rehearsed but I was quite certain she was sincere.

'How long have you been associated with *The House of Esther*?' I asked her.

'Three days.' She answered.

'Now *you're* kidding *me*, aren't you?' I said.

'I'm not kidding.' She says. 'God works in wondrous ways! Your first Sabbath here shall be my first Sabbath here as well.'

'Your first Sabbath here?' I asked.

'Yes, our entire preparation day staff must stay here for the Sabbath. We live too far from *The House of Esther* to make it back home without taking a motorized tricycle and that would be breaking the Sabbath.' She said.

'Of course. I'm just not used to being in a place where the Sabbath is honored,' I said, 'never mind spoken of. It's thrilling.'

'Yes it is!' Una bubbled with excitement.

Was she coming on to me, I wondered, or was I simply engaging in a fantasy prompted by my fertile imagination. Una set her hand on the table next to mine; each one of her fingers delicately manicured. Now I'm asking myself, is that an invitation? She searched my eyes as if reading a map. I savored the moment. I wondered, could she see the willingness in my eyes. When she smiled it ignited a spark in her black eyes like lightning in midnight skies. *Oh man*, I caught myself, *am I thinking in poetry about her already*. Certainly, Solomon was writing about such a moment. *The way of a man with a maiden.*[16]

Unabrea whispered to someone behind a curtain. '*Daniel Miller, Daniel Miller.*' Then she turns to me, 'I'm sorry Danny,' she said, 'I'm just so excited about you coming to *The House of Esther*. Everyone here will be just as excited as I am. I hope they don't ruin your food because of their excitement. Can I surprise you?'

'Well you can try.' I said.

'Even though we've added some features to *The House of Esther* that weren't in your book,' She says, 'I'm sure you'll agree that they're all in accordance with Scripture. Close your eyes, Danny.'

Una now took my hand, guiding me to my feet. Her hand was

every bit as soft as I'd imagined it. She led me across the room and through a curtain, then seated me on a chair.

'There, you can open your eyes now.' She said.

'Wow! It's exactly as I pictured it;' I said, astonished. 'Solomon's Quarters!'

Una let go of my hand and was now standing beside my table.

'Please, have a seat.' I invited her. 'I'd love to chat with you more.'

She sat down next to me and the expression on her face grew intimate once again. This time when she gazed into my eyes, I couldn't resist gazing back, my eyes full with desire. Since marrying Hannah, I hadn't looked into another woman's eyes that way.

Una responded to my unspoken desire, locking onto my gaze. I can't deny that I wanted to grab her right then and there, but I settled for more conversation.

'Una, how is it that you came to work here?' I said.

'Well, it was only a week ago,' she told me, 'that I was reading one of your books in the cafe across the street. I could see that this building was nearly completed and the name was so intriguing that I had to ask the foreman what kind of place it was. He said he wasn't sure but the owner was inside and I should ask him. Well, I'm not normally so bold but my curiosity had the best of me. I just had to know what this *House of Esther* could be. The owner told me how it was based on your book so I pleaded with him to let me work here. Unfortunately all the positions had been filled. I hope you don't mind that I have a bit of a crush on you.'

'Mind?' I said. 'Not at all. It's wonderful.'

Una appeared more relaxed now as she leaned back and continued her story.

'So anyway, the owner called me in, just three days ago, because one of the girls got engaged.'

'He fired her for getting engaged?' I asked, somewhat baffled.

'Of course!' Una said. 'All the girls who work here are NBSB.'

'Oh yes, NBSB.' I said, 'I remember having that explained to me when I first arrived here on Mindanao; No Boyfriend Since Birth; *a biblical virgin*.[17] But rather than my guessing, can you tell me why the girls here at *The House of Esther* are required to be biblical virgins?'

'Promise me you won't be angry.' Una said.

'Angry?' I said. 'I can't imagine why I'd be angry with you, but I promise.'

'All of the girls who work here want to become wives to Patriarchal Christians, and I mean wives.' She says, 'So we've all taken a vow to enter into marriage only with a man worthy of many wives. Of course the owner of *The House of Esther* knows that Patriarchal Christians would refuse to marry harlots paraded as virgins; *those girls who claim their unbroken hymen makes them a virgin even though they have allowed the breasts of their virginity to be caressed.*[18] Maybe that's why I was so excited to meet you. You're the first man I've met who I'm certain is worthy of many wives, worthy to... to touch me.'

'*To touch you?*' I said, somewhat dazed.

'*As a wife, of course.*' She answered. 'Forgive me Danny, a girl should not be so forward.'

Tears started to run down Una's cheeks. I was astounded. There was not one drop of mascara mixed with them. She was that gorgeous and exotic without a spec of makeup. It was then that I realized I'd been overcome with her beauty having never so much as seen her ankles. In fact, the only skin that her clothing revealed was that of her face, neck, and hands. Una's tears dried up as quickly as they'd begun.

'A girl should not be so forward,' Una confessed, '...unless she's found her man. Have I found my man?' Una looked into my eyes.

Just then, another girl who worked at *The House of Esther* approached our booth. Una greeted her, excitedly.

'Setia! I'm so glad that you were here for Danny's arrival. I'm sorry Danny. Is it okay if I introduce you to Setia as Danny?'

'Of course, if Setia is going to be my friend as well.' I said.

'Yes, yes.' Both of them chimed, then they began speaking to each other so quickly in their native tongue that I couldn't make out one word.

'Sit, sit.' Una coaxed Setia, pulling her down onto the cushion next to her. Setia sat gazing into my eyes.

'I haven't heard that name before; *Setia*.'

Setia was still fixed on my eyes so Una answered for her.

'Setia was born on Christmas day. She was named after your popular Christmas flower; poinsettia.'

'You're beautiful, I, I mean, that's beautiful. Well both, poinsettias and you are beautiful.' I said.

Now the three of us were laughing. Such a pleasure; the end of Friday, the beginning of the Sabbath, two biblical virgins at my sides, and I was about to have a feast. Maybe this was what the concierge meant by, 'Etcetera.'

Una and Setia's exotic scents mingled with the aromas drifting through the corridors of *The House of Esther*. They awakened a desire in me that could only be diverted by filling my now empty stomach. I could taste the air now as the smoke of braised beef, roasted chicken, sautéed vegetables, and herbs met with audible applause from my now growling stomach; the growl that precedes the taking of prey. Setia and Una, aware of the war between my two hungers, rose as one to take the simpler path to my heart. Pulling aside two heavy curtains they revealed a huge table with more dishes already prepared than could be found on most menus. They motioned me to join them, then waited, anticipating my prayer. Standing between Setia and Una, I prayed.

'*Lord, Thank you for the food we are about to eat. Help us to remember that all blessings flow from You. May each of these beautiful women standing at my sides find the man they seek. May they find him tonight and if it be Your will, Lord, let it be me.*'

My surprise that such words had jumped from my throat did not deter me, I breathed slowly and deeply, and continued my prayer.

'*As each of these women light their Sabbath candles,*[19] *may we remember your love for us and the wonder of this day. This day of rest that You, in Your great generosity have lovingly given us. Amen.*'

My closing words were met by a chorus of feminine voices as a great number of young women lit their Sabbath candles and said, '*Amen.*' Now that the candles were lit I could see that there were dozens of young ladies standing at my sides. They'd formed a circle around the great table on which the feast had been laid. They matched the beauty of Setia and Una and I'd just prayed that each of them, each one of these beauties, would find their husband in me, if it were the Lord's will. How many women had I just prayed would become my wives? In my book, I had carefully described the room named Solomon's Quarters. It had space enough for the chair of the Lord of the Room, which is the chair on which Setia and Una had sat me when I first came in. There were also forty nine other chairs, princess chairs, *in front of which now stood the forty seven other beauties besides Setia and Una!* I pinched myself, and ouch, this wasn't a dream. Were they all hoping to find their match in me?

With hundreds of Sabbath candles lit I could now see how faithfully the builder of *The House of Esther* had followed the plans from my book for this great room. Some of the girls were now filling their plates, others were taking out musical instruments, and some were doing stretching exercises.

'Oh, don't mind them.' Setia said. 'They're preparing for the performance. After we've filled our plates, the show will begin.'

'Show?' I croaked, a frog now caught in my throat.

'Yes, they'll perform the dance of the ten virgins based on the story of the ten virgins, lamps and all. It's beautiful.' She said.

'Yes, they are ...er.. *it is* a beautiful story.' I said.

Setia and Una had figured out that my propensity for Freudian Slips was deliberate, and they loved it.

'You must now tell us whether any of us are uninvited.' Una stated perfunctorily.

'Uninvited?' I said.

'Yes, although we all observe the Sabbath here, *The House of Esther* is a commercial establishment. Tonight's expenses, if all of the girls dine with you, will be fifteen thousand pesos. If you lay with one of them, that will make her your wife and her parents will expect a dowry of twelve thousand pesos. If you take all forty nine of them as your wives you could stand to spend...' She now took out a calculator, pushed a few buttons, looked me straight in the eye as if closing a deal, and said, 'Six hundred and three thousand pesos.'

'So how much is that in pounds?' I asked.

'Sorry, Danny, I don't have a pound exchange chart with me,' she apologized, 'but in dollars, worst case scenario, about twelve thousand, plus or minus. It depends on the exchange rate when it hits your bank.'

How Una was able to keep a straight face was beyond me. I couldn't help grinning. It was difficult for me to imagine how forty nine wives in one night for the paltry sum of twelve thousand dollars could be a *worst case scenario*. I gathered myself together enough to speak and said,

'So what's the deposit, considering I couldn't possibly marry them all in one evening?'

Una, sensing that I had intentions to follow through, flushed with excitement. Her lips were fuller and her eyes moist but she kept her focus on her calculator like a saleslady about to pose a closing question. She answered;

'Your expenses for the Sabbath, plus the dowry for seven wives, will be nineteen hundred and eighty dollars. Can you handle it?'

'Yes,' I said, 'I can handle them. I mean... well you know what I mean.'

Now Una turned crimson, but quickly composed herself to find out my method of payment.

'Will that be cash or credit card?'

'Do you take American Express?' I asked.

'Etcetera.' She responded.

Now it was Una making the wisecracks. We laughed. For someone from such a remote place as Mindanao, Una had a delightful East meets West sense of humor.

'All right, put it on my American Express.' I said.

Una took the card, swiped it in the machine just outside the door and came back with my receipt.

'I've simply put a hold on your card for nineteen hundred and eighty dollars. If you change your mind you'll only be charged for the meals and any dowry for which you may be responsible.'

I signed it, then Una handed me my copy.

'Please note,' Una pointed to the *Terms and Conditions* on the back of the charge slip then read them to me word for word;

'*The parents of all the girls here have agreed in advance that payment to The House of Esther represents a deposit into escrow of the dowry. Whichever girl accepts you will indeed become your wife and the dowry will be distributed the next business day to the girl's parents. By signing you have agreed to these terms and conditions.*'

Una put the paperwork into a drawer and locked it, then she sat back down next to me. The sun was disappearing behind the mountains. Such a Sabbath!

'You're finished for the day?' I asked Una.

'As far as my official duties go. But if you'd like me to stay here with you...'

I didn't let her finish her sentence.

'Of course. You must stay. You must tell me about each girl.' I could see that Una didn't care for the way I'd put that so I quickly corrected my mistake. 'But of course I want to know about you first.'

'Well, Danny, I'm only one of your besherts.[20] It's so very nice to meet you, so very wonderful.' Una's eyes were teary as she spoke. She leaned her head against my shoulder and looked up at me intensely. 'You mustn't judge me for believing I'm yours. I had a dream that you would be here, and here you are. Half of my dream has already come true. Why shouldn't I believe that all of it's true? Not to mention that some of the other girls woke up this morning and described exactly the same dream. Nobody could have known you would be here today, not even you. We are blessed virgins, biblical virgins, every one of us. Since I'm yours, wouldn't you like to know how I came to know the Lord?'

That evening at *The House of Esther* I told Una that I'd love to hear her story. I'm sure all of you folks around this table would love to hear it as well, so I'll let Una tell her own story. Please, welcome my wife as she gives her testimony."

Every one of us in John's galley applauded Daniel's wife, Una, as she stood up to give her testimony. She waited till Daniel had taken his seat among his other wives, then began.

"Well, I'm just a farm girl. The first time I came to the city was to look for work. It was horrible. There were no jobs that a decent girl could take, and when there were, the boss was always interested in something more than my work. I couldn't pay my rent and soon found myself on the street with no place to stay. I was very frightened. I fell asleep behind a park bench but woke up to a horrible odor. A man in dirty clothes was sitting on the bench, sobbing, but it wasn't an unhappy sob. Then I heard him shouting.

'*Praise God alleluia! Praise Him. Thank you Jesus.*'

He was going to wake up everyone in the neighborhood with his shouting, so I quickly came out from behind the bench to shush him.

'Shh shh, you're going to wake up the police at the checkpoint.

Stop!' I said.

He then looked at me with the most sober eyes I had ever seen. What I mean is; he had righteousness from top to bottom. He seemed to shine with righteousness,[21] except that his clothes were filthy. His first words after I shushed him were.

'I've just had a conversation with God. Do I look like I'm on drugs? I took three doses of LSD just an hour ago.'

I didn't know what LSD was except that he'd told me it was a drug and that he'd taken three doses within an hour.

'No, you don't, not at all.' I said. 'You look like a Born-Again minister.'

And he did. There was nothing street like about him, except for his dirty clothes. Even so, I suspected he might be an undercover cop out to arrest vagrants like me, then he started spouting again.

'I prayed that God would release me from the power of drugs and purge my body from all unrighteousness!'

'Why did you do that?' I asked him. I know, kind of a silly question, but it just popped out of my mouth.

'Because of Jesus' words; *He that is not with me is against me.*[22] Those words just kept going round and round in my mind till I realized God wanted me, and He wanted me right now. *Praise God alleluia.*'

'Shh Shh, please don't do that.' I cautioned him, 'The police will come.'

'Okay'. He said. 'Can you show me a place to stay?'

'What kind of place?' I asked.

'Any place, as long as they have a shower and laundry services.' He said.

I looked at him and wondered if he could pay for such a place. He pulled out a credit card.

'I have emergency funds.' He said.

'Follow me.' I responded.

He seemed so crazy and yet so sane. We walked to a local motel where they advertised laundry services on the door and he checked in. The clerk handed him two room keys and some vouchers for food at the motel's all night restaurant.

He handed me the keys to one of the rooms and a restaurant food voucher, then said, 'You look like you could use a room for the night and a good meal. Sleep well and eat. Thanks for finding this place for me.'

He left so quickly for his own room that I didn't have a chance to decline his offer as our custom requires.

'Is this room paid for in advance?' I asked the clerk.

'Yes,' he replied, 'don't worry Miss. He's paid for it as well as the voucher he gave you. I believe that man is a prophet.'

'You crazy?' I said.

Oops, I thought to myself. This clerk could put me out on the street again, but he wasn't angry with me. He just smiled and said,

'The Lord can make bread from stones, how much more a prophet from a lost soul?'

Crazy Born-Agains, I thought. The clerk had the radio tuned to one of the Born-Again stations. The song's chorus kept repeating, *The precious blood of the Lamb*.23

My room was across from the lobby desk and had two locks so I felt safe. After locking the door I went right away to the bathroom. I'd never seen such conveniences. There was a sink and a bathtub with hot and cold running water. I nearly burned myself until I figured out how to adjust the two faucets together. The bathroom had a retractable wire that stretched across it for drying clothes. I had no idea there were such luxuries! While enjoying my bath I pulled one of the knobs and the faucet on top started spraying out water. At first I was so scared because I thought that I'd broken something, then I realized this must be how tourists bathe. I felt like a silly farm girl; I didn't even know what a shower was, but now that I did, I couldn't get enough of its soothing spray. It felt so cleansing. I saw a button on the wall outside the bathtub and pressed it, thinking I could get soap from it. Instead, the music that had been playing in the lobby came on. It was a radio! I leaned back in the tub only to get poked by the corner of a tiny package. I picked it up off the ledge of the tub to place it on the chair outside the shower curtain. I didn't want to be accused of stealing. Then I smelled it. It was a bar of soap that came gift wrapped. It had the name of the motel on it. I opened it and felt even more spoiled as I washed myself with this elegant little bar of soap. The words flowed from the radio.

Alas! and did my Savior bleed and did my Sovereign die?
Would He devote that sacred head for such a worm as I?

I felt like a worm; hiding behind a bench only to be pulled out by someone dirtier than me. What a worthless life I was living. What was I worth anyway. No employer would have me because I just wanted an honest day's work. Everyone I met was strange. Now the music was even stranger. It was speaking to me. I'd heard Christian music before but it had never spoken to me like this song was doing. I listened intently.

At the cross, at the cross where I first saw the light,
and the burden of my heart rolled away.
It was there by faith I received my sight,
and now I am happy all the day!

I was remembering what had gotten me on the street and was now admitting to myself that not all my employers had been bad. In fact, the only flaw of my last employer was to tell me that while at my desk, I must place my crucifix within my blouse for he considered it idolatry. *Idolatry*, I thought. My precious Lord. I grasped my crucifix and looked at it. Just then the words on the radio continued.

Thy body slain, sweet Jesus, Thine,
and bathed in its own blood;
While all exposed to wrath divine,
The Glorious Sufferer stood.

This thing I held was not Jesus, it was *a thing* given to me by the priest of my local parish for perfect attendance at the rosary. I remembered how I had defended that priest when he was charged with molesting the young boys at my parish. I thought those boys must have been such devils; lying about the priest like that. The next verse began.

At the cross, at the cross
where I first saw the light,
and the burden of my heart rolled away.
It was there by faith I received my sight,
and now I am happy all the day!

Where was the light? Where was my faith? What was I seeing? Was I blind? I saw the priest go back into rooms with those boys. I heard the sounds. Of course I lied. I was protecting the holiness of the priesthood. Too bad they believed the other witnesses and not me or the priest would still have his holy robes and the church would be protected from those Born-Agains! I remembered the man whose shouts had summoned me from beneath the bench. That was holiness. What a strange thing. He prayed to be clean and he was made clean. The song continued.

Was it for crimes that I had done,
he groaned upon the tree?
Amazing pity, grace unknown,
and love beyond degree!

Like the shower spraying above me, my eyes burst with tears. I sobbed. The crime! I had tried to protect the guilty while condemning those poor molested boys as liars.

'Praise God they had not listened to me or the other women in the church who had tried to protect that ungodly priest. Praise God!' That came from my mouth? I realized I was talking out loud or was I praying. The song continued.

Well might the sun in darkness hide
and shut his glories in
when Christ, the Mighty Maker died
for man the creature's sin.
Thus might I hide my blushing face
while His dear cross appears
dissolve my heart in thankfulness,
and melt my eyes to tears.

'Thank You Jesus!' I began shouting, *'Thank You Jesus!'* Who am I now? I thought to myself. Then just as suddenly I shouted.

'Praise God!'

Who am I? I'm born again! There was no shame, no second

thoughts. I was simply changed, in an instant. Sure, you'll find out that I have worldly things about me that I don't seem to be able to shake but the Lord keeps me clean and keeps me away from any temptations that I might not be able to resist. The song finished as I dried off.

But drops of grief can ne'er repay the debt of love I owe:
Here, Lord, I give my self away 'Tis all that I can do.

I'd never felt I belonged to anyone but now I had a Master; the Lord Jesus. A burden had truly been lifted from me. Such a change to occur by listening to a song!"

Una broke down in tears that afternoon as she told her story to all of us at John's table. We couldn't help but sing praises to God that He'd brought about her salvation. It was a party that afternoon, a party of *praise for God* as we sang and rejoiced. By the time we'd finished our impromptu praise session, Una had gotten back her composure and was prepared to finish her testimony.

"After all my shouting," she said, "I had to peek out the door of my room to see if anyone had noticed. The clerk looked up with the same calm smile he had before but it seemed he was now related to me in some way. It was just then that I noticed there had been a ladies' prayer group in the office behind the lobby desk. I don't know why I didn't notice them before. One of them jumped up when she saw me and rushed over to my door. She handed me an envelope and said,

'The man who brought you here left us this note to give you.'

'The man who brought me here?' I said.

Well, considering what had just happened, I realized, he had brought me there. I opened the envelope. The lady stood waiting for me to announce what was written in it.

'It just has a verse written here,' I said, 'Isaiah 4:1'

The woman went back to get her Bible and read the verse out loud for me.

'And in that day seven women shall take hold of one man, saying, *We will eat our own bread, and wear our own apparel: only let us be called by thy name, to take away our reproach.*'[24]

After reading the verse to me, she walked back to her group

scratching her head. I went back into my room and fell asleep.

In the morning I visited my employer who'd asked me not to wear the crucifix and told him all that had happened. He welcomed me back to work and that night I attended my first worship service at his church. I made a lot of good friends there. I worked in his office till I started at *The House of Esther*. He was very upset that I'd work at *The House of Esther* but having heard my testimony, even before *The House of Esther* had been built, he just couldn't object. My church mates didn't understand either but they've come to accept that the Lord's hand was at work in building *The House of Esther*. About a dozen of the other girls from my church worked there as well. But that's enough of my story. I'll sit back down and let my husband, Daniel, tell you the rest of our story."

Una took her seat amid our applause. It was uplifting to know her testimony, and our *Fond Memories* gave each of us the knowledge that not one of her words was exaggerated, nor for that matter, was there any hint of false humility in her testimony. The only people left on earth who couldn't tell between a true Christian and a fake Christian were the unbelievers of the world. Our *Fond Memories* had become a powerful shield against spiritual attack.

Daniel stood up again to finish telling his story:

"After Una had given her testimony," he said, "I was free from any doubt that the great desire I had for her was from the Lord. It was not the idolatrous desire that a monogamist has for his wife, but a godly desire, a desire to make Una a member of my body in submission.[25] However, I wasn't prepared for what was about to happen. As we sat watching the girls performing the Dance of the Ten Virgins she said to me:

'They dance quite nicely, don't they?'

I was devouring my food with each step of their dance so I spoke with my mouth full.

'Quite.' I said.

'So what do you suppose your wife is up to tonight?' She asked.

'Certainly not watching the dance of the ten virgins.' I gasped, nearly choking on my food as I broke into laughter.

At that, Una and I laughed so hard that she nearly slipped off the edge of the bench, tipping one of my desserts. A few drops of chocolate fell on the back of my hand just as I reached out to grab her. She caught my hand.

'Sweet,' she said, kissing the chocolate drops off my hand. Then she nearly fell against me as she whispered in my ear.

'Do you desire me?'

'Yes.' I replied.

'And you don't lust for me?' She asked.

'No, I don't lust for you.' I assured her.

'And you won't treat me as a harlot?' She persisted.

'Never.' I said, then our lips met.

Una, clearly understood my teachings. I taught to accept the Bible and not culture to guide our lives. The Bible says that if a man looks upon *another* man's wife with desire that he commits the transgression of *adultery in his heart.* This is Jesus' way of describing the sin of *coveting another man's wife*, the breaking of the Tenth Commandment.[26] The same principle applies if the woman is single, except that the sin would be fornication for desiring to take her as a harlot and not in marriage. To desire an available single woman for marriage is never a sin. In fact, if not for that spark, or should I say that fire of desire, few marriages would take place.

Una's words that began with, *Do you desire me* and ended with *and you won't treat me as a harlot* were the exact words I'd used in many of my writings to describe the ideal betrothal. By my answers to Una, I had betrothed her to me.

'We must make the announcement.' I said.

Gazing into Una's eyes full of submission was like standing at the top of a high tower ready to fall spinning down. I literally had to shake my head to gain my balance. At that moment it hit me how prophetic was her name, Una. In her language it meant *first.* She would be the first among the virgins at *The House of Esther* to become my wife.

The girls who'd been performing the Dance of the Ten Virgins had just finished their routine, so I took Una's hand and led her to the center of the room. I handed her a simple coin which represented the dowry which her father would soon be receiving. Una kneeled and accepted the coin, then she kissed my hand.

'Una and I are betrothed!' I shouted.

The sound of tinkling glass crackled through the air as the girls tapped their glasses with silverware, their signal for Una and me to kiss. Still grasping my hand, I pulled Una to her feet, then swept her up into my arms. Her lips were fuller now, anticipating; her kiss, sensuous yet delicate. Our hearts conversed in ancient rhythms. I breathed deeply, wanting every breath that Una exhaled to fill me. I lowered her feet back to the ground. We'd barely sat down when the tinkling glasses signaled we must kiss again. Neither Una nor I tired of this ritualistic kissing which continued through the evening. There was something voyeuristic in this custom. I'd seen it many times at Filipino weddings in the U.K. but not like this; a couple surrounded by forty-eight women tinkling their glasses. It was as if they were watching the preparation of a banquet where ***husband*** was the main course, and they were simply waiting their turn. How prophetic were my thoughts, for no sooner had I thought them than the concierge shouted through the door,

'Quickly! Quickly! Your besherts have arrived!'

'We must go! Our dreams are fulfilled! Our beloveds have arrived as prophesied! We must go! God bless you!'

The room emptied now except for Una, Setia, and five of the girls who'd been performing the Dance of the Ten Virgins. They directed me to a door at the side of the room labeled Master. Una pointed to another door, labeled Maidens, then said,

'We'll prepare ourselves. Go and prepare yourself.'

I stepped through the door and was alone for the first time since my arrival. *I quickly searched for a way to escape.*"

Daniel's attempt at humor was not in vain. Every one of us in John's galley roared with laughter. When we had quieted down again, he returned to his story telling.

"Okay, so I didn't try to escape. We can't escape our destinies, isn't that right?"

This time his quip was met with applause. It was our wives who gave the loudest applause, then mine wagged their hooked fingers at me.

"All right, now that I've got your attention I'll try to finish my... *our* story."

Daniel's eyes grew teary as he looked around the table at his wives.

"I love happy endings, don't you?" He said.

Again we applauded.

Suni looked across the table at me, aware that I might also be teary eyed. Her special love brought a huge smile to my face.

Daniel's story telling reminded me how much I missed the stories John had treated us to on his mountaintop.

"Now what actually happened," Daniel continued, "was that upon entering the door labeled Master, my eyes met with a poster sized photograph in which all seven of these women; these women who are now my wives, were standing. They'd written their names beneath their images on the poster, but of course you know them today from your *Fond Memories*."

Daniel now stood behind each of his new brides as he introduced them: "Mayumi, which means pretty; Amor, in any language - love; Bituin, a star in the heavens; Dalisay, pure, as are all our wives; Malaya, freedom - something we all have through Christ; Setia, my unique Christmas flower; and of course, Una, the first at *The House of Esther* to become my wife."

We now gave Daniel's brides the official welcome they had not yet received as we stood and sang the song which is known in all Filipino churches. As we did so, every person in the galley shook hands with every other person in the galley.

There's a welcome here, there's a welcome here.
There's a Christian welcome here.

There's a welcome here, there's a welcome here.
There's a Christian welcome here.

"Thank you. Thank you so much for welcoming us." Daniel said. "Filipino hospitality is world renown and who better to do it justice than a ship full of Christians on fire for the Lord! *Amen*?"

"*Amen*!" We responded.

"Now as I was explaining," Daniel continued, "each of my brides had signed her name below her image and there was a message penned across the bottom which read:

'To our beloved, Daniel Miller, you are our beshert. We are destined to be yours. We took this photo outside The House of Esther while the sun was high so that you would know of our prophetic dream. You see us here.'

The picture included all of them standing together and pointing to a picture of me on the back cover of one of my books.

Now I'd studied God's word long enough to know that I was free to marry as many women as I cared to, and I certainly wasn't crazy, so even if all this had been a set up, a well laid plan to trick me into marrying them, what would it matter? It wouldn't be the first time God had used a ploy to get His way. Besides, *the Lord had placed within me an incredible desire to have each one of these women for my wife*. I'd had my eye on the five dancers even before they'd made their intentions clear. In fact, of the forty nine women who sat around the banquet table that evening with me, my eyes had only desired Una, Setia, and the five dancers, and it was apparent they desired me. There was no doubt in my mind that the Lord had destined these seven for me, just as it was foretold in their dreams.

I showered myself, then put on a robe that had been left for me and hurried back to the banquet table, but it was gone. A spa had taken its place. All seven of my brides were waiting for me in its waters. When I entered the spa, each one of them latched onto me and prophesied Isaiah 4:1

'We will eat our own bread, and wear our own clothing: only let us be called by your name, take away our reproach!'

I spent the next seven weeks taking away that reproach, as well as getting to know each one of my fair brides in other than a biblical sense. Finally, it was time for us to find a house that we might let, so we hired a van and headed for Cagayan de Oro. Our first stop was my apartment, to get some extra clothing. My wives waited for me in the van while I went into the apartment. It was the first time I'd been completely alone since my life had been so marvelously changed. As I put my key into the door lock, it opened suddenly. It was my wife, Hannah. Tears were streaming down her face. Then she got down on her knees, holding fast to my legs.

'I had the same dream.' She said. 'The dream that your seven new brides had. I saw each one of them in it, and you too. I miss you so much. I've been waiting for your return. God has blessed you and He has called me to repentance. Will you forgive me?'

'I already have.' I replied.

I reached down to pull Hannah to her feet but she used it as an opportunity to wrestle me to the floor, then to our mattress, the only thing left in our apartment.

'Where's our bed and the rest of the furniture?' I mumbled through Hannah's kisses.

'Oh, that. I bought you a house and had all of our furniture sent there. I figured you'd need a big house with your new wives and...' Hannah paused.

Then I saw the glint in her eyes.

'And...?'

'I'm pregnant!' This time Hannah's tears were from joy.

'So that's why you came back to me?' I couldn't help asking the obvious question.

'No, silly.' She objected. 'I'd already come back to you in my heart. When my plane stopped over in Japan I had second thoughts about leaving you. By the time the plane was about to leave for London I was in a panic. I took the first flight back to Manila and stewed there. I didn't know what to do. The thought that I'd missed my period hadn't even crossed my mind. Then I had the dream, the dream about your new wives and our new life in a larger than life family. When I awoke, I realized that you were my lord in this life.[27] My thoughts were clear for the first time in so many years. That was when I thought of making love with you and realized I hadn't had a period in nearly three months.'

Hannah was anxious to meet my new brides so we tarried no longer. It was as if they'd known each other since childhood as they chatted all the way to our new home. And, we've pretty much spent all of our time there till this voyage.

Hannah, could you please stand so that I might introduce you once again?"

Hannah stood up. She was visibly more pregnant than the rest of Daniel's wives. Yes, every one of Daniel's new brides were pregnant. In fact, I don't think there was a woman on board John's yacht that wasn't either pregnant or nursing, including John's wives of twenty-five years.

John walked up and shook Daniel's hand once more. As he patted him on the back, he said,

"I'm sure that I'm speaking for everyone here when I say that we're blessed, so very blessed, to come into fellowship with you and all your family."

Our applause filled the galley as we enthusiastically welcomed Daniel and his family. I felt such a sense of God's blessing upon me. I looked around the room at each of my wives: Ruth, the theologian; Tamisa, so soft and without blemish; Rosemary, watchful for the feelings of her sisters; Modelisa, the chameleon evangelist; Analyn, the sleeping beauty; Asina, whose speech is full of grace but seasoned with salt; Suni, the comforting comedian; and my beloved first love, Mary.

After Daniel and Hannah had taken their seats, John walked across the galley to the window and raised the blinds. The chariot of God and the angel were gone. We were in a harbor now.

"We've arrived at our destination." John said. "Sumba."

I don't think John intended to startle us, but he did. I remembered the account he gave of his first arrival on Sumba.

The sun was setting in absolute silence behind our ship and his voice shot past me like a spear. Had it been, he could easily have penetrated the lush tropical growth that began where the sand ended. One thin strand of beach separated sea from jungle. I stood between these two powers of nature. Would they wield their power recklessly against me or would the Lord use them to bless me.

Judging from how I'd already been blessed, I had no doubt that the Lord was about to pour down blessings from heaven upon me, but I wasn't prepared for what followed.

"I've got another announcement," John said, then he walked over to me, taking me by the elbow. "Come with me, there's something we need to take care of before you step ashore."

He took me to the front of the galley where he'd been standing, then spoke again, this time more formally.

"Ladies, gentlemen, children. Twenty-five years ago, King Jochan, Tatang, as we call him, left Sumba and moved to Mindanao. He and his family like it there, living not too far from my own home. It's not a *palace*, but of course, his home *is his castle* and Tatang prefers it there, having no desire to return to Sumba. For some time we thought I might become heir to his throne, but as you know, I have my own throne and my own kingdom. This brings us to the task at hand. Elkanah?"

Elkanah rushed over and placed his hand on my shoulder.

"Kneel." Elkanah said. "It shall be the last time you kneel before anyone but God."

I did as he asked, then Elkanah anointed my head with oil and proclaimed:

"It is my great pleasure to present to you: *Prince of Sumba, Husband to Many Wives*."

No sooner had those words left his lips than the voices of a glorious choir burst forth from the shores of Sumba. The sandy beach was lined with thousands of singing women in white flowing gowns. They sang praises to God and blessings upon the kingdom to which I had just become heir.

"Windowsill babies." John said. "They're still waiting for their husbands."

"Windowsill babies?" I asked.

"For a few decades now, they've been arriving from China." John said. "They were left to die on the windowsills of their homes. Their parents were limited to just one child so they abandoned the girl babies, hoping that the next child would be a boy. Chinese Christians snatched the abandoned girls off the windowsills under cover of darkness and put them on barges. Sort of like the story of Moses but on a fantastically grander scale, but I know nothing more than you. Revisit your *Fond Memories*."

At John's words I fell to the ground as my *Fond Memories* overwhelmed me. I could see millions of girl babies crying on windowsills where they'd been abandoned, then a million scenes of heroism passed through my mind in an instant. I saw Chinese Christian after Chinese Christian risk their lives to snatch those babies to safety and send them on their way to Sumba.

"They got here the same way we did!" I said, astonished.

"Yes." John said. "Their barges were pulled to safety by the chariots of angels.[28] You've got millions of subjects, from newborns to women who've spent a good portion of their adult lives here on Sumba. It's going to be quite a betrothal when their husbands arrive. Elkanah says it won't be long."

Then I thought about the other abandoned daughters, the repentant harlots of the world.[29] Who would marry them?

As if reading my thoughts, Elkanah said. "The repentant harlots are here also, by the millions. The Lord is sheltering them now but

He has chosen husbands for them as well."

Suni overheard Elkanah. "What about Cherry and Tisay? Are they here too?"

"Yes, Suni," he said, "they're waiting at your husband's palace with Mang Ricardo."

As John's sons lowered a boat for our short ride to shore, I thought back on the last few months. Those months had been so packed with love and fellowship that they had seemed like years. Now the Lord had set me at the head of a kingdom; a hidden kingdom that was supernaturally under His protection. I wondered in awe at God's great power. What task had He prepared for me and these millions of believers on Sumba? I was about to find out.

Chapter 25 Footnotes

1. "The first special hospital was the Lock Hospital near Hyde Park Corner, founded in 1746 by Martin Madan, who became its first chaplain."
A History of English Philanthropy
By Benjamin Kirkman Gray
London - P.S. King & Son, Orchard House, Westminster - 1905

2. The poor heard the Gospel with gladness, and the rich were not sent empty away.
The Life and Times of Selina, Countess of Huntingdon By Aaron Crossley Hobart Seymour, Jacob Kirkman Foster Published 1840 - Pages 165-167

3. The Church of England's hymnal began with Martin Madan's Collection of Psalms and Hymns (1760).
The New Schaff-Herzog Encyclopedia of Religious Knowledge by Johann Jakob Herzog, Philip Schaff, and others. Copyright 1909
In 1788, the publisher of the fifth edition of the Church of England hymnal, "appropriated fully two thirds of the contents of Madan's Collection."
The Princeton Theological Review - Volume XII - 1914
The Princeton University Press - Princeton, N.J. - Page 76
The first Baptist hymn-book was Rippon's (1787).
The New Schaff-Herzog Encyclopedia of Religious Knowledge by Johann Jakob Herzog, Philip Schaff, and others. Copyright 1909

4. A New and Literal Translation of Juvenal and Persius; with Copious Explanatory Notes, by which these difficult satirists are rendered easy and familiar to the reader. In Two Volumes.
By the Rev. M. Madan -Printed for the Editor, at Mr. Lewis's, No 157, Swallow-Street, Near Piccadilly MDCCLXXXIX (1789)
5. Madan not only preached against pedophilia but in 1764 the Lock Hospital bore the expense of prosecuting Edmund Thirkell for assault with the intention to ravish a very young girl who was listed by the court as over five years old but under the age of ten. A consequence of the assault was that she was diagnosed with a venereal disease. Such cases of pedophilia were extremely hard to prosecute in Eighteenth Century England and to give an indication of the difficulty, the defendant, Edmund Thirkell, a pedophile, was able to obtain the signatures of eight jurymen *indicating their disapprobation of the verdict.* The judges, may their names be remembered for their righteous judgment (Mansfield & Wilmot) thought the recantations of the jurors should be disregarded since they might have been *obtained by improper application.* (Modern English - through bribes or intimidation.)
A Complete Collection of State Trials and Proceedings for High Treason and Other Crimes and Misdemeanors Volume 20 1772-1777 Publication date 1816 - Page 912
The Secret Malady - Linda Merians, Editor Published 1996 - Page 134-135
6. "The English author is for hanging all thieves." Franklin says in a letter to Benjamin Vaughan dated March 14th, 1785.
The Works of the Late Dr. Benjamin Franklin By Benjamin Franklin 1807
Franklin obviously did not even read to page 63 of Madan's book for on that page Madan argues that a lesser but more certain punishment is the answer to England's problem of rampant crime. He says there is an "almost certainty of escape from death" [because of the pity of jurors and/or judges for the accused] and he quotes "a less punishment, which is certain, will do more good than a greater, which is uncertain."
Thoughts on Executive Justice By Martin Madan 1785
7. "The present Chapel Street was named after the hospital chapel." The Lock Hospital Chapel and its Music by Nicholas Temperley - Page 45

8. "The ensemble texture that was perhaps most fashionable in the mid-eighteenth century was that of one or two relatively high melodic lines, moving largely in parallel thirds or sixths, with a figured bass. It was the texture of the trio sonata, the chamber duet, the newly fashionable accompanied sonata, the symphony, the solo song and above all the opera, where even male parts were sung by high voices."
The Lock Hospital Chapel and its Music by Nicholas Temperley - Page 64
9. Mark 7:25-30 For a certain woman, whose young daughter had an unclean spirit, heard of him, and came and fell at his feet: The woman was a Greek, a Syrophenician by nation; and she besought him that he would cast forth the devil out of her daughter. But Jesus said unto her, Let the children first be filled: for it is not meet to take the children's bread, and to cast it unto the dogs. And she answered and said unto him, Yes, Lord: yet the dogs under the table eat of the children's crumbs. And he said unto her, For this saying go thy way; the devil is gone out of thy daughter. And when she was come to her house, she found the devil gone out, and her daughter laid upon the bed.
10. Tricycle driver - In much of Asia, motorcycles have an additional wheel added to the right of the driver in back. Between that wheel and the back wheel of the motorcycle is wedged a small seat which is barely large enough to seat two passengers. There are variations on this. Some have not just one but two extra wheels and seat as many as five passengers, if you include the one sitting behind the driver!
11. The Sabbath arrives at sundown on Friday and ends at sundown on Saturday. The first portion of a day begins with evening. The second portion of a day begins with morning.
Genesis 1:5 And God called the light Day, and the darkness he called Night. And the evening and the morning were the first day.
12. Definition: positional fornication - acting against or usurping the God ordained position of authority that a husband has over his wife.
Numbers 30:13 Every vow, and every binding oath to afflict the soul, her husband may establish it, or her husband may make it void.
Ephesians 5:23 For the husband is the head of the wife, even as

Christ is the head of the church: and he is the saviour of the body.
13. If one woman's rebellion (Eve) represents the fall then why wouldn't it be appropriate that seven women's submission would represent the restoration of God's order. If it does not then why is it that the restoration of Israel immediately follows the submission of the seven women in Isaiah 4:1?
Isaiah 4:1-6 And in that day seven women shall take hold of one man, saying, We will eat our own bread, and wear our own apparel: only let us be called by thy name, to take away our reproach. In that day shall the branch of the LORD be beautiful and glorious, and the fruit of the earth shall be excellent and comely for them that are escaped of Israel. And it shall come to pass, that he that is left in Zion, and he that remaineth in Jerusalem, shall be called holy, even every one that is written among the living in Jerusalem: When the Lord shall have washed away the filth of the daughters of Zion, and shall have purged the blood of Jerusalem from the midst thereof by the spirit of judgment, and by the spirit of burning. And the LORD will create upon every dwelling place of mount Zion, and upon her assemblies, a cloud and smoke by day, and the shining of a flaming fire by night: for upon all the glory shall be a defence. And there shall be a tabernacle for a shadow in the daytime from the heat, and for a place of refuge, and for a covert from storm and from rain.
14. Lust - to desire something forbidden
Romans 7:7b - "for I had not known lust, except the law had said, Thou shalt not covet."
15. Psalm 127:3-5 Lo, children are an heritage of the LORD: and the fruit of the womb is his reward. As arrows are in the hand of a mighty man; so are children of the youth. Happy is the man that hath his quiver full of them: they shall not be ashamed, but they shall speak with the enemies in the gate.
16. Proverbs 30:18-19 There be three things which are too wonderful for me, yea, four which I know not: The way of an eagle in the air; the way of a serpent upon a rock; the way of a ship in the midst of the sea; and the way of a man with a maid. When Solomon sets up verses this way, it is the last item mentioned which is compared to the others as being even more astounding. The last words are better rendered in modern English

as follows:
"A fourth, which I cannot comprehend; the way of a man with a young woman."
17. Biblical virgin - a woman who is set apart, and secluded till her day of marriage. She never allows anyone to touch her sensually and only accompanies a man when she has a chaperone.
18. A woman who allows her breasts to be caressed even though she has not allowed a man to penetrate her is a whore according to God's word.
Ezekiel 23:3 And they committed whoredoms in Egypt; they committed whoredoms in their youth: there were their breasts pressed, and there they bruised the teats of their virginity.
19. Sabbath candles are lit eighteen minutes before sunset on Friday night by the eldest woman of the household. A prayer such as the following is then recited:
Blessed are You, LORD our God, King of the universe, Who sanctified us with His commandments, and commanded us to be a light to the nations and Who gave to us Jesus, our Messiah, the Light of the world.
Since there wasn't an elder woman in *The House of Esther*, every one of the women lit a Sabbath candle. All together, seven times seven Sabbath candles.
20. Beshert - Yiddish for *the one God has chosen for you* or *your destiny*. In the case of women, God chooses only one beshert for them at a time. In the case of men, God may choose more than one beshert at a time. Many of today's women are denied the right to their beshert because he's already married and mistakenly thinks he may have only one wife at a time.
21. Ecclesiastes 8:1 Who is as the wise man? and who knoweth the interpretation of a thing? a man's wisdom maketh his face to shine, and the boldness of his face shall be changed.
22. Matthew 12:30 He that is not with me is against me; and he that gathereth not with me scattereth abroad.
23. Isaac Watts [Born 1674 Died 1748] was one of the most popular hymn writers of the early Eighteenth Century.
24. When a wife gives birth to her husband's firstborn son, the Lord is said to have taken away her reproach.
Isaiah 4:1 And in that day seven women shall take hold of one man, saying, We will eat our own bread, and wear our own

apparel: only let us be called by thy name, to take away our reproach.
Genesis 30:23-24 And she conceived, and bare a son; and said, God hath taken away my reproach: And she called his name Joseph and said, The LORD shall add to me another son.
Ruth 4:11 And all the people that were in the gate, and the elders, said, We are witnesses. *The LORD make the woman that is come into thine house like Rachel and like Leah, which two did build the house of Israel*: and do thou worthily in Ephratah, and be famous in Bethlehem.
1 Timothy 5:14 I will therefore that the younger women marry, bear children, guide the house, give none occasion to the adversary to speak reproachfully.
25. Ephesians 5:28 So ought men to love their wives as their own bodies. He that loveth his wife loveth himself.
26. Matthew 5:28 But I say unto you, That whosoever looketh on a woman to lust after her hath committed adultery with her already in his heart.
We must be very clear about what Jesus is saying in Matthew 5:28. He is simply giving us another name for coveting thy neighbor's wife, *adultery in the heart*.
27. 1 Peter 3:6 Even as *Sara obeyed Abraham, calling him lord*: whose daughters ye are, as long as ye do well, and are not afraid with any amazement.
Ruth 1:16 And Ruth said, Entreat me not to leave thee, or to return from following after thee: for whither thou goest, I will go; and where thou lodgest, I will lodge: thy people shall be my people, *and thy God my God*:
28. Psalm 68:17 The chariots of God are twenty thousand, even thousands of angels: the Lord is among them, as in Sinai, in the holy place.
29. Harlot - a woman who has engaged in sexual relations without the benefit of marriage. Harlots are in bondage to sin and the men they have relations with are in bondage to them. The harlot takes the place of God as head of the man. When a harlot repents she puts God at the center of her life and if she marries she accepts her husband's authority over her.

The following space is provided so that you might remind yourself of the things that came to your mind as you read this story.

~NOTES~

...There were some however, who called themselves brothers, yet like Jonah were *angry with us enough to die* and would have preferred to continue wasting water on a *withering vine*

To be continued...

PRINCE OF SUMBA

ASSAULT OF THE TARES

An End Times Novel by

Pastor Don Milton

Coming Soon

Other Books Published by Don Milton

Title	Author or Editor	Availability
Letters to Joseph Priestley	Martin Madan	Now
Exhortatory Address to the Brethren in the Faith of Christ	Martin Madan	Feb 2010
A Dialog on Polygamy	Bernardino Ochino Don Milton	Now
Thelyphthora Volume I A Treatise on Female Ruin	Martin Madan	Now
Thelyphthora Volume II A Treatise on Female Ruin	Martin Madan	Now
Thelyphthora Volume III A Treatise on Female Ruin	Martin Madan	Now
Thoughts on Executive Justice	Martin Madan	Dec 2009
Polygamy and Monogamy	Don Milton	Now
Many More Titles	Don Milton & Others	2010

www.ingramcontent.com/pod-product-compliance
Lightning Source LLC
Chambersburg PA
CBHW020659110726
47901CB00001B/255

* 9 7 8 0 6 1 5 2 9 3 2 6 4 *